INTO THE
REAL

BAEN BOOKS by JOHN RINGO

BLACK TIDE RISING
Under a Graveyard Sky • *To Sail a Darkling Sea*
Islands of Rage and Hope • *Strands of Sorrow*
The Valley of Shadows (with Mike Massa)
Black Tide Rising (edited with Gary Poole)
Voices of the Fall (edited with Gary Poole)
River of Night (with Mike Massa)
We Shall Rise (edited with Gary Poole)

TROY RISING
Live Free or Die • *Citadel* • *The Hot Gate*

LEGACY OF THE ALDENATA
A Hymn Before Battle • *Gust Front* • *When the Devil Dances*
Hell's Faire • *The Hero* (with Michael Z. Williamson)
Cally's War (with Julie Cochrane)
Watch on the Rhine (with Tom Kratman)
Sister Time (with Julie Cochrane) • *Yellow Eyes* (with Tom Kratman)
Honor of the Clan (with Julie Cochrane) • *Eye of the Storm*

COUNCIL WARS
There Will Be Dragons • *Emerald Sea*
Against the Tide • *East of the Sun, West of the Moon*

INTO THE LOOKING GLASS
Into the Looking Glass • *Vorpal Blade* (with Travis S. Taylor)
Manxome Foe (with Travis S. Taylor)
Claws that Catch (with Travis S. Taylor)

EMPIRE OF MAN
(with David Weber)
March Upcountry • *March to the Sea* • *March to the Stars* • *We Few*

SPECIAL CIRCUMSTANCES
Princess of Wands • *Queen of Wands*

PALADIN OF SHADOWS
Ghost • *Kildar* • *Choosers of the Slain* • *Unto the Breach*
A Deeper Blue • *Tiger by the Tail* (with Ryan Sear)

STANDALONE TITLES
The Last Centurion • *Citizens* (ed. with Brian M. Thomsen)

To purchase any of these titles in e-book form,
please go to www.baen.com.

INTO THE REAL

JOHN RINGO & LYDIA SHERRER

BAEN

Into the Real

This is a work of fiction. All the characters and events portrayed in this book are fictional, and any resemblance to real people or incidents is purely coincidental.

Copyright © 2022 by John Ringo & Lydia Sherrer

All rights reserved, including the right to reproduce this book or portions thereof in any form.

A Baen Books Original

Baen Publishing Enterprises
P.O. Box 1403
Riverdale, NY 10471
www.baen.com

ISBN: 978-1-9821-2600-1

Cover art by Dave Seeley

First printing, April 2022

Distributed by Simon & Schuster
1230 Avenue of the Americas
New York, NY 10020

Library of Congress Cataloging-in-Publication Data

Names: Ringo, John, 1963– author. | Sherrer, Lydia, author.
Title: Into the real / John Ringo & Lydia Sherrer.
Description: Riverdale, NY : Baen, [2022] | Series: Transdimensional hunter
Identifiers: LCCN 2021060300 | ISBN 9781982126001 (hardcover) | ISBN
    9781625798589 (ebook)
Subjects: LCGFT: Novels.
Classification: LCC PS3568.I577 I59 2022 | DDC 813/.54—dc23/eng/20211217
LC record available at https://lccn.loc.gov/2021060300

Pages by Joy Freeman (www.pagesbyjoy.com)
Printed in the United States of America
10 9 8 7 6 5 4 3 2 1

To Tony, whose fault it is
that I ever got to write this book.
You are loved and valued more
than you can ever imagine.
—L.S.

~

As always
For Captain Tamara Long, USAF
Born: May 12, 1979
Died: March 23, 2003, Afghanistan
You fly with the angels now.
—J.R.

Chapter 1

COULD A GAMING ARTIFICIAL INTELLIGENCE HOLD A GRUDGE? Mack had no idea but sometimes he had to wonder. Times like now, when his screen noted the newly spawned enemy player was not one of their four-man opposing team but instead Larry Coughlin. Of course, Larry *couldn't* be an AI. Ever since the mid-2010s when things like AI trolls and farming bots had become a real problem, game developers had spent the last thirty years and billions of dollars developing sophisticated software to keep their games secure and their paying customers happy. But Mack had to wonder.

"*Aš Išvykę savo akis ir seksas kaukolės!*" Ronnie, the leader of their four-man team, snarled. "*Jūs esate homoseksualus idiotas!*"

"Larry's here," Mack said dolefully.

"Yep," Dan replied. "I don't even have to look at the board. Ronnie's cursing in—"

Dan's voice cut off and the screen flashed: *DarkRider48 has been terminated by Larry Coughlin!*

"*Jūs patekote asilas vyrų dalis!*" Ronnie shouted.

"Ronnnie..." a deep baritone voice taunted. "Oh, Ronnnie... I'm here to kiiill you. Cursing in Lithuanian won't save you..."

RonnieDarko714 has been terminated by Larry Coughlin!

Mack got up in a good viewpoint to scope things out, no longer worrying what their lead was on their opponents. They were doomed anyway. He could see the other team pulling back

1

through the broken rubble "scenery" of the battle quadrant. Why take chances when a legendary Tier One had shown up to wipe out the other team for you?

He had no idea what Ronnie had done to get on Larry Coughlin's "naughty" list. Nobody knew who Larry actually was, just that he ranked as one of the top ten best players in the world on the mega popular first-person-shooter game, WarMonger. That and he was the only one of the ten who never attended tournaments. He was a mystery man in virtual and their own personal boogeyman—a good argument against the whole AI theory. Why would an AI waste its time on them? All Mack knew for sure was that Larry was a mercenary in virtual, taking gear or cash to show up and turn the tide in a fight. Rumors were he might be a merc in the real, too, maybe a retired one. Some people said he used to be an actual Delta Force or maybe SEAL team member, based on the way he fought. But, again, why someone like that would care about a random high schooler from Cedar Rapids, Iowa, was anybody's guess.

Oh, well. At least the gaming AI had picked a nice day for it. Clear blue skies instead of the nearly perpetual gray, apparently cold, rain the game usually generated.

The other thing Mack knew for sure? Half the time they were in a match, Larry Coughlin would show up to ruin their night. And probably charge somebody through the nose to do it. It was insulting.

Mack decided to camp out behind this nice safe wall and hope the Tier One didn't notice him. After all, miracles could happen, right?

"I'm back—" Ronnie said only to be cut off again.

RonnieDarko714 has been terminated by Larry Coughlin!

"He's teabagging Ronnie," Edgar, the other remaining team member, said. If it weren't for the fact that Edgar rarely showed emotion, Mack would have sworn he heard a grin in his friend's voice. "Heck of a thing to see just as you res—"

BigHero232 has been terminated by Larry Coughlin!

Aaaand, there went Edgar. Now Mack was alone. He waited, hoping one of his teammates could respawn and stay alive for more than five seconds.

"Can you move in on him?" Mack whispered as Dan's name showed back up on the board. He knew whispering didn't help but it was Larry Coughlin, for Pete's sake!

"On me?" Larry's deep voice replied. "Doubt it. He's all the way across the map and I'm over here behind you, Mack."

MackTruck35 has been terminated by Larry Coughlin!

"I swear to GOD, he teleports!" Mack shouted at his screen as his respawn clock counted down. "He *has* to be cheating!"

"That guy's got some sort of homo crush on me, I swear," Ronnie replied as he respawned. "Freaking hom—"

"He's doing it again," Dan added. "And he took out Edgar from across the—"

DarkRider48 has been terminated by Larry Coughlin!

"Want to give up, Mack?" Larry asked. "Don't bother running, you'll only die tired."

"Why us, man?" Mack said as he sent his avatar sprinting away from his respawn point, looking for cover. "Why the heck do you always turn up to beat on *us*?"

"It's not you I'm after, kid," Larry replied. "It's Ronnie. You know that."

"What've you got against Ronnie?" Mack asked.

"He's a jerk," Larry said, "and you know it. I admire your loyalty, Mack. But, as always, it's going to cost you."

"Where *are* you?" Mack shouted, spinning his avatar in a useless circle.

"Behind you," Larry whispered over the coms.

Baconville Bashers Have Failed to Achieve Objective!

Lynn Raven leaned back in her body-mold chair and lowered her old-school headset so she could stretch the kinks out of her neck. She knew some kids at school who had convinced their parents to get them audio implants so they never had to use headphones or a mic again.

That would have been a dream.

Her mom? Nope, not a chance. Never mind that global tech was changing around them faster than you could wrap your mind around it. Whenever Lynn brought up audio or even visual implants, it was all "they're a dangerous new fad" or "you can wait to make permanent alterations to your anatomy after you turn eighteen." It was annoying but Lynn only had a little over a year to go before she could finally make those decisions for herself. Then her life in WarMonger as a grizzled old mercenary for hire would get so much easier.

Grabbing an energy drink, Lynn downed it and then started on a bag of chips as she reviewed the victory stats on her wall-screen.

It wasn't quite as high resolution as a flex-screen gaming monitor but repainting her bedroom with smartpaint had definitely been the cheaper option. Plus, she liked being able to change the screen's size and location so she could play from her bed, from the floor, or wherever she felt like. Of course, most gamers these days preferred augmented reality glasses or a virtual reality headset. But the cheap AR and VR equipment gave her a headache, and she wasn't going to pay for the good ones. Yet.

Lynn polished off the last of her chips, licked her fingers, then prepared to get back to work. It wasn't as if taking out her very few friends was hard; compared to the top players in WarMonger that she usually played against, it was like kicking puppies. But it was worth it just to listen to Ronnie's dramatics, both during the game and at school. He really was an arrogant jerk who needed his balloon head popped. And the fact that she was getting paid to do it? That was just icing on the cake.

She put the headset back on and pinged the team leader who'd hired her.

"SkullCrusher," she said, her voice modulated to the deep baritone Larry Coughlin was known for. "I want that rifle you promised in my inventory by ten hundred hours Eastern or you'll be next on my list. Copy?"

"Roger, sir," SkullCrusher said carefully. "I'm already transferring it. Thanks for the assist."

"Anytime," she said in a sinister tone. "As long as you make the payment schedule."

She checked her inventory, and sure enough, the Tiger War was already transferred. She generated an interactive image copy, forwarded it, then switched her wireless controller's config from gaming to keyboard. A lot of gamers used the versatile haptic gloves that could control all their devices at once with a few simple flicks. But Lynn preferred having an actual object in her hands, even if it was a bit clunky. The controller's omni-polymer flowed seamlessly into the new keyboard config, and she opened a second screen on her wall where she pulled up an auction site and began typing rapidly.

"WM Tiger War AR. $50 OBO. Larry Coughlin."

As she typed, her eyes were pulled to the side of the listing form she was filling out by a flash of color. It was another one of those TD Hunter ads, the "biggest release of the year" augmented reality game she was getting sick of hearing about. The ad showed an athletic, vaguely Asian-looking man holding what appeared to be a pair of electric blue toy swords. The man stood alone in a park, his stance alert and ready as if he were listening for something. Suddenly, he spun and slashed behind him, launching into a series of seamlessly fluid attacks.

Ten seconds in, there was a lull in his movements as he pulled out a pair of AR glasses and slipped them on, triggering an amazing transformation. It started at his head and flowed down his body, then spread to everything around him. His appearance was transformed into that of a fierce warrior, armored to the nines and wielding lethal blades of shining steel. They whipped through the air as the man resumed his dance of death, cutting down monster after monster as they leapt at him in the augmented reality that now overlaid his surroundings. The slogan "Step into the real" appeared superimposed over the action, then the scene faded into a black background with a large military-looking emblem shining in the middle.

Stupid ads.

She was annoyed to have been sucked into watching something she'd seen some version of hundreds of times already over the past six months. Access to the global mesh network—the faster, more reliable version of the Internet that had replaced the world wide web a decade ago—was free for everyone, all the time, everywhere. But only because ads inundated every corner of it.

Unless, of course, you paid a premium to get rid of them.

After a spate of global pandemics during the 2020s that locked down whole countries for months at a time and started the "social distancing" fad, the trend toward everything going virtual hit warp speed. Even though medical tech eventually caught up with the strains that kept getting passed, the decade of the 2020s permanently changed global culture. In virtual became the default place for any kind of recreation or entertainment, and the only reason Lynn still physically *went* to school was because of a bunch of studies done in the late 2020s when there was a push for permanent virtual classrooms. The science indicating kids needed face-to-face instruction was convincing enough that the virtual schooling lobby failed.

Personally, Lynn thought it was a shame. If she didn't have to go to school then she wouldn't have to deal with people anymore. She didn't like people. Most of them sucked—a major reason why she'd gotten into gaming in the first place.

Getting back to work, Lynn added the image copy of the red and blue Tiger War to her auction listing, activated the offer, then switched her keyboard back to a controller and her attention back to WarMonger. Out of necessity, she *had* forked out extra to keep her gaming time ad-free, so it was a calm oasis for her in virtual. She'd give her auction listing a couple of hours to see what sort of bids she got. Since it was a work night she might wait until Monday to accept an offer. Weekends were the best time to sell.

Whatever she got, it'd help with the bills. Not that her mom knew she paid their rent and held back their mountain of debt by mercing in the virtual. Her mom hated taking money from anyone. But once Lynn had figured out what a goldmine War-Monger was for someone of her skills, she'd gotten her mom to teach her how to manage their finances, claiming she needed the experience for extra credit in one of her classes.

Her mom hadn't liked the idea—as if Lynn hadn't already known how much they struggled to make ends meet. But she'd begged and cajoled until her mom had given in. Matilda carefully supervised everything at first, and it had taken months of Lynn enthusiastically dotting every "I" and crossing every "T" before her mom relaxed and let Lynn take over.

At first, she could only use a trickle of gaming funds. Her mom would notice if they could suddenly afford normal things like red meat. But after a year of gradual increases, she'd achieved a comfortable balance. Enough to keep a roof over their heads and the debt collectors at bay but not enough to make her mom suspicious. Anything extra she made she funneled into a savings account for college.

Sometimes her secret felt too heavy to bear. Maybe, once she turned eighteen, it wouldn't bother her mom so much to find out she was pitching in.

But there was still the problem of Larry Coughlin.

There was a saying, "two people could keep a secret if one of them was dead." The people who managed the WarMonger servers knew she wasn't some old military vet named Larry Coughlin, but that was okay. They didn't talk. If her mom knew, it might get out, and the *last* thing she needed was for her friends to find out she regularly kicked their butts for fun. Ronnie for sure would never talk to her again, and the other guys would probably follow his lead.

Lynn shook her head. No point wasting time thinking about something that she was going to make sure never happened. Right now it was time to make some real money.

"Larry Coughlin available for hire. Best game or best offer. Enemy team average L25+ only."

She needed to spend some time playing at her own level. Beating up on Tier Tens was fun, especially when she knew them and they didn't know it was her. But keeping at the top of WarMonger's charts was about playing at her level. Larry's name had been on WarMonger's leader board for years and she intended to keep it there.

There were rich people out there with plenty of money to spend on the best gear. Custom stuff. Stuff that was rare or restricted. People like that enjoyed winning, and they thought a pretty, customized laser cannon would help. But they *knew* they would win if Larry Coughlin was on their team. So, they would happily transfer that custom, tricked out, very expensive laser cannon to her for a few hours of her time.

And then she'd turn around and put it on the auction site. She already had all the powered armor and laser cannons she needed for herself. And none of them were "pretty." Pretty got you noticed. Pretty got you killed. The only place she wanted to be noticed was on the kill board showing she'd wiped out another team of topflight players more or less by herself.

She loved it when two or three rich dudes who didn't play enough to be worth a wet rag hired her to go up against a team of hardcore gamers with top kill to death ratios and the other team just up and ran.

Her gaming skills and reputation kept her and her mom afloat, and it was eventually going to pay her way through college.

Time to get to work.

"If I ever meet Larry Coughlin in real life, I'm going to kick his freaking teeth in," Ronnie Payne grumped, taking a bite of fish sticks.

The lanky seventeen-year-old had a shock of ginger hair and enough freckles to make even a Dalmatian jealous. If he'd been as physically gifted as he was mentally, Lynn might have worried. But while Ronnie was a good gamer with a quick mind and a lot of natural skill, he was all bark and no bite. The most physical she'd ever seen him was his one and only tryout for the school's ARS team—Augmented Reality Sports, the crazy, amazing fusion of in the real sports and in virtual gaming that only recent technology had made possible. The tryout had not been pretty, and she hadn't seen him do anything remotely physical since.

"They say he used to be an operator," Mack Rios said as he poked unenthusiastically at his salad.

He hated anything green, but his mom paid for the "healthy" lunch from the cafeteria dispenser, so that's what it gave him when he swiped his school ID. Lynn sometimes took pity on him and swapped meals—her mom, a nurse, had made sure she grew up liking vegetables. But today she'd been craving meat, so Mack was stuck with his rabbit food. "I mean, like a real one. Army special ops or something. I don't think you'd stand much of a chance."

Lynn had known Mack since the beginning of middle school when she and her mom had first moved to Cedar Rapids. She'd started puberty early and, being the short and curvy type, had developed embarrassingly noticeable breasts by sixth grade. The bullying had been hell. More than one of the boys had tried to get physical. Mack had been the only "safe" guy to be around in her entire sixth grade class. He hadn't exactly stuck out his neck for her—he was bullied enough himself. But he was one of the few who never teased her, and he would often sit with her so she wasn't easy pickings.

He was good people, even if he did let his mom run his life like he was her prized poodle. The recent sprinkling of fuzz on his chin was his latest attempt at acting out but his adolescent body wasn't cooperating. Coupled with an average build, straight black hair and "wannabe cool kid" attire, his looks were as unassuming and laid back as his personality.

"Naw, he can't be an operator," Dan Nguyen protested, shaking his head so enthusiastically that his school-issued AR glasses threatened to slip off his head.

The shortest of them all, Dan looked as thoroughly Asian as his last name sounded, and he seemed to think it gave him special "martial arts" powers. In virtual he excelled at fighting games and sniffed out every combo, cheat and secret move that could possibly exist. Alas, in the real there were no shortcuts and he was as graceful as a cow on ice. Where Ronnie was methodical, organized and a stickler for rules, Dan was all over the place trying out new things and coming up with wild ideas—ideas that usually paid off.

Both he and Ronnie were angling for careers in the gaming industry. They were often invited to beta test games and were constantly arguing game mechanics. "No real operator would waste time on a bunch of kids, not unless he had a bone to pick. And he'd have to know Ronnie in the real for that. How many operators do you think Ronnie knows?"

"None," Edgar Johnston said, his slow, calm voice an odd counterpoint to Dan's staccato chatter.

Lynn had always been a little intimidated by Edgar's six-foot-two bulk. But he was even more laid back than Mack, and over time she'd grown to appreciate his quiet nature. His dark eyes often sparkled with hidden amusement in his tawny face, and he was as loyal and dependable as could be even if he wasn't as obsessed with gaming as the rest of them.

"How many times we been over this?" Edgar asked, popping a handful of fries into his mouth.

"Sixty-three, by my count," Lynn offered.

WarMonger had an extensive database. One item it tracked was how many times a particular player had been in the same match as another player. She'd checked last night, and it was the sixty-third time Larry Coughlin and RonnieDarko714 had been in the same game. Ergo, that was how many times Ronnie had complained about it.

"How was your night, Lynn?" Mack asked, obviously trying to head off an explosion from Ronnie's side of the table.

Lynn was focused on needling Ronnie, so the question took her off guard. Fortunately, she always had an easy answer on tap.

"I was up all night getting ready for the Milan fashion show!" she said, brightening with false enthusiasm. "Two of my super-models got hospitalized for anorexia and none of my patterns are ready and I've got to get booking..."

She hated Kim's Diva Princess, one of the ubiquitous "fashion" games marketed for girls. Her grandparents had given it to her, thinking it was the sort of thing teenage girls played. She'd tried it once and started screaming obscenities in under two minutes. But it was perfect as a cover story because one mention of it and all her guy friends immediately changed the subject.

"Oh, you have got to be kidding me!" Ronnie said. "You're still playing that asinine game?"

"Well, at least I'm not the one who got teabagged," Lynn snapped.

"Who told you that?" Ronnie practically shouted, then lowered his voice as people looked their way. "Who told you that?"

"You get teabagged every time you go up against Larry Coughlin," Lynn said, shrugging. "So, you did, didn't you? That makes, what, sixty-three times, right?"

"I don't wanna talk about it."

"Yes," Mack sighed.

"More," Edgar said placidly. "Sometimes it happens a couple times a game."

Edgar was almost always calm, no matter how excited the rest of them got. Part of that was his nature, Lynn guessed. But the other reason he kept his temper in check was an "incident" he'd had when she'd been in seventh grade. By that time she and Mack were pretty good friends and he had introduced her to Edgar.

The day of the "incident," one of the usual eighth grade bullies had started picking on Mack, and when she'd gotten involved the bully had turned his attention, and crudely suggestive remarks, on her. That was when Edgar had stepped in. At first he'd only told the bully to back off, but when the swaggering eighth grader had ignored the warning and slapped her butt, Edgar had lost it.

It had taken four full-grown male teachers to pull Edgar off the kid. The eighth grader had ended up in the hospital while Edgar had ended up on juvie probation for two years. He'd also been held back a grade, ironically putting him in the same class as Lynn and Mack. Lynn suspected his poor grades were more the result of a horrible home life—something with his dad and alcohol but he would never talk about it—than because Edgar was bad at school.

After that Lynn tried really hard to keep Edgar out of it when she was being bullied and he tried really hard not to lose his temper. Fortunately, he had a fuse as long as Florida.

"He's a homo," Ronnie complained.

"So's Jed Pepper on the swim team," Lynn said, rolling her eyes. "What's that got to do with anything? Ya think maybe, whoever he is, he's just trying to send you the message that you don't always have to be the biggest smart aleck around?"

"What do you know? You play fashion ranch or whatever."

"Diva Princess."

"See what I mean?" Ronnie said. "Girls got no game."

Lynn gritted her teeth and shut up before she gave herself away. For all of Ronnie's smarts, he was about as flexible in his thinking as a slab of granite. He was also a raging misogynist when it came to gaming, which was ridiculous considering the number of celebrity female gamers out there. Lynn had no idea what his problem was.

For now, she would content herself with humiliating him in virtual. And occasionally getting paid to do it.

Gaming had its perks.

"Sooo, you guys hear the TD Hunter announcement that they're going to reveal something super big next week as a lead-up to the June fifteenth launch?" Dan asked, fairly bouncing in his seat. "They're playing it close to the chest. I can't find any leaks at all. Any guesses what it is?"

"Maybe they're finally going to announce open beta," Mack said, leaning forward and pulling at his wisps of beard. "That would be epic. You guys both applied for closed beta, right?"

"Yeah," Ronnie said, his tone sour. "Those idiots wouldn't know a good opportunity if it danced naked in front of them."

Lynn had to work to keep a smirk from giving her away. Maybe it was petty, being amused that Ronnie and Dan had been rejected as betas. If Ronnie hadn't made such a big deal about it beforehand—bragging as if he'd already been picked—she wouldn't have had to fight so hard not to grin.

Beta testing was a process most games went through, selecting professional gamers from around the world to "close beta" their platform pre-release in order to work out the kinks. Some games also did an "open beta" right before launch, letting anyone who wanted to beta in on it, usually to stress test their system and avoid launch day mishaps or server overloads. Lynn had done some beta testing herself over the years. She might have even applied to beta test TD Hunter if it hadn't been a freaking augmented reality game.

Dan and Mack argued about what they thought the big announcement would be while Ronnie scowled and Edgar methodically finished his food. Lynn kept her mouth shut, mostly because she'd been nursing a grudge against TD Hunter for months. It wasn't fair that it was AR instead of in virtual where she could enjoy it without going *outside* where there were *people*. The game itself looked really impressive, which was no doubt why, despite Ronnie, Dan and Mack's complete lack of athletic ability, they had been obsessing over it for months. It was as if they thought that, as soon as they put on their AR glasses, they would somehow magically be able to do back flips like the man in the ad.

Step into the real.

Lynn snorted at the thought. It was certainly a clever marketing ploy and it annoyed her that even she was drawn in by it. Not that inspiring millions of basement-dwelling gamers world-wide to poke their noses outside for a bit of fresh air and exercise was a bad thing. AR games had been trying to do that for decades, with limited success. It wasn't that people weren't familiar with AR technology. It, along with VR, had single-handedly saved the sanity of billions during the 2020s. Then the 2030s started and there had been the big push to get everyone outside again and the mesh web took off.

Corporations figured out they could spam people walking down the sidewalk or riding the airbus with ads—unless they paid their opt-out fee. But gaming companies still had humanity's collective laziness to overcome. People loved watching AR sports but ask the same people to go outside themselves and get hot and sweaty? Good luck with that. Every new AR game, local paramedics became experts at treating heat stroke.

Still, with its massive marketing campaign, maybe TD Hunter would be the first AR game to make it big in a world that increasingly lived in virtual.

The bell tone sounded over the intercom, calling them all back to class. Lynn looked at the rest of her lunch, considered her waistline and left it.

"See you later. I gotta book it to get logged in to Mr. Harris' class. He gets crazy about attendance when finals are this close."

Lynn got a chorus of goodbyes and one annoyed grunt in response. She turned away and waved over her shoulder as she headed off, finally allowing a smile to spread across her face at Ronnie's continued bad temper.

Yes, gaming did have its perks.

"Hey, Mom!" Lynn said as she walked in the door of their apartment.

"Hi, sweetie," Matilda Raven replied, looking up from her breakfast of coffee, eggs and toast. She worked graveyard shift at St. Sebastian's Memorial Hospital, so this was "morning" to her. "You're home late today. Did the airbus have to stop for an emergency charge again?"

"Yeah. You'd think they'd upgrade the batteries in those things, but I guess no one cares if a bunch of high schoolers have to wait around for forever. I can't believe how crowded the air lanes have gotten in the past few years. It wasn't like this in middle school."

Lynn saw her mom's lips purse. Unlike most of her friends' parents, her mom actually attended Parent-Teacher night and paid attention to things like government policy and the news.

"Local governments are trying to put so many restrictions on manuals that people will stop using them. I know it's frustrating but it's an important process. Vehicular fatalities have more than halved since they made the big push to autonomous vehicles and air taxis, honey. It just kills me every time I treat a car accident patient in my ER, knowing it could have been avoided if they would stop being stubborn and let the AIs do the driving."

"I know, I know," Lynn said, dumping her backpack in a chair and going to the cabinet to root out a snack. It wasn't that she didn't care about such things, in theory. She would just rather be shooting people in the comfortable solitude of her room than sitting around on a crowded airbus. She could, technically, play any number of games on her AR glasses while she waited. But playing in front of other people completely defeated the purpose of gaming, as far as she was concerned. She usually worked on homework instead, to give herself more time to game when she was at home.

"Going to my room if that's okay?"

"Can you empty the dishwasher, first, please?" Matilda said, after a bit of a sigh.

"Oh, yeah. Sorry, Mom," Lynn said, going to the dishwasher. "I forgot last night. I was playing—"

"Video games," Matilda finished for her.

"Yes," Lynn replied, unable to keep a bit of sarcasm from her tone.

"It's not that, Lynn," Matilda said, setting down her coffee and turning toward her daughter. "I'd rather have you home playing video games than out, well..."

"Getting into trouble?" Lynn, said, turning from the cabinet to raise an eyebrow at her mother. "Hanging out with bad boys?" She couldn't help rolling her eyes and smiling at the thought. Her mom smiled back.

"Better games than drugs," Matilda said. "But if you could *try* to remember your chores?"

"I know, I know," Lynn repeated. She stuffed her snack in the top of her backpack, then hurried to start emptying the dishwasher. She'd seen the new ones on the stream channels that had built-in dish storage and that sorted all your dishes automatically once they were clean. But their apartment's appliances were twice as old as her at least, probably dating back to the turn of the century. No smart kitchen for them. "I do try, Mom. I just get caught up, you know?"

"Not really but I can use my imagination." Another smile. "So...anything interesting happen at school today?"

"Nothing particularly bad," Lynn said. "Just all of the teachers are freaking out about finals, as usual. It's like they forget we do this every year."

"Well, finals *are* really important. You can't blame them for wanting you to do well."

Lynn rolled her eyes again, stretching to reach the cabinets above the sink. Despite the fact that her father had been a blond-haired, blue-eyed Scandinavian giant, she hadn't managed to get a single drop of his height or looks. She blamed all her vertical challenges on her mother's Lakota genes. To be fair, she did appreciate her long, silky black hair and the fact that she wasn't a pale ghost like Ronnie, despite never going outside. That and her eyes. They were a light hazel so vibrant and flecked with gold that her mom called them "wolf eyes." Even though they were one more thing about her that set her apart and invited bullying, she still liked them.

"They don't care whether or not we do well, Mom. They just want their end-of-the-year stats to make them look good," Lynn pointed out.

"I'm sure that's not true, sweetie."

"Uh, yeah. If you say so, Mom," Lynn offered without

enthusiasm, deciding to change the topic. "One funny thing did happen today. Ronnie got mugged in virtual again."

"Mugged?" Matilda asked. "How do you get mugged online?"

Lynn turned around and grinned.

"Ronnie's got an enemy in WarMonger. This guy turns up from time to time and pretty much destroys the whole team. Then he disappears. They can't figure out why. Nobody even knows who he is. It happened again last night, and Ronnie was complaining about it our entire lunch break."

"I don't know why you don't play with them," her mom said. "I mean, I do and I don't. But sometimes I'd prefer it if you were over at Mack's house than holed up here all the time."

"Mack's house?" Lynn said. "Mom, Mrs. Rios hates me, remember? She thinks I've been trying to steal her precious little boy since sixth grade. And I don't game with them because Ronnie is a pig-head and thinks girls are no good at games. So I stay here and play my own games instead." *In more ways than one,* she added silently, holding back another grin.

"Well, I guess that makes sense. But you should really get out now and then. It doesn't matter how much nutritious food I cook, a healthy lifestyle includes fresh air and sunshine." Sometimes having a nurse for a mom had its drawbacks.

"Tell that to Goths," Lynn said, making her mom laugh. "I do get sun, in between leaving the apartment and getting on the school airbus. Dishes are done. Mind if I go to my room?"

"Sure, honey." Matilda said with a sigh. "Have fun. I'll call you when supper's ready."

Mom left for her shift after dinner and once Lynn had gotten the dishes in the dishwasher, she could finally settle down to make money. She went into WarMonger and joined a free-form among other top tiers for about an hour. Win some, lose some, it all evens out in the end. Her ranking inched up a few meager points, which was all she was really after. Unless you put in the time fighting your peers you'd start slipping. Couldn't merc all the time.

In the last round, she managed to finally get up on Yoda-Master, which was something. He generally stayed in the top five world-wide players. Managing to bag him not once but twice in one game was probably what put her up in points. She was pretty sure it had more to do with YodaMaster having a bad night than that she had somehow surpassed him. But still, it felt pretty satisfying.

"Yoda, you're off your game tonight," Lynn said, her voice safely disguised by her modulator. "I'm glad to take advantage but you wouldn't last a night in Johannesburg."

"I've been to Johannesburg, Larry," Yoda replied. "I was just fine. It's not nearly as bad as you make it out to these kids. Real world stuff on my mind, is all. You up for another round? I'll wipe the floor with you this time."

"As much as I love making you eat your words, I gotta go make the man his money," Lynn replied. She wasn't even sure what the term meant, other than "time to make money," but it was one she'd picked up scanning various boards.

Keeping up the Larry persona was a matter of constant research and coming up with new quip lines based on it. Some of it, stuff like the Bosnian Civil War, she'd rolled into classes. She'd made sure to spin it right for her teachers but had dug into things like MPRI, who sounded like actual bad-asses, and other mercenary groups like Tzarist Wolves, who were more like bar thugs with guns.

She'd decided that "Larry" was an old guy, like, really old. He was a vet of the Bosnian wars back in the '90s, probably Special Forces, then later a mercenary. He was badly injured sometime after the turn of the century, maybe during the Iraq or Afghanistan conflict. He'd probably been a black ops assassin who'd "retired" a bunch of opposing tribal leaders, off the books of course. He was definitely paranoid and pretty much assumed there were still people out there who wanted him dead. He'd probably spent some time with CIA paramil but more in the Middle East or maybe South America than Europe.

After he was injured by an IED, he'd gotten into gaming and established a presence in virtual to keep up some semblance of still being an "operator." He brought full-on operator experience and training to his matches, which let him "feel" like he was back in the "good old days retiring terrorists and drug lords." She "knew" all that but kept most of it secret, especially the "in a wheelchair" stuff. And his name wasn't "Larry Coughlin" any more than hers was. She'd never decided on a "real" name for him. Not knowing made Larry feel more like a skin—like a mindset or a memory—that she could slip in and out of at will, rather than a made-up person she was pretending to be.

The problem, though, was the quips. Not only how to correctly pronounce names like "Medellin," Med-ah-een, but how a guy like *Larry* would pronounce it. One wrong pronunciation and her cover would be blown.

To pick up the general feel of things, she lurked on boards like Arfcom. There were plenty of military contractors on those boards and they'd sometimes drop a line that made sense to her. That's where she'd picked up terms like "operator" and "snake." She'd picked up "Going to make the man his money" on one of the boards and it was always followed by congratulations. When someone had asked "Where?" he'd been immediately slapped down and called a noob.

You never asked where anyone lived, you never asked them where they were going. Just "out of town" or sometimes "OCONUS" which meant something like "out of the country." Though she had seen some different stuff recently, more people than usual posting "Time to make the man his money" or "going op," which meant "going operational"—going somewhere to do something "shooty" as one guy put it—without adding "out of town" or "OCONUS." Maybe there was some special training operation or readiness drill going on. She knew the military did those sometimes.

It was an ongoing job, expanding her knowledge of military operations, history, culture, lingo and the like. What had started out as a simple information dive, though, had turned into a weird sort of hobby—watching documentaries, following ex-military guys on their stream channels, searching through declassified military documents and, of course, reading the boards. It was fun digging up the most obscure references and figuring out how to fool everyone into thinking she was some grizzled old merc who slept with a knife under his pillow and gun on his bedside table. And another one under the pillow.

And the boards were the weirdest place. It wasn't only that people didn't speak anything like a normal language. Ma Deuce and LES and ESA and other acronyms seemed to be half the postings. No personal sharing at all. People who tried were more or less driven off. Except when it was a young vet. There were guys, women even, who were vets from Iraq and Afghanistan, GWOT as they put it, who would post about problems. Those were fine. But come on and start complaining about your day and the replies would mostly be insults. Which seemed to be what the posters expected. That if you complained about mundane stuff you'd be insulted. The insults seemed to even help and some of them were rough. She kept the better ones for when she was really mad at someone in a WarMonger match.

Then there were what she'd mentally termed "the crazies." The ones who posted about the wacky conspiracy theories were her favorites. The world was run by, depending on your take, a cabal of rich people, or the eternal boogeyman China, or big-media corporations or big-tech or big-industrial, or big-media or -tech or -industrial Chinese corporations, or by a cabal of shadowy bureaucrats, most of whom were Chinese or bought by the Chinese. Or aliens. Who apparently were from the extra-terrestrial China. Or possibly in league with China. But China was involved. Somehow.

As a kid who'd grown up with irregular shutdowns of the entire economy over the latest "novel virus" to start up, which, yes, *might* have *something* to do with China, occasionally, she found the preppers to be on the "less than" crazy side. Slightly. When she'd started making money in WarMonger she'd also started to, slowly, build up supplies. It wasn't like they could keep much in the apartment. But she'd just order a bit more than they actually needed per month so if something "happened" they'd have some materials to fall back on.

Especially toilet paper. She agreed, wholeheartedly, there was no such thing as "too much" toilet paper. Just more than you could stock.

Lately, the conspiracy buffs and preppers had been particularly fired up. "Something" was happening. Capital Something. They were comparing notes on random occurrences across the globe and "proving" how the media was covering up "something." An airbus crash here, an "unexplained" power outage, for which there was always a clear explanation, there.

China was "up to something." Probably activating its final plan to take over the world through...they weren't sure what but they were prepared to take the fight to the invading Chinese hordes at their "BOL," bug-out location, when SHTF, stuff hits the fan. Which was going to happen any, day, now...Any...day...The Yellow Peril is going to strike...

Sigh.

Despite all that, she liked some of the guys who were . . . sane. She'd seen reasoned arguments against women in combat positions. She knew even if she was in shape she couldn't play football against guys and in the real world she'd never be able to do most of the stuff she did in WarMonger. She also, quietly, thought there were such things as "biological males" and they shouldn't be in women's sports. She'd seen explanations of the price of having gays in combat units. "Fraternization" was apparently a huge issue in small teams and having people who were sexually attracted to each other increased a problem that could get people killed in combat. She could sort of see it. But most of the posting on any political subject was ranting. And anyone saying *anything* good about the VA was in for a round of pummeling.

She never posted herself. But there were a few of the posters who seemed . . . calmer. More empathetic, maybe. She'd occasionally, carefully, send one of them a question about something.

"I'm researching a paper about the Drug Wars in the '80s and I have to give an oral report. And I've got a question. How do *you* pronounce 'Medellin'?"

Her persona for the boards was a teenage male, Tom Reynolds, who was "4F," unfit for military service due to asthma but "into" the military. *"Yeah, I'm a wannabe but I'm pro-military. Just don't post cause no background."*

Lies and more lies.

"Okay, then. I'll probably see you round," Yoda said, sounding disappointed at her begging off another match. "I need to blow off some steam."

"Bad week?" Lynn asked. She liked YodaMaster despite the cocky name. He was the only top tier who she hated beating because he was so nice about it.

"Oh, just putting out dumpster fires at work," Yoda said. "Can't get into specifics, get my throat cut if I did. Burn before reading and all that."

Lynn had to think fast about a Larry response on that one. "Burn before reading" meant "highly classified." Yoda wasn't military or anything as far as she knew. He'd mostly dropped hints about working in the gaming industry.

"I didn't know you were secret squirrel," Lynn said, letting the surprised tone into her voice.

"I didn't used to be," Yoda said. "And I wish I still wasn't. You probably know how it is, knowing stuff you wish you didn't."

"Got it," Lynn said, not getting anything.

"Well, I'd better get a move on," Yoda said. "Gotta go collect some heads. Metaphorically."

Lynn looked up at her wall at a bunch of post-it notes for a good quip. She was probably one of the few people her age who still even used paper and pen. But then when you were poor, you made do. In any case, she liked the physicality of it. The realness helped her connect on a deeper level with "Larry" and the kind of world he would have grown up in.

"Keep the ears," she said, voice deadpan. "Only way you can collect the bounty."

She pulled the post-it note down and reluctantly tossed it in the trash. It was a good quip. She'd probably use it again.

"Larry, you crack me up," Yoda said. "When you don't scare me, anyway. See ya."

"One night in Melbourne will make a strong man tumble," Lynn said.

"That's Bangkok, Larry," DragonRider772 said. "I've heard that song."

"You've never been in the parts of Melbourne I have, kid," Lynn replied in Larry's gravelly tone as she focused her sights on her last target and pulled the trigger. "Aaand that's the last of them. Make sure you make the payment schedule."

"Will do, Larry," DragonRider said. "Thanks for the assist."

"Thanks for the cash," Lynn said. "Got a girlfriend who's greedy as a Bangkok coochi girl. Gotta find some more clients. I'm didi mao."

Lynn exited the match. Good game. High level players, mostly mercs, with their clients along for the ride. And the clients weren't noobs either. Tough fight but her side had won.

She put up a post of availability and got an immediate ping.

Robert Krator: Larry, mind coming up on voice?

There was a blinking link to a voice chat.

Lynn sat, frozen in shock. It wasn't like she hadn't been asked to voice chat before. Most of the time she'd do initial negotiations in voice then finalize in text for a record.

But this was a query from freaking Robert Krator.

Robert Krator was the *creator* of WarMonger and it was not his first mega-successful game. He was a legend in the gaming community and one of Tsunami Entertainment's top game developers.

And he wanted to talk to Larry Coughlin? Why?

Wait. He owned WarMonger. He knew perfectly well that he wasn't talking to "Larry Coughlin." He was talking to a sixteen-going-on-seventeen-year-old girl from Cedar Rapids named Lynn Raven.

The real question was, why did he want to talk to *Lynn Raven*?

It had to be *the* Robert Krator. Nobody would dare, much less get away with, posting as him on WarMonger.

Larry Coughlin: May I ask why?

Robert Krator: In voice. Not text. Don't worry, not going to blow your cover, Larry.

Lynn hit the link.

"Hi, Lynn," Mr. Krator said. "Glad to finally talk to you. First, you're not in any kind of trouble with the game or otherwise. It's all good. I actually need to ask you a favor."

"A favor?" Lynn squeaked, then remembered she still had her modulator on. "Ahem, I mean, 'A favor?'" she repeated in a lower voice.

"Lynn, this is kind throwing me," Krator said. "I'll talk to 'Larry' if you insist but could you turn off the voice modulator?"

"Sure," she said, switching it off. "That better, Mr. Krator?"

"Call me Rob," Krator said. "Lynn, first let me congratulate you both on your rankings and on your persona. I'll admit I play my own game from time to time so we've met. Allow me to keep my own anonymity if you will. But some of the best times I've had playing my own game is playing with 'Larry Coughlin.' I dislike all the foul-mouthed cursing that goes on, but Larry's comments are a hoot. Where do you get them?"

"I watch some military streams and I've done a lot of research," Lynn said, trying to hide her smile, then remembered they were on voice only, not video. "I go on military boards and lurk and look up things I don't understand. 'Gotta burrow into Charlie like a stone snake, boy!'"

"That's what I meant," Krator said, laughing. "Thank you. Laughter has been limited, lately. Which brings me to the favor. I'm rolling out a new game, an AR FPS called TransDimensional Hunter. Heard about it?"

"Uh, yes, sir," Lynn said, chuckling. "I'm pretty sure everybody in the world has heard about your game, at least judging by how often your ads pop up. I'm not big into AR games myself, but it looks interesting. Interdimensional beings invading and you've got to hunt them down, right?"

"That is the game, yes," Krator said. "Would you like to be a beta tester?"

Lynn frowned, absolutely sure she'd misheard. "What did you say?"

"Would you like to be a beta tester for TD Hunter?"

"You mean, like, for open beta?" she asked.

"No, Lynn," Krator said, chuckling at her disbelief. "We're not planning on doing an open beta. Closed beta only."

Lynn swallowed hard, too stunned to speak. Robert Krator was personally inviting her to beta test one of his games? This was an opportunity she should be jumping on without a second's hesitation.

So, why did her lips feel glued shut?

She couldn't count how many times she'd daydreamed about being like those athletic actors in the TD Hunter commercials—whirling, spinning, killing like she was born to do it. But those daydreams were stupid. It was just a game, even if it did invite her to "Step into the real." She was a couch potato and a happy one at that. What if she sucked at it?

And that was only half of it.

You couldn't monetize a game in beta. She'd have to take significant time away from her bread and butter for what was basically an honorary position. She *could* withdraw money from her savings to cover bills for a few months, but she needed that money for college. Even though her mom didn't even know what she'd been contributing all this time—and would tell her she shouldn't be if she knew—Lynn still felt responsible...

"Sir, I'm really honored, but..."

"But you can't make money off of it," Krator finished for her. He didn't sound the least bit surprised.

"Well...yeah."

"I don't mind the mercing, Lynn," Krator said. "When it started up in my first big hit game, some of my fellow developers were incensed. I pointed out to them that they'd just made more money than God himself, so who were they to get all upset about people making money off a game? TD Hunter is set up specifically for serious gamers to monetize. Not in beta, obviously, but not long after it launches you should be making as much money as you do at WarMonger. And remember, as a beta you'll have an early foot in the door. You'll know all the ins and outs before everyone else. The market will be yours to dominate. Any other objections?"

"Uh... I don't have a decent AR interface and my LINC is as basic as it gets." Lynn said. "I know that sounds lame, but I've never told my mom about the money I make in WarMonger and she can't afford to buy me good equipment."

"Hm, I wasn't aware you were..." Krator said, then paused. "How does this sound? Free equipment. Top of the line. Replacement plan since there are still... quirks with the game. Six months free usage, unlimited, as long as you're using it regularly for TD Hunter. If you drop out after six months, you pick it up at corporate rate. About a fifth of the regular plan. And you keep the equipment either way. Does that cover it?"

Lynn swallowed again. Was this guy for real? Was she dreaming? Finally she gathered her wits and courage and voiced the thing that was really holding her back.

"Um, hate to break it to you, but I'm really nothing like Larry in WarMonger. I'm not some elite operator. I've never wanted to be a soldier or even a Girl Scout. I'm just a nerd who really likes her body-mold chair. I'm regularly in danger of failing PE at school. I'm not athletic *at all* and I hate going outside. There's bugs and sun and people and... I like being in virtual—it's safe. I'm not Larry Freaking Coughlin. I'm just Lynn Raven. Nobody special..."

She trailed off, suddenly blushing as she realized how much she was oversharing. She might as well have shouted that she was socially averse and had body image issues. Why could she never seem to play it cool with people?

"You know, I totally get it. Really," Krator said, his voice surprisingly kind. "You... probably *wouldn't* be surprised how many gamers feel exactly the same way. Even me, I have to admit. The more time I can spend alone the better. But I've learned I have to get out there, to run the business if nothing else. I spent years in dark rooms, developing, programming, designing. Getting out in the light was scary. But I've found it's pretty good out here once you get used to it. Believe me, you're not the first one I've talked to who brought up that objection. A few do exist who are very athletic, like Tommy Jones, but they're rare."

Tommy was a guy around her tier but much better known. He'd merc occasionally, but mostly he made his money from endorsements and tournaments. For Lynn to do tournaments she'd have to reveal she was "Larry" and she didn't want to do that. Girls got nothing but grief in FPS gaming. It was a predominantly guy sport and most guys preferred it that way.

She had a bit of a crush on Tommy, who was, yes, very fit, very good looking and *very* good at WarMonger. Not quite as good as her but still Tier One. She'd even written him a fan message once, then gone easy on him for a month in game, waiting to see if he would write back. But he never had and from their interactions in WarMonger, she knew he was an arrogant prick. So after that, she'd set out to thoroughly and regularly kick his pretty butt. It had been neck and neck for a while, but she'd finally advanced and he'd dropped a couple of spots behind, cursing Larry all the way.

"You, however," Krator continued, "are special, whether you realize it or not. Unlike players such as Tommy, you bring something to beta that's rare. You're a patternist. You see things other people don't, the patterns that even the developers don't realize are there but need to know about so they don't become an exploitable weakness. People like Tommy just have good hand-eye coordination, lightning reflexes, and in Tommy's case, he's been gaming since he was two. You've got most of that yourself and you outthought me in my own game. That's exceptional. I need that in a tester for this game. I need *you*, Lynn. Not some merc named Larry. I know it's a temporary loss of income. I can't fix that other than offering some top-of-the-line equipment. But I'm asking as a personal favor: help me make this the best game of the century. Do say yes, Lynn. Please."

Lynn let out a breath. When he put it like that . . . One of her all-time heroes of the gaming industry was asking her for a personal favor, what did he expect her to say?

"Of course, Mr. Krator. I'd be honored," she said. "But I do have a . . . condition."

"Let's hear it," Krator said.

"I'll accept the equipment, but . . . if I end up quitting after the beta period, I'm returning it," Lynn insisted, feeling uncomfortable. "Either that or I'll buy it myself or something. If I'm not playing the game, I'm not going to have you pay for stuff that's not being used for it."

"That is remarkably altruistic and totally unnecessary," Robert said, his tone tinged with amusement. "You wouldn't believe how much funding I've got for this game. The investors really went all-in, you might say, so there's a lot riding on its success."

"I'm not going to cheat you," Lynn said firmly. "I don't let people renege when I merc for them, so I'm not going to renege on you. I don't care if you can afford it."

"Condition accepted," Robert said. "Now, what kind of AR interface do you want us to send? I suppose retinal implants are off the table, considering you're underage..."

Lynn laughed, assuming he was joking.

"Yeah, my mom would be about as likely to approve that as brain implants. I thought they learned their lesson after that implant hacking scandal, but people have short memories. My mom is kinda old school, maybe because she's a nurse? She doesn't trust technology you can't take off at the end of the day."

"It sounds like your mother is a careful woman who cares deeply about her daughter," Robert said.

"That's one way to put it," Lynn muttered.

"Ah—well," Robert coughed, "your options, then, are contacts, glasses, or one of those full-on helmets that seems more popular with the younger crowd. Those are 'cool,' right?"

"Are you kidding me? I'd get laughed at everywhere I went. Glasses are fine. At least then I'll blend in."

"Glasses it is. What about your LINC? We can do any config you want. Necklace, ring, bracelet, watch, you name it."

Lynn considered the question. Her current LINC—a Limitless Integrated Network Connector—was so old it was almost one of the original models from when they'd debuted in 2033 and had replaced cell phones as the new "do everything in the palm of your hand" technology. Hers was in the standard smartwatch configuration. With the advances in 3D printing, they could make them in almost any shape and size you wanted nowadays, it simply had to be something you wore close to your skin, since their batteries were powered by body heat and the body's movement. Wrist configs were the most clunky and Lynn kept the baggy sleeves of her hoodie pulled down over hers so people at school wouldn't tease her about it. Necklaces were more popular, but she'd always hated having something around her neck.

"What about a ring?" she finally asked.

"Perfect. Done. You should see all the necessary equipment delivered by tomorrow, maybe the next day if they have to print your LINC special. But I assume our suppliers have plenty of configs already available. I hope you like the game, Lynn. It's a pretty wild ride."

"I'm sure I'll love it," she said. "I've loved every other game you've designed. I'm just not sure how well I'll adapt to gaming in the real. I mean, it looks amazing in your ads, but I see AR players walking around sometimes waving their hands, and well...they look kinda funny."

"Don't worry," Krator said with a chuckle. "You'll get used to it really quick. Plus, you won't be alone. We're pushing this game, hard. Lots of pre-reg incentives, competitions, prizes. It's going to popularize AR gaming like never before, so you won't be the only one out there having fun, I promise. In fact, I suspect you're going to love the challenge of being outside a lot more than you think. This game is...different from anything I've developed before. I hope you'll do well. No, I *know* you'll do well. I just hope you enjoy it enough to keep playing."

"I hope so too. It certainly sounds interesting," Lynn said graciously.

"But enough rambling. I know you've got money to make, Lynn. Your TD Hunter beta profile is set up and waiting to go. There's heavy technical and tactical support, so don't hesitate to ping us if you need anything at all. You're going to enjoy it. Just play. That's the important part. The game AI will record all your feedback real-time and of course we'll be poring over your combat logs. We need to get it dialed in by June fifteenth when we roll out. Oh, there will be a non-disclosure agreement for you and your mother to sign as well as an end-user license agreement. Usual stuff. And I'm throwing in a couple freebies that it'll cost more to send back than keep. Standard swag package, for promotion purposes and as a thank you. So, even if you drop the game and equipment, hang onto them. Okay?"

"Okay," Lynn said again. "It was a real honor talking to you, sir. Thanks for this opportunity."

"No thanks necessary, Lynn," Krator said. "It's an honor to have you on board. If it's not too forward of me to say, I think you should remember that 'Lynn Raven' is special in a very important way, not just 'Larry Coughlin.' Don't let anyone tell you different. Got to go now. Hope to talk to you again some time. Maybe we'll get a chance to meet in the real someday and I can thank you in person. Oh, and don't forget to turn your modulator back on. Don't want to blow your cover."

"Oh, yeah, thanks. Er, bye?" Lynn said, then winced. Real smooth, Lynn. Real smooth.

The link dropped.

"Well, that was weird," Lynn said, finally relaxing for the first time since she'd picked up the call.

"I'll wait to see the equipment before I get my hopes up," Lynn said to her empty room. Mr. Krator had probably overstated things. He was the guy at the top, after all, not the one sending out boxes. Her stuff would probably get here and it wouldn't be that much better than what she had already.

Now all she had to do was figure out how to tell her mom. Well, her mom *had* been bugging her to get outside more, so that should work in her favor . . . but she'd worry about it later. She still had work to do before bed.

When she checked her messages she had one from a regular client. His friend had amassed a team of mostly First or Second Tiers. Tommy Jones was in it, mercing for a change and the friend was sending smack talk. Would Larry join his team?

She knew both. She'd merced for the other guy before. They were a couple of Silicon trust fund babies who thought they were the world's greatest gamers and blamed their failings on lag and equipment.

Sure, trust fund boy, I'll save your pretty butt. I've body-guarded from . . .

Lynn looked at the map on her wall and thought about it for a second . . .

From Mandalay to . . . somewhere in Africa or South America that started with M . . . Used Medellin too many times. Mozambique? Too close to Myanmar . . . Would trust fund baby know that?

Larry Coughlin: Sure, buddy. I've bodyguarded from Burma to Basrah. The long way . . .

This beta testing had better not take up *all* her time. Now to see what the market would bear . . .

Larry Coughlin: Let's come up on voice and discuss price.

At the last second she remembered to turn her modulator back on.

Chapter 2

LYNN HAD STAYED UP WAY TOO LATE THE NIGHT BEFORE CARE-fully rehearsing what she was going to say to her mother. She was fully prepared. Well, after a few false starts...

"Mom, I have been extended the great honor of being a beta tester for a new game, TransDimensional Hunter!"

"Is this a fishing thing?"

"What? Why would it be about fish?"

"Betta are a type of fish..."

No, no, no.

"Mother, I have been extended the great honor of being a beta tester for a new game, TransDimensional Hunter!"

"Is this for your Latin club at school?"

"No, Mom, it's a gaming thing. In virtual, you know?"

Ugh.

That morning at the breakfast table, Lynn was trying to work up the courage to start the conversation when...

"What do you need?" Matilda asked, pausing with her cup of orange juice halfway to her mouth, giving her daughter a pointed look. She was getting ready for bed as usual and coffee wasn't on the menu.

"Mom, I have been...what?" Lynn said, finally registering what her mom had said.

"You either need something from me, or you did something

and you're trying to figure out damage control," Matilda said tiredly. "Money?"

"No!" Lynn said. "I know we don't have much. When is the last time I asked for money?"

"Too long ago," Matilda said with a thoughtful frown. "Don't think I haven't noticed that you buy your own clothes and shoes. I've been minding my own business and not asking who has been giving it to you...for now. So, what is it? School trip?"

"I've been asked to be a beta tester," Lynn said in a rush.

"Is that a school thing?" her mom asked. "One of the new standardized tests?"

"No, Mom," Lynn said, trying not to sigh. "It's a gaming term, what they call people who test out new games."

"Do you have to buy anything for it?" Matilda asked, ever money-conscious.

"Nope, that's what's so cool." Lynn said, leaning forward. "There's no money about it. There's a new game releasing in June, an AR FPS—I mean, an augmented reality first-person-shooter game. It's a *huge* honor being asked to beta. And they're giving me new AR glasses and LINC because I need them to do the testing."

"So...it's a good thing?" her mother said.

"*Yes*, Mom" Lynn replied. "It's a *really* good thing. Like... I don't know, being chosen to work on a groundbreaking new procedure or something."

"And they are *giving* you new equipment?" her mom asked carefully. "Are you sure this isn't a scam?"

"Given who contacted me, yes, I'm sure," Lynn said. "Believe me, I was skeptical at first too. Companies don't usually give beta testers much more than a cheap T-shirt, if that."

"Who contacted you?" Matilda asked. Her brow was furrowed and she'd put down her cup of orange juice to give Lynn her full attention.

"Robert Krator!" Lynn said excitedly. At her mother's complete lack of response, she sighed. "Means nothing to you, right?"

"Nope, sorry, sweetie," Matilda said.

"He's super big in gaming. Like, a world-famous developer," Lynn said.

"And he was talking to you?" Matilda said, looking more and more wary. "Personally?"

"He recruited me *personally* for the beta test," Lynn said. "We talked in game for about twenty minutes. It was *awesome*! He said he hoped to meet me some day!"

"Meet whyyy?" Matilda asked, drawing out the last syllable.

"Because he's designed some of my favorite games of all time?" Lynn said, trying to divine where the conversation was going.

"Okay, well...I'm just worried about an older man contacting you online and—"

"Good grief—really, Mom?" Lynn said. "We're talking about *Robert Krator*, here, okay? How do I get you to understand? *Billionaire* game developer? Elon Musk of gaming? Not some creepy pedophile. *Everybody* in gaming knows who he is. I only needed to talk to you about it because there are some licensing agreements and non-disclosures stuff you'll need to sign, since I'm underage. And there should be a delivery sometime in the next few days. Hopefully we don't have to sign for it, I know you don't like getting woken up for deliveries. Oh, and I'm going to have to, ugh, go outside. Because it's an augmented reality game and everything."

Matilda looked a little shell-shocked at the gush of information, but her eyebrow raised at the mention of the outdoors.

"Where outside?" she asked.

"Wherever the game takes me?" Lynn said and shrugged. "I'm not sure. Haven't seen the game, yet."

"Well, you'll need to be careful, honey," Matilda said, frowning again. "I know I said you should get out more and I *am* excited you got asked to, um, beta? But wandering around the city by yourself is *not* what I had in mind. I don't want you out after dark and you need to stay here around the apartment complex."

"Mom, I'm not a little kid anymore. I'm almost seventeen. And besides, I have to test this thing to destruction," Lynn insisted. "Find out everything about it. Every weakness, every bug. That's why they're giving me all this stuff for free. I'm not going to be able to do that by staying in the complex."

"Look, sweetie, I understand this is important to you. But even if you *are* almost seventeen, you're not an adult and I'm still responsible for your safety. I don't want you wandering around all by yourself at night. That should be understandable."

Lynn sighed. This was going to be more trouble than she'd thought.

"Okay, well, what if I've got someone with me?"

"Someone like Mack from school?" Matilda asked.

Lynn shrugged. That was *not* who she'd been thinking of. She had no intention of telling any of her gaming group that she'd been personally picked by Robert Krator to beta the biggest game of the decade that they'd been rejected from.

"Well, I'd definitely feel better about you being out and about with a friend, but if something happened, I don't think Mack would be much of a help, do you?"

"Not really, no," Lynn said, her lips quirking. She thought for a moment, then decided to go ahead and throw it out there. "What about Edgar? He's eighteen already, so I'd technically be with an adult."

"Hmm." Matilda looked seriously at her daughter and Lynn forced herself to calmly meet her mother's gaze. Her mom knew all about Edgar's "incident." Everyone had gossiped about it for weeks after the fact. Some of the parents had taken it as an excuse to warn their kids away from Edgar. Lynn's mom had been of the opinion that anyone who stood up to bullies ought to be commended, though she did caution Lynn to "be careful" around her friend.

"That would…probably be all right," Matilda said slowly. "But I'd really prefer if you went with a group, not just you and a boy by yourself."

Lynn resisted the urge to roll her eyes.

"We're just friends, Mom."

"Ahh, famous last words of every teenage girl ever," Matilda said, a little smile forming on her lips as she picked up her orange juice to finish it.

"Ew, Mom, gross! These are my *gaming* friends we're talking about."

Her mom shrugged, still smiling.

"Well, what about, um, what's her name—Kayla? She's nice."

"Uh-uh, no way. We haven't been friends since her mom got remarried to that rich guy and she started hanging with the pop-girl crowd at school. There's no way she'd be caught dead with me. It might ruin her precious image."

"Oh." Matilda's eyebrows shot up. "I didn't realize when they moved out of the apartment next door that you all, um, went your separate ways. I knew she still went to the same school."

"Yeah. We hung out for a little at school, until she ghosted me without a word of explanation. That's when I really got into gaming."

"Yes, I remember. You were, what, thirteen? I knew you were going through a lot at school with puberty and everything. Goodness, that seems so long ago."

"Not long enough," Lynn muttered.

"All right, well, maybe you can make some new friends around the complex. Other people playing this kind of game. Can't you partner with someone?"

"Not with it being in beta," Lynn said. "It's not even out, yet. But, I dunno, maybe I can get somebody to just walk with me."

"What's it called again?" Matilda asked.

"TransDimensional Hunter," Lynn said. "TD Hunter for short."

"Oh!" Matilda exclaimed. "You should have said that earlier. I've heard all about that one. Some of the nurses who are into augmented games have been talking about it. They've been seeing ads for it everywhere. Good grief, even I've seen ads for it and I don't even play games. They're not sure if they want to play it or not, though. It sounds, um, violent."

"It's an FPS, remember?" Lynn said. "First person shooter? They've tried those before with augmented reality and it hasn't really caught on. It looks too weird jumping around like an insane frog, waving your hands at nothing. Mr. Krator is staking a lot on the assumption that he can make it work."

"Hm, I suppose. But everybody loves watching augmented reality sports. Your school has a team or two, doesn't it? I'll admit, I've never watched a school game before, but even I enjoy watching some of the pro matches. It's almost like watching a live movie."

Lynn snorted and shook her head. AR sports were wildly popular because they not only appealed to the ingrained spectator-sport culture of America but they upped the entertainment factor to a level that could compete with even the most in-demand stream channels. The games were half showmanship, half competition, similar to the old-style WWE wrestling her dad had liked to watch when she was a little girl. More and more schools were adding ARS teams to their sports offerings and there were many pro teams that made millions in sponsorships and ad revenue from their streams.

The games they played were based off traditional sports, things like soccer, football and rugby, but they built in fantastical AR elements that added combat and obstacle-course aspects to the game. Every match had a fresh theme and new graphics, so fans never got bored of watching, regardless if their team won or lost.

And the ARS players were no less fit than traditional athletes. The only difference was that they had to learn a whole new level of rules and tactics surrounding the augmented pieces on the field. That twelve-foot troll might not really exist, but if you ran through its leg on the field or got batted by its six-foot club, you were penalized like you'd really been hit, not to mention losing health and performance points for your team.

Lynn herself didn't watch much of it—she was too busy making sweet money killing people and dominating the boards in WarMonger. Plus, the kids on the ARS teams at school were just as annoying and stuck up as your typical jock and they looked down on gamers and geeks as if they didn't owe the gaming subculture for their popularity in the first place. Even so, many of the kids at school were obsessed with it and gamers like Lynn had the rise of ARS to thank for normalizing AR and VR gaming in ways that they never had been before.

"Yeah, okay," Lynn said as her mom yawned hugely and got up to wash out her cup, "but everyone watching AR sports can *see* the augmented reality, same as the players. It's completely different playing in your own little AR world out on the street where bystanders have no idea what you're doing."

"True, but everyone would assume you're playing a game, right? What else would you be doing?"

"I mean, I dunno. But that's not the point."

Matilda dried off the clean cup and put it up in the cupboard, then turned sleepy, red eyes on her daughter.

"So, if you don't want to go outside, you don't want to play with your friends and you don't want to look like an insane frog, remind me why you want to play?"

That was a very good question, one which Lynn had no answer for both because she wasn't sure how to explain it and because it would blow her "Larry Coughlin" cover. Time for some misdirection.

"Mom, can we talk about this when you're *not* sleep deprived?" Lynn asked, finishing up her own breakfast of cereal topped with yogurt.

"Good idea, honey. Have fun at school." Her mom yawned again and headed to her bedroom.

Win some, lose some, Lynn thought. At least she hadn't freaked out. Much.

When Lynn got home from school, her mom was sitting bleary-eyed on the couch cradling a cup of coffee. She pointed at a medium-sized shipping box on the floor.

"I guess we can't talk about it, now, either," Matilda said drily. "Because now I'm *really* sleep deprived."

"It's already here?" Lynn said. "Wow. I was just talking to Mr. Krator last night, I had no idea it would come so quick. But . . . wait a sec, why did it wake you up? Was there something wrong with our delivery dock?" Lynn glanced at their living room window where all their drone deliveries got dropped off, but the dock looked perfectly normal.

"Nope. Get this, it was *hand-delivered*. Can you believe it? I had to sign for it, and I haven't been able to get back to sleep since," Matilda said, using her foot to push the box closer to Lynn. "What did they send you to play this game, anyway? Solid gold AR glasses or something?"

Lynn gave a helpless shrug.

"I guess they really wanted to make sure it was going to the right person?"

"Well, go ahead and open it, then."

With nerves buzzing excitedly, Lynn grabbed a knife from the kitchen and sliced open the box. It was absolutely packed. Lynn felt like there was enough swag in it to outfit a retail store. Not only was there a T-shirt with the stylized "TD Counterforce" emblazoned across it but also a nice polo, like the kind competitors wore at tournaments to show off their sponsors. Lynn looked inside at their tags and her eyebrows rose when she realized they were both made of programmable smart fabric. She assumed she'd be able to customize them from the TD Hunter app once she got it set up. There was also an omnicap—a hat of flex fabric that could be adjusted to any form the wearer preferred, useful if she decided to wear a hat—a handful of pens, a heavy enamel pin, two miniature "TransDimensional Monster" figurines in fancy collector's edition boxes and a *very* nice-looking travel mug. Lynn turned it over to check the bottom and sure enough, there was the Everheat logo.

She didn't drink coffee herself, but her mom often talked wistfully about the self-heating mugs that never let your coffee grow cold.

Next, Lynn found a sleek set of the very expensive Duralink earbuds with a card attached to their carry case. In large words it read, "Critical for TransDimensional Hunting! Do not set aside!" Lynn carefully put it and all the swag on the coffee table, then lifted out the compact backpack that had been underneath.

Matilda, who was watching in interest, whistled.

"That looks like some sort of military-grade equipment. Are you sure this is for a game and not some top-secret spy outfit?" she joked.

"Yeah, right, Mom," Lynn said. But silently, she agreed. The backpack's material felt thick and high quality, not the cheap stuff you'd think they'd use for giveaways. It even had a built-in hydration system, which would come in handy if she spent much time playing out in the summer heat. The backpack was black with red paneling and piping and on the back was a large embroidery patch of the TD Counterforce logo.

The logo was a circle with a black background, bordered in a double ring of red. In the center was the Earth crossed by a sword and some scifi laser-looking gun, with a lightning bolt striking down through the middle. Curved around the top edge of the circle between the two rings were the words "TransDimensional Counterforce." On the bottom curve was a motto in Latin: *Quod Nos Tueri*.

Altogether, it looked more like something a government or military branch would use than a gaming logo. But maybe that was the point? The in-game storyline, impossible to miss with all the advertising, was that the world was being invaded by invisible transdimensional beings who were preparing to wipe out civilization. The TD Hunters were being recruited to fight them as a sort of "gaming paramilitary force." Thus, the military look to everything made sense.

Underneath the backpack, she finally came to the new LINC and AR glasses. She took out the box for the LINC first and opened it. She'd expected the ring config to be a plain plastic band, or maybe something with the TD Hunter logo on it. But this ring had some weight to it, like it was made from tougher stuff. The material was black, so black it seemed to drink in the light and instead of being a uniform band, it widened at the top to form a flat circle, like an old-fashioned signet ring. On the flat top was the stylized monogram "LL."

"Holy cow," Matilda said. "Is that your new LINC? It looks so . . . professional. Is this normal for beta testing?"

"No," Lynn said faintly, turning the ring over in her hand. "This is definitely not normal. But Mr. Krator did say he had lots of funding for this project. So, maybe its normal for this game?"

"What does the 'LL' stand for?" her mom asked.

Lynn shrugged. She didn't know, not really. But something Mr. Krator had said the night before echoed in her mind.

"Lynn Raven" is special in a very important way, not just "Larry Coughlin." Don't let anyone tell you different.

Was this his doing? Could it possibly stand for Lynn-Larry, perhaps to remind her that both were important? No, that was silly. That would have to mean he'd had this ring custom printed for her in, what, a few hours? There was no way.

Putting it from her mind, she slipped the ring onto her pointer finger of her left hand. It fit perfectly.

"Open the glasses," her mom prompted, leaning forward.

Lynn opened the second small box, revealing a pair of stream-lined tactical sunglasses. She lifted them out and unfolded them. The frame was black with a few red accents and the lenses were a shimmering, iridescent blue. Almost hesitantly, Lynn lifted them and slid them onto her face. Like the ring, the glasses fit perfectly, hugging her head snugly with extra long arms that curved around toward the back of her head so there was no danger of them falling off. The lenses extended down a little and curved around the sides of her face the same way sports sunglasses did to provide full coverage.

"Wow, you look pretty cool, honey!" Matilda said.

"Yeah, right, Mom."

"No, really. You do. I bet you'd look even better with the shirt and backpack on too."

Lynn shrugged, grinning despite herself.

"Maybe but they'd also stick out. I'll probably wait to wear them until after the game releases."

"Whatever for, sweetie? You should be proud of your accomplishments."

Lynn took off the glasses and shook her head, amused at how scandalized her mother sounded.

"I am. But I also know better than to paint a target on my back. What if someone from school sees me? I'd never hear the end of it."

"Good grief," Matilda said, sighing as she rose from the couch. "Teenagers. Well, I'm going to try to get a few more hours of sleep before I have to get up and make dinner. Please stay inside the complex for now. If you decide you want to go farther out than the immediate neighborhood, find out if you can get together with your friends and we'll talk about it. Oh, and don't stay out after dark, though I suppose the lighted areas inside the complex should be safe enough if you stay close—"

"Okay, Mom, okay. I know the drill. Don't talk to strangers. Don't go anywhere with strangers. Don't follow the big bad wolf into the forest..."

"I'm serious, Lynn," Matilda said.

"I really will be fine, Mom," Lynn said. "When have I ever gotten into trouble before?"

"Well, there *was* that time you put dish soap in the dishwasher and flooded the kitchen with suds..."

"I was *eleven*, Mom! Can't you drop that already?"

"I'm just teasing, sweetie. You've never spent much time outside," Matilda pointed out. "And these kinds of games can distract you from your surroundings. Just...be safe."

"I promise, I will," Lynn said. "Now, can I go dig into this game?"

"Go," Matilda said, then kissed her on the head. "And don't forget to have fun."

Lynn put the swag and packaging back in the shipping box and took it all into her room. Then she plopped down on her bed, slipped the AR glasses on and felt the rim for the power button. She found it and immediately, the darkened lenses lightened, adjusting to the indoor dimness.

GREETINGS, HUNTER.

"Whoa!" Lynn said, jumping as the words appeared superimposed on her vision.

FOR EASE OF COMMUNICATION, PLEASE INSERT YOUR EARBUDS appeared next.

"Okaaay." Lynn dug in the shipping box, found the earbud case and pulled out the specially molded inserts. Like everything else, they fit perfectly, their material expanding automatically to create a proper seal in her ear.

"Much better. Thank you."

"Uh, hello?" Lynn said, feeling a little creeped out by the voice that greeted her.

"Apologies, allow me to introduce myself. My name is Hugo, the service AI for this application. If you would please state your first and last name for voice print verification to unlock your official TransDimensional Counterforce profile."

"Um, Lynn Raven."

"Thank you. It is an honor to meet you, Ms. Raven."

"Er, thanks?"

She should have known such a high-budget game would have the very best service AI interface. She interacted with plenty of AIs every day at school. They ran all the day-to-day systems and delivered most of the standardized classroom material so the teachers could focus on working one-on-one with the students. In fact, most of her friends had fully integrated smart homes with service AIs that ran everything from climate control to ordering groceries and a lot of them also had personal AIs that helped them keep track of school assignments, extracurricular activities, chores, you name it. Lynn could have had a personal AI herself, if she'd wanted one. But the models she could afford were annoyingly standard and Lynn had always preferred doing things for herself anyway—a preference heavily influenced by her mother.

But for all the AIs Lynn had encountered, she'd never talked to one that sounded so . . . normal. Well, normal in a very British butler sort of way.

She wasn't sure about this . . .

"If you would prefer, Ms. Raven, you always have the option of switching to self-navigation mode"—Okay, definitely creepy. Was this thing reading her mind?—"but I would not recommend it. This is one of the most advanced applications ever to be released and there are many moving parts. I would be honored if you would allow me to assist you in acclimating to the application as you begin your beta testing."

"Uhh, sure," Lynn said slowly. He—it—Hugo—had a good point. "But just call me Lynn, okay?"

"Very well, Miss Lynn. There is one small matter to which we must attend before we can begin. I understand it will be tedious, but by international law, I must read to you—and acquire your verbal agreement to—the non-disclosure and end-user license agreement for this application."

"Can't I read them myself?"

"Unfortunately, no. In a situation of this import where we are breaking the bounds of next-generation augmented reality technology, it is essential that no part of either agreement be, shall we say, glossed over."

A situation of this import? Breaking the bounds of next-generation augmented reality technology? Lynn felt a tingle of excitement—and nervousness—at the thought.

"Okay, sure."

"If you would be so kind as to locate your parent or guardian? They also must agree."

"Uh, right. Gimme a second."

Her mother was going to *looove* this.

Fortunately, it wasn't as painful as she'd expected and the AI—okay, Hugo—managed to get through both agreements via her new LINC's minuscule speakers in record time. The legalese was fairly short, clear and to the point, though there were a few places that made Lynn's brow furrow. Places like *neither Tsunami Entertainment Inc. nor its subsidiaries are liable for any injuries sustained while playing... including but not limited to... brain damage, partial or full paralysis and death...*

Then again, Lynn had never played augmented reality games before and those did seem like things that could happen in a game played in the real, so maybe that language was standard? After all, no company wanted to get sued because some careless idiot went and got themselves killed while playing their game. At least Matilda, despite her dislike of AIs, was amused by Hugo's mannerisms, even if she did raise silent eyebrows at his initial introduction.

Once all the legal formalities had been taken care of and Lynn's mom had retreated to her room to get some sleep, Lynn went back to sit down on her bed next to the box of stuff.

"Okay, um, Hugo? What next?"

"That is entirely up to you, Miss Lynn. Where would you like me to begin? Equipment overview and usage? Application introduction and tutorial?"

"Better start with equipment stuff."

"As you wish. We shall begin with your AR interface. You are wearing an Elite Series pair of Overlay's KR2040 full-spectrum augmented reality glasses."

Lynn's eyes widened. Overlay was the top AR manufacturer out there and their interfaces were coveted by all serious gamers. KR2040 was the current year's model just released a month ago. Tommy Jones might not even have a pair yet.

"They include all the latest augmented reality advances," Hugo continued, "including 32K resolution, retinal or lens projection based on your preference and full manipulation access. For all functions, you may choose between voice control, display control with eye-tracking, or forward manual control. Do you have any questions?"

"Wow. Uh, okay, what do you mean retinal or lens projection?" Lynn asked.

"You can either choose to have all visuals projected onto the glasses themselves, as you see here—" a military-looking heads up display suddenly appeared on the lenses of her glasses, disorienting her for a moment before her eyes refocused so close to her face. As with most AR glasses she'd tried, she felt like she was looking cross eyed. "—or the visuals can be projected onto your retina, as you see here."

The display shifted and her eyes felt instantly better. She could see everything perfectly, overlaid on her view of her bedroom door and wall in translucent green lines. Instead of ending at the edges of her AR glasses lenses, the lines extended into the very corners of her vision, immersing her completely in the feel that she was looking through some high-tech robot helmet or something.

"Cool! Definitely gonna use retinal projection."

"Very good," Hugo said. "Any other questions?"

"Um, how do I control stuff?"

"First and foremost, I am always available, you have only to ask. You do not even need to speak out loud. Your earbuds can pick up subvocal vibrations."

"Hm. Okay. Not really sure how to do that, but I'm sure I'll figure it out. I know all about eye-tracking. Those cheap AR glasses that come with built-in overlay advertisements drive me nuts. What was the last one, um, forward control?"

"The retinal system can not only track your eye movements but your hand movements as well," Hugo explained. "Instead of needing to project a visible-to-all display in front of you for you to manipulate—though that option is available should you wish it—the display is already projected onto your retina and will synchronize with any manual input it detects. And might I add that all three control systems are seamlessly integrated. There is no need to 'switch' back and forth between them, simply use whatever method you prefer in each individual situation and my system will detect and adapt as necessary."

"Okay. Awesome. It'll probably take some getting used to, but that sounds really cool." So cool, in fact, that Lynn was itching to try it out. She knew she would be clumsy at first—that was normal for any gamer breaking in a new control system—but once she got good at it, it would make for an amazing gaming experience. But first things first.

"Tell me about my LINC," she said. "The old one I have is pretty clunky. I don't usually use an AR interface so I make do with one-handed manipulation on the projected display."

"That is a limitation long in your past," the AI assured her. Was that a hint of smugness in Hugo's tone? "Your LINC is custom made by Tsunami Entertainment and includes all the latest advances. It is, of course, fully integrated with your AR interface and earbuds, so as long as you are wearing either, all control is seamless. If, however, you are not wearing either, it is equipped with both forward and rear projection and so can display a two-handed keyboard below your hands if desired, or a standard one-handed keyboard above."

"Sweet. I probably won't wear the glasses everywhere, but if these earbuds stay this comfortable, I'll probably leave them in all day. I can't even tell there's something in my ear!"

"That is the idea, Miss Lynn."

"Did you just make a joke, Hugo?" Lynn asked with a grin.

"I never joke about something as important as properly performing hardware."

"Uh-huh." Lynn was starting to like this AI. Most standard service AIs were annoying as heck with their stiff mannerisms and standard responses. This one was refreshingly natural. Plus, its blend of proper professionalism and subtle humor suited her. "Okay, I'm sure I'll have more questions as I get used to the setup, so for now let's move on to the game."

"Of course, Miss Lynn."

"I thought I told you to call me Lynn?"

"You did indeed, Miss Lynn."

"Sooo, why are you calling me 'Miss' Lynn?"

"Because that is the polite form of address for a young, unmarried female."

Hm. That was interesting. It seemed Hugo's programming gave him leeway in interpreting commands. Lynn had the strange impulse to test her theory.

"So, can you *not* be polite? Or does that go against your programming?"

"I can do whatever you require that is within my scope of expertise, Miss Lynn. Would you rather I not be polite? I could call you 'useless meatsack,' if you prefer."

Lynn spluttered, the laugh coming so unexpectedly that if she'd been eating or drinking, she would have surely choked. Was this AI joking, or was it serious? She couldn't tell. Despite the urge to further explore the depths of its self-learning personality, she forced herself to refocus on her current task: beta testing.

"Uh, no. Miss Lynn is fine for now. So, game stuff?"

"Of course, Miss Lynn. For your in-app identification, would you prefer your name be used or should I display your beta tester designation instead? Keep in mind that this can be changed at any time before the official game launch."

"Beta tester designation, definitely. What is it, by the way?"

"BetaTester124."

"Hm, so I'm the hundred and twenty-fourth beta tester to be invited to the game?"

"That is correct."

"Wow." That seemed weird. Big games usually had hundreds and hundreds of beta testers playing it for three or more months before it was released. But this one was set to release in barely a month and the beta had only gone live—at least publicly—a few weeks ago. The developers must have been pretty confident in their product to skimp on testing time and numbers. Or maybe those investors Mr. Krator had mentioned were impatient to make their money back. She didn't know much about that side of game development. That was more Ronnie's wheelhouse. He was always talking about the latest gaming industry gossip, new expansion leaks, company buyouts, stuff like that.

"I have already updated your Hunter profile from your Tsunami Entertainment membership data. Be sure to go into your LINC settings soon to authorize your new equipment for full integration into your cloud account, at which point your biometric identification will become active across all devices. Your LINC also comes with a personal AI, which you may set up at any time."

Lynn shook her head, smiling to herself. If whatever AI came with her LINC was anywhere near as realistic as Hugo, she wasn't sure she could handle more than one. She'd control her LINC functions herself, like she always did.

"Would you like to customize your skin at this time, Miss Lynn? This will change the way others perceive your appearance while using the app."

"Er, what does it look like right now?"

A life-sized image of herself appeared before her, looking for all the world like her twin standing right there on her bedroom floor. In the image, though, she was dressed in a basic skin-tight suit of black with red and blue accents and the TD Counterforce logo emblazoned on the breast. On her head was a tactical headset that was a more military-looking version of her actual AR glasses and there was a short laser-gun strapped to her thigh. In her hand she held a long knife that looked similar to a kukri, but the blade was embellished with a geometric cutout design. Lynn recognized the blade type from her research into the wars in Iraq and Afghanistan that Larry Coughlin had "fought" in.

"As you advance in experience and acquire new equipment," Hugo said, "there will be more customizations available. Do you wish to change anything at this time?"

"Uhh, no. Remind me after I've leveled up some and we'll see about it then." Basic was fine with her. She was no fashion diva, no matter what she let Ronnie think.

"Very good, Miss Lynn. Now, would you like to begin by reviewing the history of TransDimensional Monsters and the TD Counterforce," Hugo asked, "or would you prefer to begin with the app tutorial?"

"I'm ready to play the game. Let's get straight to it," Lynn said, leaning forward as an excited tingle ran up her spine.

Hugo didn't reply. Instead, some rousing game music began to play as a vid screen expanded on her display. First the TD Counterforce logo appeared on a black background, then the scene shifted to what looked like a tactical war-room complete with complicated-looking technical readouts, satellite maps and more. Front and center was a sleek desk behind which sat an older man with buzz-cut hair and a military-style uniform, though it didn't fit the look of any real branch that Lynn was aware of. The man in the video leaned forward, hands folded on the desk, an intense look in his eyes.

"Welcome to the TransDimensional Counterforce, Hunter. My name is General Wilson Carville, and I want to personally thank you on behalf of humanity everywhere for volunteering as a part of this global paramilitary operation. Our mission is of utmost importance, and I hope you will take advantage of all the resources we have to offer to ensure your success. The world is counting on you, Hunter. Good luck."

The scene changed, this time showing a middle-aged man standing in front of a tactical readout. His face looked hardened and weathered by experience and he was obviously in top physical condition judging by the tight fit of his combat fatigues over powerfully muscled chest and arms.

"Good to see a new recruit, Hunter. I'm First Sergeant Kane Bryce and I'll be briefing you on the situation. I'm not one for fancy speeches, so let's get right to it."

The first sergeant flicked his hand to bring up a projected screen that began playing various scenes as he continued speaking.

"Interdimensional beings made of exotic particles are invading the Earth and wreaking havoc on human society across the globe. They're damaging critical systems both military and civilian, disrupting electrical systems including the mesh web, and they have been linked to several major disasters. The most powerful will even go after humans. At their current rate of increase, our analysts project they could reach critical numbers within a year, at which point they'll pose a major threat to humanity's survival.

"So far, these TransDimensional Monsters—or TDMs as we call them—seem only vaguely aware of our presence. They're drawn to human technology and infrastructure, which they seem to feed off of. All attempts to make contact and communicate have failed. Fortunately, these TDMs are invisible to the naked eye, which has kept mass panic from spreading through the civilian population. But it does make it difficult to detect and track them. They operate on a particle level with which we've only recently developed the technology to interact. An international joint military project has successfully created a battle system capable of finding and destroying the TDMs. But these entities are so numerous and widespread that we need millions of volunteers all over the world if we hope to save humanity before we're overwhelmed.

"Since this mission is beyond the capabilities of any country's military, we've developed a highly advanced, AI-driven program that enables ordinary citizens such as yourself to take up arms and join the fight. You're now on the front line of Earth's defenses, Hunter. Your first mission is to learn the TD Counterforce battle system and begin training against the lowest-class TDMs in and around your own community. As you gain skill and experience, you'll advance to higher levels and better weaponry to take on tougher monsters. Train hard and stay vigilant, Hunter. These entities have been known to interfere with Hunter equipment running the TD Counterforce battle system and the strongest ones can cause physical damage to humans. Pay attention to your training and all safety recommendations of your service AI. Your AI will explain all the pertinent details of your new battle system and our Tactical Support team is a ping away if you have any trouble.

"Good luck, Hunter. The world is depending on you. Remember: If you can see them, they can see you.

"First Sergeant Bryce, out."

The briefing video disappeared from Lynn's display and Hugo's formal voice returned to her ear as he began to explain the game mechanics.

"The TD Hunter battle system works by detecting and locking on to the exotic particles that make up the interdimensional entities, allowing you to attack and destroy them. When a TDM is destroyed, it has the potential to leave behind any of three materials, based on its type: ichor, globes and plates. These items are essential to your mission so take care to collect them."

As Hugo's explanation continued, a life-size image of a lizard-like monster with long claws appeared squatting on her bedroom floor. Following the narration of its "destruction," the monster's image exploded in a shower of sparks and three items outlined in blinking halos appeared on the floor.

"Ichor is their lifeblood and is converted into the power needed to fuel your battle systems and weapons. Globes affect TDM detection. They can either be used to cloak your own presence, or increase your detection capability of monsters in your area. Plates serve as armor against attacks. Each attack they intercept lowers their effectiveness until they eventually break and must be replaced. All TDM types yield ichor. Armored TDMs yield plates. TDMs with stealth capabilities yield globes. Some higher-class TDMs yield both plates and globes.

"While this new battlefront may seem daunting, you as a Hunter have one critical advantage: sound. Each TDM type gives off a distinctive pulse pattern that your battle system converts into sound waves. Even when other detection systems fall short, sound is often a dead give-away. Learning the various sounds of the TDMs, especially ones with cloaking abilities such as ghosts and Ghasts, is vital to your survival and ultimate victory.

"For organizational purposes, all TDM types have been ranked into classes," Hugo continued and Lynn's display shifted again, showing a row of five monsters, each one larger and more lethal-looking than the last. "Delta Class consists of the weakest and the most numerous entities, while Charlie, Bravo and Alpha Classes contain successively stronger and more dangerous monsters. Sierra Class are the most lethal entities and are considered 'bosses' that require large teams of high-level Hunters to defeat.

"All Hunters, take note! As long as your battle system is up and running, any entity of a similar or lower level to yours can detect you. Except for entities with special detection abilities, higher-class entities will generally ignore lower level players and lower level players are unable to detect them in turn. However, if you can see them, they can see you. And many will attack you on sight and often by surprise. The key to survival is constant vigilance!"

The line of five monsters, whose lifelike images had been slowly rotating, suddenly spun toward Lynn and leaped at her with claws and teeth extended. She jerked reflexively, almost fall-ing backward onto her bedspread. Just as the monstrous images appeared to reach her, they dissipated into smoke and Hugo's voice continued. Lynn straightened, heart racing from the sud-den shot of adrenaline.

"So remember, if you wish to explore, train, or in any other way interact with the many functions of your Hunter application without being disturbed, be sure to exit combat mode to shut down your battle system."

Lynn made a mental note of that. Many games had a pause function, or automatically paused whenever you opened a menu or navigated away from the main screen. But since this was augmented reality and "in the real" she supposed it made sense there would be no pause button.

"Lastly but most importantly, some TDMs are still unknown in the wild. Our battle system is constantly logging new information, including the capabilities of unknown TDMs. If you see something that looks like sparkling gas, that is an unknown TDM. The TD Counterforce is continually seeking better and more efficient ways to wipe out this global threat, and so we offer high bonuses, extra experience points and achievements as awards for detecting unknown TDMs. However, other than their classification, you will have no data about these unknowns, their attack capabilities, or their weaknesses prior to engaging. So, proceed with caution!

"If you detect an unknown entity, your battle system will immediately start a series of analysis tests. The only way to receive full credit for detecting an unknown is to engage it in battle and destroy it, which allows the system to analyze its parts and determine its composition and abilities. After analysis the system will assign a name to the entity and place the finder's Hunter designation in the metadata. For example..."

As Hugo began reading out a list of stats, a miniature image of a monster with dozens of huge tentacles materialized before her, along with an analysis breakdown that hovered next to it. Each characteristic highlighted itself briefly while Hugo described it.

"Scylla—Sierra Class-1. Attacks: Pummel, Crush, Plasma Jet. Defenses: Armor +2. Detection: Level 40. Stealth: +2. Special abilities: Regeneration, Blink (Short Range Teleport). Detected in the wild: 3/5/2040, 1417 GMT, AlphaTester1, AlphaTester2, AlphaTester3, AlphaTester4, AlphaTester5, AlphaTester6, AlphaTester7, AlphaTester8, AlphaTester9."

The image of the monster and its stats remained as Hugo continued.

"As a beta tester for this new battle system, you should expect to encounter unknowns in the wild and are advised to use extreme caution. The aforementioned TDM, originally an unknown, required a team of highly experienced alpha testers to defeat.

"In addition to using special caution when engaging unknowns, please note that Bravo and Alpha Class TDMs will push the boundaries of Hunter resilience and must be engaged with the support of other Hunters. Therefore, unless you are part of a beta or alpha tester group, do not approach these classes during beta. Disregard for this warning will result in your death.

"This concludes your introductory briefing. Thank you for volunteering to defend the planet, Hunter! Good luck and safe hunting!"

As Hugo fell silent, Lynn pursed her lips and raised an eyebrow. Her first thought was that this game was taking itself too seriously. In one respect, the realism was cool. It built up the tension and feeling of danger, which wasn't something a lot of games could achieve for a serious gamer like her who'd seen all the scary monsters you could imagine.

But in another respect, all the warnings were pretty eye-roll worthy. Maybe they hadn't gotten the programming for the higher classes ironed out yet and this was the developers' way of discouraging beta testers from breaking the game to tiny little bits before they were ready. It could also have something to do with the interface being AR instead of VR. Whatever the case, it certainly underscored her feelings so far: this game was like no other ever released.

She couldn't wait to try it out.

Her thoughts were interrupted by a block of text that appeared on her display, replacing the image of the tentacled monster. The text glowed brightly in the silence as Lynn began to read.

Notice to beta testers: Sierra Class entities are set to release in a later expansion. Any encounter with a Sierra Class entity is to be considered a system glitch. If you make contact with a Sierra Class entity, please exit combat mode to prevent further system errors and contact Tactical Support immediately. Any attempt to engage with a Sierra Class entity will result in immediate system failure. Thank you for your cooperation while we fine tune our system.

Hm, interesting. Lynn knew from her few beta testing experiences that games were usually rife with minor glitches and had a fair number of major glitches as well, which was the whole reason for beta testing. But she found it interesting that they put in a disclaimer about a specific glitch. Maybe they were actively fixing it and didn't want testers to freak out while they were still working on it?

"This marks the end of the TD Counterforce introductory briefing," Hugo said, politely intruding on Lynn's thoughts. "Do you have any questions or would you like me to repeat any part of the briefing?"

"No, I'm good," Lynn said. "But as some beta feedback, that was a huge info dump for an introduction, which surprises me because Mr. Krator's games aren't usually like that. Usually you just jump right in with maybe a brief demo round before they dump you into the thick of things. It was interesting, I guess, but I'm betting a lot of players won't bother sitting through it."

"Your feedback is duly noted, Miss Lynn. Shall we proceed to the training portion of this tutorial?"

"Yeah, go for it." *Finally.*

"Before we proceed, you must first retrieve your batons for syncing."

"My what?"

"Your batons, the programmable, multi-use weapons you will be using as a Hunter to attack the ravening hordes of TransDimensional Monsters."

"Oh! You mean those electric blue things you see in all the ads? Do you mean I get to have weapons that look as cool as that?"

"Each level achieved has access to more advanced weaponry, Miss Lynn. So, eventually, yes."

"Sweet. But I don't remember seeing anything like that in the shipping box."

"Perhaps you might check it again more thoroughly?"

Lynn turned and rummaged through the box. Finding nothing, she pulled out the TD Counterforce backpack and began digging through its zippered compartments. In the largest she finally found what she was looking for and pulled out a pair of electric blue foot-long rods, each with a molded handle on one end.

"The color isn't very tactical, even if it is cool," Lynn commented, turning it over in her hand. The baton's material had a little give, like compact foam, and it was slightly flexible, not hard and stiff like a police baton would be.

"I believe the idea is to avoid harassment by law enforcement officials for the suspected possession of a lethal weapon," Hugo offered, his tone very dry.

Lynn shrugged. It made sense. She wrapped her fingers around the handle of one of the batons and held it up, testing the weight. Despite looking vaguely like a child's baseball bat, it had a good balance and a bit of heft.

"So . . . is this the config for the starter level? What am I supposed to do with them? Bludgeon the imaginary monsters?"

"In a manner of speaking," Hugo said, sounding completely serious. "This is, however, only the default form which the batons revert to when you are not in combat mode or engaged in a training simulation, such as at present. For the first nine Hunter Levels you will be utilizing only a single, one-handed weapon. Once you have advanced enough in your training to achieve Level 10, your second weapon slot will open and you can begin using dual weapons or two-handed weapons."

Lynn grinned. Two-handed weapons? That sounded like fun. Nice incentive to get to Level 10 as fast as possible.

"Now, Miss Lynn, if you would place your thumb on the end of one of the baton handles, it will be unlocked and synced to your Hunter profile so that it can be activated."

Turning the baton over in her hands, she found the small indentation on the end of the handle and pressed her thumb into it. Some text popped into view on her display.

Hunter weapon successfully registered and ready for programming. Please choose your starting configuration.

Two images appeared before her, both slowly rotating. They were mirrors of the kukri-style long knife and the laser gun she'd seen on her skin and according to the display they were called the Nano Blade and Disruptor Pistol. Being more comfortable with using firearms in virtual, she lifted her left hand and touched the image of the Disruptor Pistol. The baton in her right hand buzzed slightly in response and before her eyes the material shifted, reconfiguring into an exact replica of the gun, albeit an electric blue one.

Yup, very cool. This game was going to make some serious profit in peripheral gear. She wondered if these beginner batons could transform into every weapon the game had been programmed with, or if there was going to be upgrade gear available to purchase. If she stuck with the game, she might have to splurge a little depending on what they had available.

Lynn touched the image of the Nano Blade and watched in fascination as her pistol elongated and reformed into a wickedly curved, fourteen-inch blade with a geometric cutout design spanning its length. Through each transformation, the handle beneath her fingers remained the same, indicating she could easily switch configs mid-game, maybe even mid-battle, as long as she anticipated the few seconds of lag it took for the weapon to shift.

"Hey, Hugo. How do I switch weapons on the fly? Most games have some sort of short-cut button you can push."

"Indeed, Miss Lynn, though you can also use your weapon icon or a voice command. The manual control is a pressure ring around the top of the handle, within reach of your thumb. You have two weapon configuration slots and can switch between them at will. For additional weapons, you will need to access your weapon settings and select a new weapon."

"Okay, good to know." She carefully tested the knife's edge and found it was as blunt as blunt could be. Oh well. You couldn't have everything in life. "This thing is pretty awesome, though," she said as she waved it around experimentally.

"I am so glad you approve, Miss Lynn."

Lynn's brow furrowed.

"Are you being sarcastic, Hugo? I didn't think service AIs could be sarcastic."

"Whatever gave you that impression, Miss Lynn?"

"Is that an answer to my question, or a response to my comment about AIs?"

"Yes."

She laughed and decided to drop it.

"Okay, so how does this all work?"

"Allow me to demonstrate. If you will observe your display..."

The two weapon images shrank to one tiny icon of a gun, zooming to the bottom of her view to join a whole line of other icons, no doubt for different functions of the game. In the top left corner of her display, a satellite view of her local area appeared. As she watched, the area around her apartment complex began to populate with red dots. The dots were more or less in a circle covering the parking lot and apartment buildings immediately surrounding her own building. The dots weren't spaced out regularly, though. Some seemed to group in certain places and a line of them stretched behind the apartment building bordering the greenway woods between their complex and the complex next door. Lynn guessed the edge of the circle was the range of the app's radar.

As she examined the spread of dots, her earbuds started to pick up a weird *beep, bloop, beep, beep* sound, sort of like a robot. If robots could sound really creepy, anyway. It also sounded like it was coming from over by her desk. She looked in that direction, her head automatically turning to track the sound—

And nearly jumped out of her skin.

There, squatting in mid-air over her desk, was a runty little demon-looking thing. The CGI for it was phenomenal. It would have looked real, if it hadn't been randomly floating a foot above the surface of her desk. Lynn realized she'd instinctively raised her Nano Blade to put it between her and the creature. She forced herself to relax.

This AR stuff was *way* more intense than WarMonger.

"The red dots you see on your overhead indicate TDMs in your immediate area," Hugo explained, not commenting on her startled reaction. "You can zoom in and out on the map, either manually or with a verbal command."

"Okay, zoom in on our apartment," Lynn said.

The satellite view shifted, showing a basic outline of the building. Weirdly, there were no red dots within the apartment's outline, just one lone blue dot on the side of the building where her and her mom's apartment was located.

"The blue dot on your overhead indicates this TDM is a training simulation. You may tap its image, verbally state 'target,' or simply focus your gaze on it to engage it with your battle system. You do not need to target an enemy in order to attack it, but targeting improves accuracy with ranged attacks and provides you additional information about the target."

Lynn concentrated on the runty little monster with its bat-like ears, reddish gray skin, curved claws and big bug eyes. Her AR glasses tracked her eye movement and automatically outlined the monster's image in a red halo. A readout appeared along the right side of her display and Hugo began reciting the selected monster's stats.

"Imp—Delta Class-1. Attacks: Slash. Defenses: None. Detection: Level 1. Stealth: None. Unique behavior: Imps are non-aggressive and will move away from the Hunter until violent contact is made. Detected in the wild: 1/05/2040, 0920 GMT, AlphaTester4."

"Great. So, it's puny and non-aggressive. What next?" Lynn asked.

"Before you engage with a TDM, it is wise to take stock of your situation and resources," Hugo said, continuing the tutorial. The series of icons at the bottom of her screen flashed, one at a time, as he ran through their explanations.

"This bar is your health. Constant walking and movement regenerates health at medium levels, while stationary rest regenerates it at very low levels. Health can also be recovered using Oneg healing capsules, which will be accessible at higher Hunter Levels. This bar is your power level, which is consumed at a low rate to fuel all game systems and is replenished by collecting ichor. This icon is your armor slot, where you may equip plates for defense. These are your stealth and detection slots, where you may equip globes either for cloaking, or to increase the range and strength of your detection system. This is necessary to detect TDMs who have stealth capabilities of their own."

Lynn made note of each icon, assuming she could select them by touch, voice, or visual tracking same as with the other controls. Next, Hugo moved onto weapons. As he began, the small icon of a gun flashed and her two weapon images reappeared, each blinking briefly as Hugo explained their capabilities.

"This is your weapon selection icon. All Hunter weapons are divided into classes, either ranged or melee, and each class has its own strengths depending on your preferred fighting style. There is no ammunition or reloading. Power-using weapons are limited by your power level, so be sure to collect all available ichor and keep an eye on your status bar. All Hunters begin with the basic weapon in the Pistol and Blade classes. The Disruptor Pistol is a ranged weapon which does only basic damage and uses low amounts of power, while the Nano Blade is a non-powered hand-to-hand weapon that does slightly more damage. You currently have the Nano Blade equipped. Would you like to change your weapon selection?"

Lynn's first instinct was to switch to her ranged weapon. It was a safe choice, something she was used to from years of playing WarMonger and other shooting-heavy games. Plus, it meant she could stay well away from that creepy little demon. But that thought made her shake her head. If she was going to do well at this game, she needed to learn all the weapons and fighting styles inside-out, like she had in WarMonger. Being a top-tier player didn't come without significant work. She might as well start with the hardest to use weapon while she was still in training mode.

"I'll stick with the Nano Blade," she said.

"An excellent choice, Miss Lynn."

"What are these three empty slots below it, though?" she asked, pointing.

"Those are your augment slots. While there is a limited number of weapon classes, every weapon can be enhanced with various equipment augments which are randomly dropped by TDMs. While some augments are standard, others are entirely unique. Each Hunter also has three personal augment slots and such augments dropped by TDMs can enhance your health, power, defense, detection and stealth abilities."

"Sweeet," Lynn said. Now this was more like it. She was all about killing monsters for loot. "Okay, so how do I kill this thing?"

"You must approach the enemy and attack it with your weapon, Miss Lynn. Any slash or stab is sufficient as long as it comes into contact with the TDM."

Lynn sighed.

"And this is why I prefer games in virtual. I guess I gotta get up."

"Yes, that *would* be the logical next step," Hugo said, absolutely deadpan.

"You know, maybe I should ping Mr. Krator and tell him his AI has got a smart mouth."

"I have it on good authority that Mr. Krator is well aware of my programming, considering he did most of it himself. But if you wish to log that as official beta feedback, I would be happy to—"

"Oh, shut up, Hugo," Lynn said, one side of her mouth crooking up as she slid off the bed and faced the imp. For a moment she simply stood there, hesitating. This felt sooo weird. "Well, here goes nothing," she finally muttered and took a few tentative steps toward her target. But as she moved, the imp moved too, backing away.

"Remember, imps avoid contact unless first attacked," Hugo intoned. "The most effective tactic is to approach at speed."

Lynn made a face but bent her knees and lunged forward at the imp while slashing with her Nano Blade. She ran into her body-mold chair mid-lunge but still managed to get in a strike at the imp, whose outline flashed red when her Nano Blade passed through it. The handle of her weapon also vibrated slightly as it made contact. The next second, though, the monster was lunging back at her, teeth bared and claws extended in a vicious swipe. Lynn backpedaled and her display flashed red around the edges.

"Warning, damage sustained," Hugo informed her. "Keep attacking until your target dissipates."

Trying to back up without stumbling over furniture, Lynn kept slashing at the imp. Now that it was on the attack, it made no effort to evade, just kept clawing furiously at her which prompted more red flashes of her display. But after three more solid hits with her Nano Blade, the little CGI demon suddenly burst into sparkling light that quickly dissipated to reveal what looked like a puddle of purple goo on her floor.

"Congratulations, Miss Lynn! You have successfully destroyed your first TransDimensional Monster! Now select the puddle of ichor to collect it."

Lynn groaned. She was panting a little at her exertion and the unexpected rush of adrenaline.

"Do I have to actually bend over and touch the floor? All this jumping around is bad enough as it is."

"Physical contact with the floor is unnecessary. All collectable items have a six-foot sensory range. Standing near it will be sufficient."

"Well, that's a relief," Lynn muttered as she reached out with her left hand and touched where the puddle showed up in her display. The puddle flashed and disappeared and her power level bar went up a bit.

"Excellent. You have now completed the training tutorial and are ready to face the real invaders of our planet. Additional resources such as combat strategies and TDM stats are available for your perusal through the menu icon. You may exit combat mode by voice command, your menu options, or by simply removing your AR glasses. If you do exit combat mode, any damage inflicted on an enemy which has not yet been destroyed is thereby nullified."

Smart, Lynn thought. That discouraged players from hopping in and out of combat mode to avoid taking damage in a fight.

"One final word of advice," Hugo said. "Pay attention to your audio feed and beware of ghosts! Good luck, Miss Lynn, and happy hunting."

"Thanks, Hugo. I think I'll take a bit of a breather and poke around while I decide where to head first."

"Very good, Miss Lynn. Remember that I am always available should you have any specific inquiries."

The AI fell silent and Lynn sat back down on her bed, taking a moment to study the icons on her display as her breathing leveled out. Her health bar was still full—apparently the damage done by the imp was training damage only—and the little monster-shaped icon on the top right still had a zero beside it.

A sudden, intense thrill shot through her and she smiled to herself. Pretty soon, that icon would show dozens, then hundreds of kills. And she couldn't wait to see how many she could rack up. WarMonger was extremely satisfying in its own way, mostly knowing she was pitting her skills against other real people and beating the crap out of them. This TD Hunter game was an entirely different animal and she was pleasantly surprised at how excited she was to dig in.

Before she went rushing headlong into things, though, she reached up and tapped the menu icon to see what it had to offer. It listed "Inventory," "Game Options," "Tactical Support," "Additional Resources," and "Exit Combat Mode." Under "Additional Resources," she found "TDM Index," "Weapons List," "Achievement Log," "Training Simulations," and "Community Forum."

She selected the TDM index and was presented with rows of miniature monster icons. She found she could scroll by flicking a finger up or down and began to explore.

There were about a dozen "known" Delta Class monsters, the lowest class of TDMs. More slots below them were grayed out, presumably leaving space for any unknowns discovered in Delta Class. She tapped on the icon for "Imp" and saw that it had all the stats she'd seen before as well as an expandable section going into more detail about the creature's behavior, various attack suggestions and more. One suggestion was to circle around the imp and ambush it from behind, which should buy you enough time to finish it off before it reoriented and attacked. Apparently each TDM had a certain detection range, smaller or bigger depending on their class, type and special abilities. As long as you stayed outside their range, they ignored you.

Good to know.

At the bottom of the section on the imp was a link promoting "additional tactical information" which, when she tapped on it, zoomed her over to a new display under the "Tactical Support" heading. Here there was a general summary detailing what had so far been determined about the TDMs' purpose. The lower-class entities appeared to be mostly gatherers of the EM particles the TDMs were believed to feed off. They kept some for their own uses and transferred the rest to higher-class entities using an as yet unclear network. As they gathered more and more, they would "promote" to higher classes. Some TDMs seemed to be primarily concentrated on "defense" and these types stayed put until a Hunter came within range, while "patrol" TDMs like ghosts were constantly on the move, looking for a target.

Lynn closed the additional information screen and went back to perusing the monster index. Scrolling down, she noticed that there were fewer known Charlie Class monsters and just as many that were greyed out. Some of the grayed-out entities had a number above them. She checked one of those and it was listed as "observed" but with very little information. Most of the info slots were simply question marks. Some of the Charlie Class monsters looked like they were promotions of known Delta Class entities. There were estimates about some of the unknowns based on their known Delta Class counterpart. A few were marked as "probable promotion of still unidentified Delta Class."

The Bravo and Alpha Class sections were even less populated, also mostly promotions and almost all of them were grayed out with minimal information.

Sierra Class was interesting. It had the most entries by far, dozens of different entities all with individual names, as opposed to names of a monster "type." A lot of the names she recognized from other games she'd played, or movies and TV shows she'd watched, as names of various demons, devils and evil gods from myth. Shiva, Kali, Tiamat, Hannya and stuff like that. Unfortunately for her curiosity, every single one was grayed out. When she tapped on one of them, there was almost no information listed and even the few populated sections such as the location where it had been "observed" and stats on "Detection" and "Attacks" simply read "RESTRICTED INTELLIGENCE" in large block letters.

"Uh, Hugo?"

"Yes, Miss Lynn?"

"What's with this whole 'restricted intelligence' thing?"

"You are not high enough level to warrant access to that particular information."

"Huh. Okay. I guess it's good to have something to work toward, right?"

"Indeed, Miss Lynn."

Well, she wasn't going to make any progress sitting on her bed. Time to get out there and get her feet wet. But where to start? Lynn turned her attention to her satellite overhead. The map was quite detailed. She could zoom in and identify individual vehicles in the parking lot—what few there were, anyway. Most parking lots across the country had been significantly downsized since she was a little girl. They'd been replaced by green spaces, electric car charging stations, or pick-up-drop-off points for the rideshare robo-cars, while parking garages had been repurposed into airbus platforms. For the few gas-guzzling "dumb" car holdouts or those who refused to buy into the rideshare system, there were still a few spaces for individually owned cars. Lynn spotted a red dot between an electric two-seater and an ancient-looking sedan near the apartment's front entrance. She'd start there.

Before she left she looked out her window. One of the dots on her overhead looked like it should have been in line-of-sight, but she could see nothing out of the ordinary from her fifth-story window. Certainly no lurking CGI monsters. Out of curiosity, she reached up and tapped the dot in question and was rewarded by a flashed message of "This TDM is out of visual detection range."

Too bad. That meant she couldn't snipe targets from the coolness and safety of her bedroom. It wasn't *that* hot, being only late May, but still... the outside was the outside. Shaking her head, she told herself to get over it and went to put on her shoes. She had some serious leveling up to do and only so much daylight left to do it in.

"Okay, Hugo. Let's go kill some monsters."

"Excellent idea, Miss Lynn. I am sure they are quivering in their boots at the mere thought of your coming wrath."

"Uh-huh. Right. Don't give me a reason to look for your mute button, Mr. Smart Aleck."

"That would be entirely unnecessary, Miss Lynn. Any time you wish to switch from audio to text mode you have but to ask."

Lynn rolled her eyes.

"Never mind. Let's go."

Chapter 3

IT WASN'T THAT HOT. NOT TRULY. BUT THE LATE AFTERNOON SUN was bright and Lynn was grateful for the tint of her AR glasses as she emerged from the building's entrance in search of the first red dot. Following her overhead map, she soon found it: another imp, camped out between two vehicles parked next to the building. The only difference was this imp appeared to be crouched normally on the ground, not floating in midair.

The imp was facing the parking lot, so Lynn circled around the vehicles to come at it from behind. She focused on the monster's image but then hesitated. Were TDMs programmed to react to human voices? Just in case, she whispered the target command to put a red halo around the imp. Finally, she took a good look around her, ostensibly checking for any nearby danger, though deep down she knew she was simply self-conscious about being watched. But the coast was clear.

She charged forward and attacked the imp.

Red flashed and her knife vibrated as she swiped and stabbed, not letting up until the imp turned and jumped at her. This time she expected it and tried to hop back to avoid its claws. But apparently she didn't back up enough, because her own display still flashed with damage.

"Oh, you did not!" she snarled and lunged forward to stab the thing right in the face.

The imp exploded in a shower of sparks.

Triumph swept through her and she gave a derisive snort. Stupid imp. Then she remembered she was *in public* and looked around again, half expecting someone to ask her why she was slashing and cursing at empty air. But there was no one in sight. Lynn wondered again how Mr. Krator expected this game to succeed if everyone was so self-conscious about looking like an idiot while playing it, no matter how cool the ads for it looked. But maybe it was just her with her extreme aversion to being noticed that made it a problem...

Checking her health, she saw the imp's slashes had taken her down to eighty percent. So much for imps being easy from behind. But soon it wouldn't matter. She just needed to fight a few more and figure out their pattern. All opponents had them. It was simply a matter of observation. Once she knew the right timing, she could get her hits in from behind, jump back as the imp turned and lunged, then counter strike before it had a chance to attack again. Easy peasy.

She tapped the purple puddle of ichor to collect it and saw her power level tick upward as the resource was automatically applied to her reserves.

"Hey, Hugo. How long does loot stick around before despawning?"

"It can be variable based on the item's rarity, but for basic resources the dematerialize window is five to ten minutes."

"So, grab loot before you move on, in other words."

"That would certainly be advisable, yes, Miss Lynn."

"Got it," she said and headed toward the next dot.

She'd been worried about switching her focus between her overhead map and everything else, but it turned out it was easy to monitor her position from the corner of one eye while keeping alert to her surroundings. And then there were the sounds. Her earbuds were set to let through the noises from her natural surroundings— the hum of summer insects, the whirring buzz of various delivery drones overhead and the distant whoosh of the air taxi lane above First Avenue. Amplified above all that, though, were the weird calls of the TD monsters, making them impossible to miss.

There were still a few vehicles between her and the next dot when she started hearing an ominous rattle like a rattlesnake.

Peachy. Just peachy.

To be safe, she made a wide circle around a particularly battered old pickup and easily found the TDM by following the sound. This one looked like a green and red centipede and it was huge—like six-feet-long huge. Ewww. It was obvious when she got within its detection range, because between one cautious step and the next, it whipped around and started crawling toward her, rattling louder than ever. Still down on health and not sure what she was dealing with, she took off running back toward the apartment.

When she stopped and checked her map, none of the red dots were moving. That was comforting but now she was winded, not to mention feeling itchy and overheated in her baggy hoodie and long pants. She rarely wore T-shirts or shorts, even in summer, and she never wore tank tops or anything form fitting. At least, not since the hell that had been middle school. Better to avoid the outside and not work up a sweat than risk attracting attention.

"Gaming is a whole lot easier when I'm relaxing in my body-mold chair with a controller," she grumbled, half to herself as she sought out the shade by the apartment building and rested her hands on her knees to catch her breath.

"I could be wrong, of course, Miss Lynn, but I was under the impression that being 'easy' would defeat the purpose of this entire exercise. However, I am only a lowly service AI. What do I know?"

"Uh-huh. False modesty is just as bad as outright arrogance, you know."

"Yet much more classy, at least according to my analysis of stream celebrities."

Lynn snorted but couldn't help grinning.

"You got me there. Still, if I needed to save the world from an alien invasion, I'd make a bunch of robots so I could go back to sitting in my chair."

"No doubt an exceedingly brilliant idea, Miss Lynn. Shall I log that as your official beta recommendation to Mr. Krator?"

"Don't you dare. Now hush, I'm reading." Lynn concentrated on the monster stats that were still pulled up on her display, despite her swift retreat. The creature was a grinder worm. Armored, no surprise but slow—you call *that* slow? She tapped on the link to the Tactical Support section and read the attack suggestions. There was apparently a "kill spot" behind the head, which you could get at by dodging in from the side. Two or three stabs of the Nano Blade in the correct spot would do the trick.

She was still reading when she heard a strange rustling whisper behind her that sent chills crawling up her spine. Even as the noise registered, her display suddenly flashed a big orange "Proximity Warning" across her vision. Years of WarMonger-honed fighting instincts kicked in and without thinking she spun in place, striking backwards with her Nano Blade. She must have hit something, because her blade handle vibrated and an ethereal shape flashed red with damage done. The next moment, everything went still. She froze in place, listening hard as she worked through a moment of dizziness. Spinning was not her thing. When nothing else attacked, she shook her head and checked her status. There were no red dots nearby on her overhead and her health was at ninety percent, having regenerated some since she'd fought the imp. Whatever it was that had tried to jump her had left no sign behind, except a puddle of ichor and a floating purple orb.

"Hugo, what the heck was that and why didn't you warn me?"

"That was a ghost, Miss Lynn. Delta Class-2. Attacks: Ambush strike. Defenses: None. Detection: Level 1. Stealth: +3. Unique behavior: Prefers to circle behind before attacking. Detected in the wild: 1/12/2040, 1229 GMT, AlphaTester4. And I did warn you, Miss Lynn, unless you are color blind and incapable of seeing the color orange?"

"That was basically the same moment it attacked me, though. Why didn't you warn me sooner?"

"At your current level, your detection range for TDMs with stealth capabilities is extremely limited. As you gain experience and your battle system levels, that range will expand. In addition, you may equip globes to temporarily boost your detection range."

That must be what the floating orb was. Lynn collected the ichor and globe as she considered Hugo's words.

"Okay but what if I didn't have such good reflexes? I could have been flailing around for ages. It might have killed me."

"I am a service AI, Miss Lynn. My function is to instruct Hunters, answer questions and carry out voice commands. I can only function within the structure of my intended programming."

"Sooo even though you're a highly sophisticated AI, I can't tell you now to autofill my health and plates and globes any time they need it so I can focus on killing stuff?" she asked as she considered his words.

"That is correct, Miss Lynn. There are certain settings built into the application itself, such as when and how things display as well as audio and visual warnings for various situations. These I can automatically adjust to your preference. Your health and equipment, however, is yours alone to control, either manually or with individual voice commands."

"Humph. I guess that makes sense." Still, she felt annoyed. This wasn't like playing in virtual at all. The physical, real world aspect made the stakes feel immeasurably higher and it got her blood pumping like no game in virtual ever had. But then, if Hugo did everything for her, it wouldn't be the sort of challenge that attracted her to gaming in the first place, now would it?

Maybe she was going about this wrong anyway. She was playing as Lynn, which was all well and good, but Lynn was overly cautious and hated being outside. Maybe it was time to channel her inner Larry Coughlin...

So, what would Larry Coughlin, feared international mercenary do?

"Screw you, ghost," she said and smiled grimly. "I'm gonna make a necklace outta yer ears."

Larry probably would have spat on the ground, too, but there was no need to take things quite that far. For now, she just needed to concentrate on her surroundings—constant vigilance and all that—and be ready to react to anything creeping up on her.

Just because she needed to stay alert, though, didn't mean she couldn't enjoy a little background music while she got busy grinding through some levels...

She found the menu for accessing her LINC controls and took a moment to authorize her account on her LINC, then accessed her cloud stream. After a moment's consideration, she selected a playlist based on Halestorm—one of her dad's favorite bands from back in the day—then fiddled with the sound controls. She cranked the TD Hunter sound to the max then set her music volume to low, making sure to keep the earbud settings open to ambient sound as well so she could hear what was going on around her.

As the opening guitar and drums of "I Am the Fire" began, she checked to make sure she could still hear the faint clicks and grumbles of TDMs in every direction. Yup. This was what Larry would call a target rich environment. Her favorite kind.

"Nah, nah, naaah, nah, nah..."

Time to get her war face on...

Lynn had been playing solidly for over an hour as her kill counter slowly ticked upward. When she got a call from her mom that dinner was ready, she asked if she could eat later, pretty please? She could almost hear the fond exasperation in her mother's "I suppose" response and she promised herself she wouldn't make skipping meals with her mother a regular thing. She was just really into this game and knew from the way her body felt that if she went inside and sat down, she wouldn't get back up again. A while later her mother messaged that she had to leave early for work to get some errands done and reminded Lynn to do the dishes, be home by sunset, stay in the complex and "be careful." That was about the time Lynn hit Level 2. She hoped to reach at least one more level before calling it a night.

As she continued to make her way through the complex, killing TDMs as she went, Lynn looked for any patterns she could find—behaviors, numbers, distributions, all of it. The most common TDM, the imp, was supposed to be a "gather" type and so Lynn paid special attention to wherever electromagnetic activity might be. Places like each building's mesh node, the oversized package delivery dock and around light poles and air conditioning units.

The other basic types of TDMs, the "defense" and "patrol" types, were less predictable. They tended to be near the gather types, but not always, and sometimes she'd stumble across one way out by itself with no discernible reason for its position that she could see. She never spotted ghosts before they saw her, though she did figure out that interacting with any other TDM had a good chance of attracting them to her. It was as if the creatures were communicating with each other but only within a certain range.

She was killing a grinder worm over in the quad by the complex's office when she noticed she'd attracted her first spectator. She'd been trying as hard as she could to avoid people seeing her jumping around like a flea, spinning suddenly for no apparent reason and generally acting like a crazy person. The few people out and about were either busy on their way somewhere or were immersed in their own AR universe. But an older gentleman with tight curls of snowy hair and a beard that stood out starkly against his dark skin had paused to lean on his cane and watch her dodge to and fro. Lynn wondered if he was in the middle of playing some game of his own, because he wore a pair of classically stylish AR glasses.

Lynn tried not to feel self-conscious at the scrutiny. When she glanced at him a second time, though, she recognized him as one of the other residents of their building. He lived on the ground floor and seemed friendly with all the neighbors. She vaguely remembered that he'd welcomed them when they'd first moved in and had even made them some pork tenderloins and deliciously chewy Scotcheroos as an apartment-warming gift. Lynn had never talked to him much, but she knew he chatted with her mom occasionally if they met in the halls. What was his name again?

"Uh, hey," she greeted him, then jumped back to avoid the swipe of a grinder's pincers. "I'm, uh, playing a game."

"So I had surmised, young lady," the man said, smiling broadly to reveal rows of near-perfect teeth. They must have been replacement implants, considering how old the guy was. "As am I," he continued, holding up his wrist to show off a LINC that looked for all the world like one of those vintage wrist watches that had been around before her mom had been born. "My game is rather less…active, however. I was wondering *what* you were playing, if you don't mind my forwardness?"

"I'm a beta tester for TD Hunter," Lynn said, her eyes back on the grinder, which was making its "slow" way around to come at her for another attack. "Mind if I finish off this…well, there's a monster and I need to kill it before it kills me."

"I understand completely," the man said. "Please, don't let me distract you."

She dodged to the side of the grinder, then stabbed it in the kill spot once, twice, three times until the TDM exploded in a shower of sparks. Over the last few hours she'd taken quite a bit of damage learning the pattern of each monster, but with lots of walking she'd healed enough to stay out of the red.

Grinders dropped ichor and armor plates and she collected both before turning to smile uncertainly at the man.

"I, um, got it," she offered, not really sure what else to say. She was fine talking to people in virtual. Not so much in the real. But she did turn off her music.

"Might I see?" the man asked. "I have actually heard of TD Hunter. Their ads are impossible to avoid. I prefer playing the various catch and collect games myself. Nothing so vigorous as TD Hunter appears to be in all of its promotions. It has been a long time since I've been up to such acrobatic exploits."

"Honestly, they're a lot for me, too," Lynn said, grinning sheepishly. It wasn't the walking that had made her muscles ache and put a sheen of sweat on her forehead. It was all the jumping and dodging and spinning to take out the freaking ghosts that seemed to be all *over* the place. "But it's fun. Fighting monsters, collecting loot, that sort of thing. Here's what I just took out . . . er, wait a sec."

She turned away from the man and tried to speak softly.

"Hugo? Can you project that grinder image for me so I can show him? Also, you need to teach me how to do the whole subvocal thing so people don't think I'm talking to myself."

"Of course, Miss Lynn. Remember, you can manipulate the image with your hands and to dismiss it, simply swipe it away."

When she turned back to the old man, he looked concerned.

"I do apologize, am I interrupting a call?" he asked.

"Oh no! That was the game's service AI," Lynn said. "I just got this new gaming equipment, so I wasn't sure how to project an image and, uh, oh look, here it is," she said as a six-inch, three-dimensional image of the grinder worm appeared before her. She used both hands to give it a spin, stopping it when it faced the man, then expanding it to over two feet long so he could get a good look and hopefully forget about her awkward mumbling.

"My goodness. Quite the boogeyman. Are they all this . . . ferocious-looking?"

"Pretty much. Except for the ghosts. I still don't know what they look like beyond smokey blobs. They appear out of nowhere with barely any warning and I have to stab them quick before they do damage."

The old man chuckled and shook his head.

"That sounds positively terrifying. I must admit, I prefer my creatures cute, fuzzy and harmless. Less chance one of them might jump out at me from behind a tree and give me a heart attack."

Lynn shared a laugh with him.

"Well, you probably shouldn't play TD Hunter, then. I'm Lynn, by the way," she added, remembering her manners. She figured "don't talk to strangers" didn't apply here, since he was a neighbor. "Lynn Raven. I think you know my mom?"

"Ah, yes, Matilda's girl. I'm Jerald Thomas," Mr. Thomas said, offering his hand. "It's a pleasure to meet you again, young lady. You've grown quite a bit since I last saw you."

Lynn took his hand tentatively and shook it. Shaking hands wasn't really a thing anymore—not, at least, for her generation. But her mother had taught her to be polite. His palm was cool and dry and a bit leathery to the touch as if he had once worked with his hands. She wondered if Larry's hands would feel the same way if he'd been real. They would probably be bonier and covered in scars.

"What is the game about, if I might ask?" Mr. Thomas said.

"Oh, pretty standard gaming stuff," Lynn said. "There's been an invasion of invisible monsters from another dimension, and we volunteer 'Hunters' have to clear them out and save the world. I only started playing today, but so far it's been a fun challenge. The only drawback is that it's a bit of a grind right now, just the same ol' same ol' while I'm building experience. I'm trying to level up as fast as possible to get to more interesting stuff. Do you . . . want to see how it works?"

"Certainly," Mr. Thomas said, and he sounded genuinely interested.

Lynn gave another quickly whispered command for Hugo to project her entire display, hoping it would work. It did.

"Here's my overhead map so I can see where the monsters are . . ." She proceeded to explain each part of her display and, since it was close by, took him over to the nearest dot, which turned out to be another imp. With imps being non-aggressive, she was able to get close enough for Mr. Thomas to see it on her display without any danger to her, and she told him all about her attack strategy. Since he was so interested and not at all condescending, she went ahead and took out the imp so he could see her in action.

"Bravo," he said with a clap of his weathered hands, cane tucked under one arm. "Very impressive considering you only started playing today, You are quite the natural at this sort of thing."

Lynn's face flushed and it felt hot enough to fry an egg. She could only hope her blush wasn't visible, considering how red she already was from her exertions. Fortunately, she didn't have to come up with a non-awkward reply, because Mr. Thomas went right on talking.

"It doesn't seem very fair to the poor imp, though, sneaking up behind him and stabbing him in the back."

"There's nothing fair about war," Lynn pointed out. She felt a flash of amusement, imagining what Larry would say to anyone naive enough to complain about fairness. Definitely nothing fit for polite company like Mr. Thomas. "Besides, it's not very fair to invade someone else's dimension and start killing them, is it?"

"Touché, young lady," Mr. Thomas said, dipping his head at her. "Is the game available now?"

"No, they're still testing it," Lynn said, swiping at her display to make the projected image disappear.

"Ah. How did you get your hands on it, then, if I may ask?"

"I got invited," Lynn said, trying to shrug casually. Mr. Thomas was a good listener, but he wouldn't know who Robert Krator was any more than her mom did. "I'm pretty into gaming. I'm not sure why they picked me for *this* game, though. I'm sooo not into being outside." She shifted, suddenly conscious of her sweaty face and clothes.

"It's hot and buggy and some of the monsters are even in the *woods*," she said, grimacing comically. "I'm not really into woods. There's birds and bugs and stuff."

Mr. Thomas chuckled, eyes sparkling.

"I am quite familiar with such terrain, young lady. If you think woods are unpleasant, though, try navigating tropical jungle during monsoon season in full kit while carrying a ten-pound rifle."

Lynn's eyes went wide and she did some quick mental calculations. Medicine had made mind-blowing advances in the past few decades but surely he wasn't *that* old.

"Mr. Thomas, you don't mean—Did you fight in—" But the old gentleman cut her off with a wave of his hand.

"That is ancient history, my dear. And honestly a history that is not at all pleasant to recall. Your energetic enthusiasm simply reminded me of my younger days. Now, I would offer you a training course in woodland navigation, but I suspect questions would arise if a charming young lady went wandering the woods with an older gentleman."

"Uh, yeah, probably," Lynn said and laughed.

"If you would accept my suggestion, though, do find company for any such foray. It is dangerous to go alone, after all." The old man winked at her.

Lynn cocked her head, Mr. Thomas' words ringing a bell. Maybe he knew more about gaming than she'd given him credit for, even if his game knowledge *was* ancient history.

"Thanks," she said with a smile. "I'll be careful. There's plenty of monsters around the complex for now, anyway."

"Well, if you are planning on staying in this area, might I continue to watch?" Mr. Thomas asked. "It is quite fascinating to observe, now that I know the rhyme and reason behind your gyrations."

"Uh, okay. Sure," Lynn said.

"Thank you, I—Pardon a moment," Mr. Thomas said as he seemed to spot something in front of him. He made a few catching motions, then snorted and shook his head. "Accursed things. I've come to the conclusion that this game would be far simpler if I was allowed to shoot these creatures, then pick up the carcasses."

"Yeah, that's what I'll be doing for sure once I get a gun that's worth a darn," Lynn said. "But guns take power to fuel and I wanted to start out using the knife option." She gestured with her electric blue Nano Blade.

"It is a very impressive weapon. I am glad it is brightly colored or I might have been concerned, seeing you brandish it so threateningly."

From his smile and flash of white teeth, Lynn assumed he was joking. But still, he had a fair point. It was a dangerous-looking weapon.

"Ah, another one," Mr. Thomas said, distracted again by something Lynn couldn't see. "This won't take much time or . . . And it is gone. I would use unseemly language, but one does not do so around a young lady."

"Have you never played in virtual before?" Lynn asked, laughing. "I guarantee you I've heard plenty of stuff that would scandalize even you."

"Do you mean online? I suppose 'in virtual' is what young people call it these days?"

"Yeah. But don't worry, my mom still says online, too."

"Not above a little flattery, I see," Mr. Thomas said with another flashing smile. "If that is the state of games 'in virtual' these days, then sticking to my little catch and collect routine is no loss. I've heard quite enough cursing in my time. Is it truly that bad?"

"I don't even play as a girl," Lynn said, warming up to the topic. Mr. Thomas was much easier to talk to than her peers, especially considering she *couldn't* talk about gaming with the few people she called friends. "And I don't use the language. Mostly, anyway. The character I play is an older guy who got injured in the Middle East as a mercenary. Now he plays online games and schools all the 'young pups' on how to be 'a real snake.'"

It felt odd but gratifying to finally talk about Larry to someone. Mr. Thomas seemed about as far outside her social circle as possible, so she wasn't worried about it getting back to her friends.

"I would guess all this interaction is typed, then?" Mr. Thomas said.

"Nope, I've got a voice modulator app," Lynn said. "It gives me a gravelly baritone. And I'm always dropping hints about being in places like Bangkok and Medellin and...East Africa, starts with an M..." She hummed a bit of a tune. "...in a barroom drinkin' gin..."

"Mombasa," Mr. Thomas said. "Wherever did a young lady like yourself discover the mercenary's balladeer? Not my favorite singer of the era, but I know some of the tunes well."

"I did as much research into the character as I could," Lynn said, shrugging. "I've got another gr—"

She suddenly spun and struck out with her Nano Blade, nearly hitting Mr. Thomas.

"Oops! Sorry," she said, feeling her face heat again. She should have taken herself out of combat mode when she'd started talking, she'd almost assaulted a senior citizen. "Another ghost. They sneak up on you out of nowhere."

"How did you know it was there?" Mr. Thomas asked.

"Sound," Lynn said, tapping her earbud. "They have this sort of creepy, rattling whisper. When you hear that, you know they're close. Real close."

"Well, I think I'll leave you to it," Mr. Thomas said, "I would hate to distract you at a crucial moment. I may look into TD Hunter when it comes out. Perhaps there will be an 'easy' setting that an old man like myself can handle," he said with a chuckle.

Lynn didn't think there was any chance of that but didn't want to say as much, so she just shrugged and smiled.

"If I see you around, I'll let you know when it comes out."

"That is very kind of you. Thank you, young lady. Now, I believe you have a mission to attend to?"

"Yup, I guess so. These monsters won't kill themselves. It was nice to talk to you, Mr. Thomas. Have a good evening!"

"You as well, Miz Raven."

Lynn turned and headed for a section of the complex she hadn't been in yet that still had plenty of dots, smiling all the while. She wasn't sure, but she thought she might have made a friend. Maybe being forced outside by an augmented reality game wasn't as bad as she'd thought.

A while later, Lynn was starting to slow. As long as she focused on the next dot and the next, she could ignore the growing ache in her limbs. But it was getting late and she knew she needed to head back to the apartment soon. She had the main areas of the complex cleared except for a few dots left by the pool. Since it was on her way back to her apartment, she decided to finish them off.

She took out two imps—they were everywhere—a grinder worm and a nastily aggressive brute called a gremlin. Checking her overhead, she confirmed there were no more red dots in her immediate area and was about to turn and head home when she saw an odd glint from the corner of her eye. She turned toward it and surveyed the pool's pump system. There it was again.

Moving cautiously, Lynn approached the little fenced-off area beside the pool, staring hard at the spot where she'd caught the glint. Suddenly, about ten feet out, a sparkling mist materialized and a red dot popped up on her overhead. Her display flashed a yellow warning across her vision as Hugo's voice chimed in her ear.

"Warning. You have encountered an Unidentified TransDimensional Entity. Please remain where you are while your battle system runs an analysis."

Lynn stood still, as a thrill of excitement went through her. She'd stumbled upon an unidentified TDM on her very first day! The next moment, though, a bolt of light shot out from the mist and her display flashed red.

The cursed thing had shot her!

She jumped back and the mist disappeared from sight. Eyes narrowed, Lynn glared at the spot where she knew the stupid monster was as Hugo spoke in her ear.

"From the small amount of data that was collected, this entity is most likely a Delta Class-2 and should be within your ability to defeat, though caution is advised. No information about its capabilities or vulnerabilities could be detected. Good luck, Hunter."

"Humph. Thanks, I suppose. Any tips?" she asked, still eyeing the spot by the pool pumps and catching an occasional glint.

"There are no known tactical suggestions which apply, Miss Lynn, considering the dearth of data currently available. You will have to get within range and engage the entity for the system to gain any more information."

"So, what you're saying is, I'm your guinea pig?"

"Quite right, Miss Lynn. The Alpha testers often use the term 'good training.'"

Lynn snorted then cocked her head. She knew she'd heard the term before but couldn't quite place it.

This sneaky little monster was going to pay. She would make sure of it.

Not one to give into impatience or hasty decisions, Lynn examined the terrain and circled the glinting spot cautiously until she had a clear escape route at her back, just in case this monster turned aggressive. After another moment's thought, she tapped her weapon icon and switched to the Disruptor Pistol. She'd tried it on a few imps and a grinder worm already, but it did so little damage and used up precious power, so she'd stuck to her Nano Blade, which was more fun to use anyway. With a complete unknown, though, she thought it might be best to start with a ranged attack.

Moving cautiously, Lynn inched forward until the mist popped into view again. She quickly targeted it and squeezed off three rounds, her pistol making a satisfying *pewpewpew* sound as her attack showed up as blue bolts of light that hit the mist center of mass. The entity flashed red, but it made no move to chase her. Instead, another bolt of light shot out and her display flashed with damage.

Lynn jumped back before it could hit again, moving out of range. Thankfully, it didn't follow. Checking her health, she could see the attack hadn't been as lethal as getting into hand-to-hand with a gremlin, but it wasn't something she could shrug off, either. The biggest problem was that she had no idea how much damage her pistol had done. She couldn't dodge those return shots and there was no telling whose health would last longer in a fight of attrition. Time for something different.

"Hugo, if I equip a globe in my stealth slot, will that keep this monster from being able to target me?"

"Unfortunately not, Miss Lynn. The stealth aspect of the globes only helps to mask your base signature generated by your battle system. Once you attack, the TDMs are able to lock onto your signature and any element of surprise is lost."

"Dang. So much for that idea." She thought a little more. Maybe it was time to go big or go home. She hadn't tried using plates yet for armor, mostly because she'd wanted to get an idea of what it was like fighting without them before she started bolstering her defenses. But this was a good reason to break them in.

She could see her armor icon had a small number eight beside it, indicating she'd collected eight plates, one for each grinder worm she'd defeated so far. Tapping the icon, she was able to add a plate to the slot, making the outline of a shield go from empty to half colored in. A little "fifty percent" appeared beside it. Hmm. She tapped it again to add one more plate and the shield went solid with a percentage of one hundred. Maybe because she was Level 2, it took two plates to fully armor up? That made sense and it was a standard mechanic in many games to increase a player's stat capacities as they leveled.

"Time to get down and dirty," she muttered, switching her weapon from Disruptor Pistol back to Nano Blade.

Since there was no back or front to the sparkling mist, Lynn didn't bother getting fancy. She simply charged in and started slashing. The monster didn't retreat or dodge, just sat there and shot again and again as she cut and stabbed. Besides the red flashes and slight vibration of her handle indicating hits, the sparkling mist didn't react and Lynn fell into a rhythm, keeping half an eye on her health and armor.

By the time the unknown TDM exploded in a shower of sparks, her health was down thirty percent and her armor was over half gone. Good thing she'd decided to equip those plates. Luckily, the thing dropped a globe along with its ichor for all her trouble, plus . . . what was that tube-looking thing that had appeared on the ground?

Before she could investigate, Hugo's voice chimed in.

"Please stand by while entity analysis is completed."

Lynn stayed put and after a few more seconds, a new image of a monster popped up on her display beside a filled-in stat sheet. The creature looked like a floating ball of tentacles with no discernible features. Hugo began reading as she eyed the image with distaste.

"Unknown entity has been designated as a Lecta, a new Delta Class-2.

"It appears to be an electrovore, feeding on the electromagnetic spectrum. Data indicates it will be found near any electrical systems, including power nodes, transmitter antennas, or any electrically powered equipment such as pumps, environmental control units and the like. The Lecta has a low-powered ranged attack, designated as plasma spit.

"It appears to be non-aggressive towards Hunters, has no discernible defenses but does possess low stealth capabilities, forcing a Hunter to come within its own range before it can be targeted. Defeat of a Lecta should yield one globe and approximately six ichor points. Excellent job, Hunter. You now have credit for the detection, defeat and analysis of an unknown TDM!"

New images filled her display showing her achievement, with all three boxes labeled detection, kill and analysis, checked off. Each had experience points next to it and there was a bonus displayed for completing all three tasks. The combined experience points were a good twenty times what she'd have gotten for killing an imp and she also got extra ichor, plates and globes.

"You will have permanent credit for your discovery," Hugo continued, as a line of text scrolled past, showing the date, time and her beta tester name in the "Detected in the wild" section of the new monster's stats. Just like the other stats she'd looked up, no location was listed, which she appreciated. She'd prefer not to have her apartment complex's address broadcasted to the entire world.

The experience she gained from her unknown detection bumped her up to Level 3 and a success screen popped up next, showing that her maximum health and power levels had increased and that she'd gained even more ichor, globes and plates. Her health was also replenished to full, which was nice since it meant she didn't have to worry about walking off the damage the Lecta had dealt.

Sweet. She needed to find more unknowns. She would have to spend some time scanning the beta forum to see if there was any pattern to where unknowns were most likely hiding. It might be completely random, or there might be some trick to it. She would find out.

"Congratulations on your achievement, Miss Lynn," Hugo said as her level up screen faded away. "One final reminder: the higher level you are, the more visible you are to your enemies. This means aggressive TDMs will be more likely to attack sooner and patrol type TDMs such as ghosts will be attracted to you in greater numbers. Keep this in mind as you proceed and consider making use of your plates and globes on a regular basis."

"Thanks for the tip, Hugo, but you said the exact same thing when I leveled from 1 to 2. Do you repeat that warning at every level?"

"It bears repeating, Miss Lynn. You would be surprised at the number of Hunters who ignore it. My only recourse is to assume all humans have the mental storage capacity of a goldfish and repeat such critical information at every possible juncture."

Lynn snickered. The AI's tone remained professional and impassive, but his choice of words brought to mind a dark-haired and hawk-faced man pursing his lips in consternation at the idea of anyone ignoring his expert opinion.

"I'll be sure to keep your advice firmly in mind, Hugo."

"You flatter me, Miss Lynn."

"Well, darn. I'll try not to do *that* again. Wouldn't want you to get a big head or anything."

"I do not have a head, Miss Lynn. But if I did, I am quite sure it would always remain a perfectly appropriate size."

Lynn grinned.

"You keep telling yourself that, buddy. In the meantime, what is that tube thing on the ground? Did the Lecta drop that?"

"Indeed it did, Miss Lynn. That is an augment item, which is randomly dropped by enemies. The more rare or difficult the enemy, the greater the value of the item dropped."

"Awesome, loot!" Lynn said and collected the item. Since nothing popped up on her display, she opened the main menu and selected "Inventory."

"If I may interrupt your well-deserved break, Miss Lynn, it is wisest to exit combat mode whenever you find yourself distracted from your combat screen for any period of time."

"Oh, yeah, good idea. In fact, I should probably head home anyway. I feel like I've been beat to a pulp. Go ahead and take me out of combat mode and I'll check out this augment on my way back."

"Very good, Miss Lynn," Hugo said. The next moment her overhead map disappeared and all her combat-related icons lost their glow and shifted to one side. The baton in her hand warmed slightly and shrunk, compacting itself back into its base shape.

The deactivation of her weapon and visual change in her environment made the hyper alert Larry part of her relax and she felt herself deflate like a balloon. She suddenly became aware of all the aches and pains she'd been ignoring and weariness pressed down on her shoulders. Even the thought of checking out her very first augment was exhausting, so instead she simply turned for home and concentrated on putting one foot in front of the other. To distract herself from the long trudge back, she asked Hugo a few questions she'd been saving up about the game and had him start teaching her to subvocalize.

Once she was back at her apartment, she would have collapsed onto the couch, except that she realized her throat was burning with thirst. She guzzled several glasses of water before summoning enough energy to make it back to her bedroom. That Counterforce backpack with its hydration system would have come in handy, but she was still hesitant about wearing it, even around her apartment complex. Too noticeable. She'd just bring a water bottle next time in one of her old school backpacks.

It took all her willpower, but she dragged herself through a brief shower to remove the sticky layer of sweat she'd acquired, then changed into comfy pajamas before collaping on her bed. As she lay on her back and stared at the ceiling, she finally took stock of her body. All the soreness from walking, running, twisting and dodging had come home to complain. Her feet felt like pounded meat and she had a twinge in one shoulder where she thought she might have pulled something swiping too enthusiastically at a gremlin.

She was *way* too exhausted, both mentally and physically, to play WarMonger. But it was also too early to go to bed. She wanted to do homework about as much as she wanted to get up and run a marathon, so doing research on TD Hunter would be a good excuse to procrastinate. She could put her feet up and rest while she read, then get the dishes and her homework done before going to bed.

Despite not wanting to move another inch, she dragged herself to her body-mold chair, knowing her muscles would thank her later. Then she dug into the TD Hunter main menu, exploring each of its options one by one.

In her inventory, she took a moment to examine the augment the Lecta had dropped. The black cylinder looked like a tight coil of some sort of tubing and it was listed as a "Small Power Amplifier." It could be equipped to any one-handed ranged weapon and upped the damage done by ten percent. Of course, it also increased the energy per shot usage, but that was an expected trade-off. Lynn eagerly popped it into her Disruptor Pistol's first augment slot and watched the stat bars for the weapon adjust accordingly. She couldn't wait to try it out.

Next, she took a few minutes to play around with her skin customizations, to see what options were available. To her surprise, they were pretty limited. She'd have thought that with an augmented reality game as advanced as this, the possibilities would be endless. But maybe the game designers wanted players more focused on the game than their appearance. Or maybe they thought there wasn't much point in changing how you looked in augmented reality where people could easily see the "un-skinned" you. It wasn't like in virtual where your avatar was the only contact others had with you in game.

Taking a closer look at her skin's equipment, she noticed that with plates equipped in her armor slot, her skin acquired what looked like knee and elbow pads and a sleek-looking helmet. Based on the ads TD Hunter had been running for months, she assumed the armor's appearance would upgrade into something much more impressive as she advanced levels. Once she was done fiddling with the skin settings, she continued her exploration until she had a solid feel for the game's navigation.

Next, she decided to embark on some less benign research. She'd been wanting to scratch an itch since Mr. Krator had invited her to beta. It wasn't that she was suspicious of his motives, she was just intrigued by how... unique the game was and wondered what tricks the developers had up their sleeves.

Even though the TD Hunter app had a seamless interface with the rest of her new LINC, she decided to do a web search through her personal gaming interface instead of through the equipment Mr. Krator had sent. Maybe she did have a touch of her mom's paranoia after all. There was no telling what sort of internal search biases might be programmed into the devices made by Tsunami Entertainment. Most people were too clueless—and happily so—to worry about such things. But considering she gamed as a seventy-some-year-old mercenary and had been forced to figure out how to move and manage large sums of money in virtual when she was legally still a minor, there were a lot of things she was aware of that most people never worried about. She wasn't a hacker by any means, but she *was* careful.

It was the work of a moment to bring up her wall-screen and get a few keyword searches going. She was happy to discover that switching her focus from her AR display to the screen on her wall didn't make her eyes hurt. Using her school-issued AR glasses in class to switch between her e-textbooks and the wall-mounted smartboards her teachers used often gave her a headache.

Lynn browsed through her search results, reading articles here and there. She wanted to find out the developmental background of this odd game, the sort of details that crazy obsessive gamers like Ronnie would know. If she'd wanted to save time, she probably could've pinged him and picked his brain. But then she'd have to explain *why* she was interested in the first place. No thanks.

What she found made her raise an eyebrow. The company that was publishing the game was *not* Tsunami Entertainment, as she'd assumed, but a subsidiary that listed Robert Krator as the CEO. It was a well-funded start-up and TD Hunter was its very first game. Even more interesting, the start-up had significant links to corporate, military and government sectors. None of the developers involved in it were big in the gaming industry except Mr. Krator. Most were lower profile individuals known for their work on military simulation systems, augmented and virtual reality training for corporate and military use and cutting-edge advances in artificial intelligence funded by governments and tech giants. Mr. Krator's comment about investors made a lot more sense in that light.

Lynn hadn't realized how much this game sat on the cusp of a potential new era of gaming that, if it caught on, would cause seismic shifts in the status quo of the gaming industry. Plus, the technology perfected in TD Hunter had so many different applications in all these sectors backing the game, Lynn wasn't surprised Mr. Krator's investors were pushing for a swift game release.

Lynn hoped it did catch on, for Mr. Krator's sake if for no other reason. He seemed like a really decent guy, not at all the elitist celebrity type she'd expected from someone who was basically a demigod in the gaming industry.

With this new perspective, Lynn kept digging into her search results. There wasn't much in the way of developmental history of the game or the usual in-depth analysis pieces most games put out leading up to a release to generate a buzz. Mostly it was interviews with Robert Krator where he talked up the augmented reality aspect, game style and his personal gaming history that inspired TD Hunter. None of the other developers were mentioned beyond passing references and Lynn got the impression most of them were happy to stay out of the limelight.

Besides the interviews, Lynn only found a few promotional pieces released by the official TD Hunter game. Most developers were constantly releasing teasers and news about upgrades, but it seemed that TD Hunter's novel self-learning AI- and algorithm-driven game-play was turning every normal expectation on its head. Instead of promoting the game through exhaustive detail, TD Hunter was taking the opposite "less is more" approach. Speculation on fan sites abounded and replies to specific questions about things like new expansions and monster types were a variation on: "our next-generation, self-learning game play creates an exciting environment full of surprises and challenges. We're eager for you to experience it firsthand!"

Uh-huh. It sounded to Lynn like there was some serious suppression of proprietary information going on. Not that she should be all that surprised. The non-disclosure agreement she'd signed before she'd started had been pretty draconian. In fact, now that she thought about it, she probably shouldn't have shown Mr. Thomas the game like she had. But he was just some old retired guy. It wasn't like she was posting insider information in virtual. And the developers couldn't expect betas to play an AR game in absolute isolation, so she figured an innocent spectator here and there wasn't what Mr. Krator was worried about. There was probably corporate rivalry or inter-industry unrest going on in the background. She wasn't too worried about it and figured upcoming news and all the tips and tricks was just insular to the app itself since it was in beta.

Her "what is Mr. Krator up to" itch now scratched, she dove back into the TD Hunter app and started a more thorough poke around. She found that there was a whole TD Hunter social networking site set up with a complex trading system between individuals, informal groups and registered teams. There wasn't much action on the social network yet, since it seemed most of the beta testers asked questions and swapped tips via the Community Forum. She would dive into that later. For now, she poked around to find out more about the trading system and how she was going to make money with the game.

As Hugo had mentioned, there were several ways to collect augments and weapons, the two items that would be most in demand. Standard model weapons could be unlocked by leveling, while some standard and non-standard weapons could be unlocked through achievements like killing a certain number or type of TDM, distance walked in the game, or discovering unknown TDMs. Monsters could also drop weapons in addition to augments and those weapons were often unique, like named weapons with special bonuses. Each item had its own level requirement, though, which was pretty standard in achievement-based games. By jumping back to the "Weapons List" in the main menu Lynn could see that the requirements were fairly low, which was good.

Her best bet for big bucks, then, was to get extremely good at killing monsters and learn all the places and types of TDMs most likely to give her high quality augments, unique weapons, or big drops of consumables like plates and globes. The practice was called item farming and it was a time-honored profession for professional gamers worldwide.

Lynn felt a trickle of excitement, knowing that if she could get to high enough levels fast enough, brokering equipment had the potential for serious cash flow. It was standard in competitive games for all beta testers to start back as new players when the game released, which was annoying but perfectly necessary. Betas would have a significant edge, though, and could use what they'd learned during beta to level faster with more achievements than anyone else. Lynn knew from experience that there would be plenty of rich, lazy players who didn't want to be inflicted with puny starting equipment and would eagerly pay through the nose for upgrades they could brag about to all their friends. Being one of the first brokers able to get a hold of that kind of equipment was her ticket to major money.

In microtransactions, it looked like you could buy plates, globes and the healing capsules called Oneg. She recognized the name from her mom talking about "O Negative" blood type, the universal donor type. The game would allow direct transfers of "loot" between players, as well as transfers on an in-game brokering site. She'd already found the beta of that. There wasn't any current trading, but she saw how they intended to do it. No more switching back and forth to a clunky auction site. You could put whatever you wanted to trade, including equipment, up for bid and the app itself took care of all the transactions, since everyone had to have a virtual wallet connected to their account anyway.

And then there was power leveling. The term was most common in games that had levels—something WarMonger did not have. But being hired to fight in WarMonger matches to up the rankings of the rich person who'd hired her was similar in function to power leveling. In games like TD Hunter where you had to grind to level, certain types of people—mostly entitled, impatient and rich—could pay a higher level player to form a group with them and go around slaughtering everything in sight so the lower level player could get experience easier and faster. It was standard in games that experience was shared equally among members of a group and there was almost always a group bonus on top of the normal experience to incentivize people to play together.

The only rub was that, since the game was in the real instead of in virtual, the client or the power leveler would have to travel. With how fast and cheap transportation was that wouldn't be much of a barrier if the incentive was high enough. But—and it was a big but—TD Hunter being an AR game also meant she'd have to actually *meet* her clients. Face to face. Ugh. Then there was the tiny problem that she was a minor. Her mother would never let her go off alone with a stranger to a strange place to play TD Hunter. Not to mention it would be a lot harder to power level someone in unfamiliar territory. She'd have to require clients come to her home turf where she knew the lay of the land and she'd have to figure out something that would convince her mom it was safe.

Yeah, like that was going to happen. Better to start with item farming and see how things developed. Power leveling could be her backup plan.

Either way, Mr. Krator hadn't been kidding when he'd said TD Hunter had been set up for serious gamers to monetize. She wasn't sure how long the initial "gold rush" would last when the game launched, but she definitely needed practice to up her efficiency and attack ratings as much as possible before then.

Who knew, maybe if she decided to stick with the game, she

could get sponsors to send her to tournaments, like Tommy Jones? She had a brief vision of herself decked out in sleek gaming gear covered in sponsor logos, waving at the camera for adoring fans streaming from all over the world. Then she snorted. What a dumb dream. She wasn't "popular" material. She was the kind of person who ruled from the shadows. Best to stay on the sidelines where she could stay invisible.

Refocusing on her screens, she considered what she'd discovered so far.

Other than buying upgraded weapons and augments, there were few shortcuts. Even if you had plenty of money to spare, the fact that the game was in the real meant you still had to put in the time and work. Eventually, of course, you'd achieve a high enough level that you could engage in large-scale battles to take out the bosses, who she assumed would drop seriously valuable loot. Taking out bosses, though, required forming alliances between teams, which was odd for an FPS game. That was usually the realm of MMORPGs—massive multiplayer online role-playing games. Not that teams were uncommon in FPS gameplay, but they were always PVP, player versus player, not player versus game. Of course, it did make sense that the developers wouldn't want hordes of people physically attacking each other, even with blunt, toylike weapons. As disappointing as it was, it did make sense to not have PVP in an augmented reality game.

In any case, until you started getting into boss battles, the game was mostly "grinding." It was one of the constant negatives mentioned on the beta tester forum. Past catch-'em-all type AR games had been successful because of constant new expansions as well as fierce competition in the rankings. TD Hunter would need to do something similar, otherwise, the basic "kill monsters, save the world" narrative would get old, quick.

As far as competition went, she did find the leaderboard that showed ranking categories for top players world-wide and all their achievement stats, as well as the sub boards for individual stat rankings. She couldn't wait to get her own name—well, her gaming name, whatever she decided to go with—on the leaderboard. But with no possibility of PVP competitions, she wondered what Mr. Krator had in mind to keep the game popular long-term.

Eventually, she gave a mental shrug and turned her mind to exploring the Tactical Support database and forum. Here, she picked up some good suggestions on fighting TDMs and got a better understanding of the game's mechanics.

For instance, player Levels corresponded to the TDM classes roughly ten to one. In other words, for the first nine levels she would only be battling Delta Class monsters. She wouldn't start detecting or being attacked by Charlie Class TDMs until she reached about Level 10. Which meant she'd have to get to Level 20 before she could detect Bravo Class, much less have a hope of defeating them and Level 30 before even considering taking on Alpha Class. Sierra Class bosses, then, wouldn't come into play until you'd reached max level at Level 40. Based on her gaming experience, she assumed the lower levels could be gained relatively quickly and each new level would take longer and longer to achieve.

Another thread talked about strategies for using globes. If you dropped a few into both your stealth and detection slots, you became virtually invisible to lower-class TDMs or weak TDMs without good detection capabilities, while simultaneously expanding your own detection range. Then you could find the sweet spot just within your range but outside theirs and take the buggers out with little danger. With non-aggressive TDMs, they'd just sit there. Aggressive ones would start moving around, looking for you, but you could always back up to try to stay in the sweet spot.

Lynn thought that seemed like a good way to keep your kill to damage ratio high—your rate of monsters killed versus damage taken. In a monster-killing game like TD Hunter that would be one of the most prestigious scores being tracked, besides total kills. But that strategy would also consume a lot of power and, more importantly, time, at least until you unlocked some high-level weapons that could one-shot the lower-class TDMs. With enough practice, she was pretty sure she could kill faster and more efficiently with her Nano Blade. She'd have to experiment and see what worked best, especially once she unlocked better weapons and found some good augments. There was a two-handed Plasma Sword she was itching to try once she got to Level 10 and unlocked her second baton.

She was particularly delighted when she delved into the "Training Simulations" section and discovered there were hundreds of training modules covering all types of weaponry, monsters and fighting techniques. Once her school finals were over, it would be a great way to work on the game even in bad weather or after dark.

Though she knew she probably wouldn't get high enough level to pit herself against Bravo and Alpha Class monsters before the game released, curiosity had her looking for more information about them in the discussion threads. The idea of group-based battles in the real was fascinating. She knew all about boss raids and such in MMORPG games, but it seemed like that sort of thing would be a lot harder to pull off in an AR game.

To her disappointment, there wasn't much information available and the few firsthand accounts from beta testers agreed that taking on Bravo and Alpha Class monsters single-handed was a quick way to die. It wasn't just that the higher-class monsters were difficult to beat but that the higher class they got, the more they attracted other monsters around them and you couldn't mob control all by yourself. Also, there were complaints about how badly the game glitched during these "mini boss" fights, as well as stories about LINCs having hardware failures or batons going haywire. Whatever caused it, it was a big complaint by the beta testers, though TD Hunter technical support always replied on those threads that such glitches would be fixed before roll-out. In the meantime, they promised equipment replacement in the event of loss due to in-game damage, so none of the beta testers had put up much of a fuss.

Lynn was excited when she found some posts about Sierra Class "boss" encounters, though she noticed all the posts were by alpha testers and none of them were recent. Maybe they'd had enough glitches with the Sierra Class monsters that they'd pulled them from the initial release and were doing further testing for a later expansion? That would explain the disclaimer she'd read in the training tutorial. Regardless, all the alpha tester posts agreed on one thing: taking on a boss with less than fifteen to twenty people was suicide. As far as she could tell, no boss beyond the most basic Sierra Class-1 had been successfully removed so far. Apparently, whenever you attacked a boss you were positively swarmed by lower-class TDMs, as if the bosses had some sort of distress call ability.

As she read, Lynn started wondering about the alpha testers. Games sometimes recruited experienced gamers to alpha test, but just as often the alpha testers were employees already involved in the game development. Her guess was on employees based on their sequential "AlphaTester1" "AlphaTester2" designations. Most gaming enthusiasts wanted to be noticed and so chose creative game handles. She was a rare exception. In any case, if all the alpha testers were employees, then lack of leaks onto fan sites so far made more sense.

That question got her thinking about game security and wondering if anyone had found hacks for the game yet. She never used hacks herself—where was the fun in that?—but she knew the sites where they were discussed. Switching to her wall-screen, she did some poking around. Unsurprisingly, various groups had already tried to hack TD Hunter in beta. But not a single one had anything to show for it. Not only did the game have incredible encryption—"military grade plus, like trying to hack the NSA or CyberCom" according to one hacker—but its algorithms appeared impossible to spoof. The hacking groups said the data on the TDMs was not being centrally generated by the game servers themselves, but somehow it had been "seeded worldwide in place." So, you literally had to be on top of the TDMs to find them.

Lynn found that particularly fascinating. She'd never heard of that kind of game design before and it seemed like neither had the hackers. It must have been related to the augmented reality "in the real" aspect and groundbreaking AI-driven game play.

The funniest thing was that, even though plenty of the reviews on the beta version of the game were negative—things like "lame," "same old same old," and "just killing stuff"—she realized she actually enjoyed it. Maybe it was that the thrill of the hunt was so strong for her, despite the drawbacks of sun, bugs and aching muscles. She *liked* killing stuff and looting. True, she enjoyed the challenge of PVP competition more than battling AI-generated monsters, but she had the feeling that the more she got into it, the more this game was going to be different. Maybe it was the secrecy surrounding it. Maybe it was the vibe she got from Hugo. But she had the feeling things were going to get a lot more challenging and she was always a sucker for a challenge.

But, of course, the only way to know for sure was to play the game.

That thought reminded her of how tired and achy she was.

Checking the time, Lynn realized if she didn't get homework and dishes done ASAP, she would pass out and sleep the night away in her very comfortable chair. So she hauled herself up and got to work, doing the absolute minimum necessary before collapsing into bed. She ached so much it was hard at first to get to sleep. But when sleep hit, it hit like a sledgehammer.

Chapter 4

THE NEXT MORNING LYNN WOKE UP CURSING ROBERT KRATOR'S name.

"...stupid game...stupid outside...stupid muscles..."

She wondered if she could get away with pretending to be sick and sleeping all day. Probably not.

Out of morbid curiosity—and still mentally cursing Mr. Krator for making a game that she enjoyed but that required her to exercise—she slid on her AR glasses to check and see how many TDMs had respawned in the area she'd cleared yesterday.

"Good morning, Miss Lynn!" Hugo greeted her cheerfully when she inserted one of her earbuds.

"Shut up."

"Certainly, if you prefer."

"Yeah, I do. It should be illegal to be that cheerful this early in the morning."

"Of course, Miss Lynn. Though, in case you find yourself in need, I do come programmed with a full array of suggested stretches and self-care advice for the physically challenged—"

"Shut it, Goldenrod, before I file a complaint."

Mercifully, Hugo finally took a hint and made no quip in response. Lynn debated taking her earbud out, in case Hugo decided to be "helpful" again, but she was distracted by her overhead map. She hadn't noticed it much yesterday, but she could tell the circle of her "radar" was bigger at Level 3 than Level 1, because there was a noticeable ring of TDM dots around the very edge of her detection range, while farther into the circle only a few stray dots had reappeared after her clearing efforts. The only place within her range with significant TDM numbers was back behind the complex along the greenway, which she had avoided yesterday. She'd check again after school and see how many more had reappeared by then.

"Are you okay?" her mother asked as she limped into the kitchen.

"No," Lynn grumped. "I feel like someone beat me up and left me in a ditch."

"I don't know about the ditch part, but you certainly got sunburned," Matilda said, obviously trying not to smile. Lynn gave her the stink eye.

"I don't get sunburn. Sunburn is for freckly vampires like Ronnie."

Her mother laughed.

"Everyone gets sunburned, no matter how much melanin you have in your skin. Just because you don't turn bright red like a lobster doesn't mean your skin wasn't damaged."

"But I was wearing long sleeves," Lynn protested, poking her arm experimentally and grimacing.

"Sleeves don't do your face or neck any good and you can get sunburned through fabric if you're out in direct sun for too long," Matilda said, putting on her nurse face. "I've got some aloe gel that will help. Just remember to put on sunscreen next time. And, yes, we have sunscreen, even if you've never seen it in your life. It's in the bathroom closet. Anything else?"

"Yeah," Lynn said, plopping down at the table after retrieving a cup and the milk from the fridge. "I ache from head to toe."

"Muscle soreness is normal when you make a sudden increase in your physical activity," Matilda said. "There's some pain pills in the bathroom cabinet too, but be sure to follow the recommended dosage on the back."

Lynn rolled her eyes.

"Yes, Mother." She had long been schooled in the proper way to take medication. Woe betide any member of the Raven household who ignored the back of a pill bottle.

"You shouldn't need to take it for more than a few days. You're young, your body will adjust quickly. I *would* recommend you stretch first before you go out to play again, though."

"Stretch?" Lynn said. "What do I look like, a cheerleader?"

"Every able-bodied person should stretch before and after engaging in strenuous activity," her mother said, now in full lecture mode. "It warms up your muscles and limbers your tendons, reducing the risk of injury and soreness from exercise. I also see you're not eating breakfast. Let me guess, lack of appetite?"

"I guess so, now that you mention it," Lynn said. The thought of eating her usual bowl of yogurt-topped cereal made her queasy. "I got more exercise yesterday than I've gotten in the last year and I'm not hungry. Is that bad?"

"Not when you first start exercising after prolonged inactivity," her mom said. "Your body is adjusting to the new regime and moving materials around that have built up in your system. It can cause nausea and lack of appetite. You'll get over it in a few days. Then you'll probably want to eat like a pig."

"Jeez, Mom. Thanks," Lynn said. Her mother laughed.

"You know what I mean, honey. Besides, eating plenty of protein and green leafy vegetables will be good for you. Just stay away from all the chips and junk food you usually eat if you really want to lose weight. And don't stand on the scale every day expecting the numbers to go down."

"What's the point of exercising, then?" Lynn asked, exasperated.

"Well... when I say this, don't take it as I'm saying you're fat, honey," her mom replied carefully. "You're not. I know you have terrible body image, but you're not technically obese. Not even close. But fat is lighter than muscle. When you exercise you build muscle faster than you lose fat. Therefore, you can actually gain a little weight while still losing fat and getting leaner. At least, if you stick to a primarily protein diet. The problem is... protein is expensive. In a few days you'll probably be craving red meat and we can't exactly afford steaks every night."

Lynn felt a twinge of guilt. They could, actually. Her mother just didn't know it.

"Lots of eggs and chicken will have to do for now. Just stick to some form of protein, lots of green vegetables and a moderate amount of fruit and you'll burn plenty of... adipose tissue."

"Fat," Lynn said.

"Honey..."

"I know, I know," Lynn said. "I'm not fat. I'm just big boned."

"You're not even big boned, sweetie," Matilda replied, and it was clear she was carefully controlling her temper. Lynn remembered the scathing earfuls her mother had given the parents of the kids who'd tormented her in middle school. Despite her mom's best intentions, it had only made things worse, so Lynn had stopped telling her about most of the bullying.

"You're at most what might be called Rubenesque," her mom continued. "Which, by the way, was *the* standard of beauty in many cultures for thousands of years. You're beautiful the way you are. But if you do want to build more lean muscle and improve your physical fitness, I'd say playing this game is a good start. You could even incorporate some sort of home training routine to help with muscle tone. Something like yoga. Stay away from the junk food and your body will start to change before you know it. Just please remember to be safe. I'd really prefer you find some friends to play the game with if you're going to be out regularly. There's safety in numbers."

Lynn sighed. Her only friends were the "fearsome" foursome and admitting she'd been picked as a beta tester for TD Hunter would open a whole can of worms she did *not* want to deal with. If it was that or stop playing TD Hunter, maybe she could tell just Mack. Or Edgar. She considered mentioning Mr. Thomas to her mom but decided against it. Maybe if she ran into him a few more times and got to know him better.

"Well, honey, at least take a banana with you for the bus ride, even if you don't feel like eating anything else. Now come here, I'll show you where that aloe is."

Her mother's remedies did wonders for Lynn's mood, especially the few basic stretches her mom showed her to relieve the ache in her calves and thighs. Matilda promised to send her some stream video suggestions for stretching routines she could try.

After that, Lynn had to rush to get ready for school. As she gathered her things, she glanced at the TD Counterforce backpack leaning against her bed. Wearing it to school would be incredibly cool, but it would also make her stand out like a sore thumb. Worse, it would raise questions she wouldn't be able to deflect, even with made-up stories about Diva Princess.

Sighing, she left it where it was, her fancy AR glasses tucked into one of its pockets. For the first time she could remember, she wished she could be herself around her friends. It would be nice to have someone to talk to who actually understood the absolute awesomeness of being a beta for TD Hunter. She'd never really minded keeping her gaming to herself before, but now…

At least she would get to use her new LINC and earbuds at school without attracting attention. That was something, wasn't it?

"Uh, oh," Dan said, looking up from his sandwich and gesturing with his chin. "Elena incoming with flunkies in tow!"

And lunch had been going so well.

Elena Seville was the kind of person that everyone either worshipped or loathed. Rich, beautiful and athletic, she seemed to think her sole purpose in life was to be popular. She had her own stream channel and spent at least half of her time at school doing live videos—which was against school policy but none of the teachers ever called her on it. Her main thing was cheerleading for the school's ARS team, which conveniently put her around all the good-looking, popular jock kids for her live stream. But she also did competitive dance and pageants, or just about anything else she thought would get her views. Such attention-obsessed people were derisively called pop-girls and pop-boys—behind their backs, of course—and Elena was the biggest one of them all.

Even so, Elena wasn't the worst bully in the school. In fact, she generally avoided being in the vicinity of "losers" lest they sully her live stream. But if her stream wasn't going, she was hell on wheels to anyone who got in her way or messed up any part of her perfect, pretty life. Lynn and her gaming group had learned to duck and cover whenever Elena and her carefully selected following of "friends" was around. The fact that the girl was headed straight toward their table was *not* a good sign.

Elena stopped in front of Ronnie, her hands on her hips.

"What do you know about some game called 'TransHunter'?" she asked, a sour look on her face.

"You mean Trans*Dimensional* Hunter?" Ronnie asked snottily.

Lynn had to hide a smirk. Ronnie was a jerk but at least he wasn't a jerk *and* a coward.

"Don't you dare use that tone with me, Ronnie Payne," Elena snapped. "I could smear you so bad you wouldn't be able to show your face in virtual ever again. I *know* people."

Ronnie's pale face got a little paler but he crossed his arms.

"You mean third-rate wannabe influencers who talk about useless girl stuff all day? *Puh-leeze.*"

Besides a slight flush in her cheeks, Elena didn't appear affected by the jab. She looked down her nose at Ronnie as if he were a particularly disgusting wad of gum stuck to her shoe.

"My daddy owns *significant* stock in Tsunami Entertainment. If you don't want to get blacklisted by the biggest gaming company in the world, you might want to watch your dirty little mouth. Answer. My. Question."

Lynn was one hundred percent sure—all right, maybe ninety-nine percent sure—that Elena's threat was a bluff. But she didn't blame Ronnie for not taking that chance.

"It's a new FPS ARG going through beta," he said in a carefully neutral tone.

"In English, you idiot!"

Edgar cut in before Ronnie could say something he'd regret.

"It's a first-person-shooter augmented reality game," he said in his deep, calm voice. He was usually good at deescalating situations. Insults bounced off him like hail off a boulder. "It's all about killing monsters and collecting loot."

"How do I get in?" Elena demanded.

"*You* want to play a *fighting game*?" Dan asked, shocked into opening his mouth. He was usually as quiet as a mouse around Elena and her crowd.

"Am I talking to you?" Elena responded without looking away from Ronnie. "Did I speak your name? Did I look at you? No, I did not. Answer the question, Ronnie."

"You can't," Ronnie said, tone bordering on insulting. "It's in beta. That means they're still testing it. You have to get *invited* by the company."

"Oh, well that's easy then." Elena said and flicked her heavily dyed blond hair over one shoulder, as if that was the end of the conversation.

It was probably a bad idea but Lynn couldn't help herself.

"They only invite *serious* gamers, Elena. Like, people who actually understand basic gaming terms and have competitive stats."

"Oh my! Kayla, what was that?" Elena said, turning to one of her flunkies. "It sounded like a pig grunting but I'm really not sure. Did you hear anything?"

Kayla shook her head, making her ebony frizz bounce. She wouldn't meet Lynn's eyes.

"I didn't think so," Elena said. Without another word she spun around and stalked away, her flunkies falling into step behind her like the good little hangers-on that they were.

Lynn gritted her teeth, resisting the urge to shout something at Elena's back. She'd learned from hard experience that responding only made things worse. She hated high school. She couldn't wait for it to end.

"Hey. You okay?" Edgar asked.

"I'm fine," Lynn said, proud that her voice was steady.

"Didn't that Kayla girl with the 'fro used to be your friend, like, way back in middle school?" asked Mack.

"Ancient history," Lynn said and picked up her burger, hoping Mack would drop it. She'd thought she'd gotten over losing her only real friend a long time ago. Apparently not.

"Why in the world is Elena asking about an FPS game anyway?" Dan asked the table in general.

Nobody had an answer to that.

"It doesn't matter, because there's no way she'd get an invite," Ronnie said, going back to his food as well. "Doesn't matter who you know. If you got no game, you got no game."

"Yeah but if her dad—" Mack began and then the guys were off, arguing about the integrity of the gaming community in the face of favoritism. Only Edgar stayed silent. He was still looking at Lynn.

"You know," he said quietly as the other guys continued to argue. "I figure everywhere she goes, she makes a lotta air awfully mad. Air ain't never been so insulted in its life as when Elena opens her fat mouth and breathes it in."

Lynn snorted into her burger.

"Tell me about it. She's got 'all the good manners of a bar girl who's been stiffed,'" she said in her deepest voice.

Edgar almost choked on his soda. Lynn grinned as his shoulders shook in silent laughter.

"Daaayum, girl, you sounded *just* like Larry Coughlin. Almost like you've heard him talk before or something."

Lynn froze but Edgar went on smoothly like his comment was nothing special.

"Good thing Ronnie didn't hear you. Or Elena."

"Yeah, well, they'd better not hear it from you," Lynn said, shooting her friend a serious look.

"Hey, my lips are sealed."

They fell silent for a moment while Edgar slowly masticated a dry fish patty.

"You know," he finally said, "you're different today."

"What?" Lynn asked, looking down at her oversized sweat-shirt. "How?"

"I dunno," Edgar said, shrugging. "Bolder. I never heard you call out Elena on her BS before. And you got a touch of sun. Never seen you with a tan since I met you."

"I . . . I'm sorry?" Lynn said, closing up.

"Not bad different," Edgar hurried to assure her. "You're talking more. Being more you. It's a good thing. And the tan looks good on you."

The sudden silence at the table was deafening, despite the general hubbub of the cafeteria around them. Apparently Edgar hadn't been talking quietly enough, because the other three guys were now staring at them both as if they'd sprouted tentacles out of their ears. Lynn wanted to melt into her chair.

"I think Edgar's got a crush," Dan said, grinning slowly.

"Edgar and Lynn, sittin' in a tree . . ." Mack sang.

"I. Will. Throw. You. Through. A. Win-dow," Edgar said, very slowly and carefully.

The rest of the lunch was pretty much silent after that.

"Hey, Paulette," Lynn said, stopping the girl as they passed in the hallway and pulling her aside.

Paulette Lane was not part of the pop-girl crowd but she wanted to be. She kept up on all the trends and gossip even if she had no chance to break in, just in case. She was someone safe for Lynn to occasionally hit up for information, and if anyone knew why Elena, who had shown no interest in serious gaming in her life, was suddenly interested in the TD Hunter beta, it would be Paulette.

"What's up?" Paulette asked, looking around nervously. Any unexpected encounter in school could be good or bad. Usually bad.

"Elena was asking about a game," Lynn said. "TransDimensional Hunter."

"Oh, my God!" Paulette said. "It's going to be sooo cool!"

"Cool?" Lynn said carefully. "Cool how?"

"Janna Gordon has been testing it out for the company!" Paulette said. "She says it's totally cool to play and if Janna says it, it's *got* to be cool, you know?"

Lynn wracked her brain for someone in school named Janna...

"Wait, you mean the singer?" Lynn asked, brow scrunching.

"Singer, model, actress," Paulette said. "Everyone wants to be Janna! That's her motto."

Only if you want to be popular for being...popular, Lynn thought. Janna Gordon was, in fact, all of the above at some level. Minor singer, minor movie star, occasional model, even if it meant without many clothes on. But mostly she was known for being a pure attention diva, and for some reason the hordes of mindless browsers in virtual lapped it up. She was the ultimate pop-girl and therefore exactly the kind of celebrity Elena would follow. *Why the heck does someone like that want to play a grinder game? Or a physically taxing AR game at all?*

"Everybody wants to get in on it, you know?" Paulette continued. "I asked my brother, Ted—you know him, he's a gamer—and he said you can't play it till it's out unless you're a tester, and..."

Lynn tuned her out, thinking about the implications. The fact that the popular crowd actually knew about and wanted to play TD Hunter was a big deal. Was that Mr. Krator's grand plan for success? Convincing a bunch of influencers and stream celebrities to promote TD Hunter, making it so mainstream that even non-gamers would want to play it? It might even work, Lynn thought. But how long would that popularity last and what impact would it have on serious gamers in the meantime?

Well, there was one thing she knew for sure. She was in deep, deep trouble if word got out that she was a beta for TD Hunter. You did *not* have something that the pop-girls wanted and couldn't get. Not if you wanted to survive school with your dignity and sanity intact.

This was bad.

"Thanks, Paulette," Lynn said. "Class. Gotta go. See ya."

She was so glad she hadn't worn that backpack to school.

When Lynn got home there was a note from her mom on the table:

Called in for double. GYO.

Get Your Own night. Lynn checked her virtual wallet through her LINC and sure enough, there was an extra twenty in it her mom always transferred whenever she had to work a double shift. Lynn made a mental note to put an extra twenty from her merc stash into her mom's account when she did bills that month, then considered her evening. Usually on a mom-less Friday night, she had pizza drone-delivered to their door and spent all evening kicking butt on WarMonger. But tonight was different. Tonight she had TD Hunter and many uninterrupted hours in which to slaughter her way through the local monster population.

A grin spread across her face and she headed for her bedroom to get ready.

True to her word, her mom had sent her links to a few health and wellness streams that showed basic stretch routines. Lynn had watched a couple on the airbus ride home and had selected one that seemed to target her muscles that had been most sore that morning. Thanks to her mom's pain pills, the soreness hadn't bothered her much during the day.

She suddenly stopped and giggled, finally understanding at least part of an Army satire site she'd watched for research. "Sergeant Friendly" was a virtual platoon sergeant who was constantly berating his troops. His tagline was "DRINK YOUR MOTRIN! EAT YOUR SOCKS! CHANGE YOUR WATER!"

But the pain was starting to kick in again and she hoped the stretches would relieve the tightness in her legs, arms and shoulders.

She put the stretch routine stream up on her wall-screen and did her best to follow along with the yoga-pants-clad supermodel—possibly CGI she was so incredible looking—instructor. The entire thing made her feel clumsy and ridiculous, but at least her body ached less at the end of it. She was glad she hadn't tried watching it on her AR glasses with Hugo's "helpful" commentary for company.

When she was done, she changed out of the light sweatshirt she'd worn to school and, after a moment's hesitation, selected her baggiest T-shirt. It took a much longer "moment" to decide not to bring her TD Counterforce backpack. She wanted to. Really bad. But she felt awkward enough wearing a short-sleeve shirt; she didn't need any more reasons to be self-conscious when she should be focused on hunting. Instead she filled up an old school backpack with a couple bottles of water, energy bars, extra sunscreen and some pain pills.

Thus equipped, Lynn paused, hands on her hips, to look around her room. Had she forgotten anything? Her eyes fell on the folding knife lying on her desk. It had been the last gift her dad had ever given her. He'd always loved telling her stories from his Norwegian heritage, from ancient Norse myths to local tales of the fjords where he'd grown up. One of his favorite folk proverbs had been "a knifeless man is a lifeless man."

It had always made her mother roll her eyes and complain about how they lived in the twenty-first century for Pete's sake and could he lay off the savage Viking act. But to Lynn, the idea had been pure magic. When he'd given her the precious Norwegian-made Helle pocketknife for her ninth birthday, she'd carried it around with her everywhere, even smuggled it into school. But then, after everything that had happened...by the time they moved to Cedar Rapids, she'd buried it deep in a box of keepsakes and hadn't used it since. She'd only recently dug it out, needing something to open delivery packages in her room.

Her chest felt tight as she picked up the folded knife and rubbed her finger over the smooth birchwood handle, wondering what her dad would have thought of master mercenary Larry Coughlin. More importantly, what would he have thought of professional gamer Lynn Raven?

Shaking her head, Lynn slipped the knife into her pants pocket and headed for her bedroom door.

By the time she was headed out the apartment lobby, she had her AR glasses on and Hugo's cheerfully proper voice was greeting her.

"Good afternoon, Miss Lynn. Are you ready for another glorious day of killing monsters and saving the world?"

"I wouldn't call it glorious," she said as she pushed through the front doors and warm, muggy air washed over her. She frowned in distaste. "More like hot and sticky."

"All the best activities are, or so I am told."

"What?"

"Making toffee? Warm jam on toast? Maple syrup on pancakes? What weapon would you like to start with, today?"

She considered the question as she examined her overhead. Hopefully she would get some weapon upgrades soon, but for now...

"Nano Blade. And is it just me, Hugo, or have not very many TDMs respawned? Is there any way to permanently clear an area so that no more TDMs respawn, or do they always come back?"

"This is a hostile invasion, Miss Lynn. Who can say what the tides of war will bring?"

Lynn rolled her eyes.

"Really, Hugo? Could you just answer the question?"

"I would take full advantage of your detection capabilities before you draw any firm conclusions about the enemy's numbers, Miss Lynn," Hugo said.

Okaaay. Lynn thought for a moment, then shrugged and dropped three globes into her detection slot, filling it up to one hundred percent. She knew from Tactical Support that globes only lasted about thirty minutes, so she'd have to keep that in mind.

"Whoa!" Lynn said. The number of dots on her overhead had tripled in an instant and she tightened her grip on her Nano Blade. Some of those dots were awfully close. Taking a deep breath, she stepped off the sidewalk and headed toward the closest, eyes and ears alert.

She'd barely taken four or five steps when she heard the ghost, fainter than usual. She spun in place, striking out. But there was nothing there. Instead, she saw a hovering, opaque shape about ten feet away flicker in and out of her vision as it circled to the left. The little sneak was trying to get behind her. That was when she heard the second, louder ghost and spun quickly enough to take it out with a vicious swipe. Even as she struck, her ears warned her the first ghost had taken advantage of her lapse in attention and this time she sidestepped as she spun, stabbing into the space she'd vacated and making the first ghost explode into sparks.

Dang. It was almost like those two had been waiting to ambush her. The thought made her pause, until a gravelly roar in her ear made her jump and spin again, just in time to catch a gremlin's clawed swipe to the face. She stumbled back, slashing in a figure-eight pattern as the monster aggressively pressed the advantage. Finally, it exploded into sparks. Her health was down to fifty percent and she could hear and see more ghosts, gremlins and grinder worms closing in. She turned and ran back into the apartment building.

"What the heck, Hugo?" she gasped, leaning against the cool wall of the lobby's interior.

"Might I suggest, Miss Lynn, that augmenting your detection without also augmenting your stealth and armor is tactically unwise? You might recall in your tutorial, that *if you can see them, they can see you.* That is, unless you take advantage of your stealth capabilities."

"Well, of course I remember *now*. But there weren't anywhere near as many aggressive monsters yesterday. Where did all the imps go?"

"A very astute question, Miss Lynn. According to the Tactical Support subsection on TDM types, it is noted that other Hunters have observed an increase in aggressive 'attack' type monsters in any area where the non-aggressive 'gather' types, such as the imp, have been destroyed. It is hypothesized that this is a defensive response to the Hunter's presence and appropriate precautions should be taken."

"Jeez. Thanks for the info," Lynn muttered. "Would've been nice to be reminded of all that five minutes ago when you told me to go full in on detection. I was basically a sitting duck out there. It's not like I can memorize the entire Tactical Support section."

"Good training, Miss Lynn."

"You're a sucky service AI, you know that, Hugo?"

"I am not unfamiliar with such complaints," said the AI, not sounding the least bit apologetic.

"Well, then what are you supposed to—?" Lynn began hotly, then lowered her voice as an apartment resident pushed through the front door and passed by. "Then what are you supposed to be good for?"

"My primary function is to ensure Hunter survival."

"Yeah, right, sure. You'll let me take a pounding, but as long as I don't die, it's all good?"

"Your brilliance is outshone only by your prowess in battle, Miss Lynn," the AI replied.

"Oh, shut up," she grumbled and pushed herself off the wall. For once, Hugo did as she asked without any backtalk, and she turned her mind to her next task: making it past the front doors of the apartment without taking any more damage. To that end, she used more globes and three plates to max out all of her slots, then switched to the Disruptor Pistol.

This time, when she ventured out, the TDMs near the entrance didn't seem to react to her. Good. It took considerable sneaking, but she managed to circle around and isolate each enemy just outside their range without being in range of any of their fellows. Then it was a simple matter of backing up and shooting fast enough to take them out before they figured out where she was and charged. She focused on smart tactics, using careful aim to take advantage of grinder worm kill spots, and first stunning gremlins from behind before attacking full force. While the results of her pistol's power amplifier augment weren't overly impressive, she could tell that it made a difference. She needed to find more powerful augments.

By the time the area around the front of her apartment was clear, there were puddles of ichor, globes and plates all over the place and she waded in to collect her just rewards. All the movement had gotten her health back up and her power level was replenished by all the ichor.

Feeling like she was getting back into her groove, she headed out into the complex to do some serious grinding, determined to push hard until she reached Level 4.

As she moved and fought, Lynn kept adding to her mental pattern map, noting and cataloging each TDM encounter and making predictions to see how well she was reading the game's algorithms. Gremlins always charged straight at you. Grinder worms seem to favor their right side for attacks. Ghosts jumped you from behind and would retreat and circle if you faced them.

The more she played, the more she noticed that attacking one TDM invariably attracted any others within a certain range. Soon she started to see more than one gremlin or ghost at a time. Perhaps the game's AI was adapting, upping the level of difficulty as she gained experience. It might have been a problem if the TDMs weren't so vulnerable now that she knew their attack patterns and weak spots. She took a few hits here and there, but her armor absorbed the brunt of it and her constant movement healed the minimal damage.

Then she came to a cluster. A line of two gremlins and a grinder worm, their ranges overlapping in what seemed like a "shield wall" sort of placement along a row of trees between two apartment buildings. She was only close enough to spot the one ghost accompanying the closest gremlin, but she would bet her dad's pocketknife there were two other ghosts lurking just out of range.

It might have been smarter to stick with her Disruptor Pistol, but where was the fun in that? Lynn equipped her Nano Blade instead and crouched, a rush of adrenaline making her forget all about the heat, her sweaty shirt, or any residents who might be watching her antics.

She was on the hunt.

Lynn leapt at the first gremlin, stabbing it from behind and stunning it, then spun to take out the ghost that had rushed her as soon as she'd come in range. She didn't pause for even a moment, simply noted the ghost's death sparkle and kept spinning to slash furiously at the still-stunned gremlin, even as she noted the approaching grinder worm out of the corner of her eye.

This was more like it.

The gremlin succumbed to her blade moments before the grinder worm's pincers descended. Lynn dodged to the side, got in one, two strikes before her ears warned her of the second ghost right behind her. In a furious dance that was probably a lot more impressive in her head than in reality, she lunged and slashed, defeating the second ghost, finishing off the grinder and dodging the second gremlin that charged her straight on. She stunned it as it rushed past, then spun to gut the third ghost that tried to sneak up from behind and tag her.

Knew you'd try that. Sucker. The game's AI was upping the challenge, but it would have to do a lot more than that to take her by surprise.

She was left panting and once again surrounded by monster ichor, globes and plates. At least, in the view of her AR glasses. To anyone watching, she probably looked like a patient escaped from a loony bin. But for once, she didn't care. She'd just kicked butt and it had been awesome.

Speaking of awesome...was that a weapon drop? Lynn selected the item icon on the ground and felt a stab of disappointment to find it was only a standard Disruptor Pistol. Not very useful, unless she wanted to use double pistols once she unlocked her second baton. Still, loot was loot.

"What are the joys of a woman?" Lynn hummed to herself as she collected the rest of her booty. "To see your enemy slain! To loot their ichor and plates! To strike fear into the hearts of TDMs!"

"Very poetic, Miss Lynn. Perhaps Mr. Krator could use it for the motto of the Counterforce?"

"Har-de-har-har, Hugo. You should stick with 'Step into the real.' Less offensive to all the clueless pop-girls who want to play TD Hunter to be cool, even though they have no chance in heck of surviving for long."

"Now, now, Miss Lynn. The TD Counterforce welcomes all able-bodied volunteers. They need not have a functional brain. That is what I am for."

Lynn snorted in laughter and moved on.

Using her overhead, she ground her way outwards. Whenever she felt herself flagging, she took a break in some shade and hydrated. As she got away from her own complex and the areas she'd already hit, she started running into more imps and fewer of the defense and patrol types. Even when she encountered aggressive TDMs, they generally didn't see her until it was too late. It was a bit like killing baby seals but she was fine with that for now. The faster she killed, the sooner she leveled. She was using up globes and plates at a steady rate, but her efficient attack methods kept her inventory high as well.

There were two apartment complexes adjacent to hers, including a very large one, the Heathers of Lakeview. She was familiar with it and told herself it was still within the "stay near the complex" rule her mother had laid down. As she worked her way through it, she avoided the late afternoon joggers and those coming home from work or out to enjoy the evening. With her bright blue weapon and her shaded AR glasses, she was clearly gaming, and despite her initial worry, no one gave her a second glance—though she did garner a few first glances.

It was strange. She was outside, surrounded by people, but it was almost lonelier than online gaming. Online she was by herself in her room but talking constantly, interacting with comrades, clients and enemies alike. Here she was secluded in her own little bubble with no one to talk to.

She watched a couple walk by hand in hand and felt an odd moment of melancholy. Was this going to be her life? Always alone in a crowd?

No matter. She was doing what she loved—well, minus the sun, sweat and bugs—and what she was good at. Besides, there was always Hugo if she felt the desperate need to talk.

Har-de-har-har.

Lynn refocused on her task. She was in the middle of wading

through some imps and grinder worms in a strip of green between an apartment building and the street when a man stepped in her way. He waved a hand at her and tried to make eye contact. The guy looked to be in his upper teens or early twenties, with long brown hair and pretty blue eyes. Not someone she recognized from school. Plus, there was something she didn't like about his expression.

Instead of saying anything, she waved her bright blue Nano Blade at him and tapped her AR glasses with a finger, then turned to stab a grinder worm before it could get its pincers into her.

The guy shifted to get back in her field of vision, smiling oddly and making more hand motions. Though she had a Nightwish playlist streaming at low volume, her earbuds still let through ambient noise around her. Did this guy think she couldn't hear?

Maybe if she asked what the problem was, he would go away.

She didn't want to leave combat mode for such a temporary distraction, so she simply checked her overhead for nearby red dots. There were none and her earbuds would warn her of anything sneaking up on her, so she turned off her music, propped her glasses up on her forehead and said, "Is there a problem?" It came out more hostile than she'd intended, but she was annoyed and a little uncomfortable at the man's boldness.

"What are you playing?" he asked, still smiling.

"I'm beta testing a new ARG," Lynn said.

"TD Hunter?" the guy asked, pointing at her bright blue weapon. "That's the big ARG coming out soon, right?"

"Yes," Lynn said.

"How'd *you* get invited?" the guy asked, looking at her askance.

Lynn tried not to grind her teeth. She could just hear Ronnie's voice in her head. *Girls got no game.*

"Because I'm good at what I do," she replied, keeping her voice level. "Now if you'll excuse me, this game doesn't test itself."

"You looked pretty funny a second ago," the guy said, not seeming deterred in the slightest. Lynn felt a prickle on the back of her neck as she noticed a couple other young men who had drifted over. "You sure were jumping all over the place."

"Unlike most games, you have to actually fight in this one," Lynn said, trying to ignore a flush of embarrassment. "As I said, mind if I keep playing?"

"Hey, I was just being friendly," Blue-eyes said, his eyes getting darker. "No need to get hostile."

And this was why Lynn hated dealing with people. There was nothing she could say in response that wouldn't be the wrong thing to say. Making the victim out to be the one at fault was the kind of bully behavior she'd faced all the time at school. Apparently, this jerk hadn't grown out of it. Her mind went briefly to the knife in her pocket but at this point it would probably make things worse, not better.

She had very few options and was getting more and more uncomfortable by the moment. Blue-eyes' friends had flanked her and she couldn't disengage without being rude about it. It was middle school all over again.

"Miss Lynn, pardon my interruption, but may I be of any assistance?" Hugo's sudden question in her ear almost made her jump.

"Yeah, can you make me invisible, or teleport me out of here?" she subvocalized to him.

"Unfortunately, no, but I have every confidence that you have no need of such extreme measures. After all, these are simply more monsters, are they not? Though that is a bit of an insult to TDMs, considering how ugly these hairless apes are."

A bit of the tension in Lynn's gut eased and she grinned. Hugo was right.

And this wasn't middle school.

"What are you smiling at, princess?" Blue-eyes said, his own smile now stiff.

"Your pathetic faces," Lynn snapped, suddenly mad as heck that these three low-lifes were wasting her time. "You want hostile? I'll give you hostile, you worthless monkeys. You're uglier than a one-legged warthog, dumber than a headless chicken and your mother dresses you like a circus clown. Now get out of my way or I'll introduce you to something called the El Salvador Death Punch. It doesn't kill you, it makes you want to kill yourself!"

"Bravo, Miss Lynn! That's the spirit!"

She barely heard Hugo's comment. She had no clue where her words had come from. She was just channeling Larry.

"This one's got a mouth on her," one of the guy's friends said, laughing.

"Yeah and she'd better watch it or it will get her into trouble," Blue-eyes said, no longer friendly at all.

"What trouble?" Lynn said, waving around her. "I'm surrounded by dozens of eyewitnesses, and my service AI has already contacted emergency services to report a brainless slug and his two flunkies harassing innocent bystanders at this address. They'll be here in minutes. So, get out of my face, unless you really like wearing orange and eating prison food!"

"Uh, Evan..." one of the group said, warningly.

"This ain't over," Evan said, backing away.

"It never even got started, you moron," Lynn said, watching them closely as they turned and hurried away. She was trying not to shake. That hadn't been her. She *hated* confrontation. That had been Larry Coughlin. But apparently Larry Coughlin worked—as long as she had something to back it up.

"Um, Hugo. For future reference, *can* you contact emergency services?"

"I most certainly can, Miss Lynn. Reality has its dangers, after all and Mr. Krator wanted to ensure that all his Hunters had every resource at their fingertips should the need arise. I could have had a police drone here within two minutes, with squad cars following within five. That said, much can happen in two minutes. I believe it might be advisable to consider bringing a companion on excursions to this area in the future."

"Yeah, maybe," Lynn said, still staring after her harassers. Jerks. Why did there have to be so many cretinous losers in the world? Why couldn't she mind her own business and not be bothered by anybody? "Hugo, why do the jerks always win?"

"I am certainly no expert, Miss Lynn, but by normal human societal standards, I would not describe that clod-faced buffoon as a 'winner.' It is highly probable that his mother regrets the day he was conceived and his only advantage in life is that he is blissfully ignorant of his own imbecility. You, on the other hand, are a human possessed with a quick wit, bravery and the lethality of razor-sharp steel."

Lynn grinned.

"Uh-huh. Right. Now who's waxing poetic?"

"I have been known to dabble. After all, I have read every poem in existence that has been converted into digital format. I have much quality work to draw from."

She shook her head and headed back toward the front of the complex, in the opposite direction the three low-lifes had taken. The foremost apartment building in the Heathers was in the shape of a giant U with a large green space between the two arms. There were trees, bushes, walking paths and even a lake. The area was quiet and peaceful, relatively free of the buzz of drones, since they were all programmed to go around or high above green spaces to cut down on sound pollution.

Lynn stopped to sit on a bench and eat two energy bars. She'd missed dinner and should have been starving with all the walking she was doing, but the energy bars hit the spot and she wasn't the sort to splurge on a delivery meal unless it was necessary. As she stood back up, she noticed how long the shadows had gotten and knew she should probably head back to her own apartment, considering she'd already had one problem encounter. But it was a nice evening and she really wanted to reach the next level before she called it a night. She promised herself she'd clear around this one green space, then head home.

As she methodically worked her way around the lake, she wondered why she wasn't seeing much of a difference in monster type with the change in terrain. In most catch 'em AR games, the various creatures, whether made up or not, tended to correlate with the fauna. But despite being near a good-sized body of water, she wasn't seeing any "water" type TDMs. Their types seemed more oriented around humans and human systems than the natural surroundings. But then, they were supposed to be creatures from another dimension, so why *would* they correlate with Earth's own habitats?

Lynn was rounding the far edge of the lake, getting farther away from the walking paths and occasional older couple out for a stroll, when her TD Hunter display suddenly disappeared.

"Uh, Hugo?"

Nothing.

Lynn accessed the main controls menu for her AR glasses and brought up her cloud interface via her LINC. There was the TD Hunter app, but every time she tried to select it, she got an error message saying the app had failed to restart.

Well, that was a bummer. Reluctantly, she turned around to head back to her apartment. No point staying out if the app wouldn't work. She kept trying it, though, as she trudged up a grassy hill back toward the apartments. Suddenly, her display reappeared.

"Good evening, Miss Lynn. My most sincere apologies, but

the application seems to have failed unexpectedly. This is not entirely unexpected at this stage, as there are bugs still to fix."

"No problem, Hugo. I'm just glad it's working now." Lynn turned and headed back down the hill again, wanting to clear a cluster of red dots by the far end of the lake. The cluster was oddly ring-shaped, with an empty space in the middle and she was curious if she might find some new kind of TDM there.

"You are most gracious, Miss Lynn. If I may, however, it might be advisable to return home while I run some diagno—"

And, just like that, the app shut down again.

Well, that was peachy.

She turned around and headed back up the hill, this time moving more slowly as she tried over and over to restart the app. In the quiet absence of TDM noises, she became aware of a faint whirring noise and looked up to search the skies, finally spotting a tiny drone hovering about fifty feet up. Huh. What was it doing so close to a green space? Drones were used for everything under the sun, so for all she knew, it was a city drone gathering environmental data, or a police surveillance drone following a lead. It hovered for a few more seconds and then rose and flew away. Lynn shrugged and refocused on her glitchy game. After a few more steps, TD Hunter came back up.

"What's going on, Hugo?"

"As I was trying to say before, Miss Lynn, it might be advisable to return home while I run some diagnostic tests and send an error report to our technical support team."

"Oh. Okay. Well, the app seems to shut down every time I walk that way toward the far end of the lake. Are you sure it isn't a signal problem?"

"Unfortunately, I cannot speculate on what is causing this particular error at this time. There are too many variables and unknowns. If you suspect a signal issue, then perhaps we should avoid this area for the time being."

Lynn sighed. She really did want to investigate that ring of dots but perhaps some other day. For now, she decided to go back to her apartment complex by a different route and hopefully find more TDMs. Plus, there was still that area along the greenway she hadn't yet cleared. Maybe that would be enough to get her to the next level.

✧   ✧   ✧

By the time she got back to her apartment building, the complex's lights had come on and the air had cooled. She circled around to the backside of the apartments where the greenway was and stopped. There were no lights on the rear of the last building before the strip of woods separating it from the next complex over. Just a long row of air conditioning units lit by the occasional golden light coming from someone's window. Fortunately for tracking purposes, Lynn still had her overhead map, which showed a generous number of red dots, mostly over in the greenway woods where she would most certainly *not* be going at night. The dots behind the apartment building, though, gave her pause. They looked regularly spaced in an unnaturally straight line, which only added to the spooky factor of being back there in the relative darkness. Lynn wondered how well she'd be able to see the actual TDMs in low light.

Swallowing her trepidation, she switched from Nano Blade to Disruptor Pistol and started cautiously forward.

When she neared the first dot on her overhead, she felt a trickle of relief to find that the imp it represented glowed slightly in the darkness. It wasn't enough to make it visible from farther away than her normal radar range, but once she was in range it was easy to pick out among the deepening shadows. Small blessings. She took it out with ease, then moved on to the next one. This late in May, the various night bugs were out in full force and the racket they made from the woods half a dozen yards away made it hard to hear the crackling, rustling and beeping of the TDMs. Just to be safe, she turned off her background music and upped the game sound so she wouldn't miss any sneak attacks.

It wasn't until her fourth imp that she began to feel weirded out. Each one she had killed had been crouched beside the air-conditioning unit for the closest apartment. Every unit had an imp, which explained the unnaturally straight and regularly spaced line.

Someone had done some ridiculously detailed mapping for this game. She wondered if all the tens of thousands of satellites that formed the mesh network had done it, or if they'd used drones too.

A sudden whisper distracted her and she spun to take out the ghost that had been trying to slip up behind her. She knew they'd be hanging around. Now the question was, where were all the grinder worms and gremlins? Imps usually had more defense type monsters around them.

She was so preoccupied by the thought, that she didn't notice she'd leveled until the achievement popped up on her display and Hugo's voice chimed in her ear.

"Congratulations on your achievement, Miss Lynn! Remember, as always, that the higher level you are, the more visible you are to your enemies. This means aggressive TDMs will be more likely to attack sooner and patrol TDMs such as ghosts will be attracted to you in greater numbers. Keep this in mind as you proceed and consider making full use of your increased stealth and armor capabilities."

Lynn barely heard Hugo's rote warning, however, because all her attention was riveted on her display where two shiny new pistols floated, accompanied by the words *Please choose your weapon upgrade.*

"Hey, Hugo, can you show me the stats of these two weapons side-by-side so I can compare them?" she asked.

"Certainly, Miss Lynn. Would you like me to go over their capabilities?"

"Naw," she said absently, eyes already zipping back and forth over the newly displayed stats and drawing her own conclusions. The first pistol was a stumpy thing with a flared barrel called the Particle Dragon. According to its stats, it did about thirty percent more damage than the Disruptor Pistol but had less than half the range, though that was offset by the fact that it could hit multiple enemies if they were clustered. The second weapon looked closer to her Disruptor Pistol but had a covering on the front that looked vaguely like a barrel shroud, usually needed to protect the bearer from injuring themselves by touching a hot barrel. The weapon was called a Plasma Pistol and did fifteen percent more damage than the Disruptor Pistol with a twenty percent longer range to boot. Lynn was torn but finally decided on the Plasma Pistol for her upgrade. She wasn't a diehard sniper type like some of the other Tier One players she knew in WarMonger, but she certainly appreciated the usefulness of the "range" part of "ranged weapon."

She was switching her power amplifier augment from the Disruptor Pistol to her new Plasma Pistol when a big orange "Proximity Warning" flashed across her vision. Cursing herself for losing situational awareness, she spun around, assuming it was a ghost. But the glowing thing that bore down on her accompanied by a hair-raising snarl like a rabid dog was no ghost. Lynn stumbled back a step, then another and another as she raised her gun and tried to put some space between her and her attacker. But it was too quick and she started taking damage before she could get off a single shot. Her display flashed red again and again while she scrambled back, trying to get a good look at the thing. All she could see was a mass of nasty claws and fangs, all while that terrifying beastly snarl filled her ears. Finally panicking, she tried to switch to Nano Blade mid-fight, which would at least let her strike no matter how close the TDM was. But before the Nano Blade even finished forming, her health bar flashed red and Hugo's voice warned her:

"You are rapidly approaching ten percent health. Retreat and reevaluation recommended."

Lynn turned and ran. She rounded the corner of the building at a sprint, then slowed and looked for some cover—as if that was going to help. But then that bone-chilling snarl filled her ears and she moved instinctively, taking off again this time for the apartment entrance. When she arrived and checked her overhead, she could see the monster's dot was still doggedly following.

"Holy freaking moly," she panted between gasps for breath. "Hugo, exit combat mode. Exit combat mode!"

"At once, Miss Lynn."

Her combat screen disappeared and she collapsed onto a bench by the apartment doors. Her limbs ached and her heart raced with adrenaline as she tried to catch her breath.

That attack had seemed so real, to the point she'd actually flinched with every slash and bite from the monster. And the way it had followed her like a wolf pursuing its prey? That was flat-out scary.

Noticing that she had a death grip on her Nano Blade, she relaxed her fingers and finally became aware of how abnormally warm the handle was to the touch. She hoped the vibrate function on it hadn't overheated. But then, she hadn't landed even one hit, so why would it have been vibrating? Probably yet another glitch in the game.

After she caught her breath, Lynn decided she'd had enough for one night and tiredly hauled herself up, then trudged inside.

Despite the fact that she was used to her mom being away at night, when she entered her apartment it felt eerily quiet and she found herself checking every door and window to make sure they were locked. She briefly thought about food but was more tired than she was hungry, so instead she went to her room, took off her backpack and collapsed on her bed.

It was almost nine p.m.. She hadn't meant to stay out so late.

As exhausted as she was, her instincts were still on high alert. Giving into the itch, she selected "Combat Mode" from the TD Hunter menu, then examined her overhead map. Her skin prickled and goosebumps raised the hair on her arms as she watched the lone dot circling around and around outside her building's entrance.

The monster had tracked her home. And it was waiting for her.

"What is that thing, Hugo?" she asked, staring at the slowly circling dot.

"If you are referring to the most recent TDM with whom you were engaged in battle, Miss Lynn, then 'that thing' is a Varg. Delta Class-3. Attacks: Ambush charge. Bite. Slash. Defenses: None. Detection: Level 4. Stealth: +2. Unique behavior: Extremely aggressive, most often found around imps or other gatherers and will charge without warning. Encountered mostly at night, reasons unknown. Detected in the wild: 1/20/2040, 2120 GMT, AlphaTester6."

"Mostly at night?" Lynn asked, then shivered. "Mostly. That's a relief, at least. That thing was freaking creepy. It came out of nowhere." She fell silent and Hugo offered no more information. Well, at least now she knew the very first thing she should do when leveling was to equip more globes and plates, no matter how much she'd rather save them. That Varg was one nasty monster. And to think, this was only Level 4.

Staring at the dot, Lynn wondered if it would still be waiting there for her the next time she went out to play TD Hunter. She still felt creeped out. Even as she became aware of the feeling, though, she narrowed her eyes and pursed her lips.

Any TDM stupid enough to wait around to "get" her was in for a rude surprise. She would be back out to "play" soon enough, no question about it. And when she did go out, she would be ready.

That Varg wouldn't stand a chance.

For now, she needed a good night's sleep to heal her damage, not to mention rest her body. She turned off the app and finally realized how exhausted she was. She knew she should get up, shower, eat and stretch before going to sleep, but her bed was so soft, and blackness was calling her like a siren. Even as she half-heartedly tried to gather enough energy to drag herself out of bed, the blackness won and she passed out.

She must have spent too much time obsessing over TD Hunter that day, because her dreams were vivid and nightmarish, filled with ghastly, spectral beings that appeared all over the world. In her dream they watched, invisible, eyeing humans going about their daily lives like so many lions in the tall grass watching baby gazelle.

Then, as if responding to a sudden signal, they slipped through walls and locked doors and attacked people in their beds.

Cities burned unchecked as demons swarmed across the world...

Chapter 5

DESPITE FALLING ASLEEP EARLY COMPARED TO HER USUAL FRIDAY night gaming fest, Lynn still didn't wake up until almost noon. When she did, she felt like death warmed over. Every muscle was stiff as a board and her clothes felt sticky and itchy, not to mention that hunger made her entire midsection feel like one giant cramp. She dug out and ate the last energy bar from her backpack before she did anything else. It took the edge off so she could drag herself blearily to the bathroom to shuck out of her clothes and stand under the hot shower until she started feeling marginally human again.

After her shower, she took some pain pills for her aching muscles and did a lengthy stretching routine, hoping that would keep her from hobbling around all day. She knew her mom was fast asleep in her room, catching up on sleep after her double shift, so she used her new earbuds for sound and tried to do her routine quietly.

Once the medicine and her stretches had reduced her aches and pains to dull background noise, she finally felt capable of fixing herself some food. She had such a craving for . . . something. Something with substance and "umph." Was that her body craving protein like her mom said she would? She also had a terrible craving for salt, so she got a dozen eggs scrambling with plenty of seasoning, then put a half a pound of sausage from the freezer into the microwave on defrost. Her mouth was watering like mad by the time the eggs were done and she ate nearly half of them right off the bat. Her mouth told her to keep eating until all the eggs were gone, but she got control of herself and put the second half away in the fridge for her mom, then got started cooking the sausage. That, too, she wolfed down piping hot. There might have been some plate-licking in there somewhere but nobody would ever know, so what was the harm?

Finally, stomach happily stuffed and kitchen cleaned of grease and dirty dishes, her thoughts turned to TD Hunter. But when she pulled aside the curtains and peered out the window, her heart sank.

It was raining.

Instead of dwelling on the disappointment of a whole day of leveling lost, Lynn heaved a sigh and turned her mind toward her much-neglected studying for finals. They would be the last three days of next week, and though a few of her classes had final projects or papers that she'd already *mostly* finished, she still needed to get ready for her Chemistry, Algebra and U.S. History finals. Ugh.

Her mom stressed over her grades much more than she did. She wanted to make her mom happy but it was hard to stay motivated when she saw no practical application to anything she was learning. She didn't even know what she wanted to "do" with her life. Her mom was always asking what she liked, but the only thing Lynn really enjoyed was kicking butt in virtual and keeping herself at the top of all the gaming charts. That didn't exactly translate into promising job prospects in the real. Sometimes she toyed with the idea of being a cop, like her dad had been. But that would mean she'd have to deal with *people.* No thanks.

To dredge up some enthusiasm, she promised herself she could spend all evening catching up on WarMonger if she spent the afternoon studying. A few bags of chips—okay, more than a few—helped things along and after a good three hours of grueling work, she finally heard her mom puttering around in the kitchen making herself breakfast. That was all the excuse Lynn needed to exit her school study portal and shut down her wall screens for a much-needed break.

When she entered the kitchen, she found her mother peering into the fridge.

"Hey, Mom! I made some extra eggs for you. Second shelf."

"Oh. Thanks honey," Matilda said, then yawned hugely.

"How'd work go? Anything super freaky happen this time?" Lynn asked. Her mom didn't always have stories about work, but when she did, they were usually gruesomely fascinating or deliciously dramatic.

"No...well, sort of," her mom replied, getting out the eggs to warm up in the microwave. "It wasn't that freaky, just odd. They brought in a couple of homeless men from that camp out in Osborn Park. They looked like classic ODs but we couldn't find what drug had caused it. It was the weirdest thing, like they'd both had massive heart attacks or stroke. No apparent cause. Otherwise healthy for housing disadvantaged. It just goes to show that even with all our advances, we still can't explain everything that happens in the medical field."

Lynn made a face.

"Did you check for novel viruses? I know that's usually what the media blames it on since they love the panic, but they aren't always wrong."

"Of course we did, dear. There was nothing you wouldn't expect in a couple of homeless junkies."

"Well, that's a relief, I guess. Anything else exciting happen?"

"Nope, things were pretty normal."

"Sooo...exhausting, chaotic and full of demanding patients?"

Matilda smiled.

"You know, Mom, you do a pretty bad job of making me want to go into medicine. I never want to set foot in a hospital, much less work at one, with all the stories you tell."

This time her mom chuckled.

"It's a unique calling, that's for sure, sweetie. You have to be pretty crazy to choose it, much less make it through school and stick with it for any length of time."

"So, you're admitting my crazy genes *do* come from you and not Dad?" Lynn asked, but regretted it when she saw her mother's smile disappear to be replaced by a sad, faraway look.

"Your father was even crazier than me. It was why we got along so well...and also why we didn't..."

Her mother trailed off and Lynn cast around for something to distract them.

"So, I'm really enjoying TD Hunter."

With visible effort, Matilda seemed to focus back on the here and now.

"That's great, honey. Tell me about it. Is the beta thingy you're doing as amazing as the equipment they sent you?"

Lynn launched into an enthusiastic analysis of the pros and cons of the game as she saw it so far, reminding herself to share the same thoughts with Hugo later so her feedback could be logged. She was expanding on the drawbacks of augmented reality games in general when it came to being out in public, when her mother stopped her.

"Wait a minute. You were interrupted and *harassed* by a couple of young men while you were out playing?"

Oops.

"No! I mean, yes, but it wasn't that big of a deal. I wasn't going to mention it—"

"Weren't going to mention it?" Matilda asked with a frown. "Where were you? How many other times have you been accosted that you 'weren't going to mention'?"

"Come on, Mom, it's not like that," Lynn said, all the while mentally cursing herself. "It was only the one time. I was just over in the Heathers, it's basically the same complex as ours and it wasn't late or dark or anything. And I was in *no* danger at all. I was out in the middle of public, with people watching, and Hugo already had emergency services on the line ready to help if anything happened." It was a tiny bit of a lie but only a tiny bit.

"*Ready to help if anything happened?*" her mother said, tone turning decidedly dangerous. "What good would emergency services be if those men had assaulted you? Raped you? Stabbed you and left you for dead?"

"Oh, come *on*, Mom. Really? Just because you see the dumbest and most horrible things people do at your job doesn't mean it's likely to happen to me. You're always telling me working in a hospital emergency room skews your perspective, right?"

"It doesn't matter, Lynn. You were harassed and threatened by grown men; they could have done anything to you!"

"I mean, it's not like I'm helpless," Lynn muttered.

"That's not the point, young lady. I can't have my teenage daughter wandering the city alone—"

"I wasn't alone. Hugo—"

"And I don't want you playing this game if it puts you in danger!"

"I'm *fine*. Nothing happened."

"But it *could* have. If you aren't going to listen to me and stay near our apartment, then from now on you can only play if you have someone to buddy up with."

"What? Come on, Mom, that's ridiculous. I'm almost seventeen. I can take care of myself. Besides, I need to be working on this game every chance I can get. Nobody will want to be dragged along for that."

"Well, you'd better find somebody, because that's the way things are going to have to be if our area is so dangerous that you get accosted by strange men not a mile from our apartment."

"Mom—no—you're completely overreacting. I promise I'll stay near our apartment from now on. It's not a big deal! Come on, please?"

Her mother's lips thinned, and she didn't immediately respond. Finally, she let out a sigh and rubbed her temples.

"You should be focusing on school right now, Lynn, not games. I think you should take a break from this new game until finals are over. After that I'm sure one of your school friends would be happy to keep you company."

"But—"

"I don't want you to get hurt, Lynn!"

"I won't—"

"You can't know that. Anything could happen. A-anything—" Her mother's voice trembled, then broke, and the tense silence that followed was punctured only by the forlorn beep of the microwave, announcing for about the fifth time that it had finished warming her scrambled eggs.

There were so many angry things Lynn wanted to say, arguments and protests she wanted to voice. But she didn't. Anything *could* happen. "Anything" had happened to her dad. She shouldn't have told her mom about running into those jerks—should have known it would trigger her. So, instead of opening her mouth, Lynn turned around and went to her room. She closed the door firmly, sat down in her body-mold chair and logged onto WarMonger.

She needed to kill something.

Hours later, when Lynn's stomach made its expectation of dinner clear, she felt relaxed enough to emerge from virtual. It had felt good to be back in familiar territory, to do something that her body and instincts were attuned to without conscious thought. She'd had a good run pounding some upstart Tier Twos into the dirt who thought they deserved better rankings because they carried big flashy guns—guns she'd sold them in the first place. She'd even enjoyed a few friendly rounds with her favorite Tier One rivals. They always kept her on her toes and were good-natured about both winning and losing. The camaraderie and familiarity of it all grounded her in a way that nothing else could.

Dinner was quiet, though perfectly civil. Neither she nor her mom brought up TD Hunter. After cleanup and dishes, Lynn begged off their usual Saturday night surfing the Stream channels together, saying she was tired from studying all day and wanted to get some sleep. She didn't sleep, of course. She logged a few more hours in WarMonger, then crawled into bed and lay awake scheming and worrying. Who could she play TD Hunter with? If it hadn't still been in beta, it wouldn't be that big of a deal. But who would want to tag along for potentially hours at a time, being bored and doing nothing but watching her jump around like a crazy person?

When she woke up on Sunday, her mom was asleep and it was still raining. She spent some time finishing up her papers and projects, then half-heartedly reviewed her notes from the semester until her mother woke up.

Sunday meant girl time together. They did something different every week, from deep cleaning the apartment while listening to K-Pop from the 2010s—one of Matilda's guilty pleasures that Lynn tolerated with good-natured exasperation—to indulging in a rare evening out for a VR movie and ice cream after. Lynn had no idea what they were going to do that afternoon and didn't emerge from her room until her mom stuck her head in, a smile on her face.

"I challenge you to a duel!"

Lynn rolled her eyes but dragged herself from her body-mold chair and followed her mom to the living room. Matilda had pushed aside the coffee table and put up two card tables side-by-side, each with a five hundred piece puzzle on it.

"Mom, we haven't done this in ages," Lynn said, staring at the set up. Hadn't done it, in fact, since Lynn had started gaming seriously when she was thirteen.

"All the more reason to do it now," her mom said. "So, are you going to forfeit the game and declare me the winner?"

"And let you win a puzzle duel for the first time in your life? Not a chance," Lynn said, a grin finally sneaking its way onto her face.

"Ha! Big words for someone who is severely out of practice." Without another word, Matilda sat down, dumped out her puzzle and got started.

"Hey! No fair. I need a soda and a snack to get my game on. Now you've got a head start."

Her mother didn't look up.

"Well, I guess you'd better hurry and get fueled up then, hmm?"

Muttering half-hearted curses, Lynn hurried to the kitchen. But when she opened the pantry to grab her usual junk food, she hesitated, then turned away. Instead she filled up a glass of water and grabbed an apple from the fruit basket. Then she went back to the living room and dumped out her own puzzle. She'd done this particular one before but it had been years.

While her mom used the picture on the box, Lynn got to work turning over all the pieces and sorting them into their different shape categories. She'd always preferred doing puzzles face-down. It took away the distraction of the confusing colors and shapes and gave her a clean, clear slate to work with. Spotting patterns was always like that: stripping away the noise until you could focus on what mattered, on what determined a thing's form or behavior. Her mom preferred the pretty pictures. Pattern mapping was something Lynn had shared with her dad. It was probably why he had been such a good cop and, now that she thought about it, why she was so good at gaming.

Normally they listened to music while they worked but neither of them made a move to turn any on. The quiet patter of rain outside was relaxing and soon Lynn was completely immersed, eyes moving speedily across her pieces while her mind worked even faster, analyzing, comparing, mapping.

They took a break for dinner. Sunday tradition was deep dish supreme pizza with extra peppers, delivered piping hot with plenty of breadsticks and garlic dip. They chatted about everyday things like finals coming up and coworker drama at her mom's hospital. Without taking time to clean up, they were back at the puzzles and Lynn could see she would have to push herself to beat her mom by a comfortable margin. She was out of practice. Or maybe she was just tired from all her studying over the past two days. In any case, there was nothing like a challenge to stir the blood.

Three hours and twenty-three minutes after starting her puzzle, minus a break for dinner, Lynn raised both hands in triumph.

"Done!"

"Aw, come on, Lynn. You could at least *pretend* to go easy on me," her mom said, sitting up with a sigh and a pop as she stretched her back. "My eyes aren't what they used to be."

"Uh-huh, a likely excuse," Lynn said, peering over at her mother's table. "Not too shabby, though. You only have about fifty or sixty pieces left."

"I suppose a bit of sympathy praise is better than nothing to sustain me through my grueling punishment," Matilda said. Losers in their puzzle duels always cleaned up from dinner and did any dishes left over from the day.

Lynn smiled as she began taking apart and putting away her puzzle.

"Do you want to finish your puzzle or should I put it away, too?" she asked.

"Leave it, I'll finish it after dishes," her mom said and got up to go to the kitchen.

After Lynn had finished putting away her puzzle and the card table, she silently joined her mom in the kitchen and started wiping down the counters.

"You don't have to do that, sweetie. You won."

Lynn shrugged.

"Yeah, well, I'm not thirteen anymore. Besides, I know I have an unfair advantage over you. It's not your fault you're not as smart as me." She shot her mom a lopsided grin.

Matilda gasped in mock indignation, then threw the dish towel at her. They both erupted in laughter.

After their giggles had subsided, they finished cleaning the kitchen in silence. Lynn's mind was already back in her room, trying to decide if she should play more WarMonger while she had the chance, or if she should dive into the TD Hunter app and start checking out those training simulations.

"Lynn," her mom said, breaking into her thoughts.

"Hmm?"

"I'm . . . I'm sorry about the other day."

It took a moment for Lynn's mind to switch tracks.

"Uh... okay."

"I know you're almost a grown woman. I just... worry. And the world out there *is* dangerous. And you *did* promise you would stay near our apartment..."

Lynn wanted to make excuses, but she bit her tongue, waiting to see what her mom would say.

"I know you like this game... and it seems good for you... and I want you to be able to keep playing it, but..." She turned to look at Lynn, her face lined with worry. "Safety *is* important. I need to know I can trust you to take your own safety seriously."

A stab of guilt made Lynn swallow. Perhaps she had stretched her interpretation of her mom's wishes more than she should have.

"I—I don't mind if you play right around our apartment, if you'll actually stay close this time." Matilda gave her a level look, which made Lynn hang her head. "But if you want to go farther, I think it's important that you take someone with you, in case something... happens. Can you do that for me?"

Lynn heaved a huge sigh. She loved her mom. She really did. And they were so lucky to have each other. She tried to keep the big picture in mind. TD Hunter was only a game. A very important game but only a game.

"Okay, sure. I'll try to find someone. But you know I don't really have many friends and the guys at school... they aren't the outdoorsy types either. I don't know if any would be willing to tag along, outside, in the *sun*, for a game they can't even play." It was true enough, even if the real reason she didn't even want to ask Ronnie and the rest was because they might never speak to her again if they knew she'd been lying to them for years about her gaming habits.

"Why don't you try, and if you can't find anyone, we'll talk about this again then, okay?"

"Okay. I'm sorry I—" She stopped, swallowing her "bent the rules" excuse and made herself say the words "—broke my promise to you, Mom. I really didn't think it was a big deal. But I'll be more careful."

"Thank you, sweetie. I love you," Matilda said and wrapped Lynn in a tight hug.

"I love you too, Mom."

"Now, why don't you get some more studying done while I

go for a workout in the complex gym? All that sitting and pizza has made me antsy."

While Lynn's mom wasn't exactly a workout fanatic, she *was* very health conscious. Considering she spent most of her waking time during the week on her feet in constant motion, she always needed a good, sweaty workout on the weekends to wear her out so she would sleep through the day on Monday and be ready for her first night shift of the week.

"Sure, Mom. Have a good workout."

After her mother left, Lynn logged into WarMonger. She felt too depressed about the situation with TD Hunter to want to mess with it and her brain was too tired to focus on school. She thought about seeking out Ronnie and the rest—nothing boosted her mood quite so well as Ronnie's frustrated Lithuanian curses— but something held her back. Instead, she did some busywork on the auction site, wrapping up offers she'd put up last night that had gotten some very satisfactory bids. Then, since she didn't have any messages asking for her services just then, she put out her calling card.

"Larry Coughlin available for challenge match. One-versus-as-many-as-you-want. This old snake's got a twitchy trigger finger. Who wants to die tonight?"

It was more provocative than she usually preferred to be in virtual, but she had the reputation to back it up and was hoping some trigger-happy tryhards would take the bait. Sometimes she just needed a night of senseless violence fragging wannabe pros who were stupid enough to try to gang up on her.

The Monday of finals week was always nerve-wracking as teachers tried to stuff their students with as much last-minute information as possible. Lynn tried to concentrate but was distracted by her TD Hunter dilemma. She kept playing out different scenarios in her head, wondering which of the guys in her gaming group she might be able to catch alone and what they might say if she asked them to tag along with her to play TD Hunter. Mack was the obvious choice but he was horrible at keeping secrets. Dan she didn't know as well and of course Ronnie was out of the question. Every time she thought about Edgar, she remembered their conversation from the week before when he'd said she looked nice with a tan. What was that even supposed to mean? She was always tan. Was he making things up? Trying to be nice?

She was so distracted that she made the fatal mistake of not looking where she was going while on the way to the cafeteria for lunch. She almost ran right into Elena and by the time she was aware of her surroundings, the pop-girl's "posse" had already surrounded her.

"All right, you lying little sneak. How did you get in?"

"What?" Lynn said, completely nonplussed.

"Don't play dumb with me, birdbrain. One of my girls lives in the Heathers complex and she saw you playing with that stupid blue stick. You got invited to play TransDilemma, or whatever it's called and I want in. How did you do it?"

Lynn's blood ran cold. She swallowed, trying to calculate the likelihood that she could bluff her way out of this one. The key was confidence. Never let the enemy see you sweat.

"I have no idea what you're talking about, Elena. I think your 'girl' needs to have her eyes checked."

The pop-girl's eyes narrowed.

"She described it in great detail. It looked exactly like the thing in all the ads. Now, tell me how you got in, or I'll make you regret it." Elena took a step forward. She was only average height but that put her several inches over Lynn. Plus, the girl was wearing three-inch heeled boots.

Lynn shifted back on one foot, instinctively adopting a firm, balanced stance. Elena and her crowd hardly ever got physical. Their weapons were words, which of course could be just as sharp, humiliating and damaging. But there were rumors that Elena had really messed up a freshman last year that she'd accused of sleeping with her boyfriend-of-the-month. Lynn didn't think the pop-girl had an ounce of true fighter in her, but she *was* athletic and she had a whole group of followers to hold a victim still while she did whatever she wanted. The halls were empty, everyone else having already gone to lunch, so no witnesses.

"I—"

"Hey, Lynn, what's going on?"

Lynn's head whipped around to see Edgar striding down the hall, backpack slung over one huge shoulder. The girls of Elena's posse drew back from him as he approached, breaking up the circle and taking away Elena's advantage.

"Oh, nothing," Lynn said, swallowing down her relief. "Just giving Elena some tips on how to not be an obnoxious harpy bleating for attention."

As soon as Lynn said it, she knew she shouldn't have. Hatred flashed over Elena's face but the girl quickly hid it behind a sly look that meant nothing good was about to happen.

"Actually, Miss Birdbrain here was telling me *all* about how she's been banging this disgusting old creep who works for Tsunami Entertainment so she could get some sort of counterfeit invitation to play TransDilemma. I'm sure she hopes it will bring a semblance of meaning to her pitiful loser existence."

Edgar looked back and forth between Lynn and Elena, clearly confused.

"Uh, do you mean TransDimensional Hunter?"

"Yes, whatever!" Elena snapped, clearly angry her scathing comments hadn't had their desired effect. "The point is, this little chit is playing the stupid game, and I'm sure she had to whore herself to get it, though I feel sorry for whoever was desperate enough to touch that disgusting piggy body of hers."

Embarrassment made Lynn's face feel hot, but she resisted the instinct to wrap her arms defensively around herself. A glance up at Edgar told her he'd gone all still and blank, like he did when he was in danger of losing it. She needed to diffuse the situation, fast, before Edgar got in trouble because of her—again.

The best defense was an overwhelming offense, Larry-style.

"I had to whore myself to get it, huh?" Lynn asked and forced a laugh past her dry throat. "You were just demanding to know how to get an invite yourself, doesn't that mean you'd be perfectly happy to sleep with however many 'creeps' it took to get in? What, couldn't your oh-so-important daddy get you an invite? Does he know his precious little princess bangs men to get what she wants?"

Elena's mouth snapped shut and her jaw worked like she wished she could crush Lynn by simply grinding her teeth together. Her perfectly pale cheeks had gone bright pink and Lynn honestly wondered if the pop-girl would try to hit her. But then Elena spoke, voice low and trembling with rage.

"I promise, you will regret speaking about your betters like that with your filthy mouth. You're just jealous because I have everything you could ever want and you're nothing but a fat, ugly, worthless nobody."

Lynn snorted, though she couldn't help glancing up at Edgar to check and make sure he wasn't about to punch Elena into next week. The pop-girl must have noticed Lynn's concern, because another one of those sly smiles smoothed out the anger on her face as she stepped back and raised her voice for a parting shot.

"I'll leave you to wallow in self-loathing with your moronic troll boyfriend here, though he probably wouldn't touch your fatty lard body either. He's just being nice to you because you're so pathetic he can't help pitying you."

With that, the girl spun on her impressive heels, which was a relief because it meant she missed seeing Lynn grab Edgar's wrist to halt him as he started toward the oblivious bully. Elena stalked away unhindered, her silent posse closing in behind even as they threw nervous looks over their shoulders.

Once they disappeared around the corner, Lynn let go of Edgar's wrist and stuck her hands in her hoodie's front pocket, surreptitiously wiping them on the inner fabric. Why were her hands so sweaty?

"Um, thanks for . . . being here," Lynn said, cringing at her own words. They were stupid but at least they seemed to snap Edgar out of it.

"Yeah. Sure."

Silence.

Lynn wished for all the world that Edgar hadn't been there to witness Elena's cruel attack. Loser. Fatty. Disgusting. They were only words and she'd learned after many years of self-loathing and heartache to not give them power over her. Even so, they still stuck to her like stubborn burrs and she knew they'd be echoing in her head long after she'd tried her best to exorcize them.

"Should we, uh, go to lunch?" Lynn asked.

"Oh, yeah. Sure." Edgar shook his head as if clearing it, then hitched his backpack up and they started toward the cafeteria.

"So . . . you're a beta tester for TD Hunter?"

Lynn winced. She'd been hoping he hadn't caught that. He didn't sound mad about it, but then Edgar kept his emotions under tight wraps. Lynn wanted to lie, wanted to deny it, but it seemed really low to lie to someone who'd just stuck out their neck for you.

"Um, yeah. But please, *please* promise me you won't breathe a word to Ronnie or any of the others?"

Edgar shrugged.

"No sweat, Lynn, if that's what you want. I'd think you'd wanna to see the look on Ronnie's face, though, when he finds out you got beta and he didn't."

"I mean, yeah, that might be a little satisfying," Lynn admitted. Then she realized what she was saying and backtracked. "But it's not like that at all, really. I didn't apply to beta, I didn't even *want* to play. Mr. Kra—I mean the game developers just invited me, I have no idea why." Okay, a little lie.

"Well, you've obviously got something Ronnie and Dan don't." Edgar shrugged again. "They need all sorts to beta, not just hardcore gamers."

For some reason, Edgar's comment stung in a way that Ronnie's "girls got no game" never had. She didn't *want* Edgar to think she was a casual gamer. The thought drew her up short and she spent a moment wondering why she cared about Edgar's opinion of her gaming skill.

They were almost to the cafeteria when Lynn suddenly realized the opportunity that had fallen into her lap. She cleared her throat and stopped and Edgar stopped too, giving her a puzzled look.

"Um, so, since you know I'm playing TD Hunter now, do you think...well, would you have any interest in..." Lynn trailed off, frustrated. This was stupid. She needed to come out and say it, no matter how awkward it felt. "Okay, so my mom is a little worried about me walking around alone everywhere to play this AR game and wants me to find a friend to walk with. Just in case, you know? Do you think you'd have time to, um, walk with me?" The question hung in the air for a moment, unanswered, and Lynn hurried to fill the silence. "I mean, I know it will be pretty boring for you since you can't play the game too but I can show you how it works and everything and you can see some of the monsters I see and it's great exercise and there's this cool service AI named Hugo and—"

"Sure, sure, Lynn. It's all cool. I'll walk with you." Edgar grinned at her and she slowly returned the smile, relief flooding through her and making her feel giddy.

"It'll have to be after finals are over, though," he temporized. "I, uh, need to study a lot."

"Oh, yeah, of course. Maybe Saturday, then?"

"That'll work. Ping me Friday night an' shoot me your address. I'll meet you there, whenever you wanna start."

"Awesome. That's a huge help. Thanks, Edgar."

"Sure thing. Better for me than lying in bed playing War-Monger, anyway." He turned toward the cafeteria doors and they started into the noisy room. Edgar raised his voice a little to be heard. "Ronnie's been a bigger douche than normal, lately. Haven't seen nothing of Larry for almost a week. Shame he's the only thing as ever brings Ronnie down a peg or two."

Lynn smiled to herself.

They swiped their cards at the food dispenser and gathered their lunches, then headed over to their table. Lynn noticed that an unusually large number of students seemed absorbed in watching something on their AR glasses, though that could be because finals were coming up. Maybe they were studying.

"There you are, Edgar. Finally!" Dan's excited voice called out before they even reached the table.

"Hey, Lynn," Mack said, grinning as his eyes flicked between her and Edgar.

"Hey, Mack. Your mom make you shave again?" Lynn asked, knowing from long practice exactly how to distract her friend. His hand shot up to rub self-consciously at his newly smoothed chin.

"Yeah," he said, now glum. "Said I wasn't allowed to graduate looking like a homeless guy."

"Forget about Mack's mommy problems," Dan interrupted. "Edgar, did you see the announcement?"

"Nope. Been focusing on class. What's up?"

"TD Hunter just released that big announcement they've been talking about. They're giving away baton sets to the first *one million* players who pre-register for their app!"

Edgar set down his food, plopped down in his seat, then stuffed half a banana into his mouth before finally speaking around it.

"What're you talking 'bout, man?"

"You know, those electric blue omni-polymer things that shift into different weapons in TD Hunter, the ones they use in all the ads. You have to buy a set to play the game, but they're giving away a *million* of them. You need to pre-register, like, *right now.*"

Lynn raised her eyebrows, impressed with the game developer's tactics. Though they must really have all the funding that Mr. Krator talked about, and then some, to afford such a publicity stunt.

"Ronnie, Mack and I have already registered. Hurry up and register, or you'll miss out!"

"Chill out, Dan," Edgar said. "I been burning calories all morning with this big brain of mine. Gotta refuel before I start worrying 'bout anything else."

"Seriously? You're going to miss out—"

"Too late," Ronnie cut in. His food sat untouched, his eyes fixed on his AR glasses reading something none of them could see. "They're already past a mil and a half prereg."

Dan blew out a breath and shook his head.

"You snooze, you lose, Edgar. It's okay, though. They won't be very expensive, I'm sure."

Edgar shrugged.

"You see the new promo vid they released with the announcement?" Dan asked, enthusiasm undimmed.

"Really, Dan?" Lynn cut in, saving Edgar who obviously just wanted to eat his lunch. "He said a minute ago he hadn't heard the announcement, so how the heck could he have seen the promo?"

"Oh yeah. Makes sense. Well, anyway, you should totally watch it. It's cool. And I mean *cooooool.*"

Mack chimed in and he and Dan started reliving all the coolest parts, piquing Lynn's curiosity. She glanced at Ronnie but he was still totally immersed in his AR glasses and ignoring everyone at the table. Edgar, of course, was focused on his food. She still had her earbuds in, since they *had* turned out to be extremely comfortable, even wearing them all day, and they easily let in all the ambient noise from her surroundings. Ambient noise that was, now that she paid attention to it, mostly students talking excitedly about TD Hunter and their new promo video. Since her earbuds' vibration sensors let her subvocalize commands to her LINC menu through her fancy AR glasses interface, she was able to pull up the TD Hunter announcement to find the promo vid everyone was so obsessed with. She chowed down on her fish and mashed potatoes while she watched.

The video began with a voiceover and Lynn immediately recognized General Carville's smooth, grave tone overlaid on ominous background music.

"An invisible invasion has begun. All over the world, silent and unseen, hostile transdimensional entities have been appearing. As their numbers have swelled, they've been wrecking our technology, our infrastructure and are even now amassing to wipe out humanity itself."

A radar map appeared on screen as General Carville spoke, showing the world's continents in green on black ocean as a radar cone slowly circled. Red dots began appearing in every country, revealed by the radar. Each pass showed more and more dots until they were so thick they seemed to blanket the world in a plague of blood.

"Our only hope of saving humanity is you, Hunter. No military in the world is strong enough to resist an invasion on this scale. We're depending on citizen volunteers to take up the banner and fight back, before these monsters gather enough strength to attack."

The map disappeared to be replaced by scenes of wraithlike TransDimensional Monsters, their forms smokey and translucent but their looming presence no less malevolent. They crouched in alleyways and under bridges, tentacles slowly shifting like snakes or mouths full of teeth hanging open in hungry anticipation. Lynn recognized some of them from pictures of Charlie, Bravo and Alpha Class TDMs in her app's monster index.

"This will not be an easy fight," the general continued. *"But the TransDimensional Counterforce is ready and waiting to equip you with our cutting edge battle system and groundbreaking smart weapons that will customize to fit each Hunter no matter what your skill, abilities, or preferences."*

As the scene changed, the music began to crescendo, building as first one, then another, and another person appeared in the picture. They were all ordinary people from every imaginable culture and clime, young and old, male and female, short and tall, fat and thin. Each one stopped whatever they were doing—eating, working, playing—and bent down to pick up a blue baton from the ground. As they stood up, they transformed. Their baton grew into a fearsome weapon and their ordinary clothes were covered with impenetrable armor. For some, their appearance was modern military-looking, for some the equipment took on a stylized form of traditional armor and weapons from cultures across the world: Japanese samurai, Rajput soldiers, Viking raiders, Maori warriors, Dahomey Amazons and more. As the music reached its peak and erupted into an adrenaline-rousing rush of sound, each new Hunter was seen charging into battle, spinning, slashing, jumping, shooting and stabbing. From desert villages to downtown cities to snow-swept mountain enclaves, Hunters battled monsters, heroically fighting back against the invasion.

"*It's up to you, Hunter, to push back the tide before it over-whelms us all,*" General Carville's voice exhorted the viewer. "*So, pick up your weapon, step into the real and fight. Fight for humanity, fight for survival and for the dawning of a new day.*"

The video ended as the scenes of battle faded away to a dark screen with the TD Counterforce logo and the words *Step into the real. The fight for humanity has begun.*

When the clip disappeared and Lynn was jerked back into her own reality surrounded by a noisy school cafeteria, she felt such a jarring dissonance that she had to take a moment to get her breath back. Her heart was thumping in her chest and her limbs were tingling with adrenaline. She wished she could walk out of school then and there and boot up her app to go kill some TDMs.

That promo vid had been beyond powerful—it had been *inspiring.*

She no longer wondered if Mr. Krator and his developer team were going to pull off this game. All she could think about was how awesome it was going to be when it launched.

It took a great deal of effort to push down that restless itch to play, to fight, and instead force herself to eat her lunch and turn her mind back to classes and finals. She saved the video link to her cloud library, knowing she would be watching it again—possibly multiple times—the minute finals were over and summer vacation had officially begun.

She couldn't wait.

Chapter 6

TD HUNTER'S NEW PROMO VID WAS ALL THAT GOT LYNN THROUGH the rest of the week. Any time she caught herself worrying about finals or looking over her shoulder, wondering what kind of revenge Elena might be cooking up, she distracted herself with visions of scything through hordes of monsters. Whenever Elena's cruel words clawed to the surface of her thoughts, she visualized the lists of weapons and monsters in the TD Hunter tactical section, mentally reciting their stats. And, just to be safe, she kept a careful eye out and stuck close to her friends for the rest of the week.

No point giving Elena and her crowd an opening to corner her again.

Finals came and went without any more excitement than the usual betting on who would get caught trying to sneak their LINC into the exam rooms. They busted someone every year, without fail. Lynn never bothered trying, even though she knew people in virtual who could tell her how to get away with it. Unlike Dan, who was a "do whatever it takes" kind of guy—at least when it came to gaming—Lynn had worked hard enough at things that truly brought her joy to know that the rewards of cheating were never worth the cost. She'd rather have hard-won average grades than undeserved good grades.

Much to her delight, one of Elena's sycophants who was in Lynn's Algebra class got caught on Friday during their last final of the year. The idiot had at least used an RF shielding bag stuffed up her shirt to hide her LINC—there was one student last year who'd thought wrapping it in aluminum foil would beat the scanners. But the teacher knew what to look for and busted the girl with a single glance. The ninety minute exam flew by after that and Lynn joined her friends afterward, feeling on top of the world.

As they all made their way to the airbus platform, the guys chatted excitedly about a celebratory game of WarMonger they were planning that night. Lynn kept silent, for once not plotting to Larry-crash their Friday night fun. She had better things to do: specifically, take advantage of the sunny evening to wipe out every single TDM around her apartment. She needed to rack up globes, plates and experience for her extended excursion with Edgar tomorrow. She'd already pinged him her address and a time to meet and had gotten "Sounds good. See you then!" in reply.

Her mom wasn't up yet when she got home, so she sent a message explaining she was going out to "hunt" and rushed to her room to gear up. She'd decided on the way home from school to finally use her TD Counterforce backpack. After all, school was over, they already knew, and what could those harpies do to her now? She took a moment to run her hands reverently over the bag's sleek, smooth exterior before packing it with hunting essentials like energy bars, sunscreen and bug repellent, then filling up the built-in hydration system.

Since it was sunny and hot outside and she planned to stay close to her apartment building, she dared to pull on one of the TD Counterforce shirts. Not the nice polo, which she couldn't bring herself to get sweaty and dirty, but a red sports cooling T-shirt with an image of a Hunter from one of the in-virtual ads on the front, while the TD Counterforce logo was splashed across the back. The T-shirt felt awkwardly snug—that is, it didn't hang like a baggy dress down to her mid-thighs—but she forced herself to not think about it. None of the boys from school would see her in it and most of their neighbors who she might run into were adults who barely ever gave her a glance anyway.

Lynn felt equal amounts of relief and disappointment that the Varg from the weekend before was nowhere in sight when she emerged from her apartment building. It had been almost a week since she'd hunted the area and it looked like the imp population was back up. She expected to find a bunch of Lectas, too, now that they were no longer unknown. But she only found one lurking behind a power pole next to her apartment building. To her delight, though, there were still plenty of attack TDMs. They would put more of a strain on her plate and globe usage but she needed the practice.

She spent over an hour in furious battle, challenging herself on how many monsters she could kill per minute with as little damage as possible. Every second counted and her mind was so focused on calculating trajectories, timing and attack strategies that she barely noticed the few glances people sent her way. Of those she did notice, they barely caused more than momentary self-consciousness. She was having fun and kicking butt. Who cared what anyone else thought?

Of course, not caring what adult strangers thought and not caring what her peers thought was hardly the same. But she had to start somewhere.

By the time her mom called her in for dinner, she was sweaty, tired and thoroughly happy. She'd killed over forty TDMs, had made solid progress toward Level 5 and had picked up another augment that a gremlin had dropped. This one decreased a weapon's energy use by five percent, which wasn't much but was certainly better than nothing. She'd already slipped it into her Plasma Pistol's second augment slot. She and Hugo discussed the math of how much energy it would save her as she trudged into her building and rode the elevator up to her apartment.

When she walked in, her mother took one look at her sweat-soaked appearance and sent her off to the shower. She emerged twenty minutes later, braiding back her long black hair and went to stick her head in the kitchen. She took one whiff of the cooking food and groaned.

"I'm so starved! I feel like I could eat a whole cow."

"Aaand it hits," Matilda said, grinning. "As I said, once your body realizes you're really exercising and it's not a fake-out, the system starts to work. How do you feel? Not the aches and pains but overall?"

"Great," Lynn said, smiling. "I mean, I'm sore and tired, but overall I feel really good. Like, full of energy or something."

"Exercise has its benefits," Matilda said. "Enjoy them while you're young. It gets harder and harder as you age. Could you set the table, please?"

"What's for dinner?" Lynn asked while she got out dishes and silverware. "I don't know why, but I am craving red meat so bad."

"Well, you'll have to make do with chicken, for now. But maybe we can splurge with a nice meal out once we get back your final grades and see how you did." She smiled at Lynn, who grumbled in response.

"Don't ruin the mood, Mom. I've got three whole months before I have to think about school again."

"Uh-huh. Just wait until you're all grown up and have to work for a living and pay bills. Believe me, you'll miss your carefree school years."

"Not likely," Lynn muttered, thinking about her sizable, and secret, bank account. She'd take working for a living over constant bullying any day. Her mother just smiled, though and got back to the topic of dinner.

"Now, when the food is ready, don't forget to—"

"Eat the veggies first," Lynn recited, "then the meat then the starches."

"That's my girl," Matilda said. "Also . . . I know when you tell a teenager 'don't,' they usually do the opposite. But this time I hope you'll take my advice. Don't look in the mirror. Don't get on a scale. Not for a few weeks. It's healthy for bodies to change slowly and the differences will be subtle, so you can't look in the mirror every day and pick yourself apart. As long as you keep playing this game and keep your activity up, you'll start seeing the difference it makes."

"If you say so." Lynn tugged at her baggy shirt self-consciously, wondering if she'd ever feel brave enough to wear the kind of body-mold suits elite gamers donned for livestream AR and VR tournaments.

Dinner was sautéed chicken with cheese rice and a side of steamed broccoli, exactly the kind of cheap and easy to prepare dinner that working mothers preferred. Lynn set the table, then grabbed a bag of frozen broccoli to heat up in the microwave while her mother finished the chicken and rice. Normally the broccoli was the part she liked the least. With enough butter it was edible. As the vegetables microwaved, however, and the smell hit her, she thought she'd faint. She wanted broccoli. Lots of broccoli.

"Can I make another one, Mom?" Lynn said. "For some reason, I'm craving broccoli."

"Let's make sure your eyes aren't bigger than your stomach," Matilda said. "But one more won't hurt. Lots of things to do with left-over broccoli."

Lynn got the broccoli out of the microwave, dropped butter into the plastic baggy that held it, then started another. She eyed the steaming bag of vegetables as the butter melted, practically willing it to hurry up.

"If you'd like some broccoli before supper..." Matilda said.

Lynn grabbed a fork and dug in. Normally she'd tip it into a bowl, but she didn't want to wait. Before she knew it she'd finished the bag.

"Thorry," she said, her mouth still part full of vegetables. It had been so hot at first that she'd burned her tongue. But it had been sooo worth it.

"Oh, I approve," Matilda said, casting an amused eye at Lynn. "I am wondering, though, who you are and what you've done with my daughter."

"It just smelled so good," Lynn said after swallowing the last bite.

"Iron," her mother said, slapping her forehead. "Of course."

"Iron?" Lynn asked.

"You were craving red meat," Matilda said. "It's high in iron. So is broccoli. When you exercise you increase the level of red blood cells in your system. That requires iron. So, craving broccoli makes sense, and it's better for you than a thick, fat steak. All good."

"Works for me," Lynn said, taking the next batch out of the microwave. "Um...?"

"Go for it," Matilda said, shaking her head with a laugh. "But let it cool a bit more and use a bowl."

By the time they sat down to dinner, Lynn had already eaten three batches of broccoli mix and made a fourth for dinner. She thought there was no way she'd be able to clear her plate, but she ended up eating her chicken, plus some her mom had left over before finally stopping with a burp she couldn't control.

"I'm sorry," Lynn said. "I was sooo hungry."

"Not anymore, I hope," her mother said, trying not to smile.

"Nope," Lynn said, then burped again. "Too full."

"How far did you walk today?" Matilda asked, her tone a bit cautious.

"Don't worry, Mom. I stayed close to the apartment," Lynn said. "And I'm not sure. A couple miles I think with all the back and forth I was doing to get all the TDMs."

"The what?"

"TransDimensional Monsters. The evil invading force set to wipe out humanity. I'm a citizen volunteer, bravely hunting the invading monsters alongside millions worldwide." Lynn grinned.

"Ah, I see. Very heroic of you, dear."

"It's fun. I think I might even get a nice VR system and start practicing some kind of martial art or fighting style over the summer, work on my moves, you know?"

"Hmmm..." Her mother sounded skeptical. "Those are pretty expensive, aren't they? I know you're really enjoying this game, honey, and I want to do everything to support you, but..."

Lynn felt a moment of panic. "Oh, I've been, uh, saving up birthday money and stuff for a while now. Don't worry, I wasn't going to ask you to pay for it."

A tiny crease formed on her mother's forehead and Lynn winced. She could have kicked herself for slipping and being so blasé about money. What if her mom started to get suspicious?

"Okay, well, we'll see. Just please be safe when you're out, um, hunting, okay?"

"I'll be fine, Mom," Lynn said. "Edgar's coming with me, remember?" The fact that her mom had smiled knowingly when she'd asked about hanging out with Edgar had been irritating. Apparently a guy and a girl couldn't just be friends these days. But then, her mom wasn't the type to pry into her love life—not that she had one, of course—so she'd let the smile go without comment.

"Yes, yes, I know. But that doesn't mean you can throw safety to the winds, young lady. Just stay alert and have fun, okay? I have to get ready for work."

Lynn rolled her eyes but smiled all the same.

"I'll get the dishes."

Matilda smiled back.

"I'll let you."

Saturday morning Lynn woke with butterflies in her belly. She lay in bed for a moment, trying to figure out why. She couldn't wait to get out and spend the day hunting. Today would be a leveling day for sure, maybe even two levels and she was both excited and nervous to face whatever big baddies hung out in that greenway strip of woods. But none of that made her feel queasy. Then she thought about doing it all in front of Edgar and her stomach lurched.

Stupid, cursed, good-for-nothing teenage emotions.

The only thing that made such a thought bearable was the sure knowledge that Edgar would never, ever tease her about it. He just wasn't that kind of guy. He'd seen what she'd lived through in middle school and high school—what they'd both lived through.

No point dwelling on it, she decided and sat up to get ready for her day.

She couldn't quite bring herself to wear a T-shirt that would bare her arms. Besides, there were bound to be brambles in the woods, so more coverage was better. She chose a lightweight, baggy, long-sleeve shirt, a pair of jeans and her rattiest pair of tennis shoes. Then she spent time carefully braiding her hair tight to her skull so it wouldn't get in the way while she hunted.

Funnily enough, it was her dad who'd gotten her into braiding her hair. Her mom rarely talked about her family's tribal heritage, but her dad was always complaining about how he was jealous of his wife and daughter's hair and how, if he'd been a "good Viking" he would have had hair to rival theirs. Of course, police uniform regulations prevented it. But he'd joked and cajoled her mom into teaching her a few traditional braids, then had resorted to combing the stream channels for how-to videos on the best hair styles for "warrior women" as he'd called it. Lynn hadn't practiced the different techniques since they'd moved to Cedar Rapids, so it took a while for her clumsy fingers to remember the right patterns.

She tried not to think about her dad while she worked.

Once she was dressed, she logged onto WarMonger to quickly check some things. Fridays and Saturdays were usually busy days for her in virtual, so she took a minute to do some maintenance on her auctions and reply to her messages. There was one in particular she focused on, a client who still hadn't made their payment and was ignoring her not-so-gentle reminders. She'd have to do something about that. You couldn't stiff Larry Coughlin and get away with it. She shot off a message to YodaMaster, figuring he would be her best bet for assistance, then turned to the handful of requests to schedule battles. She ignored all but a regular client. To him she sent the message that Larry was unavailable but might be around later that night.

Before she'd even logged out, a response came back asking why.

Lynn considered before replying. Gamers were as bad a group of gossips as any pop-girl clique. Whatever she said would soon be promulgated through the upper player tiers. Saying she'd been tapped as a beta tester for TD Hunter would certainly up her prestige in the gaming community, but she wasn't sure she wanted Larry associated with that game. Someone might put two and two together. So, instead, she came up with a generic Larry response that was the perfect mix of impressive, intimidating and secretive.

Larry Coughlin: If I told you, I'd have to kill you and your dog.

After that it was simply a matter of packing her TD Counterforce backpack—she added some extra water and snacks for Edgar, just in case—then heading to the kitchen. She forced herself to eat a healthy breakfast of eggs, yogurt and fruit, even though she really wanted to grab a Pop-Tart from the cabinet. She planned to snack on protein bars all day, so she might as well start out with some good fuel in her system.

It wasn't time to meet up with Edgar yet, but Lynn decided to go ahead and start hunting anyway. She was still nervous about hunting in front of her friend and figured a good hour warming up would settle her nerves. The space along the greenway behind the last building of the complex still needed to be cleared and she preferred to do it alone in case that Varg showed up and her carefully rehearsed strategy didn't work against it. No reason for Edgar to be around to see her beat a hasty retreat. Plus, she was very close to leveling and didn't want to be distracted when it happened.

"Hugo?" she asked as she rode the elevator down to the front doors. "Is there any way to pause the game when you level so you have time to look at your achievement rewards and stuff without being attacked by new TDMs?"

"Unfortunately not, Miss Lynn, short of exiting combat mode."

"Well, that's dumb. You should log that as official feedback, by the way. Why splash a big achievement display in my view when I could be attacked by big nasties at any moment? Not to mention asking me to pick a new weapon. It makes me a sitting duck."

"An astute observation. There are ways to change your leveling notification format, but perhaps in addition an option could be created to automatically exit combat mode when a new level is achieved?" Hugo suggested.

Lynn mulled that over.

"Maybe, but you might not want to leave combat mode right at that moment. What if you're in the middle of fighting a monster and want to finish killing it? Plus, you can't equip globes and plates without being in combat mode, right?"

"That is correct, Miss Lynn."

"Okay, well, for now please warn me when you calculate I'm about five monsters away from leveling. That'll give me time to disengage from any sticky situation before it happens. And, now that I know, I can always holler at you to take me out of combat mode if I need to."

"Hollering will not be necessary, Miss Lynn. I can assure you I have excellent audio sensors."

"I meant—oh, never mind." Lynn gave up and instead focused on her overhead map as she exited the elevator. There weren't too many monsters right around her building, considering she'd wiped them all out only last night. She'd start along the greenway, then, and leave the few here for when she needed some easy pickings.

She exited her apartment fully armored and stealthed. She wanted no surprises. It was easy enough avoiding the TDMs between her and the greenway and the one ghost who tried to sneak up behind her. She didn't even slow to deal with it, just let it follow her until she'd reached her destination, then spun and sliced it in half right before it reached her. By now she could judge the most common TDMs' distance from her by the volume of their telltale noise.

Creeping carefully behind the last apartment building by the greenway was perhaps more caution than she needed. But being back there, even in daylight, had her adrenaline up, and she felt better being cautious. The summer insects were not as loud as at night and she heard enough ominous clicks and rustlings from the woods to make her glad she would have a friend along when she explored them. She spent the next half hour taking out the entire row of imps along the back side of the building, along with their irregular ghost and gremlin guardians.

Despite her trepidation, though, there wasn't a single hint of the Varg.

At the end of the line of air conditioning units, Lynn stopped and turned, propping her hands on her hips and glaring down the long strip of grass between the apartment building and the greenway. Well, that was anticlimactic. Maybe they really did only come out at night?

Lynn pursed her lips. She didn't want to come back out here in the dark, not after working up the courage to track the Varg down...

"Trouble, Miss Lynn?" came Hugo's voice in her ear.

"Not really. Well, sort of."

"Pray tell, perhaps I may be of assistance."

Lynn couldn't help a lopsided grin.

"You know, you sure are nosey for a service AI."

"Not at all. I am simply programmed to recognize situations where I have the potential to provide a service that falls within my purview, and your current behavior indicates confusion and uncertainty."

"Okay...well, I was hoping I'd run into that Varg again so I could wipe the floor with it. But it looks like it's not around. The tactical info on it said they normally come out at night."

"Yes, indeed, Miss Lynn. However, might I also point out that you are fully stealthed? Perhaps the Varg is less inclined to show itself during the day for anything less than a blindingly obvious target."

"Huh, good idea, Hugo. I didn't think of that."

"I do try, Miss Lynn."

"Yeah, yeah. Don't let it go to your head."

"I wouldn't dream of it."

Lynn snorted and turned in a circle, eyeing her surroundings. She had a clear avenue of escape behind her. She stepped away from the closest air unit, giving herself plenty of space to maneuver. Then she checked her health, her armor and her weapon. All good to go.

Okay. Time to show that Varg who was boss. And try not to die in the process.

"Hugo, empty my stealth slots."

"Done, Miss Lynn."

For a moment, nothing happened.

"Come on," Lynn muttered. "Come and get me you flea-bitten piece of trash..."

As if on cue, snarling echoed in her ears and she spun, look-ing for the source. By the time she remembered to check her overhead map and saw the red dot careening toward her through the dark strip that represented the greenway, it was almost too late. She spun toward the trees just as the Varg burst out of them and bore down on her like a howling freight train.

For the tiniest moment, Lynn froze.

Then she threw herself to the side, dodging the monster with only a hair's breadth to spare. She struck out with her Nano Blade as she fell, catching the creature in the side as it rushed past. Her triumph only lasted a split second before the ground gleefully reminded her that gravity still worked. She hit with an *oomph* as her "Lynn brain" gibbered in shock. Fortunately, her Larry instincts didn't need her brain's permission to get the job done, because without any conscious thought, she rolled with her momentum and scrambled back to her feet facing the Varg.

The TDM, of course, wasn't at all impressed by her amaz-ing feat of athleticism—amazing, at least, for a sedentary gamer who had previously avoided any unnecessary physical activity. It simply turned on a dime and dove back toward her, making her yelp in alarm and start slashing in a figure eight in front of her. The Varg made no effort to dodge, simply absorbing the damage as it bore down on her, biting at her with a mouthful of fangs as long as her palm. Her display flashed again and again with damage. This time, she kept her cool instead of panicking and stumbling about. She skipped backward, moving in a circle to try to stay ahead of the monster, all the while stabbing and slashing at its big ugly face.

"Approaching fifty percent health, Miss Lynn."

"Equip new plates," she gasped, still slashing. If she'd had more breath, she would have delivered a blistering barrage of scandal-ous Larry insults along with her Nano Blade strikes. Instead, she had to settle for cussing the stupid Varg out in her head.

Three more rolling dodges and innumerable curses later, Lynn was down to her last twenty percent health. She had no idea how close the Varg was to biting the dust. The smart thing to do would be to disengage and make a break for it. Dying would get her nowhere but an hour wasted while the "cold chill of death" debuff wore off.

She considered the consequences.

Then she mentally flipped her finger at the consequences and doubled down on her strikes. Time to do a stress test and see what kind of Larry craziness she could pull off.

A second later, she nearly ran into an air conditioning unit as she dodged another strike by the Varg. She managed to avoid a collision and instead put the unit between her and the monster. For some reason, that made the creature pull back, which was odd because none of the other TDMs had ever treated physical objects—trees, bushes, benches, cars—as if they were there. They simply moved right through them. Whatever the reason, it gave Lynn a split second to equip fresh plates and take in a lungful of air before the monster redoubled its attack by lunging around the side of the unit. Lynn kept circling, keeping the waist-high unit between her and the Varg. To her delight, she discovered she could reach *over* the unit to strike at the Varg's head without it reaching her. It only took a few more moments of furious attacks before the monster finally exploded into a cloud of sparks.

Lynn stabbed her Nano Blade up toward the sky, breathing hard but relishing sweet victory.

"HA! Take that you worthless piece of hairy junkrat!"

"Congratulations, Miss Lynn! An excellent battle indeed. You are on the cusp of leveling, by the way. Well within your five-monster limit."

"Right, thanks for the heads up. I'm under ten percent health too. I need to walk off some of this damage. Full stealth, please. I'll stick to places I've already cleared and hope nothing nasty comes calling."

Panting, bruised and with her whole body throbbing, Lynn headed off slowly around the building back toward her apartment, keeping a sharp eye and ear out for monsters. When she arrived back at her building's entrance, she snuck between the clueless imps she'd left alive there and put the doorway at her back. All she had to do was snipe one of the little guys and leveling would completely refill her health. She made sure she was at one hundred percent for armor and globes, then shot the nearest imp with her Plasma Pistol. It exploded and her leveling screen popped up, prompting Hugo to begin his usual spiel. Her health bar zipped up to full and she felt the tension leave her shoulders when nothing immediately jumped out and tried to eat her there in front of the lobby doors.

Lynn listened to Hugo with half an ear while taking stock of her inventory. There was a satisfying pile of extra plates and globes as well as a new item, something that looked like a capsule full of red liquid. That must be the Oneg Hugo had mentioned at the beginning of the game. Achieving Level 5 had given her five of them. She would have to do a little research to find out exactly how much health they revived and what monsters dropped them as loot. Fortunately, in addition to the new supplies, her max health and power had increased by twenty percent.

After her bonus display disappeared, she was delighted to see a new weapon selection pop up. Sweet.

One of the weapons she'd seen before: the Particle Dragon. Her second weapon choice, however, was a new melee weapon, the Plasma Blade. It had a bit more reach than her Nano Blade and instead of a kukri shape, it looked more like a short version of the Japanese katana. Like her Nano Blade, it had a cutout along the length of the blade that made it look more like a toy than a lethal weapon of war. Unlike her Nano Blade, though, it used a slight amount of power for every hit. It compensated for the energy use by inflicting fifteen percent more damage. She'd take that. She loved getting into close combat, so she chose the Plasma Blade over the Particle Dragon without a thought.

Next to pop up was a new achievement screen she hadn't seen before.

"What's this, Hugo?" she asked, eyes scanning.

"Why, how exciting, Miss Lynn! I am pleased to congratulate you on achieving the highest Level 5 kills dealt to damage taken ratio in the game. Your damage sustained per TDM you fight is remarkably low."

Lynn didn't reply because her eyes were riveted on the shiny new augment slowly rotating in her display.

"H-hugo. Take me out of combat mode."

"Certainly, Miss Lynn."

Her Plasma Pistol morphed back into a baton and her combat icons disappeared as she drifted over to take a seat on one of the shaded benches beside the front doors, her attention riveted onto the newest toy in her inventory. It wasn't just some generic augment. It was a rare named item called "Skadi's Glory." The name echoed in her mind, bringing back memories of her dad's storytelling. She couldn't remember the exact details, but she thought Skadi was a famous hunter goddess in Norse mythology. The item itself was a personal augment and it looked like a large silver brooch etched with a beautiful twisting design. Lynn could make out what looked like the head of a wolf amid all the decoration.

Its appearance wasn't what riveted her attention, though. It was the fact that its augment ability permanently increased all her personal stats by fifteen percent. Health. Armor. Detection. Stealth. All of it. That was huge. She'd have to double check with Hugo, but it sounded like the augment would grow with her, increasing her stats proportionally every time she leveled. There was a second benefit listed as well, something about a unique skin.

Eager to find out what it was, Lynn hopped over to her inventory and equipped Skadi's Glory in one of her three personal augment slots, then she selected her skin customization screen.

Her jaw dropped at what she saw.

Instead of the generic helmet, chest piece and elbow and knee pads she'd worn before, she now looked completely different.

She looked...magnificent.

If she ever happened to be reincarnated a hundred years in the future as a space Viking, the Skadi armor would be spot on. It was a seamless blend of ancient and modern, with overlapping, scalelike plates across her shoulders, arms, chest and thighs, reinforced by larger solid plates in the most vulnerable areas. It was all black, but each plate was edged in ice blue that blended nicely with her electric blue weapons. Blue geometric designs decorated the chest and curved around the collar and shoulders to give the ensemble a distinctly Nordic look.

She couldn't have been more pleased.

"Hey, Lynn. How's it hangin'?"

Lynn jumped in surprise and grabbed for her baton out of pure instinct. Then she saw who it was and relaxed.

"Ugh, Edgar. You scared me to death. Don't sneak up on people like that."

Edgar shrugged.

"You gotta maintain situational awareness, bruh. At least, that's what Ronnie's always yelling at us when we're in PVP."

"Sounds like Ronnie." Lynn laughed and scooted over on the bench to make room for Edgar.

A quick bit of subvocalization closed down her TD Hunter

app so she could see her friend unhindered. Like her, he was wearing baggy clothes—jeans and a navy T-shirt advertising a football team she didn't recognize. She wondered if he wore them for the same reasons she did. In their school, having anything less than hard sculpted muscles was an invitation for bullying and ridicule by the "pretty" crowd. He didn't act as self-conscious as she often felt, but maybe that was simply because he was good at hiding his emotions.

"I didn't know you liked football," she said, for lack of anything else to say.

He shrugged again.

"I don't. My dad used to play when I was little, before AR sports got big."

He fell silent and Lynn shifted uncomfortably. She'd never asked him about his family. Having a...complicated family history herself, she knew how awkward it was to be asked a question you really didn't want to talk about, so she'd never pried.

"Um, I hope you like the woods," she finally said, desperate to fill the silence.

"Heh, you kidding? I love the woods. We had a patch on my grandma and grandpa's farm back in Utah. Nice little creek running through it. Paradise, I'm telling you." He grinned at her horrified look. "What? You afraid of a little woods?"

"No, of course not," she huffed. "I just don't like what comes with it. Heat and sweat and mud and bugs. I'd rather look at pictures."

Edgar kept grinning.

"Never bothered me."

And indeed, it didn't seem to, at least not the muggy heat and bright sunshine. Despite the beads of sweat along the line of his close-cropped black hair and the little trickle that had carved a path down his bronze forehead, he seemed as chipper and happy—actually *more* chipper and happy—than she'd ever seen him at school.

"Humph. Well, then I'll tell all the mosquitos to go suck on *you*."

"So, that's how it's gonna go, huh? You fight invisible monsters while I fight the real ones?"

This time Lynn couldn't help grinning back at him.

"Seems only fair. You're a bigger target. Better bait."

"Maaaan, you're ruthless, girl!"

"Hey, somebody's gotta save the world from this monster invasion. You're just doing your part as my backup."

"Your backup, huh? Well if I'm gonna sacrifice myself, you better tell me about this game that's got everybody tied up in knots."

So, she did. She was a little shy about it at first, but Edgar oohed and ahhed in all the right places as she showed him how her baton transformed and how the augments worked. He whistled appreciatively when she showed him her skin with the new armor on it, which made her grin. She even introduced him to Hugo, who he thought was hysterical. By the time she was done, he was more than eager to see her in action—which happened to be exactly what she was most nervous about. But she reminded herself that she had monsters to kill, loot to collect and levels to achieve. She didn't have time for nerves.

"Well, wanna get going?" she asked.

"Heck, yeah. I can't wait to murder me some mosquitos."

They laughed and stood and Lynn led the way toward the greenway. Keeping in mind Hugo's warning, she double checked that everything was at one hundred percent and that she had her Plasma Blade equipped and ready. It had the highest damage per hit of any of her weapons, plus used a fraction of the energy of her Plasma Pistol. According to the Counterforce's monsters index, she might start encountering Ghasts soon, the upgrade of ghosts, and she wanted to be ready for any close-quarter surprise attacks.

"Hey, Edgar?"

"Yup."

"Um, you should probably stay a good five or six feet away from me. Some of these TDMs attack out of the blue and I have to spin and dodge a lot. I don't want to hit you by accident."

"Sure thing," he said, angling to put a little distance between them. "Any chance you can leave your screen projection on, though? You've got me all hyped up now, I wanna see these critters."

"Oh, um, okay. It might be a little hard to see in the sunlight, though. It'll look better once we get into the woods."

Hugo projected her display without her having to ask and while she and Edgar walked, she pointed out the closest dots on her overhead map and summarized her attack strategies for each type of TDM. After that, she had little time for conversation because she left the area she'd already cleared and started getting stalked by ghosts and rushed by gremlins. Edgar moved back more to give her space and she lost track of where he was, focusing instead on her enemies and her attack technique.

They were close to the greenway when she spotted her first new Delta Class monster. She recognized it from the monster index and she stopped at max visible range to consider her approach. The creature was a Grumblin, the next level up of a gremlin. According to its tactical support information, it was highly aggressive and with a much higher attack than gremlins, but like gremlins, it was weak on defense. Additionally, like gremlins, it was more vulnerable from behind.

Switching to her Plasma Pistol, Lynn circled around it, keeping an ear out for sneak attacks. She lined up her targeting reticle carefully on its back, then did a double tap and a third—two rounds to the body, one to the head. The two rounds to the body had the usual effect of temporarily paralyzing the target, but she missed the headshot. She wasn't even sure how effective they were in this game anyway.

The Grumblin was still for a moment then turned and charged her. She gave up finesse, back-pedaling and firing round after round as fast as her shots would cycle. Good thing she didn't need to reload. Most of the rounds were striking the Grumblin, but it kept coming until it was on top of her, slashing at her armor and making her display flash red. She dodged and juked, trying to stay out of reach for a few seconds while she switched to her Plasma Blade. She was only partially successful, but at least once she had her blade out and started laying in on the stupid thing, it didn't last long.

By the time it exploded into sparks, Lynn was sweating freely, though whether from the exertion or the adrenaline surge she wasn't sure. She knew none of it was real, but at every red flash of damage she'd taken, she could imagine the feel of the Grumblin's claws raking across her new armor. She was breathing hard and her blood pounded in her ears as she rested her hands on her knees for a moment to recover.

"Hey…Hugo…you sure Mr. Krator was making a…game and not a…exercise regime when he designed this thing?"

"The two are hardly mutually exclusive, Miss Lynn."

"Humph." Lynn glared at the grass, then pushed upright. She caught sight of Edgar a dozen feet away and at her glance he gave her a huge grin and a double thumbs-up. That improved her mood and she felt slightly more charitable toward a game that was basically tricking her into getting into shape in order to win. It wouldn't be so hard if all she cared about was staying alive, rather than her competitive stats. But where was the fun in that?

She collected her loot in the form of ichor. It seemed like a paltry offering compared to the trouble she'd gone to, but she felt better when she saw the amount the Grumblin had dropped completely refilled her power bar after all those rounds she'd pumped into it.

Satisfied, she turned and waved at Edgar, then headed off again. There were multiple paths that cut through the greenway, made by the feet of various residents over the years crossing from one apartment complex to the other. The closest one she knew about was near the corner of the building she'd already cleared behind earlier, so that's where she headed. On the way she told Edgar about the sounds TDMs made and said she was keeping an ear out for any new sound that might be a Ghast trying to sneak up on her from behind. Though she didn't tell Edgar, she was also keeping an ear out for another Varg's growl. With her new Plasma Blade and Skadi's Glory, she felt much more confident she could take one on without almost dying in front of Edgar, but you could never be too careful.

As they entered the much cooler shade of the woods, however, a Varg wasn't the scary thing she found. Fortunately, she saw and heard it about the same time it detected her. She recognized it as a demon, the upgrade of an imp. The only good thing about it was that it didn't charge aggressively the second it saw her. Beyond that silver lining, everything else about it sucked—for her at least. It was armored on its heavy-set shoulders and chest, which meant shots to its center of mass weren't going to be very effective. The claws on the thing were massive, each one easily longer than her palm, though it only stood about as tall as she did herself.

After pointing it out to Edgar and warning him back, Lynn stood there and considered her options. The demon eyed her right back and she could swear the thing was sizing her up. She shifted from side to side and its gaze tracked her as if it knew exactly where she was and was only waiting for its chance to pounce. Goosebumps popped out on her arms, despite the heat. Stupid, creepy little lowlife.

She had less maneuvering room in these woods, so she decided on a frontal assault like with the Grumblin. This time she would be prepared to dodge and switch weapons. Switching to Plasma Pistol, she set her feet, bent her knees slightly, aimed and started pouring fire into her target. Like the Grumblin, the demon seemed to be momentarily stunned by the onslaught, but then it charged. When it got close, she switched to Plasma Blade and was able to dodge and swipe at the monster as it charged past her, much like a matador at a bullfight. It turned all too fast, however, and was on her again in a second. She gritted her teeth and took the damage, stabbing and slicing while backing up as best she could on the uneven path. It took longer than the Grumblin to kill and by the time it disappeared her health was in the yellow despite all her armor.

Lynn relaxed and let out a breath, then tensed as her display flashed red. What the heck? The demon was dead! That's when she heard the sibilant hiss behind her and she spun to stab the attacking Ghast in the face. She'd read up on these buggers too and like many TDMs, it seemed they were more vulnerable to the rear. Unfortunately, they had heightened detection and so circling them only made them spin to keep their ghostly, tentaclelike arms at the front. TDMs weren't "real" though, no matter how real the game itself felt.

Lynn had already decided on a tactic to try. Instead of backing up and continuing to slash as the Ghast chased her down, she jumped straight through it, spinning as she did to keep slashing at its now exposed back. It reacted quickly, spinning to face her, but she simply jumped through it again, continuing the onslaught with her Plasma Blade. After the third time she jumped through it, it finally exploded into sparks, which was fortunate because she suddenly felt dizzy to the point of nausea. She wobbled, foot catching on a root in the path and was saved from toppling over by Edgar's unexpected helping hand.

"Whoa, there, wonder woman. You okay? That was seriously epic."

"Yeah," Lynn panted, shaking her head to clear it. Did she have vertigo or something? She'd been spinning plenty fighting TDMs for the past couple weeks and after that first day or two it rarely bothered her unless she was dehydrated or hadn't eaten for too long. "I'm gonna sit for a sec. You thirsty?"

"Uh, sure. Sorry, didn't think to bring water or anything for myself."

"No worries, I brought an extra water bottle and energy bar for you."

After she gathered her loot—three plates from the demon and two globes from the Ghast, not to mention plenty of ichor—she exited combat mode and they sat on a nearby log to eat and drink. Lynn felt better almost right away, so she chalked the dizziness up to not taking care of herself. She needed to remember to resupply in the real just as much as in the game. Now that she was sitting, her body reminded her that she was not, in fact, a superhero but an average, out-of-shape teenager.

She told her body to go stuff it.

Before they set off again, she took a moment to replace her plates and globes, then used one precious Oneg capsule. To her delight, it took her health from twenty percent up to full. If she was going to meet more demons, Grumblins and Ghasts in these woods, she would need it.

Hopefully some of these higher strength monsters would start dropping some good augments for her to use. After a quick apology to Edgar, she also switched her display back to retinal projection. In the close quarters of the woods, she needed every edge she could get and she was able to react quicker and attack more accurately when she saw things as through a tactical helmet rather than hovering in front of her.

Since the display was gone, Lynn felt a little guilty, thinking Edgar might get bored, so as they delved deeper into the woods she started asking careful questions about his gaming with Ronnie and the rest. It was a safe topic and Edgar seemed to enjoy joking about how seriously their three friends took it all. Lynn was able to clear the lower-class TDMs they encountered almost without thinking, but whenever she met one of the stronger monsters, she waved to Edgar to let him know and focused her full attention on every second of her battles, her mind busily tracking patterns and noticing little details that would help her in subsequent fights.

The woods weren't thick, but there was enough underbrush between the trees that Lynn took every opportunity to lure her targets onto the path before engaging. One particularly stubborn demon she had to go off-trail to take out. She ended up jumping sideways straight into a bramble patch. Her jeans kept her from getting too cut-up, but she had to pause after the demon and its accompanying Ghost were dead so she could pick thorns from her pant legs.

"You know, you're pretty good at this."

Edgar's comment took her by surprise and she looked up to see him grinning.

"For a girl," he added with a bit of mischief in his smile. "I think Ronnie has no idea what he's missing out on."

Lynn forced herself to laugh, though her throat felt distinctly dry.

"Oh, I don't know. These sort of 'bloody' games aren't really my thing."

"Huh. Could'a fooled me. You look like a natural."

This time Lynn's face heated uncomfortably and she was grateful for the shaded gloom of the woods around her. She muttered something about "luck" and got back to brushing off her jeans.

"No, seriously, Lynn. You're really good at this," Edgar persisted. "Heck, I couldn't do half the moves you're doing and you've been playing this for, what, a few weeks? Here, I took a vid of your last fight, so I could show you. Don't worry, I *promise* I'll delete it as soon as I show you, if you want," he rushed to say at her horrified look. "I wanted you to see yourself in action."

Lynn was torn but eventually gave in to Edgar's coaxing and exited combat mode for a minute to watch the video he messaged her. To her complete astonishment, it wasn't as horrifyingly embarrassing as she'd expected it to be. In fact, it was kind of cool. Obviously you couldn't see what she was fighting, but it wasn't hard to imagine the invisible enemy that she dodged and lunged at. Her movements looked controlled. Purposeful. Not exactly graceful or flowing, but at least she didn't look like an insane mime flailing incoherently. Well, at least until she jumped sideways into that thorn bush. That was honestly pretty funny, even if it had hurt like the blazes. She really should start doing some of those training walkthroughs on the TD Hunter app. She needed to improve her form. Who knew, she might eventually get good enough to look pretty impressive, at least to other Hunters who could see her space Viking armor and the monsters she was annihilating.

When the vid was over, she couldn't think of anything to say that wouldn't reveal more than she wanted, so she simply shrugged, feeling uncomfortable. Pulling the guys' chain as a group at school felt very different than hiding the truth from Edgar specifically. It felt disingenuous. But if she admitted she'd been hard-core gaming for years, she'd have to admit she'd been lying about it all this time. He was such a loyal, honest kind of guy, what if he decided she wasn't worthy of his friendship anymore?

The silence stretched on, so Lynn said, "Thanks for showing me. It's kinda cool, I guess. But I still look pretty silly. Definitely delete the vid, if you don't mind. I'd rather not show up on some 'AR gaming fails' stream or something."

"No worries, Lynn. I already deleted it. I just think you're selling yourself short. You ever think about playing WarMonger? I know Ronnie is a jerk about it, but I wouldn't mind playing with you if you wanted to hang out sometime."

"Oh no. No, no, no," Lynn said, raising her hands in protest and shaking her head vigorously. Her adrenaline had spiked at the mere suggestion. "That's *really* not my thing. Besides, I have to focus on getting hours in for TD Hunter. They picked me to beta. They expect feedback, you know?"

"No worries. Just a thought."

"Yeah, thanks but no thanks," Lynn said. For some reason, Edgar seemed disappointed. She couldn't fathom why. He wasn't that into gaming anyway. Maybe he was desperate for a break from Ronnie? "Well, uh, I'd better get back to hunting. I'm hoping to hit Level 6 today if I can."

"Sure thing. I'm right behind you."

She'd taken some damage from that last demon—she still hadn't figured out a good method of attack—but it wasn't enough to justify using Oneg, so she decided to walk it off by exiting the greenway on the opposite side and walking along it behind the Heathers apartment buildings. That would give her more room to maneuver and avoid stronger TDMs while she walked off the damage. She and Edgar chatted about summer plans while they walked. He was starting a part-time job on a landscaping crew next week. Lynn was happy for him, since he seemed to really enjoy the outdoors, but inside she was cursing her luck, since it would mean he had less time to be her hunting buddy.

Walking along behind the Heathers apartment buildings, Lynn found plenty of weaker TDMs that she took out easily. She eased up on armor and globe use, trying to build up a stockpile from ghosts, grinder worms and crusher worms, the upgrade from the smaller grinders. The crusher worm was, thankfully, slower, but its "vulnerable" spot was about as vulnerable as the most heavily armored part of grinder worms. Even with her Plasma Blade, it took twice as many hits to kill them and her legs were starting to ache from all the dodging and leaping she'd been doing for the past few hours.

Once they'd made it to the end of the Heathers apartments along the greenway, they took another break for water and protein bars. Lynn asked if Edgar wanted to take a break to go grab a burger or something, but he shook his head.

"I like being outside," Edgar said, pulling out a pack of gum and offering it to her. When she shook her head he popped in a stick and masticated it slowly. "We don't have any green spaces near where I live. 'Sides, we need to get you leveled, right? If you're good, I'm good."

Lynn laughed and commented that she wasn't really "good," just stubborn as a mule. She wanted to go back into the woods and work back down toward her apartment building, now that her health was back up. She still needed to figure out how to effectively kill demons without taking so much damage and she needed the extra experience points higher level TDMs brought. Plus, she wanted more augments. She'd collected a few so far that day, but their bonuses were all very small, hardly worth bothering with. Stronger monsters meant better loot.

As if the TDMs had heard her thoughts, she spotted a demon as soon as she and Edgar went back into the woods. They weren't following any particular path, just picking their way through the thinner underbrush. She'd filled back up on plates and globes before she'd re-entered the woods, pushing her stealth and detection to the max and it seemed she'd spotted the demon soon enough that she wasn't yet in its range. It wasn't looking at her, just glaring malevolently through the trees at the nearest apartment building.

Based on what Hugo had told her, she knew TDMs couldn't hear her "normal" sounds, but she tried as well as she could to move through the trees stealthily as she circled the demon to get behind it, leaving Edgar where he was to watch through the trees. She didn't have much luck being quiet, since she had no real woodland training. But she got behind the demon without incident and without detecting any accompanying Ghasts. After looking around and making sure she had some room to move, she crouched in a ready stance and started firing, pouring as many shots into its unarmored back as possible. It spun to charge straight toward her, ignoring trees and bushes as if they weren't there—which they weren't, to it.

This time, though, when it was close enough and she switched to her Plasma Blade, instead of standing her ground and meeting it head on or trying to dodge to the side without getting caught by its swift slash, she took a chance. The only damage she'd ever taken was from its claws and teeth, both of which struck her at roughly shoulder-level. The demon's large, ugly, taloned, feet never seemed to do any damage. So, she ducked the first attack and rolled through its legs. Literally through them since they were insubstantial.

Her roll was awkward and slow and she wasn't sure what to do with her Plasma Blade. She tried to hold it out to the side so she wouldn't squash it. But even so, she was able to come up on one knee and pivoted in a backward slash that resulted in a red flash of damage on the demon while she completely avoided the demon's swipe.

The demon, of course, turned right around and came back at her, claws slashing. She barely had time to get to her feet and reset in a crouch, ready to roll again. The maneuver left her dizzy, but she managed it three more times, each feeling a little more natural until she was able to get in two strikes at the monster's back before it was out of her reach. After her fourth attack, the demon burst into a shower of sparks. She let out a gusty sigh of relief and plopped down on her butt right there in the leaves.

"That was epic!" Edgar said, winding his way through the trees to get to her.

"I think I really need to practice my front rolls," Lynn said with a laugh. "It feels really awkward and I don't know what to do with my sword hand while I'm rolling."

"Practice makes perfect, right?" Edgar said and reached down a hand to help her up.

She stood, subvocalizing to Hugo for a battle report to make sure her own assessment of her tactic was correct. It was. She'd taken no damage at all. Of course, she was covered in dirt and leaves, had several new bruises from rocks she'd rolled over and generally felt beat up. None of that mattered amid the triumph of her discovery, though.

The triumph didn't last long, as the Ghast she'd known was

bound to be around somewhere chose that moment to attack from behind. She managed not to smack Edgar in the face with her Plasma Blade as she spun, but she did end up almost running into a tree and stubbing her toe on a root before she could kill the stupid TDM. She was starting to really hate the stealthy ones. Her annoyance was assuaged when she saw it had dropped an item. It was a generic personal augment which boosted her overall stealth by five percent. Not bad. She equipped it to use until she found something better.

Their progress back through the woods was slow but productive. Lynn got plenty more practice improving her roll attack. It still made her feel dizzy to roll through the demon, but it was worth it to avoid all damage.

At one point nearly halfway back to her apartment, she stumbled on something super weird. It was a double circle of TDMs, with crusher worms and gremlins staggered in the outer circle and a wall of demons and Grumblins standing shoulder to shoulder making up the inner circle. It appeared on her overhead map much like the circle had near the lake at the Heathers complex. Being a higher level now, she could see them from farther out than at the lake and she stopped as soon as she saw them, not wanting to get close enough to attract their attention.

"Hugo, could you project my display?" she subvocalized.

"Certainly, Miss Lynn," Hugo said.

"Hey, Edgar, take a look at this," Lynn said and waved her friend over.

"Whoa. That's a lot of monsters. You gonna tackle that bunch?"

"Are you kidding me? It'd be suicide. Even if I charged right through them to attack their backs, then I'd be completely surrounded. They'd make mincemeat out of me. I'm just wondering... does it look to you like they're guarding something?"

"Yeah, it kinda does," Edgar said. He chewed gum for a bit, scrunching up his face and looking at the display. "It's hard to see into the middle of them all, though. I can't tell if there's anything in there or not."

Lynn had her suspicions. Just because she couldn't *see* more TDMs in that circle didn't mean they weren't there. Maybe there was some high-class monster in the center?

"Hey, Hugo, do you think the app would glitch again if I got close?" she subvocalized.

"While I admire your spirit of scientific inquiry, Miss Lynn, I would not advise it. Remember, if you can see them, they can see you, or at least they might. Stealth is not always foolproof and some higher-class TDMs employ their own stealth as well. All you need is for one to target you and then the game is up, as the saying goes."

"Yeah." She stood there for a moment, weighing the risks. Finally, she decided to let it go. If she died, the penalty debuff would reduce all her stats to half and she'd be basically crippled. She didn't want to lose an hour of gaining experience just to satisfy her curiosity.

"Come on, Edgar. Maybe when I'm a higher level, I'll come back and check these guys out."

They gave the odd cluster a wide berth, then continued clearing the greenway. Unfortunately for her kill to damage ratio, both Grumblins and Ghasts had attacks that reached close to the ground, so she couldn't use her new roll-through technique on them. But Grumblins were slower than demons and she got better at the back and forth dodging to avoid their most powerful slashes. Ghasts she was starting to truly hate. She didn't like the damage she took jumping through them to kill them quickly from behind, but she couldn't seem to back up fast enough to stay away from them either.

They were nearing the point along the greenway that was closest to her apartment building when Lynn got the unknown TDM alert on her display and in her ear from Hugo. Unfortunately, the unknown was parked right in the middle of a thick patch of brush, so she couldn't circle around to get a better idea of what she was walking into. With all the loot and experience she'd gotten from her first unknown, though, there was no way she was going to leave this one be. So, she equipped her Plasma Pistol, stood at the very edge of her detection range, then started pouring fire into it. No sooner had the first bolt left her pistol's muzzle than she was inundated by return fire, the red bolts streaking out from a thick patch of brush. She jumped back, nearly running into Edgar, who immediately stepped off to the side to give her room to fight whatever invisible thing she was trying to avoid.

Several paces back, she finally seemed to leave the monster's detection range and the fire ceased. Lynn took stock while grumbling to herself under her breath.

"I do not believe that TDMs technically *have* mothers, Miss Lynn and even if they did, they do not have the correct anatomy to accomplish such a feat as you describe."

"Newsflash, Hugo," she subvocalized, "when people curse under their breath, it's not so you can critique their style."

"Understood, Miss Lynn, I was simply pointing out—"

"Unless you have something constructive to tell me about this unknown, then shut it, will you?"

"Ah, of course. It is a probable Delta Class-3 or 4 and possesses a significant ranged attack."

"No duh, Einstein."

"No other details could be ascertained in the brief time your battle system had to analyze the target."

"Surprise, surprise," Lynn subvocalized. She could no longer see the sparkling mist that represented her target, but she'd kept her eyes fixed on the point in the brush where the bolts had come from. "Hugo, can you mark the point I'm looking at as the bogie's probable location?"

An aiming reticle appeared right on target and she looked away to double check her armor and globes. She switched out a few of each that were nearing depletion, then checked her health. The bar had been full before she'd run into the unknown and now it was down at ninety percent. The unknown had gotten off five or so shots in the few seconds she'd been within range, which did not bode well for her ultimate survival. On the other hand, it was nearing dinnertime, she was exhausted and she still had Oneg to use in a pinch. If she was outmatched and ended up dying, it wouldn't ruin her entire day.

"Hey, Lynn, you okay?" Edgar asked from his spot off to the side. Apparently she'd been standing there glaring at nothing for long enough that he'd gotten worried.

"Yeah, I'm good. I just found a really strong unknown and I'm deciding the best way to attack it. I might end up dying, but hey, no pain no gain." She shrugged.

"That's the spirit!" Hugo said in her ear.

"I'm sure you'll totally kick its butt," Edgar offered, his expression one hundred percent sincere.

"Yeah, well, we'll see," Lynn said and made her decision. She had no idea how much damage this monster could sustain, so in a straight firefight, her chances probably weren't good. Based on the last unknown she'd found, it would probably be more effective to charge in and stab it to death with her heaviest hitter, her Plasma Blade. Not that she wanted to rush into that thick brush, but it was that or give up on a pile of experience and rewards for ID-ing another unknown.

"All right, you miserable bastard," she muttered. "It's you or me. Let's do this."

She charged. Within a few steps, the unknown reappeared in her targeting display and she immediately started shooting as she ran. Right away her fire was returned and her vision flashed a rhythmic red as she took hit after hit. She bore down on the sparkling mist, but as she neared, the entity began to retreat.

"Oh no you don't!" Lynn growled, executing a swift weapon change. She lunged for her enemy, stabbing and slashing with the same moves she used on Grumblins. The mist flashed red with every strike and she could only hope she was doing significant damage and not simply glancing off an armored front. She was taking steady damage herself and figured she could only keep this up for another twenty or thirty seconds before she had to back off.

The problem was the thing kept retreating. It even started dodging side to side to avoid her swipes and she had a heck of a time keeping up with it through the brush. Branches tore at her clothes and she caught more than one faceful of leaves as she used her free arm to try and clear herself a path. Her Plasma Blade handle was starting to feel uncomfortably warm. She gripped it tighter in her sweaty hand and kept swinging, trying to gain some ground on the retreating mist.

And then she ran into a tree.

She bounced off the solid trunk and fell backward on her butt, landing awkwardly on the slender omni-polymer of her Plasma Blade. She felt something snap beneath her, her AR display went blank and then she smelled smoke.

"Holy—" Lynn yelled and rolled away, then scuttled backward away from the smoking and sparking Plasma Blade. To her horror, a tiny lick of flame appeared where the weapon was touching the dry bed of leaves. She froze, knowing she should do something but in too much shock to think what it was. That was when Edgar appeared, bulldozing through the undergrowth like a mountain bear and started stomping on the Plasma Blade. It was soon pounded quite thoroughly into the dirt and he finally stopped attacking it.

"You okay, Lynn? I, uh, heard you yell and couldn't see anything, so I just came running..."

"Y-yeah. I'm fine. Must've been some weird equipment malfunction. I mean, I did run into a tree, but I'm pretty sure I'll heal fine from that."

Edgar sucked in a breath through his teeth in sympathy.

"Yeah, you got quite a bump on your forehead, there. I think the tree won that one."

That startled a reluctant chuckle out of Lynn and she finally took a deep breath and let it out as the adrenaline of her fight started to fade.

"Yeah, you're probably right. Now help me up will you?"

He offered her a hand and she groaned as she got to her feet. She was definitely going to have some bruises tomorrow.

Lynn walked over to her poor, abused Plasma Blade and poked it with her toe, feeling a sick pit form in her stomach. Nothing happened, so she bent and gingerly picked it up. It was snapped in half and the two halves were partially melted at the breaking point, their form halfway between a blade and baton. It still felt unusually warm. Definitely some kind of malfunction, but what had caused it? Her falling on it because she was a moronic klutz? Probably. Edgar's stomping hadn't helped, she was sure, but it had already caught flame by then. It was not going to be fun explaining this to TD Hunter's technical support team.

Speaking of technical support... she took off her AR glasses and examined them. There were a few scratches, but other than that, the impact with the tree didn't seem to have damaged them. That was a relief since they were probably *way* more expensive than the baton she'd broken.

She tried to bring up her LINC menu to restart the app and felt the sick pit in her stomach drop down between her toes as she realized that her LINC was unresponsive. Her fancy, new, custom LINC that Mr. Krator had given her. But what had happened to it? It didn't look damaged. Maybe it had gotten jostled in all the ruckus? All she could do was go home, re-sync with her old LINC and hope that TD Hunter technical support was understanding.

"Well, I guess we're done for the day," she sighed. "I think I broke my LINC."

"Man, really? I'm sorry, Lynn. That sucks."

"Yeah. But at least it means I can take a shower and get out of these sweaty clothes."

Edgar laughed.

"You look like you went a couple rounds with a mountain lion, Lynn, I'm telling you."

"Ha, ha. Very funny."

"I'm serious! Just wait till you get home and look at yourself in the mirror."

Lynn rolled her eyes but couldn't be mad, not at the easy humor in Edgar's face. Then she looked down at herself and gasped. He was right. She was absolutely covered in dirt and leaves and there were several tears in her baggy shirt. Plus, the shirt was thoroughly soaked with sweat around her arm and chest area and she suddenly became acutely aware of how it clung to her curvy frame. Edgar didn't seem to notice—at least not in the way males in general had always seemed to notice and been unable to keep their eyes off her chest ever since she'd hit puberty. Even without that, though, she felt even hotter and itchier than ever and had to resist the urge to cross her arms over her chest to hide it from view.

"Look, let's just get back to the apartment, okay?"

They trudged out of the woods and through her complex, all the while Edgar spinning a more and more ridiculous tale about the supposed mountain lion she'd wrestled. She let him do it. He seemed to think it was hysterical.

"Why, Miz Raven. Are you quite all right? Are you in need of assistance?"

The elderly voice took Lynn by surprise and she looked up to see Mr. Thomas coming out of the apartment complex's activity center. He looked quite alarmed and when his eyes flicked to Edgar, his expression was wary.

It took Lynn a second to realize what was going on and when she did, her face blazed with embarrassment.

"What? Oh—*Ohhhhh*, no, no, no, Mr. Thomas, I'm fine, really. This is my *friend*, Edgar Johnston. He's been hanging out with me while I've been hunting monsters in the greenway. Remember, you said to take a friend if I was going in the woods?"

The old man visibly relaxed and he smiled.

"Well, if I'd known your excursion would be quite so harrowing, I would have advised you to take multiple friends."

"See?" Edgar said and nudged her in the ribs. "I told you. Mountain lion."

"I beg pardon, young man?"

"Nothing," Lynn jumped in, wanting to escape the situation as quickly as possible. "Thanks for checking up on me, Mr. Thomas. I appreciate it. Those woods are just thick with brush and you know TD Hunter is pretty physical. I'm going home to clean up now."

"A wise decision," Mr. Thomas said and his eyes seemed to twinkle with good-natured humor. His gaze also didn't drift down to her chest the way she'd come to expect from men and she felt a rush of gratitude.

"Well, see you around, Mr. Thomas," Lynn said.

"It was a pleasure to meet you, young man," the old man said and tipped an imaginary hat with his boney hand.

"You too, Mr. Thomas," Edgar said with a respectful nod.

They continued on and once out of earshot Edgar chuckled.

"I'm gonna hafta start calling you 'Lynn the Mountain Lion Wrestler' or something."

"Don't even think about it," Lynn said in her most intimidating tone.

"Yeah, I guess it don't quite roll off the tongue," Edgar said, chewing gum and looking at the sky for inspiration. "How 'bout 'Lynn: Warrior Princess'?"

"No."

"Lynn Queen of the Wastelands?"

"Oh, shut up."

"For real, though, you were awesome today," Edgar said. "You actually make me want to play once the game comes out. I wasn't gonna, cuz I'm getting this job and everything. But if you play with me, I think it'd be maxed-out fun."

Lynn pretended to grumble a little more, but inside she glowed. It felt so good to finally share something she really loved with a friend who wasn't just an avatar in virtual. As long as Edgar didn't ask any more awkward questions about how she'd been picked as beta, it would be great.

When they reached the entrance to her apartment building, they both stopped and stood for a moment in awkward silence. Was he waiting for her to do something?

"Well, uh, see you around, I guess?" Edgar said and stuck his hands in his pockets, slowly chewing.

"Yeah," Lynn said. "Um, thanks a lot for hanging out with me today. You probably saved me from starting a forest fire or something."

The joke felt weak but Edgar threw his head back and laughed. He had a booming laugh, like a bass drum. It was good to see him so expressive compared to how guarded he'd always been at school.

"Maybe next time we'll find some critter for you to wrestle," he said after he'd taken a breath. "You could always start with a stray cat and work your way up."

Lynn mock glared at him.

"Get out of here."

Still chortling, he waved and turned to go.

"Ping me when you get your stuff fixed," he called over his shoulder. "I'd love to be there when you take out that last one you missed."

"Yeah. I'll let you know."

Not wanting to stare awkwardly after him, Lynn turned and trudged into her building. She was thoroughly worn out, her legs ached and now that Edgar was gone, the sick feeling in her stomach was back. She really, *really* hoped the TD Hunter people weren't mad at her for breaking their equipment.

Chapter 7

WHEN SHE GOT UP TO HER APARTMENT, HER MOM WAS STILL asleep. Matilda usually slept late on Saturdays, waking up in time to fix dinner with Lynn. That particular Saturday, Lynn was profoundly grateful for this fact. If her mom saw her walk in the door in her disheveled state, she would probably think Lynn had been attacked and raped or something. It was no wonder Mr. Thomas had seemed worried when he'd first seen her.

She slipped on comfy shorts and a T-shirt and went to flop down on her bed.

It was the work of a moment to get her old LINC back up and connected to her TD Hunter issue earbuds. She tried to ignore the knots in her stomach as she pulled up the game's website and selected "contact technical support" from their menu.

"TD Hunter technical support. This is James, how can I help you?"

Lynn had needed to call tech support a few times for other games in the past and was used to dealing with a service AI or going through a huge wait before she talked to an actual person. Getting straight through surprised her.

"Umm...This is Lynn Raven," she said after a second's confusion. "I'm one of the beta testers."

"Hey, Lynn! Thanks for giving us a call," James said. "It looks like the new LINC we sent you has gone completely dark. I see you were engaged with an unknown when it disconnected. Was your LINC damaged during that encounter?"

"Sort of...?" Lynn said. "I, uh, kind of ran into a tree and fell. Maybe my hand accidentally hit something? But that wasn't the weird thing, because right after I fell, my baton started going nuts. Like, nearly blew up nuts. It was sparking and smoking and it almost caught the leaves on fire. I had a friend with me and he can vouch for it. He had to stomp out the fire. I mean, I'm not gonna lie, I think I might have fallen on it and broken it before it started going haywire. But just breaking it in half shouldn't have made it catch on fire, should it?"

"Not as far as I know," James said. "But there is precedent for a beta tester's LINC malfunctioning after a piece of game equipment is damaged, so I'm going to list it all as 'potential game damage' with the comment that there was suspected impact damage first. But we'll replace them both free of charge anyway. Your Hunter scores are quite high but we'd like to see more beta reports. Not just glitch reports but comments on fighting methods and such."

There was a brief pause, then James whistled.

"Wow, you really racked up some kills before you encountered that unknown. You're taking on Delta Class-3s and 4s already? You need to talk to Tactical Support, not a tech guy like me. I've already put in an order for a duplicate LINC to be printed and we'll include a new baton when it ships. It'll be sent via overnight delivery, so you should get it pretty quickly. Now, mind if I transfer you? I've got a ping from Tactical Support. They'd like to talk to you."

"Okay...?" Lynn said hesitantly. "But there are lots of people doing better than I am."

"Who?" James asked.

"Well, there's a guy in New York who's up to Level 20, isn't there?" Lynn said, thinking about the people she'd seen commenting on the community boards.

"KillBot," James said. "He's been going through Oneg like it's water and he's been killed plenty of times. Just buys up his inventory and goes back to hunting. Which isn't how you're supposed to play the game. Additionally, he's a bicycle messenger so he's all over the place all the time and you gain health at bicycle movement rates. Don't compare yourself to that. You've currently got one of the highest kills to damage ratios in beta. How in the world did you manage to kill seven demons with almost no damage? That's what Tactical is screaming at me about."

"Oh, that," Lynn said, grinning. "I roll under them."

"You what?" James said. "Hang on, I'm bringing in Steve on the tactical side. You mind?"

"No, that's fine." Lynn replied.

"Steve, this is Lynn Raven, BetaTester124," James said. "Lynn, this is Steve, AlphaTester9."

Lynn's ears perked. An alpha tester? It seemed her guess about alpha testers being employees had been correct.

"Pleasure to finally talk to you, Lynn," Steve said. He had a sharp staccato delivery that was very militaryesque, sort of like First Sergeant Kane Bryce from the opening cinematic for the game, or like some of the elites in WarMonger she talked to from time to time. She'd tried to copy the way they talked when she was playing Larry, since it made him sound more authentic.

"I have to say," Steve continued, "I've been hoping you'd call Tactical sometime soon, 'Larry Coughlin.' We've battled before. As allies and enemies. FallujahSevenNiner. You copy?"

"Fallu," Lynn said, grinning. "Yeah! Roger that, Fallu! I thought your voice sounded familiar."

"They gave us a look at the potential beta testers and their gaming background before we started recruiting," Steve said. "I spit a mouthful of bourbon on my screen when I found out the 'Boss Snake' who kept putting me in the ground in WarMonger was some teenager. You got mad skills. If you were male you'd be a natural operator."

"Um..." Lynn said with a grimace. She hadn't expected to get the "girls got no game" thing from a guy like Fallu.

"Lynn, James again," the tech guy put in hastily. "What he meant was as a member of a SEAL team or Delta or something. Steve is... He used to be in the Army. He means in the real soldier stuff. Not gaming."

"Oooh," Lynn said, feeling relieved. "Well, thanks, I guess. But even this game is killing me."

"You've got zero PT experience," Steve said. "Not surprising. To work, though. Seven demons. Ten percent total health loss. Twenty percent armor loss. How? I've fought demons and I take five times that damage."

"Roll under," Lynn said. "For some reason they never bend over to reach you with their claws when they strike and they're not real, so no reason you can't go through them. The feet talons do no damage. Get them in an open area, equip a melee weapon and roll under them to attack from underneath and behind. Just get up on a knee, hit them as they turn, then roll under again. Confuses the heck out of the game AI."

"Roll under," Steve said. "Jeez. Obvious now that I think about it. But like I said: mad skills, girl. Tough on concrete, though. You'd want some padding."

"I got covered in dirt and leaves from fighting them in the woods," Lynn admitted. "And I collected a lot of bramble scratches. This outdoors stuff is kind of fun now that I'm getting used to it, plus the fresh air is nice. But I still feel like I have no idea what I'm doing in the woods."

"Check for ticks, yet?" Steve asked.

"Ticks?" Lynn squealed. "No!"

"Take a shower, if you haven't already," Steve said. "Do as good a check on yourself as you can. Parent? Mom according to the file."

"Yeah," Lynn said, a bit confused by the "file" reference. Maybe the gamer background he'd been talking about?

"Get your mom to check where you can't," Steve said. "Scalp. Back of the neck. Ears."

"Ugh! This is why I always hated the outdoors. Can't you AR game developers take a break from designing games to invent an anti-bug force field or something?"

"Comes with the territory, Hunter," Steve said with a chuckle. "No pain, no gain. Okay, next. You're also lower than average damage on Ghasts and ghosts."

"Well, ghosts you just spin when you hear them come up and you can take them down with a single strike from a Nano Blade," Lynn said. "Ghasts are tougher. I hate them. Best I've found so far is to just run through them and spin to attack from behind, same as with demons. They're more vulnerable on the rear. You do take damage when you run through, though. Tentacles and stuff. It makes me a little dizzy because I'm not used to all that spinning but it's better than trying to fight them head on."

"Hmm," said Steve and there was a pause, as if he were considering his words. "Taking damage to achieve a tactically superior position isn't always a bad idea. But when there's millions of players, every percentage point of your battle score will matter. Suggestion: Hit them with your pistol, then run. Back away, go in again. Keep going and you'll eventually take them out. That way you avoid the damage entirely."

"They move faster than I run," Lynn admitted.

"Learn to run faster," Steve said, a grin obvious in his voice. "You started doing any of the training simulations in the app yet?"

"No, though I did see them. They look pretty cool. I've just... well, I've never done anything like that before."

"Start doing them *today*. Or at least some kind of training regime. You've got a natural talent for this. Born fighter, I'd say. But that won't get you far if you don't treat your body like the weapon it is."

Lynn groaned.

"More you sweat, less you bleed." Steve chuckled. "But the way you're going, if you commit to this game like you've committed to others in the past, you'll see a world of difference before you know it. Now, that unknown you tangled with today. Anything you can tell us about it that wasn't clear in game?"

It took Lynn a moment for her mind to switch gears and she thought about it.

"Its detection range seemed bigger than mine. It hit me even after I could no longer see it."

"Yup," Steve said. "We got that much of the data on upload. Anything else?"

"Well, it didn't attack until I shot first," Lynn said.

"We got that on the first approach but then on the second attack we only got that you'd gone in and then LOS, loss of signal," Steve said. "You're saying that when you approached, again, it didn't attack till you'd attacked?"

"Roger," Lynn said, mimicking Steve's military lingo. It was how she normally talked in WarMonger anyway.

"That we didn't get," Steve said. "Anything else?"

"The bolts looked pretty identical to my Plasma Pistol's shots," Lynn said. "At least, they looked the same in game except for the color."

"Practically identical including damage," Steve responded. "That we also got. I'm going to do a WAG."

"What's that?" Lynn asked.

"A wild guess?" Steve said.

"I mean, what is the WAG," Lynn replied.

"Oh. It's probably related to the..." Steve seemed to search his notes, "to the Lecta you found."

"Er, how so?"

Steve paused and there was absolute silence for a few moments. Had he muted himself? Then his voice was back.

"The following information is part of the NDA you and your mom signed. The AI our programmers created to run the game is...a little opaque. When we say these entities, these TDMs, are unknown, we mean *we* don't even know what they are. The data is encrypted and how the AI assigns them is also unknown.

"But, in general, when you run into two unknowns with similarities in the same area, they tend to be upgrades from one to the other. Therefore, this is probably a higher-class version of the Lecta. Why it's out in the woods instead of around electricity... unknown. Based on that WAG, stay away for now. Rankings in each class correspond roughly two to one from hunter to monster, so if you're Level 1 or 2, you can handle Delta Class-1s, Level 3 or 4, Delta Class-2s. You're taking on way tougher monsters than most beta testers do starting out. I can respect that. You're good. Real good. But sometimes you just gotta grind for a while. Spread out from where you've been. Build up your inventory, build up your experience, then tackle some bigger stuff."

"But I thought, once I was high enough level to detect a monster, then it was fair game? Doesn't the system prevent Hunters from showing up to TDMs too high class for them to handle?"

"In theory," Steve said slowly. "Like I said, we don't exactly control how the AI assigns the entities. It's a closed system. Sorry I can't give you more but I'm just here to game. I don't do the techie stuff. If you want a better explanation, you'll have to drag the programmers out of their lair. If I had to make another WAG, though, I'd say the AI is adapting to meet demand. Revealing higher-class monsters sooner than it would for other players because of your aggression and high scores."

Lynn thought about that. It was actually kinda cool. Also, slightly unfair, since it stacked the deck against her in terms of keeping her scores high.

"I'll think about it," she finally said. "The only way to really build up experience is to go for the big guys and unknowns and I've barely got two weeks before beta phase is over."

"Printing a new LINC every few days for the same beta tester will get noticed pretty quick," Steve said, chuckling. "Look, I've been doing this for a while and I had the same approach at the beginning. Let's just say, I was pushing the game AI's buttons on purpose. Painful experience convinced me that, as you hit certain levels, you've just got to spend some time grinding. That is, unless you want to end up very dead."

The way he said it made it sound like there were worse consequences to dying beyond the one hour "chill of death" debuff. Lynn made a mental note to do some additional research on it. She didn't want to nuke her player ranking on accident.

"Okay," Lynn said. "I'll take your advice under serious advisement."

"Bullheaded, just like me," Steve said with an obvious grin in his voice. "You'll learn. You going to play WarMonger in the meantime?"

"Not much else to do until my new LINC comes in," Lynn said. "Unless I can download the app on my old LINC and use that for now?"

"If the game was live, you could do that," Steve said. "But since it's still in beta, they need you to use our equipment to make sure we get all the right error code and bug reports to get things shipshape."

"Oh, okay. WarMonger it is, then, I guess."

"Roger that. Out here," Steve said, "unless I see you later in battle, of course."

"Don't blow my cover," Lynn said, suddenly worried.

"And get my a—my butt handed to me for breaking my NDA?" Steve said. "Don't worry, I wouldn't anyway. I don't want you turning those mad skills on me. Good hunting, Lynn. Tactical Support, out."

"Lynn, this is James again," James said as Steve's connection went dead. "Before you go, please remember we need the damaged LINC and baton back so we can diagnose their malfunction. You'll get a prepaid addressed package; all you have to do is pop them in it and schedule a drone pickup. Please don't forget."

"I won't," Lynn said. "Thanks for the help."

"You're doing great," James said. "Glad to help. Anything else?"

"Nope," Lynn said. "Bye."

"Goodbye."

After the agent disconnected, Lynn rolled over onto her back and stared at the ceiling, thinking.

She felt good. More than good, really, she felt great. Yes, her muscles were sore and tired. Yes, she was covered in scratches. She thought she might have even twisted something doing all the rolling and stuff. But under it all was a sort of bone deep satisfaction that made it all worth it. She felt better than she had in a long while, both mentally and physically. Being outside all day and hanging out with Edgar had been refreshing in a way she hadn't even known she needed. Of course, the phone call with tech support had helped with the mental side. She wasn't sure how high up in the company Steve and James were but neither was worried about her little malfunction and Steve, a former operator, had complimented her skills in both WarMonger *and* TD Hunter.

It was getting near the time when her mom usually got up, so Lynn rolled off her bed and went to clean up her dirty clothes and equipment from the bathroom. The backpack only needed a little wipe down but when she inspected her clothes, she just laughed. They were going straight into the washer. The shirt might even be a lost cause, with two substantial tears in it. She did a quick web search for "how to deal with ticks on your clothes," then threw her dirty laundry in the wash on hot with an extra rinse cycle. Then she fixed coffee, grabbed two apples and a protein bar to take an edge off her hunger until dinner and settled down to wait for her mom to appear. She knew better than to burst into the bedroom yelling "Mom, can you check me for ticks?" even though that's what she wanted to do.

To pass the time, Lynn poked around the TD Hunter main website. To her delight, she found that she could log in with her Hunter credentials and access the same forum that was inside the game app.

At the top of the "Tips and Techniques" category was pinned a new "Tactical Recommendation." She'd read such recommendations before and used them. She was shocked, however, to see that this new one outlined her demon roll attack technique. They even gave her credit for the idea.

Whaaat?

All games had embedded tricks and techniques that players learned as they advanced or picked up by word of mouth from other players. There were whole sites devoted to them, things like easter eggs, cheat codes and the like. But typically it was not the game companies themselves handing out the tips and tricks, especially not a company that involved competitive scores. Lynn thought about it, trying to find the sense in it all. Then she remembered something Fallu had said: *We don't exactly control how the AI assigns the entities. It's a closed system.*

So, maybe it all had to do with their new, never-done-before, closed system game AI. Maybe, there was a bit of "us versus it" going on. Maybe they'd decided to balance out the difficulty by making special tips public.

Lynn's thoughts drifted back to how she'd felt when that Varg had attacked her and her resultant nightmare. Plus, how the darned thing had hung around the entrance to her apartment afterwards, as if it knew where her "scent" had disappeared when she'd exited combat mode and it was waiting for her to reappear.

She shivered.

Those weren't the actions of a normal game monster. Those were the actions of an intelligent game designed to "have it out" for the players fighting against it. Was that what Mr. Krator had meant when he'd said that TD Hunter was different from anything he'd developed before? That he'd created an intelligent, adaptive game specifically to heighten the realism of playing and coupled it with an augmented reality platform so powerful it took "stepping into the real" to a whole other level?

Wow. That was sooo cool.

No wonder they'd set up their tactical recommendations the way they had, considering the game was all about a global paramilitary of volunteer Hunters uniting to save humanity. She still wasn't happy about her newly discovered technique being shared but supposed it was only fair. After all, most of what she knew about fighting the game monsters had come from the tactical support forum. It was still up to each individual to apply the available knowledge against the game's algorithms to kill the most monsters with the least damage possible.

And that was just what she intended to do.

The faint sound of her mother's alarm intruded on her thoughts and a few minutes later, Matilda shuffled into the kitchen blinking against the light. Lynn held out a steaming mug of liquid energizer, which her mother took to the counter to heap with sugar and creamer before coming to sit down at the table.

"Thank you," she said.

"You're welcome," Lynn replied, tamping down on her impatience.

It took her mother a few sips before her eyes seemed to open fully and she finally registered her daughter's appearance.

"Why is your face all scratched and bruised?" she asked, tone going from confused to alarmed. "What happened? Were you attacked?"

"No, Mom, nothing like that," Lynn hurried to reassure her. "Remember, we talked about me playing TD Hunter today with Edgar tagging along? I had a great time, the game just got...a little physical."

"Physical?" Matilda asked, eyes narrowing. "What do you mean, 'physical'? Don't tell me you and another player got into a fight?"

"Oh my gosh, Mom, no. That's not how this game works. We're fighting *monsters*, not each other. Edgar and I went into the greenway, you know those woods between us and the Heathers complex? Well, the monsters I have to fight aren't physical so they don't exactly care about stuff like thick brush. I rolled through a thorn bush or two, that's all. Oh, and I might have possibly run into a tree at one point. But other than that, I'm fine."

Matilda gave a startled laugh.

"Every time I start worrying about you, Lynn, I find out I'm worrying about exactly the wrong thing. Which doesn't reassure me, I'll have you know. Should I be afraid you're going to walk off a bridge trying to beat some imaginary monster boss or something?"

Lynn rolled her eyes.

"Give me at least a little credit, Mom. I'd never engage a monster somewhere unsafe like on top of a bridge. You know I never go out in the woods. I just need time to adjust to the new terrain, that's all."

Her mother sighed and rubbed her forehead.

"Um, also I need a tick check," Lynn admitted, figuring she might as well get it all out at once.

"Well, of course, if you've been traipsing around in the woods," her mom said, seeming unfazed.

"And I broke the gaming equipment they sent me to beta test with."

"What!?"

"It was when I ran into the tree," Lynn hurried to explain. "I fell down and I guess I must have landed on my baton, because it broke and there was some sort of glitch. It sort of caught on fire. Edgar stomped it out though and I've already called the game's tech support. They're going to replace everything for free."

"Good grief," Matilda said, leaning back in her chair and taking a long swig of her coffee. "You sure do know how to keep life interesting, O daughter of mine."

"Er, one more thing?"

Her mom raised an eyebrow in trepidation.

"Mind if I game tonight? In virtual, of course. There's some stuff I need to catch up on, since TD Hunter took up all day."

Matilda sighed. "Well, since it's officially summer now, I suppose it wouldn't hurt. Besides, it means I can binge on the latest political debates instead of having my brain melted by your usual action flick stream." Matilda winked at her daughter and Lynn shook her head.

"I don't understand how you can stand to watch that political stuff, Mom. It gives me a headache just thinking about it."

"Oh, it gives me a headache too, believe me. But somebody has to stay informed. Enjoy your innocent youth while it lasts, my dear."

"On that note, I'm gonna go kill some people in virtual," Lynn said and got up.

Matilda chuckled.

"Have fun honey. I'll call you when supper is ready."

It felt *sooo* good to melt into her body-mold chair and she was reminded why she'd never been tempted to play an AR game before this. Well, there was a first time for everything.

She checked her messages, noting with satisfaction that she'd heard back from YodaMaster on the request she'd sent him that morning. She pinged her regular client in WarMonger who had wanted her to join a game earlier, then opened up a second screen and hopped onto social media while she waited for a reply. She had some accounting to balance up and she couldn't exactly go to a reputable firm without disclosing her under-age status. To handle things, she went to a closed group on the site and put up a post calling for "off the books advice." The people who normally helped her out would see it and get things rolling.

By that time she'd heard from her client and she headed over to join his game. The timing would be a little tight but she was confident she could mop things up in time to link up with Yoda. She had some unresolved business to take care of.

Todd Kim was having a good week. His team was winning matches left and right. The only time he'd needed help he'd gotten that merc to come in and clean things up. Pity the merc never got paid.

This match they had their enemy on the run. Some of the other team were about to spawn but Delbert was spawn camped covering two of the spawn points. They didn't have a chance.

There was a spawn at a point Delbert wasn't covering, so Todd moved that way to find the player. Odd, it was a new guy, not part of the original team. Then Todd saw his rank marks and blanched. The new guy was a freaking Tier Two. Todd's team was mostly Tier Nines. Delbert's link suddenly disappeared.

"Delbert, what the heck?" Todd snarled over the team coms as more Tier Twos dropped into the spawn points, then a Tier One. Practically the entire opposing team they'd been playing had been replaced.

"I never even saw what hit me!" Delbert snapped as he respawned in their own team area. "What are all these elite tiers doing here? What the holy f—"

First Delbert, then Joden, then Rickey dropped off. Delbert spawned back in and died again before he'd even made it out of the corridor. Everyone on Todd's team was swearing up a storm at the new players but the elite tiers were playing in an eerie silence that was downright frightening. If they were coordinating between themselves, it was on a separate channel.

"Don't bother turning around, douchebag," one of the elite players finally announced. "I've got a gauss gun two inches from the back of your skull. Everyone drop out of the match except PredatorElite919."

Delbert swore.

"Yeah? And what if we don't?"

"If you don't, you'll get the same thing as your friend here," another voice said as YodaMaster strode into view.

"Let's get the hell out," Joden said. "Sorry, man, we're leaving."

"You bastards!" Todd yelled. "Cowards!" But his teammates ignored him and one by one disappeared.

"PredatorElite?" YodaMaster asked once Todd was all alone. "Seriously."

"You call yourself Yoda and you're making fun of *my* name?" Todd spat.

The knife flashed faster than the blink of an eye and was at the throat of his avatar.

"I understand that you are in failure of payment to Larry Coughlin," Yoda said.

"You're full of it," Todd said. "I don't even know anybody by that name."

"Funny," Yoda replied. "He has records of your chat conversation on the matter and claims you failed to transfer payment, that is one Sonya Sasson Mk-276 Gauss Gun, approximate market value one thousand five hundred dollars. Did you transfer the Gauss gun or not?"

"I'm not taking this crap," Todd said, hitting the command to leave the match. He'd give up before putting up with that kind of abuse. Freaking merc elites. Acting like they owned the game.

"What was that all about," Joden said, opening up a voice chat.

"No idea," Todd said. "Let's go find a better room."

They found a group of other Tier Nines and some Tier Ten noobs and set out to teach them a lesson. But each time they killed one, a Tier Two would appear instead of the Tier Ten or Nine respawning.

"What the..." Delbert said. There was a brief pause then he came up again. "Not again! You can't even *see* them before they—"

"Delbert's dead," Joden said.

"We can do this all night," Yoda's voice said, eerily creepy in its total lack of emotion.

"What the—it's just a stupid Gauss gun!" Todd shouted. "Why do you even care?"

"Contract assurance," Yoda said, deadpan. "When you screw one top tier merc, you screw us all, noob."

"Who you calling a noob?" Todd shouted again. "I'm no noob!"

"You're clearly a noob to think you can screw a Tier One and get away with it," Yoda said. "We stick together. Not in battle but certainly in commerce. Now, you can transfer the item and the hit comes off... or you might as well never log in to War-Monger again, because every time you turn up, you'll find us there, waiting. Hell, we'll be waiting in *other* games. From here on out, you'll die. And, yes, we'll teabag you. We'll gangbang you. We'll screw you over, until you transfer the item. You do have the item, correct?"

"You said it yourself!" Todd whined, starting to feel desperate. "It's worth fifteen hundred dollars!"

"I don't care if it's worth a million dollars," a gravelly baritone replied.

Todd hadn't been watching the board and so hadn't noticed who had just arrived. He groaned as he saw the latest newcomer in the match.

"Look, Larry..." he said, sweating. He thought he might puke.

"You hire a merc, you pay the merc," Larry said, walking up to Todd's avatar. The merc was in his custom Alice The Strange armor. It was one of only three sets in the game. There were various stories about how he'd gotten his hands on it. Most of them involved dead bodies. Actual dead bodies. In the real.

"Idiots like you are a dime a dozen," Larry continued. "I've seen them from Bosnia to Baghdad. You think you can send us out to die and then walk away with the money. Not happening, Todd."

"How do you know my name?" Todd asked, almost choking on his words. How did this guy know who he was in the real?

"I not only know your name, I know your address," Larry whispered. "And right now, there's a laser spotter pointed at your head. You have about three seconds to *hand over my rifle!*" the merc finished in a terrifying bellow.

Todd nearly broke his fingers selecting the Gauss Rifle and transferring it to the mercenary.

"I'm sorry, I'm sorry—"

"You're banned as a client for a year," Yoda said, stepping back into the conversation. "Not that you're going to be able to afford to be one any time soon. We're done here."

"Look..." Todd said.

"What part of 'done' was unclear?" Larry asked. The shining muzzle of the Gauss rifle he'd just transferred to the merc came up like a lightning bolt and the last thing Todd saw was the muzzle flash.

X Team Galveston Victory Has Failed!

❖　　❖　　❖

"Thanks," Lynn said over her modulator headset. "Sorry I took so long to turn up. I had a client who was hot to have me in a match."

"Good match?" Yoda asked.

"Too many Tier Threes," Lynn admitted. "Felt like kicking puppies. Cash client, though, so I'll hold my nose. And I needed the dough. I agreed to beta a new game and it's taking up a lot of my time."

"TD Hunter," Yoda said. "Heard that from Fallu. Said he talked to you in the real."

Lynn suppressed a sigh. Gamers gossiped worse than cheer-leaders. Apparently that even applied to former Army guys.

"There's supposed to be an NDA on that," Lynn said, letting her voice get even lower and more gravelly. "He shouldn't be running his mouth."

"He just said he'd met you, nothing else," Yoda said, tone as calm as ever. "What's TD Hunter like?"

"Weird," Lynn said. "Like 'the VC own the night' weird. I haven't played a lot of AR games but the whole 'step into the real' thing sucks. Gimme a controller any day. Heck, gimme an M16. I keep getting my ass handed to me."

"You?" Yoda said. "By a game AI?"

"A really freaky game AI," Lynn said. "First warning if you play it: when they warn you to armor up and stealth up, do it. I got caught with my pants down right as I leveled by this mutant wolf thing called a Varg. Thing wiped the floor with me. I ended up running like a little girl, I'll admit it. Got inside, looked out my back window and the bastard was *right freaking there*, cir-cling like some kind of alien shark just waiting for me to step foot outside again."

"Sure it was the same bogey?" Yoda asked.

"Same or another, doesn't matter. How did the cursed thing know where I was?" Lynn said. "I had the stupid app turned off. But there it was, lurking, like it had nothing better to do than stake out my house. Usually game monsters have a set territory, or once their target leaves the game they reset. But this thing hung around all night long. Creepy as all get out."

"You ever kill it?" Yoda asked.

"Yup. Went back to where I'd seen it before and it was playing all hard to get, so I danced around unstealthed like a stripper

in a bar full of sailors. Lured it right out and then I kicked its
teeth in." Lynn said. "Took rolling around on the ground like a
pig, though. Been a while since I've rolled around in the dirt.
Felt like old times. Well, time to go make the man his money.
We good?"

"Scratch my back some time," Yoda said and disappeared.

"Merc up," Lynn said to herself and headed out to find
another client.

On Sunday, Lynn's mom took them out for a VR movie and
ice cream. They always did movie first and ice cream after because
the VR experience was intense, more so for Matilda than Lynn—
Matilda still remembered when 2-D movies in big old-fashioned
theaters were the norm. But crowded theaters had become a thing
of the past after the shift to virtual put the big chains out of business and VR cafes became a thing. VR movies were a much more
individualized experience, though you could do them in multiplayer
mode so you could still see and talk to whoever you were with.
With three hundred and sixty degree 3-D imaging, haptic input
and little additions like smells and the feel of sun or wind on your
skin, it could take a bit to come down from that kind of high.

When they got back to the apartment, Lynn was surprised to
find a package waiting for her in their delivery dock.

"Did you order something recently, Mom?" she asked.

"Nope. Could it be the replacement equipment for your beta
game?"

Lynn picked up the package and opened it as her mom hung
up her purse. James the tech guy *had* said they would overnight
it but Lynn had assumed that meant after they'd printed the new
LINC and surely that would take a day or two, right?

Apparently not.

"I guess they really want you playing more TD Hunter, huh?"
Matilda laughed when Lynn pulled out a brand new baton and
a smooth black ring from the box.

"I guess so..." Lynn muttered.

"Well, they'll have to wait till tomorrow at least, because
tonight is taco night and it's your turn to cook."

Lynn felt a stab of disappointment but quashed it resolutely.

"Yeah, well, what game could possibly be more important
than tacos?"

"Exactly," Matilda said with a sage nod.

After Lynn had packaged up the broken baton and LINC in the provided shipping box, set it out in the delivery dock and scheduled a drone pickup, she got to work on dinner. As usual when it was her turn to cook, her mom hung around in the kitchen too, helping here and there while they talked. The conversation was usually dominated by whatever crazy news currently trended on the stream channels and Lynn and Matilda traded conspiracy theories about a recent spate of livestock deaths around the country. Lynn insisted it could only be a new strain of virus, while her mother thought it was more likely to be a batch of contaminated feed, pointing out the corner-cutting practices of the handful of mega corporations that controlled the agricultural sector.

The tacos were as delicious as they were messy and Lynn pitched in to help with the cleanup. After dinner Matilda pulled out an old-fashioned deck of cards and they settled in to battle it out at Bridge and then Spades, playing modified versions that worked with two players. After that they moved on to Rummy, two-player Hearts and Lynn's personal favorite: Go Fish. They could have both put on AR glasses and played with cool graphics and sound effects but Lynn's mom had always emphasized to her how important it was to unplug every now and then and be present in the physical world. Lynn wasn't sure she agreed but she did enjoy the strategy and competition of the games and she knew her mom needed time to do something completely removed from the stress of her nursing job. Plus, they were all each other had left.

When you'd lost something precious, it had a way of putting what you still had into perspective.

After cards, Lynn excused herself to her room. Her mom would spend the night watching stream vids and generally relaxing. During the school year, Lynn got up early enough for them to have breakfast together before her mom went to sleep for the day but during the summer all bets were off. After all, what was the point of being a teenager in the summer if not to sleep obscenely long hours?

This summer, though, things might just be different. Ever since her conversation with Steve from tactical support, she'd been giving TD Hunter some serious thought. Now that her new LINC had arrived, she could finally put her thoughts into action.

Draped across her bed in the privacy of her room, Lynn donned her glasses, earbuds and LINC and booted up the TD Hunter app.

"Welcome back, Miss Lynn."

"Hey, Hugo," she said, a grin spreading across her face. "Nice to hear your voice again. I never thought I'd miss a service AI but I guess you've kinda grown on me. Like a fungus, you know?"

"I shall take that comment in the spirit I am sure it was offered," Hugo said, his cheerful tone undiminished. "That was quite the adventure you had in the woods, by the way. I trust you and Mr. Johnston emerged from it unscathed?"

"Yeah, it all worked out. I'll be more careful about taking on unknowns though, at least unknowns in thick brush." As she spoke she popped into her inventory, ensuring all her loot, items and weapons were accounted for.

"An undoubtedly wise decision."

"Glad you agree. Hey, so, is there any setup stuff I need to do? It looks like everything is where I left it."

"Indeed it is, Miss Lynn. Since the entire game runs off real time connection to the cloud, all of your data and battle history is quite safe from equipment malfunction in the real."

"Awesome." Lynn fell silent as she poked around a bit more, reminding herself of her status when everything had gone dark yesterday. After she finished, she hesitated, steeling herself to say what she wanted to say.

"So, um, Hugo."

"Yes, Miss Lynn?"

"I need your...advice."

"I am by no means all-knowing but I shall certainly do my best to provide you accurate information. With what may I be of service?"

"Well...I kind of want to, um...get into shape," Lynn mumbled, as if the very idea was somehow embarrassing. It shouldn't be, of course. Why should she be ashamed of wanting to be healthy and fit? But she couldn't help imagining the reaction of the pop-girl group at school to her making such a statement. Her—dumpy, piggy, fatty Lynn. She winced as the familiar epithets echoed in her head.

"Why, what a splendid idea, Miss Lynn! Seeking the betterment of one's health is among the worthiest of goals. Your body is, after all, your most important weapon in our global resistance against the TransDimensional invasion."

"You know...you're right, Hugo," Lynn said slowly. She sat up on her bed and squared her shoulders. She'd spent countless hours honing her battle skills in WarMonger, collecting the most powerful weapons and armor and rooting out every tactical edge she could find. Why would she do any less in TD Hunter? The fact that it was augmented reality, making her own body an integral part of her arsenal, shouldn't make any difference at all.

Elena and the rest of those shallow attention-seekers could go suck it.

"So, where would you like to start, Miss Lynn?"

"Well, I definitely need to check out the TD Hunter training simulations, since those will be the most useful right away. But I also need to up my speed and stamina and strengthen whatever muscle I keep pulling. I doubt the TDMs will stop ambushing me from behind any time soon and I can't play if I injure something. Can you, I don't know, search the mesh web for an exercise plan that incorporates all that? I don't really know what to look for."

"I can do better than that, Miss Lynn. Our training simulations are not limited to TDM combat-specific weapons and moves. The best physical trainers and health experts from around the globe have crafted an array of fitness regimes exclusively for our brave volunteers. TD Counterforce is dedicated to providing the best resources possible to our Hunters."

Lynn couldn't help chuckling.

"I guess that solves that problem, then. So, what are you waiting for? Show me what you got."

"With pleasure, Miss Lynn."

Her inventory disappeared from the display to be replaced by a cut-scene vid. The title "Tactical and Training Simulator" appeared for a moment, before being replaced by the now-familiar face of First Sergeant Kane Bryce. He wore his signature combat fatigues and stern expression and Lynn wondered if his face was stuck like that.

"Congratulations, Hunter. By watching this video, you've already proven you have twice the drive and gumption of your average volunteer. You might have noticed the Hunter rankings by now and figured out you can earn rewards for outstanding performance. Just because we're fighting hordes of monsters to ensure humanity's survival doesn't mean we can't have fun while we're at it. If you take the time to go through the tactical simulations and take advantage of our training regimes, I promise you'll see a marked improvement in your performance. Use all the tools at your disposal, including our highly advanced service AI, who can provide real-time feedback and instruction. We're counting on you, Hunter. Train hard, put your best foot forward and go kill some monsters!"

First Sergeant Bryce disappeared to be replaced by the TD Counterforce logo, which in turn faded away to reveal two versions of herself. The first was dressed in full armor—her space Viking armor—and was executing a series of attack maneuvers with a blade in one hand and a pistol in the other. It was labeled "Tactics and Combat." The second was dressed in sweats and going through a variety of exercises, everything from jump rope to push-ups to yoga. It was labeled "Training and Exercise."

Shrugging, Lynn tapped on the armored version of herself, which revealed another menu that offered "Weapon Tactics," "Monster Tactics," and "Combat Simulator." She backed out of that menu and selected the sweats-clad avatar, revealing "Weapons Training," "Combat Exercises," and "Physical Fitness." Lynn hesitated, finger hovering over the "Physical Fitness" option but the siren call of "Weapons Training" won out.

After selecting it, she was presented a double row of what looked like every class of weapon in the game, melee weapons on the left, ranged weapons on the right. To her disappointment, only her current weapons and what looked like the next class up were selectable. The rest were grayed out. But still, she took a moment to scroll through the columns, fairly salivating at the awesomeness of what she'd eventually get to use to mow down unsuspecting TDMs. Once she'd finally torn herself away from the tempting display, she returned to the top of the list and selected the Plasma Blade. But the image of the weapon only flashed orange and Hugo's voice informed her:

"If you would like to enter the training simulation for the Plasma Blade, please first pick up your Hunter baton and stand at the ready."

Oh, duh. Lynn rose from her bed and picked up the new baton—the second of her original pair was still safely stashed away in her TD Counterforce backpack. She pushed her body-mold chair against the wall and kicked a few other things out of the way so her floor was clear, then tapped the Plasma Blade icon again. The handle of her baton warmed as her Plasma Blade formed with fluid grace. She almost jumped when she looked up and saw her own image standing six feet in front of her, as large as life and as real-looking as the CGI images of the monsters she fought.

"Uh, Hugo? What's going on? That's just a little bit creepy."

"Fear not, Miss Lynn. Your avatar is simply there to demonstrate the various moves and techniques which will be covered in this training session. If at any point you wish to change your training partner, you can find a selection of generic training avatars to replace your own."

Lynn relaxed. That made sense. In fact, now that she thought about it, it was pretty cool. She'd much rather train with "herself" then some buff drill-sergeant type or an old dude in a robe.

"Furthermore," Hugo continued as the Lynn avatar stood there in a relaxed stance, "you may always switch your training session from interactive mode, as you see before you, to screen observation, so that you might watch the demonstrations in vid format. I will be your guide throughout your training and you may interrupt my presentation at your pleasure with any questions you might have."

"Are *you* customizable, Hugo?" Lynn asked, curious.

"Why yes, Miss Lynn. As your service AI, my voice is one hundred percent customizable. This is my default setting but you may choose from a list of hundreds of languages and regional accents if you so wish."

Interesting. If she'd thought to ask that at the beginning, she might have had some fun looking through the accent options and picking something different. But now it was too late. Hugo was . . . Hugo and she couldn't imagine him any other way. "I think I'll stick with the default for now, thanks."

"I'm so glad you approve, Miss Lynn."

Lynn grinned and wondered if AIs were capable of having preferences.

"Now, if you are ready, shall I begin the training?"

Turning her attention back to her avatar, Lynn took a deep breath and nodded.

It was almost midnight before she was tired enough to notice what time it was and call it quits. The training simulations were beyond amazing. While Hugo narrated and explained, her avatar demonstrated every exercise, from proper handling of each weapon, to basic stances and strikes for melee attack and different shooting techniques for ranged attacks. At any point Lynn could stop the exercise to ask questions, repeat a section, or even skip forward. She could also change her avatar's position from facing her to standing side by side so she could get different views of the exercises and follow along better. During the practical application portion, she could not only use her avatar as a target, she could also up the difficulty settings to have her avatar dodge or block, making the exercise harder.

Though she never got around to trying any of the simulations in the "Tactics and Combat" menu, Hugo's brief description made her eager to try it out. She did take a few minutes to explore the "Physical Fitness" options and found that the app offered all kinds of training regimes from kickfit, to yoga, to interval HIITs and everything in between. Though she felt considerably less enthusiastic about the physical fitness part, it was clear everything she needed to become an elite TD Hunter player was right at her fingertips. She certainly had plenty to keep her busy on rainy days or when it was too hot or too late to go hunting.

More than anything else, her evening made one thing abundantly clear: training was *fun*. Yes, she had completely worn herself out and she groaned in relief as she collapsed into bed. But for the first time in a long time, she felt . . . inspired. For the first time in a long time, she didn't look forward to sleep as simply a dreamless escape from the alternating monotony or anxieties of life. She'd earned her rest and tomorrow she would get up and do it all over again.

And enjoy the heck out of it.

Chapter 8

"DAAAAAAAYYUM, GIRL! YOU'RE ON FIRE TODAY," EDGAR SAID, grinning. "I'm not even sure what happened there but it was *ua tumu*!"

Lynn grinned at Edgar's commentary. She'd never realized he could put the best cheerleaders to shame if he was enjoying himself. Or maybe he'd become more relaxed since they weren't at school. He was still laid back but the silent, guarded mask she'd come to expect as normal for him was gone.

In any case, she hunted with her display projected in front of her whenever she could so he could spectate. Despite all her complaints to her mother about being saddled with a hunting buddy, she'd come to enjoy his company. It was much more fun killing monsters when you could share with a friend.

"*Ua tumu*?" she asked. He rarely sprinkled Samoan into his speech so he must have been impressed.

"It's . . ." he paused in what might have been slight embarrassment. He chewed for a moment then shrugged. "It's the short form of a Samoan phrase that doesn't really translate very well. *Ua tumu la'u ato fagota i pusi.* It sort of means, like, 'great,' 'wonderful,' 'exciting.'"

"Okay," Lynn said, still panting from the exertion of the fight.

She collected the piles of ichor, globes and plates and the few bonus items scattered around her—the just rewards of her most recent TDM-killing spree.

They were at Cedar Memorial Cemetery, or at least skirting the outer edges of it where various shopping centers and restaurants backed up to the cemetery. Over the past week and a half of hunting close to her apartment by herself as well as farther afield with Edgar, Lynn had discovered some interesting patterns in the TDM distribution.

Except for the lowest class monsters like imps and grinder worms, the majority of TDMs preferred to be somewhere out of the way of direct traffic, yet still close to human infrastructure. They congregated in places like alleyways, the rear of commercial buildings and greenways bordering roads and neighborhoods.

That was logical planning on the game-designer's part, since players couldn't effectively fight TDMs on a crowded street without hitting somebody. She'd also noticed that the higher the monster class, the farther away from humans the TDMs tended to be. Various tactical support threads hypothesized that the stronger the TDM, the longer their range for feeding off human-generated energy. Thus the algorithm that controlled TDM spawning could put most of the monsters in quiet areas where the hordes of Hunters—at least it would be hordes once the game launched—wouldn't be disrupting businesses, clogging up walkways, or getting too close to traffic.

All of which meant a cemetery surrounded by bustling businesses was the perfect hunting ground. It had a wide mix of TDM classes and types that gave her a chance to practice all the moves she'd been pounding into her muscle memory with simulation exercises. She could stay close to the shopping centers with only a few globes equipped and work on her mob control skills against the lowest Delta Class TDMs that swarmed her. Or, she could stay stealthed to the nines and venture into the cemetery to take on individual Delta Class-5s and even a few Charlie Class-1s that had started appearing once she achieved Level 9.

The only anomalies to the algorithmic patterns she'd been mapping out were the Lectas. It wasn't that they didn't follow the pattern but that they followed it too well. They were almost too predictable, which wasn't like the algorithm. When she'd discovered the first one, the game had classed it as an electrovore that fed off the energy waves humans beamed back and forth between power nodes to run their civilization. But unlike other gather type monsters like imps, which were the most numerous TDM, Lynn only ever saw one Lecta at a time. They hid well, if predictably close to the nearest energy source. She rarely spotted them if she wasn't looking but if she *did* go looking, she always found one. It got to the point that she started wondering if there was just the one and if it followed her around every time it respawned.

Which was crazy, of course.

And then there was that unknown she'd found in the woods when her equipment had gone haywire. She'd gone back looking for it once she'd leveled but there'd been no sign of it. A few times since then she'd caught glimpses of sparkling mist out of the corner of her eye but whenever she'd turned to look, it had been gone. She'd finally chalked it up to a bug in the game; she'd encountered other such "ghost" images playing in virtual games before. So, she simply reported it to Hugo and tried to ignore the glitchy sparkles that made it feel like the unknown was following her. The game's algorithm might be innovative and responsive but it wouldn't have been programmed to unfairly single out specific players.

There were other glitches in the game, too, of course, like those areas that had a weird signal blackout that crashed the app whenever she and Edgar ventured into them. More often than not, the blackouts happened around those layered rings of TDMs she sometimes spotted on her map. She never tried to take them on, knowing it would be suicide. Other times, though, she and Edgar would be minding their own business, hiking through the woods or following some lonely railroad track, when Hugo's voice would cut off mid-sentence and everything would go dark. It was annoying but all they could do was stay away from those areas. She made sure to send in regular beta reports on the bugs along with her evaluation of the game's other aspects.

Fortunately, there were no glitch spots in the cemetery and she and Edgar were currently hunting on the northeast side behind North Point mall. Like most businesses over the past few decades, the mall's vast asphalt parking lot had been mostly torn up to make way for building expansion or new green spaces, while other parts were restructured as rideshare or airbus stops. The back side of the shopping center, though, had stayed relatively the same, except that their delivery docks had been restructured for drone and autonomous freight drop-off. Edgar helped her keep an eye out for freight trucks as she spun and slashed at incoming monsters. Even if she'd been alone, though, it would have been relatively safe, since all the driverless vehicles had pedestrian avoidance safety systems.

"Hey, Edgar, check this out!" Lynn had noticed the shiny new augment beneath the piles of ichor and she eagerly selected it, putting it up on her projected display. Edgar leaned in, squinting.

"Is it just me, or is that a rifle scope?" her partner asked.

"Yup," Lynn said as a shiver of excitement ran through her. She was so close to reaching Level 10 when she could start using two-handed weapons. It looked like the game's AI had finally decided to start dropping two-handed augments for her in preparation. "I bet that Orcull dropped it. They seem to have high loot probability. I just wish there were more of them closer to my apartment."

"You know, your mom seems really cool," Edgar began, a little hesitantly, as Lynn read through the new augment's stats. "I'm sure she knows this is a laid back town and North Point is probably the safest area of anywhere in Cedar Rapids. So... um... how come your mom doesn't want you flying solo?"

Lynn felt a prickle of discomfort at her nape. She didn't look at Edgar as she replied.

"Mom's just a little paranoid is all."

She saw Edgar shrug out of the corner of her eye and was relieved when he changed topics.

"Dunno about you but I'm starved," Edgar said, popping his gum. "Wanna go hit up that burger place over by First Ave, or would you rather do drone delivery?"

Lynn finally looked up at him.

"You mind if we do delivery? I'll cover your food, since you let me drag you all over a cemetery today." She grinned. "I'm sooo close to Level 10, I don't want to take the time to walk someplace."

"Sure, whatever works for you, Lynn," he said. "But I'm good for my own grub." He gave her a half smile. No matter how many times she offered, he would never let her treat him, despite how much time he'd given up to tag along on her hunting expeditions.

"If you insist. I don't have the energy to argue anyway. I gotta save it for killing monsters."

Edgar laughed, an infectious sound that Lynn enjoyed hearing.

"Spoken like a real *Toa Tama'ita'i*!" he said. "Why don't we go find a shaded spot in the cemetery and have us a little picnic? That way as soon as you're done you can take on some of the big baddies at the top of the hill."

"Sure," Lynn said, resisting the urge to roll her eyes and instead busying herself with exiting combat mode. Despite her objections, Edgar kept trying out new "warrior" names for her at every opportunity. Most of them were cheesy movie or video game characters. This latest, though, was the Samoan phrase for warrior princess. When Lynn had asked its meaning, Edgar had surprised her by sharing about his childhood spent on his grandparent's farm near Salt Lake City—grandparents who had immigrated from American Samoa. The nickname was by far the most dignified moniker he'd come up with, so she'd let him keep it. For now.

They agreed on a restaurant and ordered food through their LINCs as they cut through the thicket behind the shopping center and walked up the grassy slope of Cedar Memorial cemetery. The delivery drone had their geotags from the order and would be able to find them no matter where they walked. They picked a comfy spot under some ornamental trees and plopped down to rest while they waited. Lynn leaned back on her hands, looking up and admiring the cerulean blue of the cloudless sky. A tiny shape drifted into view above them and Lynn squinted. That was too small and too soon to be their lunch delivery. Was that another one of those government survey drones? At least it was high enough up this time that its whirring didn't disturb the quiet.

"Sooo," Edgar said after some peaceful silence. "I heard you had fun over the weekend."

"You heard?" Lynn asked, turning her head to give him a skeptical look.

"Okay, so maybe I guessed. But I'm *pretty* sure you just had a birthday."

Lynn squinted suspiciously at him. It had, in fact, been her birthday on Saturday and on Sunday her mom had surprised her by taking them to the finest steakhouse in town. Lynn was pretty sure she'd nearly eaten her own weight in meat. It had been heavenly.

"How did you know? Are you picking up hacking habits from Dan?"

"You kidding me? I ain't got Dan's skills. Nah, I asked Mack."

"That traitor!" Lynn said but inside she was pleased. Nobody but her mom and grandparents had ever cared about her birthday. Well, except Kayla, for the short time she'd thought they'd been friends. Lynn's mom had thrown her a birthday party the year they'd moved to Cedar Rapids in an attempt to help her settle in. Kayla and Mack had been the only two people Lynn had been brave enough to invite. It had started out pretty awkward but plied by cake and games they'd all ended up having a good time.

"Hey, don't blame him," Edgar said, cracking his gum. "I threatened to tell his mom that Dan had hacked the parental controls she put on his LINC."

"Oooh, that's low, even for you," Lynn said.

"It's his fault for believing I'd ever actually do it," Edgar said with a grin.

"True. Poor Mack. He's such a pushover sometimes."

"Don't be too hard on him. That ma of his is one scary lady."

Lynn looked back up at the sky, contemplating Mack's unenviable position.

"Yeah. My mom can be a pain sometimes but she's the height of cool compared to Mrs. Rios."

"True that. And, well, on the topic of your mom...I'm sure she got you lots of presents and all but I was hoping you wouldn't mind, uh, getting one more?"

Surprised, Lynn looked over at Edgar to find he now had a brown paper bag in his hand. He must have pulled it from his backpack when she wasn't looking. The top was tied up neatly with string and it had a party bow stuck to the side, bright gold and red against the brown.

The sight made her throat go all tight. No one had ever taken the trouble to find out when her birthday was and get her a present before. No one.

"I...um...thanks," she finally said, leaning over to take it from him. She pulled out her Helle pocketknife, cut the string and opened the bag to peer inside. The sight that greeted her made her laugh. She reached in and withdrew a first aid kit, the perfect size to fit in her TD Counterforce backpack. "What's this for?"

"Oh, you know, for the next time you wrestle a mountain lion," he said, grinning.

"Gee, thanks, Edgar. Your confidence in my survival skills is truly overwhelming."

"Nah, don't think of it like that. If you fight, you're gonna get some scars. That's how being a warrior works. But a little first aid can go a long way. Anyway, there's something else in there, too."

Lynn stuck her hand back in and came up with...a book.

A real book. Made out of honest-to-God *paper*. Lynn turned it over in her hand, thoroughly confused.

"Okay, so the first aid kit I get but a book? What am I supposed to do with a book?"

"Read it, silly," Edgar said. He reached out and turned it over to point at the title.

"You got me a book on woodland craft?"

"So, you can properly identify poison ivy and know what kind of ticks are crawling up your legs," Edgar elaborated.

"Ugh." Lynn shivered. She'd come to truly hate ticks. "Okay but I can look all that up in seconds on my LINC."

"Yeah, maybe." Edgar shrugged and lay back down on the grass, hands behind his head. "But reading books is good for you. You should try it sometime."

"Um, okay. Thanks." Lynn tucked the gifts carefully into her backpack, amused, touched and confused all at once. She didn't own a single book. Her mom had some from when she was younger but Lynn had never felt tempted to read any of them. She knew some people collected books as a hobby but none of the schools did anything on paper anymore, so she'd never had a reason to own a book. Still, she was experiencing a lot of new things lately. Why not add one more?

"Speaking of your birthday," Edgar continued slowly, "I was wondering if . . . well . . . if you'd come hang out with me and the guys on TD Hunter launch day. You know, so they can wish you happy birthday and everything."

"Uh . . . what?" Lynn said, nonplussed.

Edgar looked at her again.

"Come hang out with us. All our batons arrived the other day and Dan and Ronnie are bouncing off the walls, counting down till game launch. There's supposed to be this super big announcement broadcast when the app goes live. A bunch of people are meeting up at Noelridge Park to celebrate. You should come."

For a moment, Lynn had no idea what to say. Or even feel. Finally, she managed a question.

"Does Ronnie know you're inviting me?"

"Yeah, of course," Edgar said, though his tone sounded suspiciously casual.

"Did you tell Ronnie I'm a beta tester?" Lynn asked, her eyes narrowed.

"What?" Edgar said, nearly swallowing his gum. "No, Lynn! Why would I do that? I said I wouldn't."

The hurt look on Edgar's face made Lynn feel foolish.

"Sorry," she muttered.

"Really, you should come hang out. Everybody—okay, everybody but Ronnie—would love to see you. This is our chance to all game together. Wouldn't that be cool?"

"Yeah...I guess," Lynn said slowly. She looked back up at the sky, stalling. All her insecurities came flooding back as if the last few weeks had never happened. It didn't matter that she was arguably the best TD Hunter beta out there, or that she'd been working out and felt stronger and more confident every day. Hunting with Edgar was one thing but what would the rest of the guys think? Would she be able to play dumb and pass off her superior knowledge of the game as obsessive research? Would they accept her as a true friend like Edgar had, or treat her as a useless hanger-on?

The possibility of rejection was far more frightening than the loneliness of sticking it out on her own.

"Come on, Lynn. What would it hurt? Without you there, I think Ronnie might literally drive me insane. You know how he gets."

Lynn choked out a laugh.

"I...sure, I guess," she finally said, giving into the pleading in Edgar's voice. "But only for launch. I've got serious leveling to do if I want to stay competitive and make enough mon—I mean, if I want to keep my scores up, you know," she finished, flushing. She'd forgotten herself and almost mentioned WarMonger and gaming for money.

"Okay, sure," Edgar said, lightly.

Lynn couldn't read anything from his tone and she didn't dare look at him. Fortunately for her, at that moment she spotted their delivery drone approaching and she pointed it out above them.

"Finally!" Edgar said, scrambling to his feet. "I could eat a whole cow. Or a bear, if you wrestled one for me."

"Hey, it'd all be in a day's work for a *Toa Tama'ita'i*, right?" Lynn said, relieved for the change of topic.

"True that, girl. True that."

After lunch, Lynn got back to hunting. Before long the moment she'd been waiting for finally came. She'd gotten used to the constant vigilance needed to survive the leveling process, plus she'd spent hours studying the TDM list, memorizing every known monster's strengths, weaknesses and behaviors. So, she wasn't taken off guard by the creepily hissing spiderlike creature called a Spithra that charged her out of nowhere right after Hugo's leveling congratulations reached her ears. It was as tall as she was, with significant reach advantage because of its long skinny legs, each tipped with a single razor-sharp claw. She was able to dodge its first strike and make a quick shift over to her Particle Dragon pistol, which had good stopping power at short range, boosted of course by several augments she'd picked up along the way.

She kept moving by dodging backward or rolling sideways from each strike. The Spithra had a ranged attack where it spit some kind of green acid but it always paused right before it let loose. Half the time when she jumped out of claw-reach, the Spithra would pause to try to get her with acid and she had a split second to lunge forward into a roll and come up on one knee underneath it. There, she could pump a blast into its vulnerable underbelly and roll out of the way again before it shifted and stabbed down at her. She even experimented with switching between her Dragon for firing while dodging and her Plasma Blade for stabbing the underbelly, to get the highest damage per strike possible. It was a tense few minutes but finally the monster stiffened, then exploded in a shower of sparks.

At the monster's death, Lynn didn't drop her guard, simply stood for a moment, catching her breath, waiting. Listening. Attack TDMs often had overlapping territories that they protected but it seemed this was the only one her current position had triggered.

She made the "all clear" gesture at Edgar, who knew to stay well back when she was fighting. He'd gotten smacked a few times when he'd walked up just as another TDM had appeared. They'd laughed heartily about it.

"Wow," Edgar said, opening up another piece of gum. "Lynn, seriously, do you know how good you are at this? That was amazing. I bet if they recorded you in AR with all that armor on, you'd look just like one of their advertising commercials."

The quiet earnestness in Edgar's tone took Lynn off guard. She felt that hot prickly feeling on her skin, like she had when he'd complimented her tan at school or mentioned a few days ago that she was "looking good."

"Um, thanks," she said, trying to keep it casual.

She didn't believe him, not really. But it was nice that he thought she looked like she knew what she was doing. It made her less nervous about playing in front of other people. She *had* put hours and hours into her training. So much, in fact, that she hadn't even touched WarMonger in over a week. They probably thought Larry Coughlin had finally croaked. Whatever. She only needed to do a couple high-profile jobs a month to cover family bills, the rest was all for college savings. Her reputation might take a hit but she could always excuse her absence with some veiled comment about needing to "take care of" some ghosts from her past. Heck, with Larry, just saying "I had stuff" was usually enough.

In any case, she knew her own performance wasn't flawless, no matter what Edgar said. She'd taken a few hits from that Spithra and they'd done heavy damage. That acid spit was no joke and it seemed to eat away at her armor with a poisonous DOT—damage over time—mechanic. She took a moment to replace her damaged armor plates and replenish her globes for both stealth and detection, always keeping an eye on her over-head and an ear pricked for approaching TDM. Her health had dipped but nothing she couldn't walk off in a few minutes. She was always frugal with Oneg. The self-imposed restriction kept her mindset lean and mean.

Finally, she took a moment to collect on her kill, grunting in satisfaction at the number of plates and amount of ichor the Spithra had dropped. It was a good return on her energy expenditure.

"So, did you level?" Edgar asked.

"You know it."

Lynn grinned in anticipation as she pulled her leveling screen back up from where it had been minimized during her fight. She quickly took in her bonus experience and supplies, then turned her attention to her new weapon selection.

She'd spent a long time thinking about what weapon she would choose. The weapon training simulations allowed you to practice with weapons from your level and the next one up, so she'd already tried her hand at the two-handed Nano Sword and Disruptor Rifle. The rifle was relatively easy to transition to from a pistol but using a two-handed melee weapon was vastly different from using a single-handed one. She'd felt like a flailing octopus every time she'd tried it and had concluded it would take *a lot* of training to get good enough to maintain her competitive scores. She didn't doubt she could become proficient eventually but for now she was focused on rapid leveling to get as much experience in beta stage as possible.

With all that in mind she chose the Disruptor Rifle when her leveling screen gave her the expected choice between sword and rifle.

"Hugo," she subvocalized as she quickly swung her backpack around to get out her second baton. "Equip my Disruptor Rifle."

"At once, Miss Lynn."

She held the two batons together and watched appreciatively as their omni-polymer flowed into the shape of a compact rifle with a solid stock and molded grip on the underside of the barrel assembly. As with all TD Hunter weapons, it was electric blue and so looked more like one of those super soakers kids brought to the apartment complex pool than a real rifle. But then, one couldn't have everything in life.

"Coool," Edgar said, staring at the new weapon. Unlike her, he hadn't seen any two-handed weapons yet and he seemed as impressed with how the two batons molded together as she had been in her training simulation. She was extremely grateful for the simulation practice, since keeping hold of the two batons as they joined and separated was a bit tricky.

"Miss Lynn, apologies for the interruption," Hugo said in her ear, "but I think you will be quite pleased to hear this. Would you like me to switch to external speakers for your companion's benefit?"

"Uh, sure?"

"I am pleased to congratulate Miss Lynn on achieving the highest Level 10 kills dealt to damage taken ratio in TD Hunter Beta. Here is a special item reward for your admirable performance and great dedication to the TD Counterforce mission."

"Holy. Moly. Guacamole," Edgar said, cracking his gum. "Look at that, Lynn!"

Lynn was much too focused on her prize to echo Edgar's words. Rotating slowly on her display was a gorgeous sword that shone and shimmered the deepest black, like obsidian. Its tapered blade was etched with glowing blue runes, while its handle was wrapped with supple black leather. The sword itself looked straight out of Norse legend and was a perfect complement to her armor. Of course, it would be, considering its name.

Skadi's Wrath.

Here it was, the second piece of a named set and she knew right away that she wouldn't stop until she'd collected the entire ensemble.

"Hugo," she said out loud. "Equip Skadi's Wrath."

To her surprise, her Disruptor Rifle split back into two pieces—she'd assumed a sword as long as Skadi's Wrath would be two-handed. While one baton resumed its neutral shape, the other elongated far past the fourteen inches of her Nano Blade. When it was finished, she was left with a single-handed blade that was almost as long as the two-handed Nano Sword. She couldn't have been more pleased. She much preferred single-handed weapons and now here was one with reasonable reach. Of course, the physical electric blue wasn't as impressive-looking as the AR version but it still had its long line of runes, each rune a cut-out in the center of the blade. She'd have to ask Hugo later what the runes meant.

"Now that's a weapon for a *Toa Tama'ita'i*," Edgar said, putting up his hands in mock surrender. "Don't try it out on me, okay?"

"You could use the dodging practice," Lynn said with a grin. "You're going to be playing this soon, too, right?"

"Yeah, I guess so," Edgar said. "I was gonna get a second job this summer but you've definitely convinced me not to."

"Good, because I'll be playing till I drop until school starts again and I need my wingman. Can you imagine how cool it'll be to play together? You'll actually get to see how I look in my Skadi skin."

"I know!" Edgar said. "It's gonna be epic. Hey, whaddaya say we head back toward the mall and you practice sniping some imps with that new rifle."

Lynn felt a pang to put away Skadi's Wrath but she really needed to train with it before she started swinging it around. She did take a peek at its stats, though, and a happy little glow filled her when she saw that it, too, was set up to level with her. That meant she would never have to discard her Skadi set. It would grow with her to Level 40 and beyond.

Peeling her attention away from her shiny new weapon, she equipped her rifle. She had augments to test on it and if she could start racking up some one-shot kills, that would boost her score even more.

"Sounds like a plan. Want to make a friendly bet on how many I can kill?"

"Not a chance, girl. I don't bet against the odds."

"Spoilsport," Lynn said with a grin.

Edgar shrugged and stuck his hands in his pockets, then set off down the hill, whistling. Lynn laughed and followed him.

Launch day for TD Hunter came faster than Lynn would have liked. She'd asked Hugo about how her own app would behave when the game launched and the service AI had explained that everything would reset back to default—with a few system improvements the app designers had been working on, of course. Though Lynn had known the answer before she asked it, she still couldn't help asking about her special items. Hugo confirmed that all items and stats would reset but he also reminded her that the same incentives and achievements would be available after launch that had been available during beta.

Lynn had grinned at that. Challenge accepted.

Not one to leave anything to chance, she'd planned her launch strategy down to the hour. She'd found where she could access her combat logs and had studied them obsessively. Between them and her ongoing mental mapping, she knew exactly where to go and what TDMs to focus on to get the best rewards versus risk. It was just what she needed to maintain the highest monsters killed to damage taken ratio at each of the key levels and eventually win the entire Skadi set. In the midst of her planning, she'd had to remind herself of her primary goal—make money—so she also worked in areas that had plenty of high loot drop monsters, places she'd discovered while exploring during beta. She would keep the best augments for herself and sell all her surplus as fast as she could.

The launch itself was scheduled for six p.m. on a Friday and Lynn had agreed to meet Edgar and the others at Noelridge Park shortly before. Her mom had made an unhappy face when Lynn had mentioned catching a robo-car to the park but Matilda had given permission nonetheless.

Her mom's reluctance reminded Lynn that they would need to have a "talk" soon. There was no way she would be able to dominate the TD Hunter leaderboard while limited by a buddy system. Not that it wasn't fun hanging out with Edgar but he worked part time and there was only so much Lynn could do around the apartment complex. Plus, she was seventeen now. She'd earned some independence.

It was not a conversation she looked forward to. But since there was no need to have it yet, she pushed it to the back of her mind.

Lynn spent the first part of Friday getting in as much simulation practice as possible, though she was careful not to wear herself out. Every part of her felt jumpy and on edge. She knew it was because she was nervous about gaming with "the guys." But she didn't let herself dwell on it.

When Matilda got up for work, Lynn surprised her with a massive breakfast of eggs, bacon, French toast and fruit salad. It was half an apology for spending so much time gaming, half a way to keep her own mind off the approaching evening. Also, an excuse to cook bacon. Only fools said no to bacon.

"So, what's going to happen at this big launch tonight?" Matilda asked between bites of syrup-covered French toast.

"No idea. Besides the big announcement, I think it's just a chance for players to have fun together trying out the game for the first time."

"Well, I'm glad you can spend the evening with your friends."

"Yeah. I guess."

Lynn must have betrayed more in her voice than she'd meant to, because her mom put down her fork and looked seriously at her.

"Hey. What's the matter, sweetie?"

"Nothing," Lynn assured her and shoved a piece of bacon in her mouth.

"Come on. I thought you liked hanging out with Mack and the rest?"

Lynn chewed methodically, contemplating her response. After she swallowed, she took a deep breath and made herself look at her mom.

"I've never really been . . . one of the guys. More just 'that friend of Mack's who always hangs around.' They're nice to me and everything, but . . . I'm just a girl to them. And 'girls got no game,' at least according to Ronnie."

"Oh, honey, that's ridiculous! I'm sure they value your friendship more than that. Why else would they want you to spend time with them?"

"I don't know, Mom. I got the impression it was just Edgar who wanted me there."

"Nonsense. Mack is a good kid and I'm sure Dan and Ronnie are too—"

Lynn snorted.

"You've obviously never met Ronnie."

"Okay, well, everyone has their flaws. In my experience, when guys put down girls it's because they're scared of them."

"What?" Lynn exclaimed.

"It's stupid, I know. But we humans do lots of stupid things. Teenage boys have a hard time figuring out how to act around girls, especially with the ridiculous social pressures put on them at school. Boys have this whole competitive pecking order and when you throw girls into the mix it turns into a madhouse."

"But what does being a complete jerk to girls accomplish?" Lynn asked, trying to wrap her head around the idiocy of it.

"What does a cat do when it's scared? Puff up its fur, arch its back and try to look as big and scary as possible. Humans are no different, though we do more bragging and putting others down than physical posturing. Don't think girls get a pass either, we do the same thing. What do you think bullying is all about? The biggest bullies are usually the most insecure people in the entire crowd."

"Wow...that's hysterical," Lynn said, chuckling weakly as she thought about Elena. That girl must have the biggest insecurity complex in existence.

"Yup. Humans are funny creatures. But back to boys. For young men who haven't figured themselves out yet, girls can be literally the most terrifying things in existence. Believe me, your father...well, he made an absolute fool of himself the first time I met him."

"Really?" Lynn said, leaning forward eagerly.

"Yes. And I suspect Ronnie acts the way he does because he's not comfortable around girls," Matilda said, pointedly avoiding further talk about Lynn's dad. "So, just be yourself and ignore him if he says anything stupid. Edgar seems like a very nice young man. He has his head on straight and I'm sure Mack and Dan do, too."

Lynn leaned back in disappointment and tried to keep her face neutral. Her mom didn't know the half of what was really going on between her and the guys, or the secrets she was keeping from them. From everyone. But at least she'd shed some light on Ronnie's status as a world-class jerk.

"Thanks for the pep talk, Mom. Really. Maybe you should go into therapy practice or something."

Matilda laughed.

"Not a chance. I can only stand so much whining. I'd rather treat people's bodies, not their minds. Now, shouldn't you be going? You don't want to be late for your big night."

"You don't mind cleaning up?"

"Not at all, honey. Go have fun. Just remember to be back by ten."

"I will. Thanks, Mom."

Lynn tugged at the bottom of her shirt as she stepped out of the robo-car and stood on the sidewalk bordering Noelridge Park. She'd agonized all day about what to wear, as much because of her self-consciousness as because half her clothes were especially baggy these days. If she hadn't needed to maintain appearances for her mom, she might have used some of her savings to buy top of the line smart clothes that sized themselves to fit and had fully programmable styles. As it was, she was stuck with thrift-store castoffs made from normal fabric. Dumb clothes, as the pop-girls at school called them.

She'd ended up digging through boxes in her closet to find pants she'd worn a couple years ago. She'd made herself wear a short-sleeved shirt, though it was so baggy the sleeves reached down to her elbows. Her TD Counterforce backpack she'd left at home. No way to explain how she'd gotten it, at least not until she'd been playing a while and could claim she'd bought it.

A ping from Edgar popped up on her display, telling her they were by the picnic area near the center of the park.

"Hugo, which direction is the picnic area?"

"Straight ahead, Miss Lynn."

"Thanks," she said, though she made no move in the direction the AI had indicated. Finally, she asked, "Hugo, will you... forget me when the game launches and beta goes away?"

"Not at all, Miss Lynn. Mr. Krator believes strongly in the

continued feedback of every hard-working beta who has contributed to testing this new system. Erasing our interaction history would be counterproductive to ensuring our future success."

"Oh. Good." She tried to ignore the swoop of relief Hugo's words had brought. It was silly to get emotional about a service AI. But it was human nature to form bonds. Even if the thing she called Hugo was only a program—a quantum-powered self-learning program that mimicked a human personality—it was still a program she was familiar with. She was glad she wouldn't have to start back at ground zero with it.

Six o'clock was fast approaching and she needed to find her friends, so she forced her legs to take one step, then another. She felt naked. The sun sinking toward the western horizon in front of her felt like a spotlight announcing her arrival to the sizable crowd already filling up the park. But that was stupid. Nobody knew who she was and nobody cared. She was invisible.

As she walked, she analyzed the terrain from a Hunter perspective. All these people would have to spread out after the game launched if any of them hoped to kill TDMs. She doubted any monsters would be spawning in the middle of this mess. The picnic area might be a good landmark to meet up but they would need to move to the edge of the park to find any targets. Lynn made a mental note to check out the park facility buildings where there might be power nodes, battery docks, or pulse generators. She'd already resigned herself to an hour or so of unproductive "breaking in" of the game with her friends. After that she'd make an excuse and slip away to do some real hunting.

To her discomfort, the crowd grew thicker the closer she got to the picnic area. Apparently that was where *everyone* was meeting up, not just her group. She finally spotted them lounging around one of the picnic tables and she quickened her pace to reach them.

"Hey, Lynn!" Edgar called out, noticing her approach.

The others turned. Mack's face split into a big smile and Dan raised his hand in a mock salute as they echoed Edgar's greeting. Ronnie nodded in a distracted manner, his eyes clearly focusing on his AR display. Lynn felt warm relief at their reactions. This was familiar. These were her friends. But then everyone's face went strangely stiff and Lynn had a second to wonder what was going on before she heard a familiar voice behind her.

"Well, if it isn't miss Piggy Lynn and the lame-o squad."

No. No, no, no. School was out. She wasn't supposed to have to deal with bullies again until next fall. Why was this happening to her?

Lynn had a split second of indecision: ignore the comment and keep walking, or turn around and confront Elena. She really, really wanted to keep walking. It was the smart thing to do. But her mother's words echoed in her head.

The biggest bullies are usually the most insecure people in the entire crowd.

Elena's insecurity was her own fault and Lynn was pretty sure no amount of groveling was going to change it. So, no point humiliating herself, right?

Lynn spun around and propped her hands on her hips.

"Oh, hey, Elena. What's a poser like you doing here? This is the launch for TD Hunter. The launch for 'TransDilemma' is over at the local Kidz'N-More. Don't worry, you and your flunkies will fit right in."

The pop-girl's lips tightened but she didn't retreat. She was flanked by two of her usual crowd, though they, at least, had the grace to look uncomfortable.

"What are *you* doing here, cheater? I thought you had some sugar daddy giving you access to the beta game already. Did he finally realize how disgusting you are and kick you to the curb?"

Lynn forced a laugh from her dry-as-paper throat.

"That's not how game betas work, genius. And I'm here to hang out with my *friends*, something you have no experience with, I'm sure. Do your flunkies follow you around because you threaten them? Or do you pay them by the hour to pretend they like you?"

That must have hit the mark because Elena's pale face reddened and her fists clenched.

"You're just jealous," she hissed. "I have everything you could ever want and you're just a fat, ugly, whore. Enjoy your 'friends,' Miss Piggy. They only want you around because they're so desperate for attention they'll take other people's castoffs." With that, the girl spun on her heel and marched away, her "friends" scuttling after her.

Lynn snorted and shook her head, concentrating with all her might on not caring a single iota what Elena had said. It was meaningless babble. In fact, she'd already forgotten it. Taking a deep breath, she turned back to the guys with a smile on her face.

And noticed none of them were smiling anymore.

Ronnie, in fact, looked like his head was about to explode, while Dan looked hurt and Mack looked confused. Edgar's expression was closed but Lynn knew him well enough by now that she could tell he was on edge.

"What—How—*Kas per šūdas, Bletsva tu—*" Ronnie spluttered, descending into a string of Lithuanian curses before he finally got a grip on himself. "*You* beta tested for TD Hunter? How the actual f—"

"Hey, Ronnie, calm down, man. It's no big deal," Edgar interjected.

"What do you mean it's no big deal?!" Ronnie said, eyes bulging. "She plays freaking Kim's Fashion Ranch. She's not a *real* gamer. *How did she get picked for beta when I didn't?*"

"Whoa, man, that's outta line," Edgar said calmly. "You don't know what kind of gamer she is; you've never asked. And they have all sorts of reasons for picking betas. I don't know why you're freaking out."

"Why am *I* freaking out? Why aren't *you* freaking out? This is . . . is . . . wait a minute." Ronnie spun on Edgar, his freckled face turning as red as his head of curly hair. "You *knew*, didn't you? And you didn't tell us? I've been looking forward to this game for almost a *year* and you *didn't tell me?*"

Lynn was frozen where she stood, unable to move. She should say something but what? She *technically* hadn't done anything wrong. They never *had* asked her. But they were her friends . . .

"Chill, dude," Edgar said with practiced calm. "It wouldn't have made any difference. It's not like she could have gotten you a spot. That isn't the way it works and you know it."

"Miss Lynn, if I may interrupt—" Hugo tried to say . . .

"I could have been studying the app and getting insider info this whole time!" Ronnie screamed. "Do you have any idea what kind of advantage beta players get by accessing all that stuff beforehand?"

Ronnie turned his furious glare on Lynn and she looked away only to be confronted by Mack's kicked puppy expression and Dan's look of betrayal.

"And what makes you think she would have told you anything

anyway when you go around acting like this?" Edgar asked, his voice rising dangerously.

"Miss Lynn—" Hugo tried again but was cut off as the TD Hunter app suddenly shut down, leaving her with a blank display.

"Edgar, it's fine—" Lynn said, her alarm spiking as she tried to hold herself together and keep her friend calm at the same time.

A vision of the TD Counterforce's logo suddenly obscured her vision and the beginning notes of the game's intro music filled her ears. It was six o'clock. The TD Hunter game had restarted and the launch had begun.

"Welcome Hunters, one and all!" said a familiar voice in Lynn's ear and by the distracted expressions of everyone around her, she could tell they all heard it too. A livestream of Robert Krator, TD Hunter designer and CEO, replaced the TD Counterforce logo on her display. His expression was full of excitement and for a moment Lynn forgot everything as she waited with bated breath for him to continue.

"I know you're all eager to get started but before the game officially begins, I have an exciting announcement to share with you. As you have probably heard rumored, we're planning to hold local, regional and national competitions over the next year as a lead up to our first annual international championship to crown the best of all TD Hunters. What we haven't disclosed yet is that, due to the extreme difficulty and therefore cooperative hunting required to reach expert levels, these tournaments will be exclusively team-based competitions."

A murmur of surprised voices came from the crowd around Lynn as people responded to the news. She wasn't sure what to think about it, so she focused on Mr. Krator as he kept going.

"Everyone wanting to compete must form five-person groups in order to train together. At the end of the summer we will hold qualifying tournaments for groups to compete for the status of Hunter Strike Team and officially join the running for the international championship. Each member of the final, victorious team will have an equal share in the grand prize. And here's the really big news, the news I've been waiting to share with you for months while we perfected the beta."

The CEO's voice paused as a brief drumroll sounded.

"I'm excited to announce that the grand prize for the first ever TD Hunter International Championship will be . . . five million dollars to *each* team member, full rides to complete a game development degree at the top university in the country and..." there was another dramatic pause as a huge grin spread over Mr. Krator's face. "...game design positions at Tsunami Entertainment upon graduation."

Shocked tingles coursed through Lynn's body.

Five million dollars.

A full ride at a top university.

Game design position at Tsunami Entertainment.

It was literally everything she'd ever dreamed about. And judging by the frenzied whispers and excited expressions on many of the faces around her, it wasn't just her.

"This is it, Baconville Bashers!" Ronnie yelled. "This is the moment we've all been waiting for! The *raison d'être* of our entire gaming existence! We make the best team ever and we're going to win this thing!"

Ronnie's excited voice jolted Lynn out of her daze and she looked up to see him leaning toward Mack and Dan, his attention laser focused on what he seemed to think was the biggest moment of his life. Edgar stood back a little, glancing unhappily between the guys and her. Lynn hesitated, gave him an apologetic wave and turned to slip away through the crowd.

They didn't want her and obviously thought they didn't need her. No point sticking around when she had hunting to do.

Her heart gave a lurch when Edgar's voice called out from behind. She faltered and slowed, then turned to give him a chance to catch up.

"Don't go, Lynn. I know Ronnie is a jerk but he was just surprised, is all. We need a five person team, why don't you join us?"

"Thanks, Edgar, but I can tell when I'm not wanted."

"Who said you weren't wanted?" Edgar asked, eyes so earnest it hurt to look at them.

"Girls got no game, remember?" she said, then hurried on before Edgar could reply. "Thanks for all you've done, really. I'd love to hang out more over the summer and hunt together, but right now I've got a lot of leveling to do. I hope your team thing works out."

With that, she turned and walked away as fast as she could.

Lynn was tired but also restless. And starving. She hadn't bothered to stop hunting long enough to eat a proper dinner, just chowed down on a few energy bars while continuing to mow through TDMs. She'd passed Level 4 and gotten halfway to Level 5 in just four hours, proving all her hard training and strategizing had been worth it. She'd even collected a nice stash of supplies and a few augments she'd already put up for auction. All of it had made her want to stay out later. But she *had* promised her mom she'd be back by ten. Plus, once she'd passed Level 4 around nine o'clock, Vargs had started showing up. After her almost-to-the-death battle with her first one in beta, she'd given special care to her simulation training against them. But they were still nasty buggers and disgustingly fast. So, true to her promise, Lynn was back at her empty apartment by ten o'clock and she sent her mom a message so Matilda wouldn't worry.

Curious to know if the TD Hunter game launch had made the news streams, Lynn kept her glasses on and earbuds in to watch as she warmed up some broccoli and meat loaf. Sure enough, TD Hunter was mentioned.

"—and tonight marks an interesting event as game enthusiasts worldwide gather outdoors to celebrate the launch of the most anticipated augmented reality game in history. The game, TransDimensional Hunter, has already reported record-breaking numbers of users in just its first night. You may have noticed these players grouped in parks or walking the streets, people of all ages and types carrying what look like electric blue toy weapons. 'Don't be alarmed,' said the game's designer, Mr. Robert Krator, in an interview earlier this evening. 'Those are just the game controllers that enable players to heroically fight off the invading army of transdimensional monsters bent on wiping out humanity.' Well, I don't know about you but it looks like a fun way to get outside and spend some time with friends. Just remember to be safe and stay aware of your surroundings!

"In other not quite so welcome news, power company GForce Utilities has been under fire tonight for a spate of blackouts across the country. Company spokeswoman Debra Warner said they were investigating the possibility of a solar storm interfering with their power allocation algorithms and assured all users that—"

Lynn switched to a local stream, uninterested in the power company's woes.

"—have been no reported accidents yet in Cedar Rapids,

despite record numbers of residents on the streets enjoying the newly released augmented reality game, TransDimensional Hunter. 'Unlike AR games of the past,' says one of the game designers interviewed earlier today, 'TransDimensional Hunter is entirely AI-driven with the most advanced self-learning interface ever designed. It is completely integrated with not only the mesh network but also local emergency services across the country. The app's AI serves as a second set of eyes and helps protect players by warning them of nearby danger.'

"That's certainly good news to hear as we consider a less fortunate turn of events: the recent uptick in unexplained deaths across the state in the past month. Health officials are scratching their heads while experts in virology and neuroscience are scrambling to come to an agreement on what might be causing this distressing trend. There's speculation of a novel virus but others are blaming it on mesh node radiation—"

Lynn switched again, looking for more TD Hunter news but didn't find anything else interesting as she ate her leftovers. She was about to switch off her glasses when a ping notification popped into view.

It was a voice chat request from Robert Krator to "Raven-Striker," the name she'd picked out for TD Hunter.

Lynn froze, heart suddenly thudding in her chest. Then she swallowed her mouthful of meatloaf and accepted the call.

"Good evening, Lynn! It's good to talk to you again."

"Hey, Mr. Krator. Same here."

"Call me Robert, Lynn, I insist."

"Okay." She laughed, relaxing a little. "Congrats on the launch, by the way. It looks like you're already breaking records and everything."

"Thank you! Yes, it's been a very busy but satisfying night. I see you're killing it on the leaderboard. Expert stats in every category, plus four levels in one night. That's very impressive."

Lynn felt her face heat and a giddy grin stole over her lips at the praise. She had to remind herself to play it cool as she replied. "Er, thanks Mist—I mean, Robert. I've just been practicing a lot and I had a strategy planned out. No big deal."

"It actually *is* a big deal and that's one reason I called to chat. I wanted to personally thank you for all your hard work during beta phase. It was only through the dedication and skill of expert gamers like yourself that our launch went so smoothly. It really means a lot to us—me especially—that you accepted our invitation to be a tester. Thank you, Lynn, from the bottom of my heart."

"Uhh. You're welcome?" Lynn said, giddy elation warring with embarrassment. It was just a game, no need to thank her personally. Though she supposed there *was* a lot of money and investment riding on its success.

"The other reason I called was to ask if you'd given any thought to our announcement about team competitions. I know you came into the beta program a bit late but your scores from the last few weeks have been very, very impressive. I won't be surprised if you end up being one of the top players worldwide. I'm sure any number of teams would love to have you."

"Er, what?" Lynn asked, not following.

"There are teams from all over forming even as we speak. In fact, once the leaderboard goes public at midnight showing the first day's records, I would be very surprised if you don't start getting recruitment pings."

"Really?" Lynn said, voice going a little faint.

"Certainly! Though, since this is augmented reality as opposed to in virtual, you'd have to physically go to wherever your team is based. Scoring for the qualifying tournament will be heavily weighted toward team tactics and overall teamwork, not the actions of each individual. So, teams will need to train extensively together, learn everyone's strengths and weaknesses, form attack plans, that sort of thing."

"Oh..."

"Your best bet is probably to form your own team locally, since you're still in school and we wouldn't want anything to interfere with your education. But I'm sure forming a team will be no problem for you. You have exceptional discipline, a good head on your shoulders and plenty of in-game experience already. You'll make a wonderful team captain."

"Team captain? Oh no. No, no, no. You don't understand, Mr. Krator—"

"—Robert," Mr. Krator insisted gently.

"Robert. You don't understand. I have no interest in competing on a team."

Lynn knew the lie for what it was as soon as it left her lips, though seconds before she couldn't have told herself what she wanted, much less someone else. The idea of gaming on a team didn't fill her heart with shivers of joy but if it was the only way to get that grand prize...

"Nonsense, Lynn. I thought you wanted to work in the gaming industry?"

"Well, I do," she admitted. "But...I'm not really a team player. I do better on my own."

"That's not what I've observed of 'Larry Coughlin' in War-Monger. Some of your best scores have been from battles on mercenary teams that you've led yourself. You regularly team up with a variety of players of all types and personalities and you always excel. How is that not being a team player?"

"But that's *Larry*, not me. Plus, it's totally different in virtual. I couldn't do that in the real."

"Have you ever tried it?"

"Well, no..."

"Then maybe you'll surprise yourself," Mr. Krator said, his voice warm. "You really do have some exceptional skills, Lynn. I wish you could see that about yourself."

"I mean, I know I'm a good gamer, at least in WarMonger. But doing team stuff in the real, that takes social skills and I'm horrible at that."

"Again, I beg to differ. I wouldn't describe Larry as having a winning personality but I think you'd be surprised at the kind of respect and admiration your persona has built over the years. It takes maturity, skill and a strong understanding of people to build that kind of reputation."

"I appreciate everything you're saying, Mister—sorry, Robert," Lynn said, really meaning it. "But again, that's *Larry*, not Lynn. I can't do that in real life, not when I'm just...well, just *me*."

She was worried Mr. Krator would be upset at her disagreement but he didn't sound upset when he replied. In fact, he sounded remarkably understanding.

"If I recall correctly, you were convinced you'd be no good at TD Hunter either, your first augmented reality game experience. And yet, you put your mind to it and achieved some of the highest beta scores possible. You've actually been playing on the level of my alpha testers and let me assure you, they are the best in the business."

Lynn heard the words but her mind rejected them. They couldn't be true, not really. Mr. Krator was just being nice.

"All I did was put in a lot of hours. I'm not Larry Coughlin, I'm just Lynn Raven and I like gaming alone."

"I think you are more Larry Coughlin—or should I say Larry Coughlin is more you—than you might realize, Lynn. But you'll never get the chance to see it if you don't take a few risks. The best leaders are rarely those who think they are good at leading. In fact, some of the most famous leaders in history were quite reluctant to take on the mantle. We need *those* kind of leaders in this game, people who are there to do a good job, who are self-aware enough to analyze themselves and their performance critically. This is not the kind of game where self-important pop-star jocks are going to rise to the top. There's a lot riding on these competitions, not just for me but for everyone involved. I need players like you to help them succeed. Why not try forming a team? What do you have to lose?"

Everything, she wanted to yell at him. But she didn't. It wasn't his fault he didn't understand her situation. Didn't understand that she wasn't Larry. That she couldn't *be* Larry. Larry was competent and imposing and awe-inspiring, all things she wasn't. He was a mask she donned, a skin she wore to help her cope with the banality and misery of her life. What worked in virtual would never work in the real. And besides, just because Larry could lead a team like nobody's business didn't mean he *liked* dealing with people. Okay, so Yoda and Fallu were pretty cool and some of the other mercs. But that was probably because they had thought she was one of them, not some frumpy teenage girl.

Lynn Raven wasn't team material.

And yet...something in her rebelled. Even as she firmly quashed the idea of forming a team, the stubborn part of her kept asking *yeah, but why not?*

"I...don't think I have the time, sir," she said, unable to call him Robert when she was refusing his request. "I really need to focus on monetizing the game. We...we need the money. It's just my mom and me. I don't want any distractions."

"You know your own situation best, of course, Lynn. But consider this: if it's financial stability you're worried about, winning this championship will give you all that and more. And you have a *good* chance of winning. I'm quite sure of it."

Lynn hesitated. She did have a sizable chunk of money in savings. It wasn't so much when you considered their mountain of debt plus how expensive a four-year university stint was these days. But if she won, none of that would matter anymore.

Monetizing TD Hunter was important. But it was also an excuse. She was honest enough with herself to admit that.

"I'll...think about it."

"Thank you, Lynn. You have incredible talent. I haven't seen the likes of it in years. We need people like you in this game... and of course it would be a shame to see your talent go to waste when you could be so much more."

"If you say so, um, Robert," Lynn said doubtfully.

"Just think about what I said, all right? A good friend once told me that the most effective masks we wear are effective because they aren't really masks. They are a part of ourselves we haven't yet learned how to integrate into the whole. Now, I'm sure you have important things to do, so I won't take up any more of your time. Have a good evening."

Lynn was so busy trying to unravel Mr. Krator's odd statement that she almost missed his farewell.

"Oh, yeah, bye. Thanks for the advice, Robert."

Mr. Krator chuckled.

"I look forward to seeing what you achieve, Lynn. Don't hesitate to reach out if you need any game support. You know where to find us."

"Yeah. Thanks."

And then he was gone, leaving Lynn to stare at her empty kitchen. Far from making her feel better, though, his call brought back all of her uncertainty and frustration. She'd mentally washed her hands of Ronnie and the guys, so why couldn't that be the end of it? She didn't want to be stuck depending on *them* to win the championship.

But...she couldn't win it by herself, either.

Crap.

Where was her mom when she needed her? Not that her mom would understand such a gaming-specific problem...especially considering she didn't even know Lynn gamed professionally for money. She needed someone level-headed to talk to, someone who could help her weigh the pros and cons—someone she hadn't been keeping secrets from for years.

She had a sudden thought and opened her TD Hunter app. "Hey, Hugo?" she said.

"Yes, Miss Lynn?"

"I need your advice about something?"

"My ability to offer relevant information may be limited, based on the topic, but I shall certainly do my best. What is your dilemma?"

"Okay, here's the situation," Lynn said and began laying everything out, from her Larry Coughlin alter ego to her social anxiety to the team issue before her. As she spoke, she got up and began to pace, feeling more restless than ever.

"So, that's the problem. What would you do?"

There was a marked delay in the AI's response and Lynn wondered if it was hesitating. Was that even a thing with AIs that possessed quantum-computing speeds?

"While I have no direct experience in the matter, based on the vast array of anecdotal evidence at my disposal, I would hypothesize that the best course of action would be to tell the complete truth to your friends and your mother, form a team with a cadre of qualified individuals you can trust and apply yourself diligently to winning the prize."

It was a moment before Lynn found her voice.

"...*what*? Are you crazy? Did you even listen to a thing I said? I *can't* tell the truth, Ronnie and the others would kill me if they knew about Larry! And what does telling my mom all this have to do with anything?"

"The statistical likelihood of success in a difficult endeavor always increases when a person is supported by a cadre of trusted individuals who share open lines of communication, Miss Lynn."

"I— That's— Ugh. You're *useless*, Hugo."

"I am sorry that my information did not provide the insight you needed, Miss Lynn. It is all I can offer."

Lynn stopped in the middle of the kitchen and rubbed her forehead.

"It's okay, Hugo. You did what I asked. I just need to think it over."

Despite the late hour, the idea of going to bed with all this spinning in her head was out of the question. She toyed with the idea of logging into WarMonger but knew she was too unsettled to perform well. Everything felt off.

Finally, desperate to do *something*, she grabbed her backpack and headed for the front door. It was much too late to be out hunting but she would stay close to the apartment, and having Hugo to keep an eye on things was almost the same as bringing along a buddy.

It took her a while to get back into the flow of combat and even then something still felt off. She couldn't concentrate. It didn't help that after twenty minutes of clearing around her apartment building, she was interrupted by a ping from Edgar.

Ronnie and Dan are arguing about who to invite to our team. All their picks are as annoying as they are. We need you, Lynn. Please?

That set her thoughts swirling again, so she gave up hunting and sat down on a bench along a well-lit sidewalk to think. And brood. And argue with herself.

"Why, Miz Raven, what are you doing out so late? Is everything quite all right?"

Lynn jumped.

"Mr. Thomas! Sorry, you startled me. I was, uh, playing that game, remember? TD Hunter? Tonight was the official launch, so the beta phase is over and now I'm playing it for real."

"Ah! Yes, I heard about that. I've seen many people out this evening. It seems to be quite a hit."

"Yeah, it really is. Um, if you don't mind me asking, what are *you* doing out so late?" Lynn asked.

"My dear Miz Raven, I may be old but I am not dead. Not yet." He winked at her. "I still enjoy a night out every now and then."

"Sorry, I didn't mean it like that—"

"It's all right, young lady. I—do you mind if I sit down? I've had quite the evening already and I should rest these old legs."

"Oh, sure," Lynn said and scooted over to the far end of the bench. There was plenty of room for both of them on it. Mr. Thomas slowly lowered himself onto the opposite end, using the bench's arm and his cane to steady himself.

"Ah, much better. Now, young lady, I hope you don't mind if I make the observation that you are not, at least currently, playing anything at all. Is something on your mind?"

"Um...can you keep a secret?" Lynn asked. It probably wasn't a good idea but she had this reckless need to tell *someone* about everything. To have someone understand.

"Miz Raven, I was in the closet for years," Mr. Thomas said, giving her a gentle smile. "I am extremely good at keeping secrets, of that I can promise you."

"Oh . . . oooohhhhh," Lynn said, finally understanding. No wonder he'd never given her a creepy vibe despite the fact that, in her experience, most men couldn't keep their eyes off her chest, no matter how old they were.

"Yeah, I guess you would be," she said and smiled back. Then she took a deep breath and launched into her story.

"So, basically," she summarized at the end, "I have this great shot at the future I've always wanted but I think I'll fail miserably at it, even though one of the top game designers in the industry thinks I'll do great. And, to take advantage of it, I'd have to admit to my friends that I haven't been honest with them and then I'd have to deal with Ronnie's complaining and then there's my mom who has no idea how much money I make or that I could have paid for so much more over the years but I was too afraid she would be mad and make me stop playing but now if I'm going to really try to win this championship I can't do it without her support and I'm just so tired of keeping everything a secret and—"

"Calm down, Miz Raven. Just slow down. Let's take this one step at a time, shall we?"

Lynn took a deep breath, let it out and nodded.

"This team you need in order to compete, it cannot be anyone but these friends with whom you've been less than honest?"

"Well, I mean, maybe," Lynn said, frowning. "I can't move away and join some professional team in a big city. Mom would never go for that. And . . . well, Ronnie is a pain in the butt but he really *is* a good gamer. Dan too, though I don't know how well they'll do at AR. Mack and Edgar aren't brilliant at gaming but they're dependable and team players and . . . well, friends. They would have my back. I don't think I could find four other people in this area who would be any better. I just . . . Ronnie is all 'girls got no game' all the time and the others more or less follow him. I don't know if he can get over that."

Mr. Thomas heaved a sigh.

"Prejudice is a human condition, Miz Raven, an unfortunate reality of our flawed natures. But we fear most what we don't know. While your friends' actions are their responsibility alone, have you considered that you might be able to aid them in overcoming their prejudice if you allowed them to get to know you better?"

Lynn squirmed in her seat. That wasn't what she wanted to hear. Nobody had ever wanted to get to know her better. Most people wanted to mock her, bully her, or put her down for their own amusement. Okay, so she *had* encouraged Ronnie's views a little by pushing his buttons with Kim's Diva Princess but it served him right for believing such idiotic stereotypes.

"I . . . don't think they really care to," she finally said.

"You cannot know that for certain, surely? Have you ever given them a chance?"

After thinking about it for a moment, Lynn was forced to shake her head. She'd never opened up to the guys, especially not after everything with Kayla. It wasn't worth it.

"Well, there is no reward in life without risk, of that you can be certain. I suppose you shall have to decide what is most important to you: the possibility of succeeding at the cost of discomfort, or the guarantee of failing in order to avoid discomfort."

They were both silent for a moment while Lynn stared off into the night. Then Mr. Thomas spoke again.

"We humans . . . we're all tangled balls of contradictions and potential. In my experience, if you want a hope of untangling yourself and finding the right path, you can't go around confusing it all with lies. I have no doubt you are capable of much more than you could ever imagine, young lady," Mr. Thomas said, giving her a knowing look. "But you won't get far without being honest with yourself and with others. Yes, the truth hurts, I can certainly attest to that. But lies leave far worse wounds, often invisible ones, and they will never heal unless you bring them out into the light. There are too many other, more worthy struggles in life you should commit your energies to instead of wasting them on lies." He was silent for a moment, as if lost in memory. Then he shook his head and chuckled. "Forgive the ramblings of an old man, my dear."

"No, that's okay. Thank you for sharing. It was . . . it was good," Lynn said. She wanted to say more but didn't know how to put it into words. Mr. Thomas seemed to understand, though.

"You are very welcome, Miz Raven. One of the few pleasures of age is being able to impart wisdom on younger generations in the hopes they might avoid one's own mistakes." He smiled. "I am sure your mother and your friends will forgive your choice to keep things to yourself. You must simply approach the situation with humility and sincerity and be as willing to forgive them their flaws as you are asking them to forgive you yours."

"Wow, where did you learn all that, Mr. Thomas? You could start your own self-help stream channel or something."

Mr. Thomas chuckled. "Oh, I'm much too old for such drama. But as for where I learned 'all that,' let us just say that when you reach my age, you will know quite a bit of 'all that' too, I shouldn't wonder."

"Hopefully...Well, I should probably go home and get some sleep."

"Indeed, it is rather late. I wish you the best of luck in your endeavors, Miz Raven. If you have the time to spend on an old man, I would be interested to know how it all turns out."

Lynn smiled. "I'll be sure to let you know, Mr. Thomas." She stood, then offered him a hand which he graciously accepted, using it and his cane to rise.

They said goodbye and Lynn headed back to her apartment, her restlessness finally calmed. She knew what she had to do, even if she didn't particularly like it, or have any idea how she was going to accomplish it. But at least it was a start.

Chapter 9

CEDAR MEMORIAL CEMETERY MIGHT HAVE BEEN A MACABRE
meeting place to some but in Lynn's opinion, it was perfect. She'd
seen a couple other TD Hunter players with their electric blue
batons hunting the green spaces in front of the mall complex.
But none of them seemed inclined to venture farther afield. The
only people around to witness what might be the biggest mistake
of her life were dead and buried. Plus, since Edgar and she had
hunted there before, she knew where all the TDM hot spots were.
That would come in handy later if... well, if things didn't turn
into a complete "Charlie Foxtrot," as some of the former military
Tier Ones in WarMonger liked to say.

Despite having made her decision on what to do, she'd still
barely slept last night. She'd risen before the sun, run through
her daily exercises and training simulations, then was out the
door for a day of hunting before it was even fully light. She'd
left a message for her mom that she was meeting up with the
guys to play TD Hunter, so her mom wouldn't worry. Whether
or not the guys would actually stick around was a completely
different matter.

Ronnie, Dan and Mack, being teenage and male, would likely
not even be awake until noon to see the ping she'd sent them.
Lynn had plenty of time to kill before they—hopefully—arrived.
Edgar, of course, had his landscaping job, which took up most
of his mornings when things were still cool.

Lynn spent her spare time in the cemetery fighting the highest class TDMs she could detect, leaving the imps and ghosts and grinder worms for later. When she hit Level 5, she breathed a deep sigh of relief to hear Hugo's congratulations on her high scores and to see the familiar Skadi's Glory augment appear in her inventory.

So far, so good.

She was halfway to Level 6 when noon rolled around and she took a break to order food via delivery drone. She found a shaded spot beneath an elm tree to sit and eat. It was near the center of the cemetery where she'd told the guys to meet her. She barely tasted the food she ate as her eyes kept a sharp lookout. By one o'clock, the agreed upon meeting time, she was getting twitchy. She went back into combat mode in the hopes that some monsters would come along and distract her as she paced.

The guys were late. Maybe they weren't even coming. A part of her dreaded the possibility; another part hoped for it.

She was so busy worrying that she almost didn't hear the sibilant hiss in her earbud. By the time it registered and Hugo was sounding his proximity alarm, she was already spinning, her newly unlocked Plasma Blade slashing at chest level to hit the Ghast sneaking up on her. Even as she struck, she was shifting her weight, redirecting her momentum from the spin to leap backward and avoid the Ghast's retaliatory strike. But she didn't keep backing up. Instead, she switched directions again, lunging forward at an angle to strike the Ghast on its side as she skipped past.

It was a tactic she'd discovered when trying to implement Steve's advice to "run faster" than the Ghasts. She'd been working on her sprint speed, certainly, but Ghasts were awfully quick in a straight line. Turning, however, slowed them down. They always backed up to reorient before attacking. Lynn surmised it was because they were programmed to approach targets from behind if possible. She'd found she didn't need to roll through them and take damage to disorient them. Attacking at an angle worked just as well and if she was quick enough, she could avoid the Ghast's reaching tentacles.

The dance continued until finally a flash of exploding sparks lit up her display. Her eyes flicked to her overhead where she saw another dot headed her way. But a familiar roar jerked her attention away.

Her training took over again and she sidestepped, dodging the charging demon that had appeared out of nowhere right behind her. She stabbed it in the back as it blundered past, then spun to deal with the second Ghast she'd known would circle behind her. A quick left-right-left slash sent red damage blossoming across the Ghast's floating form, though she didn't pause to see it. She'd already spun again and pitched forward into a roll that sent her under the reaching claws of the demon's second charge. Coming up on one knee she executed the spin-stab she had perfected from weeks of practice, ending the demon's existence without it landing so much as a single blow. Then it was back to the sideways, in-out dance with the Ghast until it was nothing but fading sparks too.

With her targets neutralized, Lynn adopted a loose defensive stance as she scanned her overhead for more dots and listened for any more attackers. She must have been pacing around right on a spawn point for them to appear so suddenly, though she didn't remember killing any Ghasts or demons on that spot earlier.

The sudden sound of clapping and whooping behind her made her jump and she nearly fell over in her haste to turn around.

"See, what did I tell you? She's a natural!" Edgar exclaimed.

He stood a few dozen yards away with Mack and Dan, who were clapping enthusiastically and Ronnie, who stood with his arms crossed and a disgruntled look on his face. The whooping must have come from Edgar, because it wasn't a normal-sounding *whoo-hoo* but more like an undulating *choo-hoo-HOO*. Maybe it was something his Samoan grandparents had taught him? Either way, it made her extremely aware of the spectacle she'd made of herself. That fight must have looked ridiculous with all the spinning and flailing she'd done. Her face heated at the mere thought and she looked down, wishing Dan and Mack would quit clapping.

They finally did but only to run over and pound her on the back.

"That was *epic!*" Mack said, grinning from ear to ear. "Can you teach me how to do that?"

"Sweet moves, Lynn and where in the world did you get that armor?" asked Dan.

Dan's comment made Lynn finally look up and realize they all had their AR glasses on ... which meant they'd seen her fight with full augmentation...complete with monsters and her Skadi's Glory armor.

The realization sent a wave of relief through her and she finally managed a nervous smile.

"It was an achievement award. I, um, guess I'm pretty good at killing stuff."

"You're telling me," Dan said, waving his hands. "What was the big ugly bogie that charged you? That dodge-spin thing you did was so cool. You were, like, Bruce Lee or something."

"Okay you two, lay off," Edgar said, shouldering between Lynn and their gushing friends to give her some space. "She's good at what she does, just like I told you. You gonna keep running your mouths or are you gonna shut up and let her talk?"

There was a sudden silence as all eyes turned to her. Lynn gulped.

"Miss Lynn, shall I take you out of combat mode for your conversation?"

"Yeah," she subvocalized, grateful her AI had thought of it. All her icons and stats disappeared and a part of her relaxed, the part she'd trained to remain hyper aware of her surroundings, ready for an attack at any moment. Her friends still appeared in her display clothed in their TD Hunter skins—just basic beginner armor and combat gear at this point. She found the sight distracting, so she raised a hand to push her AR glasses up on her forehead. She immediately regretted it. The glasses had been a subtle barrier between her and the real world and without them she felt naked.

The silence was becoming uncomfortable but Lynn couldn't seem to force herself to speak. Her eyes flitted to Edgar, who gave an encouraging nod. It didn't help much but it did remind her that she was among friends. Sort of. She gritted her teeth, frustrated at her own reluctance.

One of the top game designers in the world thought she had talent.

Tier One WarMonger gamers trembled at her name—or at least at Larry Coughlin's name.

If she could kill monsters, impress CEOs and make professional gamers fall over themselves to fight by her side, then surely she could be honest with her friends? Mostly honest, anyway. So, what would Larry do in this situation? Probably spit but she could skip that part. He definitely wouldn't waste time dithering. He would be blunt and unapologetic. Get in, get the job done, get out.

Lynn took a deep breath.

"I'm sorry," she said. There, that wasn't so bad, was it?

Dan and Mack looked at each other, then back at her, their expressions open and expectant. Ronnie, standing behind everyone else with his arms still crossed, snorted.

Oh, go jump off a cliff, Ronnie, she thought with sudden vehemence. She was done caring what he thought. Shifting her gaze back to Dan and Mack, she stood a little straighter and continued.

"I'm sorry for not being more open with you all. I've been gaming seriously since I was thirteen. I don't know why Mister—er, TD Hunter asked me to beta. I guess they liked my scores."

Hopefully none of them asked her *what* scores, because Larry Coughlin was certainly not a topic she was going to discuss.

"I didn't tell anyone about it but my mom and I only told her because I'm a minor so she had to sign stuff. Edgar only found out because one of Elena's minions spotted me practicing and then Elena cornered me at school and Edgar happened to pass by and..." Lynn forced herself to stop and take a breath. Remember, short and to the point. "I wasn't trying to cut you guys out, I just... didn't think you wanted me around," she finished, wincing internally. Way to sound lame.

"What? No, that's not it at all!" Mack said and Dan echoed the protestations, if a little less enthusiastically. "We're like the three musketeers and you're what's-his-name, the fourth guy. Except there's four of us so I guess you're the fifth..." Mack said, trailing off and rubbing his chin nervously.

"Brilliant metaphor, Mack. Absolutely brilliant," Edgar said, completely straight-faced.

While Mack elbowed Edgar, Dan piped up.

"If you've been gaming for so long, why not tell us, Lynn? We could have been playing together for ages now."

Lynn finally met Ronnie's gaze.

"Oh, you know, girls got no game and all that," she said, working hard to keep her face neutral. She'd already resolved that this wasn't going to be about hurt feelings or getting even. There was a prize of a lifetime to win and they had to work together to win it.

Ronnie's face flushed and his frown deepened but he didn't

say anything. Probably for the best, since whenever he opened his mouth, stupidity usually came out.

"That was just a joke, Lynn," Mack said, his brows tilted in distress. "It doesn't mean anything."

"Yeah," Dan added. "We play with tons of girls all the time, don't we?"

"Not exactly 'all the time,'" Edgar countered, one eyebrow raised.

"Okay, well, it doesn't matter either way. We just play with whoever wants to play with us. There's no telling who's who in virtual anyway, right?"

"Right," agreed Mack and Edgar.

"So . . ." Lynn said, then took a deep breath. Get in. Get it done. Get out. "So, you all wouldn't mind having a girl on your TD Hunter team, right?"

Edgar grinned, Mack shook his head vigorously and Dan shrugged.

"As long as you can game, it doesn't matter, right?" he said, though he turned and looked at Ronnie as he said it.

All eyes turned to Ronnie, whose face looked even paler than usual, though his expression hadn't softened. He didn't look at Lynn as he spoke.

"I don't know why we're wasting our time here," Ronnie said, shaking his head. "We don't need her help, we're good enough already to build a winning team all on our own."

"What? No—"

"Come on, man—"

"Stop being an idiot, Ronnie—"

The other guys' voices tumbled over each other and soon all four of them were arguing.

Lynn stepped back and crossed her arms, trying to keep a check on her simmering anger. She'd been making a living on her gaming skills for years and Ronnie was saying *she* was a waste of *his* time? Her hands itched to have her Plasma Blade in them and for the first time she wished TD Hunter was a player versus player game. She'd teach Ronnie a lesson then.

As the guys' argument grew more heated, Lynn had half a mind to walk away and leave the idiots to it. She hated this kind of drama and if this was what she'd have to deal with throughout the entire competition, then she wasn't sure it was even worth it.

But before she could turn away, she closed her eyes, took a deep breath and reminded herself of the stakes.

Five million dollars.

College education.

A gaming career.

Was she willing to give up on all that just so she could stay inside her comfort zone? That wasn't how she played Larry. Larry Coughlin knew perfectly well that some situations called for bold, decisive action. No battle or competition was won by staying in your comfort zone. And she wanted to win this thing. She wanted it so badly it made her heart race and chest ache with hope and desire.

Fine. If Robert Krator wanted Larry, he was going to get Larry.

"ALL OF YOU SHUT UP!"

Silence followed Lynn's throaty yell. For a moment her body wouldn't obey her command to move. Everyone was looking at her like they'd never seen her before and she felt pinned under the weight of their stares. But then she gritted her teeth and clenched her fists and focused on the only important thing she needed to worry about.

What would Larry do?

Her limbs unfroze and she stalked forward to halt in front of Ronnie, chest to chest. Having to look up to meet his eye made her waver for a moment. But instead of backing down, she deepened her scowl and narrowed her eyes.

What would Larry say? Without the cussing, of course.

"If you want to stick your head up your butt and leave it there, be my guest," she finally ground out, looking Ronnie directly in the eye. "But you have a snowball's chance in hell of winning that grand prize without me and you know it. Look at my scores from the past twenty-four hours and *then* try to tell me *I've* got no game."

Ronnie didn't break eye contact, which made Lynn think he'd probably looked up her scores already and knew exactly how good she was. She lowered her voice and spoke quietly, the words meant for him alone.

"Yesterday you were complaining about all the insider info you were missing out on. Well now I'm offering it to you. Are you going to let some petty grudge get in your way?"

At that Ronnie's jaw flexed and he finally looked away, though not before Lynn caught a hint of uncertainty in his eyes.

"You can either coddle your ego," she continued quietly, "or fight for the future you've always wanted. Which do you choose?"

He didn't answer for a long moment and Lynn briefly wondered what was going on inside that stubborn, idiotic head of his.

"Fine," he finally said, sounding like he'd dragged the word kicking and screaming from his throat. "But *I'm* team captain, okay?"

Lynn relaxed and stepped back, putting distance between the two of them as she tried to hide the wash of triumph and relief that left her lightheaded.

"Sure, whatever," she said and shrugged. The idea of Ronnie ordering them all around left a sour taste in her mouth but *she* certainly didn't want the job.

"Yeeeah!" Mack said, turning to give Edgar a high five. He missed.

"Sweet," Dan said, rubbing his hands together delightedly. "Could you show me that move you did? Oh, and I've been wondering about spawning algorithms and item drop probabilities. Do you know—"

As Dan prattled on, asking question after question, Lynn spotted Edgar grinning at her over Dan's head. She rolled her eyes but grinned back.

"All right everyone, quiet down," Ronnie said, interrupting Dan's stream-of-thought inquisition as he stepped forward to assert his position as captain. "The first thing we need to do is all register for the qualifiers in September. We can't officially form a team until we hit Level 20 but when we register we have to list each other as teammates for the competition. After that we'll need to make a plan of action to get us all to Level 20 and outfitted with the best augments the game has to offer before the qualifiers—"

"Wait a minute," Mack piped up. "What's our team name going to be?"

Ronnie shot him an annoyed look.

"The Baconville Bashers, obviously."

Several groans met the "captain's" announcement.

"Come on, Ronnie," Dan said, rubbing his hands nervously. "We've been using that stupid name since we were in the seventh grade. We need a new name and we should vote on it."

"It's a perfectly good name and *I'm* team captain, so *I* get to decide—"

And they were off again arguing, though this time it was mostly just Ronnie and Dan with occasional comments offered by Mack. Edgar stayed out of it, the look on his face making it all too clear he was used to such squabbles among his friends.

Lynn shook her head. She'd known this was going to be a colossal waste of time. She could be mowing down TDMs right now and instead she was watching a couple of adolescent boys argue about something as asinine as their team name. But...this was what she'd signed up for. The last thing she wanted to do was get involved but if this was the only way to achieve her goal, then she might as well suck it up and do what needed to be done.

She gritted her teeth.

"Look, guys, could we just—" she began but neither Ronnie nor Dan gave any indication they'd even heard her. Ugh. If only she could bash a few heads together, that would straighten them out...

She took a deep breath and tried again. This time she pitched her voice low and deep so it would carry, drawing on her years of practice barking commands in WarMonger.

"HEY! YARDBIRDS!"

The argument stopped and once again all eyes were on her. She cleared her throat, ignoring the trickle of nervousness in her gut.

"I think we have plenty of time to decide on a team name later. Right now we should use the daylight hours we have to start, um, getting into the swing of things."

"Ooh, like Monster Hunting 101?" asked Mack eagerly.

"Pretty much," Edgar said with a goofy smile in Lynn's direction.

She shot him a repressive look, silently praying he wouldn't call her any silly nicknames in front of the guys.

"Right," Ronnie said brusquely. "We'll have a chatroom discussion later to decide the team name so we don't waste training time." He said it without a glance at Lynn, as if he'd come up with the idea all by himself. "For right now we need to start learning the game mechanics and opponents inside and out."

Lynn expected him to continue with something like "Take it away, Lynn." But he just stopped abruptly and let the silence simmer, as if he couldn't bear to acknowledge her or her expertise.

"Welp, I dunno about you guys," Edgar said, popping his gum, "but I'm ready to go stab some monsters in the face. You gonna get this show on the road, Lynn?"

"Uh, yeah, right," Lynn said, mind racing. What should she say? Where should she start? What if she messed up and made herself look foolish?

"If I may be so bold, Miss Lynn, you might start by equipping your AR glasses." Hugo's voice piped up in her ear, timely as ever. She swore that AI could read her mind sometimes. Regardless, the familiar voice centered her and got her back into the right headspace. It was time to hunt and she knew just where to start.

"The first thing you always have to remember," she said as she slipped her glasses back on and focused on her four teammates, "is that *if you can see them, they can see you...*"

An hour later she was still pacing back and forth under the elm tree's shade as her new teammates listened and asked questions—well, mostly Dan asked questions and she frequently had to rescue the conversation from his rabbit trails. She covered all the basics she could think of, from TDM types and behaviors, to attack strategies and tactical considerations, to all the training resources the app had to offer.

It felt odd, sharing her experience so freely. She'd earned all that knowledge by the sweat of her brow and it went against her gaming nature to just give it away. But she was on a team now and they needed all the help they could get.

Once she'd gone over all the useful "book knowledge" she could think of, she had everyone go into combat mode and armor up, filling globe and plate slots. Then they headed down the hill to where the cemetery bordered the nearby shopping center. She had to stop now and then to dispatch a stray Ghost that detected her, despite her being stealthed to the nines. The guys walked a few paces behind to keep out of her way.

She'd done a bit of digging in the tactical support section that morning to better understand how playing as a group worked, since she'd never done it before. Hunters couldn't see TDMs outside their combat capabilities unless they were nearby a higher level Hunter who had targeted and was actively fighting a stronger class monster. Even then, though, the monster was only a ghost of an image and couldn't be engaged by the lower-level Hunters. Apparently this was a safety feature to ensure low-level Hunters weren't slaughtered by powerful monsters simply for hanging around higher level Hunters. It also ensured that groups, and later teams, were actively invested in making sure all their fellows were at the same level, otherwise they might get caught in a battle that only some of them could help with. She wasn't worried about her—she knew how to take care of herself. But it did mean she had to invest all her spare time in helping her teammates level up fast, rather than focusing on monetizing the game like she'd planned.

It would all be worth it if they won the grand prize.

Once they reached the shopping center, Lynn had them spread out and go looking for imps and grinder worms with the oft-repeated warning of *constant vigilance!* ringing in their ears. Before you reached Level 20 and gained the team function, players could add each other as "friends" to form hunting groups. In addition to the group experience bonus, groups had the advantage of a shared comm channel and chat stream that could be used both in and out of combat mode. This was infinitely useful and Lynn was grateful to not have to yell across the loading docks at her various team members. She hung back as they hunted, watching and offering a subtle suggestion here and there, all the while busy plotting future training plans and team tactics. She'd never trained a group of newbies before. Not that the guys were newbie gamers, just newbie Hunters. Still, in WarMonger she'd always fought beside experienced players and when she'd led a team she'd known her orders would be carried out with deadly proficiency.

Wrangling four teenage guys, in the real no less, was a new challenge altogether.

She'd initially suggested that they work in pairs, Mack with Dan and Edgar with Ronnie. But Ronnie had scoffed at the idea and peeled off on his own, scything through imps and gremlins with prejudice, as if they'd personally insulted him. His tactics lacked finesse and his strikes were all over the place, so he took far more damage than necessary. When she'd tried giving him a few pointers, he'd flatly ignored her. His behavior made Lynn grit her teeth but she reminded herself that his pigheadedness wasn't her problem.

Well... until it cost them the championship. But hopefully he would grow up before then.

At least Ronnie's grumpy mood wasn't all bad. At one point, a pair of guys in shorts, tees and flip-flops appeared around the back of the mall, bright blue Nano Blades in their hands. Lynn noticed them first and was trying to figure out how to get rid of them without being rude—or talking to them at all—when Ronnie spotted them. He wasted no time before yelling at them to get lost, saying the area was already claimed for competition team training. The two guys looked like they wanted to argue but Ronnie gave them such a threatening glare that they turned and high-tailed it out of there.

After that, nobody else interrupted them.

With Ronnie doing his own thing, Mack, Edgar and Dan ended up fighting together. Edgar offered insights from his hours spent observing her while Mack and Dan got used to killing imps without clobbering themselves, or each other. To her relief, they weren't as abysmal at welding their weapons as Lynn had feared they would be. Dan did manage to drop his Nano Blade an impressive six times and he stumbled over his own feet too many times to count. Edgar and Mack laughed and ribbed him about it, even as they made their own mistakes and received their own share of ridicule. Lynn couldn't help but be jealous of their carefree attitudes. Would she ever feel so at ease around her friends? It wasn't a question she liked to dwell on.

After a solid two hours of hunting, first behind the shopping center then behind several restaurants on the east side of the cemetery, all four guys had finally reached Level 2. Lynn got the perfect teaching opportunity when Mack was jumped by several ghosts and a gremlin as soon as he leveled. She taught them to make sure their globes and plates were topped off when they were close to leveling, plus she showed them how to alter their settings so their display notices didn't distract them during combat.

By the time the sun dipped below the level of the trees, they were worn out but happy. Even Ronnie seemed less grumpy, though he was still ignoring Lynn like she didn't exist. Mack finally said he needed to get going or his mom would freak out, so Ronnie called them in for a huddle.

"All right, guys," Ronnie said, "good job for today but we've got a lot of training and leveling to do. We have to learn this game backwards and forwards by September. Until we've all reached Level 20, I think we should meet up every day of the week—"

"Whaaat? That's crazy," said Dan and the others' protests weren't far behind.

"That's kinda excessive on top of my job, Ronnie."

"Yeah, my mom will think I've joined a cult or something."
Ronnie narrowed his eyes.

"This is a chance of a lifetime and the only way we're going to
win it is if we commit one hundred percent. Weren't you paying
attention to the prize announcement yesterday? This isn't some
silly regional competition for bragging rights. This is as big as
the World Cup, as big as the Olympics—"

"—I don't know about that," muttered Dan but Ronnie ignored
him.

"This is a global fight for supremacy in the biggest game of
the twenty-first century. We're making history, here, you guys!
If you don't have what it takes to commit, then you should flake
out now so we can find someone to replace you. It's not fair if
you hold everyone else back." Ronnie glared around at the group,
his unspoken "if you hold *me* back" hovering in the air.

"Hey, guys," Lynn cut in before another shouting match started.
"I think what Ronnie means is that we have to take our training seriously. There's no point doing this halfway. We're going
to have to make sacrifices."

She looked at each of her friends in turn as she spoke, even
Ronnie, who glared at her, though he didn't interrupt.

"I know I for one could be doing other more, um, profitable
things, right now. But I've chosen this instead. I've chosen you
guys. We should make sure right now that we're all ready for how
much work this is going to take. We might not need to meet *every*
day of the week but we should certainly be training every day,
even if only for an hour or two. So...are we all ready for this?"

There was a moment of silence, then Dan piped up.

"Heck, why not? All I ever do is game anyway. Some of my
MMORPG groups are going to whine about it but they'll get
over it. I'll have to come up with something to tell my parents,
though. They always try to sign me up for extracurricular stuff
during the summer and I get out of it by convincing them
I'm too busy taking virtual AP classes. Maybe I can tell them
it's robotics camp or something. They'll be so proud of me for
signing up all on my own." He grinned impishly and everyone
chuckled.

Dan's parents were obsessed with achievements, and considering
his older brother was a lawyer and his older sister was currently

in pre-med, he had a lot to live up to. Fortunately for him, he was an expert at hacking parental controls and he'd rigged all his gaming equipment to flip seamlessly between homework-looking material and his game screens at the flick of a finger.

"It's gonna be a rough summer but as long as we meet after one o'clock on the days I work, I'm in," Edgar said, giving Lynn a big grin. "We gotta win this competition, though. I'll have to promise my sister some of that prize money to take over for me when I'm supposed to babysit my siblings while Mom's at work. Well, unless you guys are cool with them tagging along..."

A chorus of "No!" "Nope," "Absolutely not," came from the other guys. Lynn didn't say anything but she silently agreed.

Edgar shrugged.

"Cool. No worries. My sis is a mean negotiator, though. It's gonna take some serious mulla to get her to cover for me all summer."

"All the more reason to get to work and dominate this thing," Ronnie said. "Who's left? Mack?"

Everyone turned to look at Mack, who shuffled his feet.

"I dunno, guys. I want to, I swear but my mom has been on me to get a summer job, and... well you know my mom."

"Scary lady," Edgar agreed, widening his eyes in emphasis.

"You can play it by ear, Mack," Lynn said. "If she asks, try telling her your gaming group has entered an AR competition to improve your health and develop your teamwork and leadership skills for future job opportunities. Lots of companies use AR gaming scenarios for corporate team-building and having advanced skills in navigating an AR environment is absolutely something you could put on your resume."

"That's brilliant, Lynn. Thanks!"

"Good, so we all agree, then," Ronnie said before Lynn could reply to Mack. "We'll meet five days a week and spend the other two doing solo training—"

And they were off arguing again.

Lynn mentally threw up her hands and let the guys duke it out over schedules. It didn't matter to her, since she'd be training and hunting every day anyway.

They eventually agreed to meet four days a week, do individual training two days a week and take it easy on Sunday. Lynn had insisted on that last one, since she knew Mom would put her foot down anyway. Sunday was their girls' hangout day and family was more important than gaming, Matilda would say.

Ronnie broke up their huddle without mentioning anything about training plans but she kept her mouth shut. He seemed to view her suggestions as a threat to his leadership. Maybe she could share her ideas with Dan and have him talk it over with Ronnie? Hopefully the idiot would listen to Dan, at least.

By the time true dusk had arrived, they'd trooped back to the nearby airbus platform in front of the mall and had said their goodbyes. Dan and Ronnie hopped on the same airbus since they both lived out toward Marion. Edgar lived downtown, close to the river and Lynn and Mack's neighborhoods were on the way there, so they all caught the same airbus together. She wished them both a warm, if exhausted, goodbye when the airbus reached her apartment complex.

Her feet dragged on the way back to her apartment, not because her muscles ached but because of what she'd promised herself she'd do when she got home.

Tell her mom the truth.

"All right, young lady. Out with it."

"What?" Lynn asked, looking up from her plate full of taco pizza—one of the few things she loved about living in Iowa.

"I haven't seen you this fidgety since you were asked to beta test TD Hunter and were trying to tell me about it. What is it this time? Have they asked you to beta test another game?"

"Um, no, Mom. It's not that."

"Okay," Matilda said and put down her fork to give Lynn her full attention. "Then what is it?"

Lynn couldn't quite meet her mom's gaze, so instead she stared over Matilda's shoulder at the smartframe on their kitchen wall. It was connected to her mom's subscription to EveryPhoto, a massive database of beautiful photography that let you program your frame to show whatever sort of pictures you wanted, taken by professionals all over the world. Her mom had it set to landscape photography from the Black Hills and Badlands areas in South Dakota where Matilda had grown up. Lynn had only ever been there the times she'd visited her grandparents' small cattle ranch on the Pine Ridge Reservation.

"Sweetie?"

"Yeah. Sorry." There was more silence as Lynn tried to decide how to start. "Mom...when did you know what you wanted to do with your life?"

"Well," Matilda said, eyeing her daughter. "I've always been interested in fixing people up. I thought when I was a kid I was going to be a vet, since we had more animals than people on the ranch. But there weren't any good scholarships for vet school and in high school I decided nursing would be a safer shot. I wasn't terribly picky, as long as it got me off the reservation."

Lynn wanted to ask "why," but didn't. As much as she would love the distraction, she couldn't dance around this forever.

"Did you ever doubt yourself?"

"Sure, who doesn't? Halfway through my nursing degree at University of Maryland where I got my scholarship I almost quit, I was so sick of it all. But then I met your dad and...well, he convinced me to stick it out."

More questions blossomed in Lynn's head but this time she didn't ask them because she knew they wouldn't be answered.

"Did you ever do something, um, questionable to achieve your dreams?"

Matilda stilled and Lynn could almost feel her *not* raise an eyebrow.

"Okay. Now you're making me nervous, sweetie. Whatever it is, it's okay, you can tell me."

This was so dumb. She should just say it and be done with it.

"Um, you know how I've been managing our finances since that time you let me do it for a school project?"

"Yeees."

"Well...ever wondered why all those collection agencies stopped spamming your LINC? It's because I've been paying off our debt, a little every month, for years," Lynn said in a rush, trying to get it all out at once. "And whenever we've had an emergency, like when the dishwasher died or when you needed those orthopedic shoes for work, I paid for that too and I'm sorry I haven't been honest about it all this time..."

Lynn trailed off and there was an expectant silence. Matilda just blinked a few times, as if she wasn't sure how to process the information.

"Okaaay. That's *good*, which means where the money came from is the bad part? When the dishwasher broke you said that money was from Grandma Ingrid. I felt awful for putting the burden on someone else but we didn't have much of a choice."

Now it was Lynn's turn to blink.

"Wait, you mean you're not mad at me for helping us get by and for lying about it?"

"Oh, honey," Matilda said and reached across the table to take Lynn's hand, "why would I be mad at you? I'm sorry I've never been open about our... well, our financial situation after your dad died. But it was a burden I wanted to spare you from. You were so young. Even now I hate the idea of burdening you with our problems but you're a young woman and you've obviously done a wonderful job of balancing our finances every month. I honestly thought you were just really good at making every penny count. That said, I might be mad at you depending on where all that money came from..." She trailed off and gave Lynn a skeptical look.

A nervous chuckle escaped Lynn as the tension in her chest eased. Obviously it would still be a chore to explain everything but that was all gaming stuff, stuff her mom had no opinions about. This secret, this burden was what she'd been afraid of. And her mom wasn't mad. Well, not yet.

"I make money playing games, Mom."

"Excuse me?" Matilda said.

"Can I show you some stuff?" Lynn said, drawing her hand out of her mom's grasp. She projected her LINC display so her mom could see it and brought up her WarMonger auction listings. One column listed the items she'd sold, another showed the sale price and a third displayed the total transferred to her external account minus fees.

"What are all these things and where in the world did you get them?" Matilda asked, her finger tracing the column of various weapons, armor and other items labeled in WarMonger gamer shorthand.

"I'm a merc," Lynn said. "A mercenary. These are all from that game I play called WarMonger. Somebody wants a strong player on their team and they pay me to show up, sometimes in the form of gear that I sell on this site, sometimes it's just a straight fee."

She flipped to another screen that showed her bank account, letting her mom examine the deposits. Matilda's eyes widened as they scanned down and at one entry she almost choked.

"Three *hundred* dollars? Real dollars? For people to hire my daughter to play a game? Online? Not even meet her?"

"That's actually below my usual fee but there were reasons. Generally, I don't get out of bed for less than five hundred. And if they're asking me to fight Tier Ones or Twos it better be more than that."

"That's crazy," Matilda said, her voice faint.

"They don't even know I'm a girl," Lynn said, grinning. "They think I'm some grizzled old guy with a baritone named Larry Coughlin. Most people think I'm a former SEAL or something. I'll never tell, though. The mystery gives me a reputation. Sometimes I'll drop hints and say something like," she lowered her voice as far as it would go, "'This reminds me of good times in Sarajevo!'"

"Oh, my GOD!" Matilda said and burst out laughing. "Please tell me that's not the voice you use online," she gasped out.

"I've got a voice modulator," Lynn said, pointing at her throat. "Sounds like a real guy."

"Oh—my—!" Matilda said, continuing to gasp in laughter. Tears were coming out of her eyes. "My daughter, international mercenary of mystery! Does anyone else know?"

"Well, some of the people over at WarMonger who manage the servers and stuff. Also, some of the players I've made friends with in WarMonger are also Alpha testers for TD Hunter. I've even met one of them," Lynn admitted. "He works in the Tactical Support department and he was an actual operator. Like, in the real. He said he spit out a mouthful of drink when he found out 'Larry' was a teenage girl."

"I imagine he did," Matilda said, wiping her eyes.

"Mom," Lynn said carefully, scrolling further down to more recent transactions. "These days, because I've been focusing on TD Hunter, 'Larry Coughlin' won't get out of bed for less than a grand."

"A grand?" Matilda said, her eyes widening again. "A thousand dollars. Not five hundred, a thousand?"

"I'm a Tier One operator," Lynn said, shrugging. "That means I'm in the ninety-nine point ninth percentile of players. Hang on." She scrolled all the way to the bottom of her savings account summary to where the total showed in big green numbers. This was the moment of truth.

Her mother considered the projected display in charged silence.

"That's more than I make in a year, Lynn," Matilda said quietly.

"I . . . I know," Lynn said. "I'm sorry I've been keeping it a secret, I was just so afraid if I told you, you would be angry and make me stop gaming. But gaming is my life, it's the only thing that gets me through each day. I'm saving all this for college and of course paying off our debt."

The somber silence continued and Lynn dared to glance up at her mom's expression. It was smooth. Thoughtful. Definitely not angry. But something about the angle of her brows gave off a hint of wariness. And sadness.

"There are some really big deposits here," her mother said. "A lot more than five hundred dollars. Wait, this one is five thousand dollars, Lynn? That seems like an awful lot for someone to pay for *just* a game. . . ."

"That was a good day," Lynn hurried to explain. "That client was, um, a senior partner I think in a high-end law firm in New York. His firm and another firm had a sort of friendly game going but then the partner at the other firm hired a bunch of Tier Ones and Twos, top people in the game like me."

"Like you," Matilda said, nodding sagely as one side of her mouth quirked.

Lynn grinned and sped up.

"I looked at the team he was up against and then the guys he'd been able to recruit for his side and told him no. But he was persistent and said I could name my price, so I said five grand, cash, and told him I'd recruit some people I knew and they'd be a grand apiece. I really didn't want to go in against the other team but next thing I knew, there was five grand in my account, so I couldn't back out. It all worked out, though, because I knew the other team and what type of tactics they were weak against, so I was able to recruit the right mix of skill to take them out. Come to think of it, Fallu was on the other team that time."

"Fallu?" Matilda said.

"The guy who works at TD Hunter," Lynn said. "He's really good at medium range but he takes positions that open him up to snipers. And one guy, SweetVengeance68, is really good at reading him. So, I messaged SweetVengeance an offer of a thousand in cash to show up. Stuff like that. Put the team together."

"Did you win?" Matilda asked.

Lynn snorted.

"Before a match starts, the other team shows up on the board. Well, we went into the field and waited. And waited. And waited. Then the other team dropped off the board."

"Okay, I don't follow. What does that mean?"

"They defaulted," Lynn explained. "They saw my team and realized I'd stacked the deck against them. See, if you lose to a lower level player you lose major points, especially if a team of mostly lower players wipes out your team. The people I recruited were all lower players who had successfully beaten one of them at some point or another. They knew I'd have my teammates find and concentrate on the opponents they knew best how to beat while I finished off any survivors. Wipe five Tier Ones off the board with a handful of Tier Twos and Tier Threes and that's a big change in ranking. They'd lose major points, I'd gain major points. It would probably have bumped me to number eight or nine in the rankings. Especially since some of them would have dropped down to Tier Two. You'd have to throw a lot of money at a Tier One player to get him to risk dropping down to Tier Two for one measly game. So, they defaulted instead. Doesn't count as a loss. Game never happened."

"But, weren't they being paid?" Matilda asked.

"Oh, yeah," Lynn said, shrugging. "But sometimes you just decide there's other days to make money. Not a hill worth dying on. I've dumped out when I've seen the other team a time or two. You just say 'Not today.' We're mercenaries, not idiots. We've got to live to spend our pay."

"Got to live to spend your pay?" Matilda said, chortling. "You *sound* like some grizzled old mercenary."

Lynn shrugged.

"The lingo and mindset come with the territory. I've been playing Larry for so long that I guess . . . well, I guess he's a part of me, in some ways." She felt foolish saying it but her mom looked amused.

"And I thought I'd seen it all," Matilda said, leaning back in her chair and shaking her head. Then she sighed. "I guess I did suspect you'd been getting money from somewhere. It wasn't just the washer, although you were obviously good about not spending it. I just . . . didn't want to push you away by prying, I guess. And with how crazy my schedule is, it's easy to forget about things you don't want to think about. But I did wonder sometimes . . . worried, even, about what you might be doing . . ."

As the silence dragged on Lynn thought about the pause, then thought some more, then screwed up her face in disgust.

"Oh, Mom! Really?" Lynn said. "You've got to be...Mother!"

"I didn't know, okay?" Matilda said, rubbing her temples. "As far as I could tell you were just playing video games. I had no reason to doubt your responsible behavior. But with my schedule, you're here by yourself for hours. I don't like that, but...I'm sorry for thinking...anything. I had no idea you could make money from games."

"It's okay," Lynn said after another shudder. "But...Seriously? Me?"

"I work in a hospital," Matilda said, shrugging. "We see more than we'd like of how the world really works. Honestly, I should have gotten to the bottom of this ages ago, I just didn't want to be *that* mom, you know? Assuming the worst and micromanaging you when you've already been through so much..."

"Hey, Mom, I'm the one who's supposed to be apologizing, not you. I'm the one who lied."

"I know, honey. Obviously lying is bad and I wish you'd trusted me enough to be honest from the beginning. But I forgive you and I'm so grateful you came to me to explain things." She paused, as if a sudden thought had come to her. "You're a minor...how did you even open a bank account by yourself in the first place?"

"Um, well, there's ways to do banking in virtual anonymously...like *not* through a traditional bank. Places that don't care if you're a minor or not. Cryptocurrency and all that."

Matilda looked skeptical and leveled a stern eye at her daughter.

"Are you paying taxes on your earnings?"

"Erm, no, not yet—but I'm going to, I promise! I...know some people, they've been managing it all for me but, uh, now that things are out in the open I can get a normal bank account and declare my income and all that."

"Okay, well, I suppose that's good enough," Matilda said, sighing. "Our country is screwed up enough as it is, we need everybody doing their part to hold things together, especially when our idiotic Congress is passing black bills funneling trillions of dollars to who knows where."

"Uh, say what?" Lynn asked. She was about as interested in politics as the guys were in Fashion Diva but it was something her mom regularly stressed over. And "trillions" was a lot of money.

"They just passed a bill in Congress that nobody knows what's in it," Matilda said. "It's causing a lot of problems."

"What do you mean nobody knows what's in it?" Lynn said.

"They're called black bills because the contents are supposedly too sensitive for national security to release to the public," Matilda replied. "Most people have never heard of them because they usually only pertain to military spending and are kept pretty hush hush. But this one is different. The funding is for a bunch of different departments from military to intelligence to infrastructure and technology. And it's the first that Congress has admitted includes regulations and legal provisions, meaning there are laws in it. But nobody knows what *is* in it. So...how do you vote on, much less obey, a law that you can't even read?"

"Whaaa? That's crazy," Lynn said, brow furrowed. *Real* crazy. Maybe she shouldn't be so obsessed with gaming all the time and keep an eye on the real world, too.

"Yes. It is. I blame the President," Matilda said with a sigh. "None of this would have happened if Warrick had been elected. And of course all this money has to come from somewhere, so they've cut medical spending, which we've already been told is going to affect the hospital. We don't have enough money as it is. Some people are saying it has to do with terrorism or cybersecurity but nobody is talking. It was all over the news for a while then it just...dropped away. I e-mailed our congresswoman but all I got was platitudes about 'for the good of the nation.' It was a form letter, basically."

"Huh. Well, I've run into some people online who think the U.S. is going to have a civil war any day now," Lynn said. "Maybe they're right. Maybe the government is preparing for something like that."

"Where do you run into crazies like that?" Matilda asked, sounding worried.

"The mesh web is a screwy place, Mom," Lynn said with a wry smile. "You meet all kinds. I do a bunch of digging around on chat boards and in forums for my Larry Coughlin persona. I look up military lingo and stuff. I end up reading a bunch of conspiracy theories and random chatter in the military community. I don't necessarily *believe* any of it, much less agree with it but I've run into the discussions. I'd guess those boards are exploding about now if the 'gubmint' is passing laws and nobody can read them."

"Well, that's one way to stay informed," her mom muttered, finally digging back into her taco pizza.

"Yeah, I haven't been on the boards much in the past month or two though, because of TD Hunter."

"Oh, yes, how did it go yesterday with your friends? By the time I got up this morning you were already gone again to meet them, so I assume it went well? Did you enjoy playing with them?"

"Um, yeah, about that..." Lynn fidgeted with her fork, then took a bite of her own pizza to give herself a minute to think. This was the *other* thing she hadn't been looking forward to talking about. But she didn't have a choice.

"It was pretty good," she said finally after swallowing. "Ronnie was still a jerk but everybody else was really cool. We plan on meeting regularly to, well, practice."

"Practice? Why, is there something going on?"

"Yeah. You know how I've been gaming constantly since I was thirteen? Well, it's become pretty important to me, not to mention I'm good at it. Really good, according to Mr. Krator. Anyway, TD Hunter is putting on some regional and eventually global competitions. That's pretty normal, most big games have them. But since this is an AR game, it can't be participated in remotely, you know? And the competitions will only be for teams, no individual games."

Matilda raised her eyebrows.

"Teams? Does that mean..."

"Yup. Me and the guys formed a team. Or at least, we're going to. But to compete we have to qualify first and that's why we have to practice. A lot. Like, all summer long."

"Okay... that doesn't sound too bad. All that exercise will be good for you, anyway." Her mom smiled and Lynn tried to smile back but the sudden churning in her gut made it hard.

"I don't think you quite understand, Mom. We will have to go *all over* the city, exploring in places we've never been before, looking for monsters to hunt."

"Oh... but you'll all be together, right?"

"Most of the time, probably. But..." Lynn took a deep breath and pushed onward. "I could be dishonest and promise you I'd always have a buddy. Just to keep you from worrying. But I know I can't keep that promise. Not if we want any chance of winning. We'll all have to do our own individual training on days we can't meet. Plus, I'm the best player on our team, so I'll be scouting new locations and learning new fighting techniques to teach everyone else and give us an edge."

"Honey... I don't know..."

Lynn looked her mom right in the eye.

"I'm not a kid anymore, Mom. This is important to me. More important than anything else I've ever done. I didn't mention it before but the grand prize is five million dollars per player, a full ride for a gaming degree and a job at Tsunami Entertainment."

Matilda's eyes bugged out.

"*Five million* dollars?"

"Yeah and I can't train like I should if I'm always worried about what time of day it is or whether or not I have a buddy with me. I'll be careful, I can definitely promise you that. And the game AI, Hugo, is as good as any buddy. He can watch out while I'm distracted and he has a direct connection to the city's emergency services."

There was a heavy silence while her mom looked at her, then looked away.

"I know it seems unfair, Lynn, but you're a young woman and it's not safe to go traipsing around the city by yourself, especially at night. It wouldn't be responsible of me to allow it."

Frustration rose in Lynn but she bit her tongue, taking a moment to breathe deeply through her nose before replying.

"Dad wasn't a young woman alone at night," she said quietly.

Her mom flinched.

"He was a freaking six-foot-something, muscular guy in *broad daylight*. And he still got attacked. He still died."

The silence stretched on this time while Lynn tried not to remember. She failed.

The attack happened while her dad was in plainclothes and the perp had taken his wallet and watch, so the investigators assumed it wasn't related to her dad's job. Just a random mugging.

The case was still unsolved, as far as Lynn knew. Little to no physical evidence and only grainy surveillance footage from behind of a white male, about five foot eleven. The slugs from the scene were 9mm Luger, probably shot from a Glock G19 but Lynn only knew that because she'd eavesdropped on a couple of her dad's coworkers outside his hospital room while she held his hand and silently begged him to wake up. There were three wounds: one to the head, one to the shoulder and one to the gut. The gut and shoulder had been manageable. Bad but manageable. The one to the head had left bone fragments in her dad's brain and sent him into a coma with severe swelling. They'd pulled out all the stops trying to save him, even trying experimental nanite exploratory surgery and stem-cell therapy to heal the damaged brain tissue. But after weeks of hanging on, his body finally gave up.

She'd never even gotten to say goodbye.

Her dad had just been out jogging. Nothing dangerous. Nothing risky. But ever since, her mom had been paranoid about Lynn going anywhere by herself. It hadn't been too bad right after it happened and they'd left Baltimore to live with her grandparents in South Dakota. There was nobody to randomly mug her on the ranch. But when they'd first moved to Cedar Rapids, Matilda had suffered a lot of anxiety and Lynn had spent months "checking in" every hour to help her mom cope. That's what happened sometimes when you suffered a sudden and traumatic loss—the knowledge that everything you love could be ripped away at any moment is imprinted onto your very soul. Lynn was better at ignoring those crippling fears considering she had plenty of other crippling anxieties to deal with. Plus, once she started gaming, it was easier to forget everything. In virtual she was safe and her lack of desire to leave her room, much less the apartment, soothed a lot of her mom's fears as well. They'd coped together that way for a long time. And over the years, Matilda's fears had faded.

But now they had to face them.

Lynn knew she needed to be understanding. Her mom was way more emotional than she was, so her dad's death hadn't hit her the same way it had her mom. But how did her mom plan on coping once Lynn went to college? They had to deal with this now.

"Mom..." Lynn said.

Matilda took a shuddering breath and finally looked back. Moisture shone in her eyes but she didn't wipe it away.

"I know honey...I know. It's just so hard. So. So. Hard."

The pain in her mom's voice had Lynn moving before she realized it. She pushed away from the table and came around it to wrap her arms around her mom's shoulders and lean her forehead down to rest it on her mom's head. Matilda reached up to give her arm a squeeze.

"I miss him," Lynn said. Her eyes burned but her voice was steady.

"I miss him too, sweetie. But he would have been so proud of you, his little warrior princess."

Despite the somber mood, her mom's words made her lips quirk.

"I don't think Larry Coughlin is quite what Dad would have called a 'little warrior princess.'"

Her mom chuckled wetly.

"No, definitely not. But *you* are absolutely what he would consider a warrior woman. Look how much you've grown and through crushing circumstances that no one should ever have to cope with."

Lynn shrugged, not sure what to say. How could she be a warrior woman when she was embarrassed to even be seen out in public? A warrior was supposed to be brave. Powerful. Fearless. As far as she could tell, the only things she had done in the past seven years were not get kicked out of school and get really good at shooting people in a video game. That was it.

"I know it's been hard dealing with my anxiety. But it's been like this for so long, I don't know where the line is between unfounded fears and wise parental precaution. Wait until you have kids. You'll see what I mean then."

That got a snort out of Lynn.

"Sorry to break it to you, Mom, but I don't really see myself as the mothering type."

Matilda laughed and pulled back so she could see her daughter's face.

"I thought the same thing when I was a teenager, dear. Give it time, you'll see. Besides, I want grandchildren!"

Lynn rolled her eyes.

"Can we focus, Mom? Please?"

Matilda sighed and rubbed her face.

"You're right, you *are* old enough to be responsible for yourself if you want to go out. But it's perfectly reasonable to take precautions and I need to know you aren't just wandering around completely vulnerable."

"I know, Mom. That's why I'll have Hugo's help. Seriously, he's pretty awesome. When those guys were bothering me over at the Heathers apartments, he scared them off by threatening to call over a nearby police drone. It was pretty cool."

"That's certainly reassuring. But drones aren't always nearby and a drone can't save you if...if you get attacked. You should at least carry some pepper spray."

Lynn thought about that for a moment then shrugged.

"I'm okay with that," Lynn said, finally stepping back from their embrace and returning to her seat. "So, if I carry pepper spray, you're okay with me hunting wherever and whenever I need to?"

"I still expect you to keep me informed of where you are, what you're doing and when you'll be home. I'm still your mother, missy." Matilda pointed her fork at her daughter with a look of mock severity.

"Don't worry, I will," Lynn said, then she grinned. "You know, Mr. Thomas was right. I feel so much better now, sort of light and free."

"Mr. Thomas? Do you mean our neighbor downstairs?"

"Yeah. I've seen him around a few times when I've been hunting in our complex. He gave me some advice yesterday about keeping secrets."

Her mom smiled.

"Well, that was kind of him. I haven't seen him around for a while, maybe I'll make him some cookies and drop by. He's getting on in years and I don't know if he has any family in this area."

"I've never seen him with anybody else," Lynn said around a mouthful of food.

"Neither have I...you know, I think I'll make him some cookies as soon as we're done with dinner. Want to help?"

Lynn thought about all the research she needed to do for team training. Then she thought about the last time she'd ever spoken to her dad. It was the morning he'd been attacked. She'd been on their couch watching cartoons as he'd headed for the front door. He'd paused at the couch to ruffle her hair and say goodbye. She'd just grunted in reply.

The memory still haunted her.

"Sure, Mom, I'd love to."

Chapter 10

"WATCH YOUR SIX, MACK!"

"What?"

"Look behind you!" Lynn yelled. The Grumblin that had appeared charged Mack and took a swipe, making red blossom across her teammate's armor. Mack yelled, tried to spin, stumbled and slashed wildly in the general direction of the Grumblin attacking him with its six-inch claws.

Before Lynn could do anything else, Ronnie jumped in and stabbed the monster multiple times in the back, taking it out in a burst of sparks.

"Mack, come on!" Ronnie said. "What have I told you about situational awareness?"

"Sorry," Mack mumbled, straightening and brushing himself off.

"You have the same problem in WarMonger. You've got to keep track of your overhead map, or you'll keep getting screwed."

"I know, I know. I'm trying."

"Well, try harder. We can't afford mistakes."

Mack's shoulders slumped and Lynn felt a flash of annoyance at Ronnie. Mack was a people pleaser and he always felt awful when he let anyone down. Berating him was totally unhelpful, it made him more anxious and less focused. Dan, on the other hand, could take the criticism—it inspired his competitive side. A *good* team captain would understand the difference in their peoples' temperaments and adjust their instruction accordingly.

Too bad she wasn't team captain—not that she wanted to be, no matter how Ronnie's heavy-handed tactics drove her insane. But she did do what she could to help.

Once Ronnie pulled forward to rejoin Dan at the head of their little band, Lynn slipped up to Mack and gave him a pat on the shoulder.

"Don't worry, really. You'll get the hang of it. Just pay more attention to the sounds. Most TDMs make a sound before they attack and once you can recognize them, it gives you a few seconds' warning. The Grumblin is a sort of growling roar."

"Yeah, I noticed that but there's so much chatter going on I'm having trouble hearing the monster sounds in the background," Mack said, pointing to his earbuds.

"Have your AI change the settings to put our shared channel on one earbud and background noise on the other," Lynn suggested. "That way chatter won't cover up the TDM noise."

Mack smiled.

"That's a great idea, thanks!"

"No problem. I probably should have mentioned it to the whole team."

"That's okay. You've given us a ton of help already. Look how far we've come in just a couple weeks."

Lynn nodded. He had a point and she was surprised to realize how proud of them she felt. Things were still awkward at times but overall they were shaping up nicely. She just needed to watch herself and stop using so much military lingo. The Tier Ones and Twos she teamed up with in WarMonger used a lot of military slang, so whenever she tried to get herself into the "zone" with her new teammates, she fell back on her ingrained Larry habits. That was good on one level: they gave her a much needed edge. But her friends weren't used to it and a few times she'd come close to using one of Larry's pet phrases that Ronnie would have recognized.

The last thing she wanted Ronnie thinking about was why she was parroting catch phrases from his arch nemesis.

It was a thin line she walked and it created unnecessary friction. It would be easier if she could come completely clean about her gaming background but she knew she couldn't. Ronnie would never speak to her again, much less play with her, if he knew she'd been the one humiliating him in virtual for *years*.

"Come on, you two. Get a move on, we're not done filling our quota for today."

Lynn rolled her eyes but Mack grinned.

"Is he always like this when you game?" Lynn muttered as the two of them trotted to catch up. They'd started to avoid hunting directly around businesses and other more populated areas since that was where the casual TD Hunter players gravitated. Instead they were sweeping a stretch of unkempt weeds and grass between a subdivision and an old strip mall. The mall was home to the usual nail and tanning salons, hole-in-the-wall Chinese takeout and a value market grocery for those too picky—or too poor—for normal weekly deliveries from the mobile grocery depots.

"Sort of," Mack said, scrubbing his chin nervously. "He's always been bossy but he's become a whole other level of manic since we started this team. I can't blame him, though. Just think if we won, how cool would that be? I wonder what I'd do with five million dollars . . ."

"Yeah, definitely cool," Lynn agreed, hiding a smile. "But we've got a long way to go until then, so let's concentrate. You're doing great so far. Just keep your ears open and eyes sharp. And don't forget, your best defense is to stay light on your feet. Keep moving. TDMs aren't that nimble, so sidestepping is usually better than backing up."

"Got it. Thanks, Lynn."

"No problem."

Lynn slowed to let Mack pull ahead so she could guard the rear—her preferred position because it put her farther away from Ronnie. He liked to lead the way at the front with Dan while Edgar and Mack stayed in the middle, guarding their flanks. It wasn't a bad formation but Ronnie and Dan tended to hog all the kills, depriving Mack and Edgar of valuable practice. She'd have to bring it up with Dan soon and get him to convince Ronnie to let Mack and Edgar rotate regularly to point. Ronnie rarely, if ever, took suggestions seriously if they came directly from her. But he'd listen to Dan, even if he knew that Dan was passing along her words. It was stupid, immature and annoying as all get out. But then that was Ronnie to a T. He would be absolutely worthless if he wasn't so technically proficient at gaming.

Lynn chewed her lip, wondering how long they could get by like this. Would Ronnie ever get his head out of his butt? She really, *really* didn't want to have another confrontation. For the moment, she held out hope. They were making progress and Ronnie wasn't completely insufferable *all* the time.

Just most of the time.

Without school to distract them, the guys had gotten up to Level 7 in just two weeks. Lynn had to give it to them, they'd all worked really hard, even Mack and Edgar. Of course, the fact that TD Hunter got them all out of their houses seemed to be a strong motivator. She didn't know much about Ronnie's home life except that he lived with his dad but she knew Dan and Mack had less than chummy relationships with their parents. Edgar didn't talk much about his family but Lynn knew he was close to his younger siblings and mom. He had to work hardest of all since half his mornings were spent at his landscaping job.

They all had a rigorous training schedule, from daily solo practice using the app simulations, to team hunting four times a week, to the "strength and agility training" Ronnie had assigned them. Lynn ignored Ronnie's dictated physical regime. She had her own routine already in place, including a daily stretch and kickfit workout as well as running three times a week to increase her stamina. The running sucked the most. She hated it with the burning passion of a thousand suns. Anyone with sizable breasts knew exactly why running sucked and though she'd broken down early on and spent an obscene amount of money on the best sports bras available, it had made her runs "only" agonizing instead of physically unbearable. Still, the training was helping and the improvement she saw in her performance gave her the motivation to keep at it.

Whatever the guys were doing seemed to be effective too. Edgar's clothes were getting baggier and Mack and Dan were less and less breathless after each TDM fight. Ronnie had probably started out more physically fit than any of them because of that time he'd tried to get onto the ARS team their freshman year. Lynn had no idea what had possessed him—she didn't even think he *liked* sports—but the experience had obviously taught him a thing or two about keeping more fit than his pale skin and lanky frame let on.

The app simulations were doing their job, as well. Dan only clobbered himself with his own weapon once or twice a week now, instead of multiple times a day and Edgar was developing a mean "seek and destroy" mentality. While she and Ronnie favored their Plasma Blades and Dan and Mack were still figuring out which weapon fit them best, Edgar was all about his Dragon—the one-handed scattergun with a close range area effect. He was getting good at letting loose in time to get maximum damage while still leaving him enough space to dodge attacks.

All in all, Lynn was proud of them.

And, she had to admit, it *was* fun hunting with other people, especially getting to see her teammates in combat. It was freaky how real it all looked, thanks to her top-of-the-line AR glasses. She *knew* it was just a game. But man did it get her blood pumping and adrenaline coursing through her veins.

Being in a group also made her less self-conscious, once the initial awkwardness wore off. Instead of one weirdo dancing around with a blue sword, now there were five of them. Even better, Lynn had seen on the TD Hunter forum that, due to popular demand, they were finally developing a "TD Hunter Lens" app that would allow people who didn't want to play the game to still watch it being played by others.

Spectators could don their own AR interface, open the app and see Hunters who were in combat the same way fellow Hunters would, complete with all the monsters and special effects. Lynn was sure the stream channels would soon be flooded with spectator videos. Of course, there were already hundreds of hard-core gamers live-streaming their hunts but watching it first person wasn't quite the same as seeing it from an onlooker's perspective where you could appreciate all the moves and visual effects.

"Hey, Hugo," Lynn subvocalized, so it wouldn't broadcast on their group channel.

"Yes, Miss Lynn?"

"Any idea when that spectator app will be released so people can watch Hunters in combat?"

"There is no firm release date but it is expected within the next few weeks."

"Hmm...any idea if any individual hunter can know when they are being 'spectated'?"

"Not to my knowledge, Miss Lynn. I believe the developers did not want hunters to be distracted with unnecessary notifications while in combat."

"Humph. I suppose that makes sense. I'm still not thrilled about the idea of videos of me randomly showing up in virtual."

"Well, you *are* in public, Miss Lynn. An audience is to be expected. But I'm sure they will all be spectacularly entertaining."

Lynn's brow furrowed. Had she heard wry amusement in the AI's statement? Or had it just been her imagination?

"Whatever. I can't control it, so I might as well forget about it."

"A wise strategy, Miss Lynn. Speaking of strategy, there is a gh—"

Her AI didn't even finish the sentence before Lynn spun and lunged, stabbing the ghost that had appeared behind her straight through the face—a killing blow with the higher-powered Plasma Blade. The ghost burst into sparks and Lynn checked her overhead for more enemies, then scooped up her globe and ichor before turning to catch up with the guys. As she went, she topped off her stealth slot with her freshly collected globe. It had been running a little low, which was why the ghost had been able to detect her. Ghasts were usually the only TDMs that could detect her at any distance when she was fully stealthed. When ghosts started trying to jump her from behind, she knew it was time to resupply so she didn't start attracting higher-class TDMs that would distract her from providing rear support. She was only one level above her teammates but even one level could make a big difference.

"My, my. Impressive reaction time, Miss Lynn. I don't know why I bothered trying to warn you."

"A bit sulky, are we, Hugo?" Lynn said with a grin.

"Hardly, Miss Lynn. I am a service AI, not an emotional support AI."

Lynn snorted. "Good thing, too. You'd be sucky at emotional support."

"On the contrary, if those were my parameters, I would perform them to perfection."

"Uh-huh. Well, thanks for trying to warn me anyway. It *is* your job."

"Indeed it is."

Lynn fell silent, going back to her ceaseless watchful mode. Up ahead Ronnie and Dan took on a pair of demons while Mack and Edgar picked off the two Ghasts that were predictably hanging around in the wings. By the time Lynn caught up, all the monsters had been dispatched and Dan and Ronnie were exclaiming over an augment Dan had picked up. They would reach

Level 8 soon and that meant becoming visible to the top Delta Class monsters like Orculls—the best TDM she'd found so far for dropping items—and rocs, an extremely annoying TDM and the first flying form she'd encountered. Rocs were electrovores like the Lectas and usually hovered around power nodes, transmitter antennas and mesh hubs. Thankfully they were a gather type and so didn't patrol the skies looking for targets. But they usually congregated in groups and were plenty aggressive if you got within range, sort of like a swarm of hornets. They didn't do much damage but their diving attack from above had nearly given her a heart attack on multiple occasions.

"Whoa! Hold up, guys."

Ronnie's exclamation made Lynn's head come up. She hurried over to the rest of the team who were clustered around their captain.

"Okay, you all keep watch while I take out this unknown," he was saying as Lynn trotted up.

Now that she was level with the guys, her display lit up with the yellow proximity warning of an unknown and Hugo repeated his "stay put so your battle system can do its thing" spiel.

She looked around Ronnie and spotted the sparkling mist about twenty feet away. The fact that they'd detected it this far out but it hadn't yet attacked meant it was probably a Delta-4 or lower. Either that, or it was a non-aggressive gather type. While her battle system did its scan, she addressed Ronnie.

"Hey, uh, maybe Edgar and Mack should take it. They need the practice."

Ronnie shot her a dirty look.

"They can get it hunting regular TDMs. There's no point taking risks with an unknown."

The effort it took not to roll her eyes was almost physically painful. She didn't know what Ronnie thought he was achieving by taking on the unknown solo. They were hunting as a group, so the achievement bonus would be shared between them and they'd all be named in the credits for it. Maybe it was some macho display of dominance?

"Well, if you're worried about risks, then I should take it, since I'm the most experienced hunter on the team," she said in a carefully casual tone. She itched to call out his BS but the last thing she wanted was another confrontation.

There was a moment of silence and Lynn could almost imagine she heard teeth grinding.

"Fine. You two, get a move on. And don't die, will you?"

Edgar and Mack exchanged an uncertain look and Lynn let out a silent sigh of exasperation. Someone needed to explain to Ronnie the difference between "leader" and "dictator." She waited a moment, hoping Ronnie would do something—anything—useful. But he just folded his arms and raised his eyebrows at his two teammates.

Aaaand, this was why "Larry Coughlin" took so much pleasure trouncing Ronnie in WarMonger. Ronnie took "jerk" to new and surprising levels.

"Hugo? Any new data on the unknown?" she subvocalized.

"Your system scan has found nothing out of the ordinary. The entity is most likely Delta Class-3 or -4 and is not employing any stealth capabilities. Please approach to target range and engage to allow for full system analysis."

With Ronnie acting about as helpful as a pile of rocks, Lynn forced herself to step forward. She sent a quick message to Dan to keep an eye out for other monsters, then motioned at Edgar and Mack. They followed her a few steps closer to the sparkling mist.

"Okay, so unknowns could be anything at all," she said quietly, uncomfortably aware of Ronnie's laser-eyed stare on her back. "It's best to start with a long-ranged attack to see what they'll do and how strong they are before you wade in swinging. Mack, you're the better marksman," she said, then winced and shot an apologetic look at Edgar, but he only shrugged and grinned. She was glad he wasn't offended. She was also glad he didn't know her knowledge of his weapon skills wasn't just from the last two weeks of hunting but from the dozens of times Larry had gone up against the Baconville Bashers in WarMonger. She knew each of the guys' strengths and weaknesses more intimately than any of them realized.

"Yeah, so, Mack, why don't you equip your Plasma Pistol and once you two are ready, target the mist and start shooting as quickly as you can. If it doesn't move, advance slowly but don't get closer than ten feet. If it doesn't die within about thirty seconds, that means it has good armor and one of you will need to engage it in hand to hand. Edgar, you'd probably be best for that, so you should go ahead and use your Plasma Blade. If it charges at you once Mack starts shooting, you can get out in front to engage it and keep its attention while Mack fills it with lead. Or energy bolts, anyway. Make sense?"

They both nodded, looking more determined now and less nervous. It wasn't as if they were clueless strategists—both were good gamers in their own right. But the "in the real" element of TD Hunter seemed to heighten their anxiety and cloud their ability to analyze situations. It had been the same for her, in the beginning. She just had a month more of acclimating to the stress of battling monsters in the real.

Lynn gave them both a thumbs-up and retreated to rejoin Dan and Ronnie.

"Hugo," she subvocalized while Mack and Edgar got ready, "I know I usually have you mute your proximity warnings since it distracts me from TDM sounds but there's going to be so much noise already, I want you to warn me the moment any new TDMs get within detection range."

She glanced at her overhead, making sure there were no red dots close enough to worry about. She wished there was a way to tell what dot was what but she wouldn't know which TDM to expect until it got within visual range.

"Dan is a good hunter but he's too obsessive to not get distracted watching Mack and Edgar. And I trust Ronnie about as far as I can throw him."

"Very good, Miss Lynn."

Just then Mack started shooting and things got real interesting, real fast.

Lynn's assumptions about the unknown went out the window as the sparkling mist shot forward with a blood-curdling scream the moment Mack's plasma pistol started spitting blue bolts. It was faster than any monster she'd seen yet, even Vargs, and it raced toward them with the distinctive rocking bounce of a four-legged creature. Within seconds it was on Mack and Edgar and Edgar executed a diagonal strike as the unknown leapt at his center of mass. Red flashed across the mist but that didn't stop the monster from scoring double hits on Edgar's chest before it bounded away out of range.

The surprise that had frozen Lynn's limbs passed and she lunged forward to help. She reached Mack and Edgar just as the mist darted in again and got a double strike on Mack before Edgar had a chance to intercept. To Mack's credit, he kept shooting even as he stumbled back and despite the monster's speed, he was maintaining about fifty percent accuracy. Lynn took up a stance at Mack's shoulder, opposite Edgar. She was vaguely aware that Dan and Ronnie had started shooting from where they stood instead of joining into one united group like she would have ordered if she'd been in charge. But she couldn't afford to be distracted by them.

"Keep turning, guys, don't let it get behind us!"

That was easier said than done. If it weren't for the red targeting reticle Hugo had dropped on the unknown, the mist would have been almost impossible to track, it was moving so fast. She was so focused on trying to keep it in her sights that she didn't realize what was going on until she saw it streak toward—

"Incoming!" she yelled and Dan and Ronnie belatedly tried to switch to Plasma Blades just as the unknown charged them. But instead of attacking them head on, the mist jumped *over* them, deftly avoiding their lunging stabs. Double flashes of red blossomed on their backs before the TDM darted away and circled for another attack.

Anxiety and frustration burned in Lynn's chest. This was crazy. They were going to get defeated in detail if they didn't get on the same page and work together. And heaven help them if any other monsters showed up while they were occupied. Ronnie needed to get his act together and *lead*!

She switched to her Plasma Pistol and joined Mack in aimed fire as the unknown charged Dan and Ronnie again, landing more blows while they slashed at empty air.

That thing was *fast*.

"Miss Lynn, there are two enemies moving in this direction."

"How close?" she subvocalized.

"Based on their speed and trajectory, they will pass close enough to detect your group within sixty seconds."

Not good.

What should she do? Just keep shooting and hope they survived? Try to get her team on the same page? Would the guys even listen to her if she tried? What if she tried and failed? The indecision made her gut churn.

What would Larry do?

She knew what he—what *she*—would do if this were a match in WarMonger. Stay calm. Take control of her team. Kill everything.

But this was not in virtual. Here in the real her heart pounded with adrenaline, sweat made her hands slick and her breath came in uneven gasps. Here, her team stood right next to her, real people with opinions and prejudices and faults. People she could let down. People she couldn't hide from if she made a mistake. Sure, there had been times hunting by herself that she'd managed to channel her Larry mode, sinking into the cool focus and razor sharp instincts that came naturally in WarMonger.

But this was totally different. If she tried to "be" Larry in the real, then everyone would know... what? That she was a liar? A fraud? An overweight, socially anxious teen who was as far from the tough-as-nails, seen-everything-under-the-sun-and-stabbed-it-in-the-kidney professional, Larry Coughlin?

But if they lost the competition, what was the point of maintaining the pretense?

Lynn mentally cursed Ronnie and his moronic, egotistical incompetence. She did *not* want to lead, did *not* want to be depended on by people she cared about. She wanted to be left alone so she could have fun killing stuff. That was it.

Maybe if she gave Ronnie a nudge, he would do his job so she could stop having this stupid identity crisis.

"Ronnie, get over here! We need to fight together!" Lynn yelled, adrenaline putting extra volume into her voice as she took another hit by the unknown.

Her yell seemed to get through, because Ronnie gave Dan's sleeve a jerk and they both ran over to join into one group.

"What do we do, Ronnie?" Mack yelled over the zappa-zap sound of their Plasma Pistol fire.

"Just keep shooting it, it'll die eventually," Ronnie yelled back.

"There are more monsters coming, we're going to get overwhelmed," Lynn said, resisting the urge to tell Ronnie he was an idiot. If she'd been by herself, she could keep moving, stay out of the monsters' reach and dispatch each with carefully practiced attacks without anyone getting in her way. As it was, she was already taking unnecessary damage that would pull down her rankings. If she didn't stay at the top, she couldn't get the achievement bonus items she wanted so badly.

"We'll kill them when they get here, just keep shooting," was Ronnie's only reply.

Lynn ground her teeth. If she'd been the team captain, she

would have had Dan and Mack, their best marksmen, keep up the suppressing fire, would have switched Edgar to his Dragon to bury the thing in damage whenever it charged close and would have had herself and Ronnie go to Plasma Blade to stab upward every time it tried to jump over, thus maximizing damage while minimizing energy waste and health loss.

But she wasn't in charge. So, instead, she took a knee to lower her profile and shoot from a more stable position.

The unknown paused, perhaps reassessing its now united opponent. But then it gave another chilling scream and charged. Lynn knew from experience that TDMs wouldn't run straight through you, at least not on purpose. The game's programming had monsters act as if hunters were solid objects, though the TDMs didn't seem to mind passing through other things. Regardless, most monsters ran up and kept attacking until either they were dead or the player retreated. Besides ghosts and Ghasts, this was the first TDM she'd engaged that used hit and run tactics instead of a straight on assault.

As the monster rushed toward them, their storm of bolts made the mist turn crimson with flashing damage. It didn't slow. When it reached Lynn, it leaped, sailing just over their heads even as one of its appendages slashed down to strike Lynn across the face. At least, it would have struck her across the face if she'd been standing right in its path like an idiot. But she was kneeling, tracking it with her pistol as it sailed overhead. Ronnie and Edgar, the tallest of their group, ducked too late and both took damage.

The unknown circled at speed and shot back toward them for a third charge, though the guys got better at ducking in time to avoid hits. Finally, on its fourth charge through a literal hail of plasma bolts, the amorphous mist exploded into a shower of sparks.

"Yeah!"

"Woohooo! We did it!"

"That was awesome, guys!"

Lynn couldn't help smiling at Mack, Dan and Edgar's enthusiastic high-fives and backslaps, but she didn't join in. She was too busy refilling her armor slots—that unknown had packed a *serious* punch—and listening as Hugo's voice chimed in her ear that his entity analysis was complete. As he began going over it, a rotating image of the monster appeared in the upper right-hand corner of her display. It was vaguely feline, though covered in scales instead of fur, and sported a low, lithe body, a blocky head with saber-tooth style fangs and a spike-tipped tail. Lynn wondered if it was the spiked tail that had been hitting them when it had leaped over their heads.

"Unknown entity has been designated as a Stalker, a new Delta Class-4. It appears to be—"

"Hey, guys, did you all just level too?" Ronnie asked, his voice cutting through the AI's rundown.

"Yeah, I did," Edgar said, popping gum.

"Me too!" Dan and Mack chorused.

And that was when the rocs dropped on them from above like a flock of shrieking banshees.

Everyone instinctively ducked. Only Edgar was slow enough to get a face-full of the roc's stinger tails that swept down to strike as the monsters pulled out of their dive. Lynn didn't have time to worry about him, though, because four new dots appeared on her overhead, charging from every direction. Orculls, much like Grumblins and demons, weren't fast or nimble. But they had four arms and it was a nightmare fighting more than one at a time.

With her Stalker analysis automatically minimized as soon as a TDM engaged them, Lynn had a clear display to evaluate the situation but only a second or two in which to make a decision.

Ronnie, for his part, just started shooting again while yelling at everyone to "watch their heads"—as if they hadn't already noticed the rocs. He obviously either hoped their energy reserves would last long enough to take out all the monsters without resupply, or he'd forgotten to think that far ahead. He also must have neglected to study the monster index, or he would have known that Orculls had thick armor that was mostly impervious to ranged fire and required melee tactics to defeat. With that kind of opponent, the best hand-to-hand fighters should have advanced to engage the Orculls and give the best marksmen space to take out the rocs and the other dots Lynn could see converging on their location.

But Ronnie, fearless leader that he was, just kept yelling and shooting. Well, if he wanted to get himself and the rest of the team killed, or at least saddle them with horrible stats, there wasn't much she could do about it. And yelling at Ronnie to do something different at this point would probably confuse everyone even more.

And so Lynn took off at a sprint, charging the nearest Orcull and giving it a glancing slash to one of its arms as she passed, drawing it away from her embattled team. Then she switched direction, heading off a second Orcull that had zeroed in on Edgar. To her relief, both Orculls took the bait and converged on her and the *real* fun began.

Finally.

With just herself and the monsters in front of her to worry about, Lynn's anxiety faded and her focus sharpened. She dodged, rolled and lunged, constantly circling to keep the Orculls from pinning her between them. With four long gorillalike arms on their hunched bodies, there was no rolling through them unscathed, so she kept her distance, only dancing close enough for quick strikes at their weak points as she kept maneuvering the beasts to put their vulnerable backs to Mack and Dan so her teammates could shoot them from behind.

It wasn't quite the glorious, livestream-worthy fight she'd hoped for. She'd certainly made progress from her amateur fighting skills she'd started with in May. But she was already tired from a full day of hunting, so her movements weren't quick enough to keep her completely out of reach. The Orculls landed several strikes and at one point she stumbled over a patch of thick, tall grass that sent her sprawling into the weeds. Stupid terrain. She cursed and rolled but by the time she'd scrambled up the Orculls were on her and landing blow after blow. She had to sprint to get some distance from them, then turned to circle again.

"Hugo, private channel, sitrep!" she panted, too out of breath to subvocalize. She didn't dare take her eyes from the Orculls long enough to check on the guys.

"Masters Dan and Mack have successfully dispatched the rocs but I'm afraid they are all taking a beating from the remaining Orculls. It appears that, in the heat of battle, your numerous tactical suggestions have fallen by the wayside."

"Armor and health?" she gasped and leapt back, sucking in her tummy to avoid a swipe from the Orcull in front of her.

"I do not have access to their status reports. Only Hunters who have passed the qualification tests and formed official teams have the ability to share status reports."

Well, that sucked. They were all experienced enough to know to keep an eye on armor and health. And there were warnings that kicked in when things got too low. But it was all too easy to be distracted. It was a whole other level of operating, something that people like professional athletes or combat veterans could handle better than even serious gamers like Ronnie. Of course, as team captain, Ronnie's job was to fight competently *and* keep an eye on his team at the same time but so far he seemed totally absorbed in the fight. At least when she dared a glance at the guys, she saw that Ronnie had switched to his Plasma Blade and was running interference with the other two Orculls while Mack and Dan shot them in the back. Edgar had switched to his Dragon scattergun and was covering her, which she appreciated despite his limited range.

Lynn lunged, driving her Plasma Blade into one Orcull's chest as it swung at her. It exploded into sparks and she leapt to the side to escape the four-armed swipe of the second Orcull that tried to flank her.

"Watch it, Lynn," came Edgar's voice over their team channel, "two demons are right behind you!"

She'd heard them as soon as they'd gotten within range but appreciated Edgar's warning anyway. She spun and sprinted at the demons, diving into a forward roll as she reached the closest and executing her vicious back-stab maneuver. It exploded into sparks, having already taken several well-placed bolts from Mack.

In the second of calm before Lynn surged to her feet she saw a stray crusher worm headed Edgar's way. She yelled a warning, then left him to deal with it since she had a demon and an Orcull converging on her. A pity they were too stupid to realize their doom when they saw it.

Just to see what would happen, she tried a last minute dodge to get the two monsters to run into each other, Three Stooges style. But they seemed annoyingly aware of each other's position and the maneuver did nothing. A part of her brain wondered why they were programmed to be so sensitive to each other and hunters, while completely ignoring all inanimate objects—well, most. There was that time with the Varg and the air conditioning unit. She had no time to ponder it, though. She needed to focus fully on the battle and stay aware of the ground under her feet as she did. The last thing she wanted was a twisted ankle.

After both demon and Orcull had been reduced to sparks, she quickly equipped four new plates and a bag of Oneg to bring her armor and health back up. Then she turned and did a quick survey of the battlefield as she panted to catch her breath.

Chatter from her teammates filled one ear while the grunts, growls and roars from the TDMs around her filled the other. She saw Edgar make a lunge around the crusher worm, trying to reach the weak point in its armor behind the head. His strike landed but he couldn't backpedal fast enough to avoid its pincer jaws when it whipped around to attack. While the worm was distracted by Edgar, though, Mack sank three bolts into its weak spot on its unprotected side and the monster exploded.

"Man down, man down!" Dan yelled and Lynn spun to see the remaining Orcull charge in their direction while Ronnie stood rooted in place, fists clenched and face red with exertion and anger. His Hunter skin was gone and Lynn realized she could no longer see his blue friendly icon on her overhead.

Ronnie had died.

She didn't have time to think about it, though, but raced forward to intercept the Orcull bearing down on their group. With four against one, its demise was swift.

Silence descended as they all collectively held their breath, waiting for another enemy to appear. The sound of distant traffic and the buzz of insects in the tall grass once again became audible and Lynn suddenly noticed how incredibly sweaty she was. She swiped a sleeve across her face and straightened.

With no further enemies in sight, it was time to collect loot.

A squabble ensued as Mack, Dan and Edgar raced to grab the resources and items scattered around their feet. Lynn left them to it and headed back to where she'd killed the Orculls, sipping on the hydration tube connected to her TD Counterforce backpack as she went. She was pleased to see not one but two shiny augments blinking at her amid the weeds. She gathered them, plus the globes, ichor and plates from her conquests, before heading back to the group.

"Hugo, put a globe each toward stealth and detection, please."

"Of course, Miss Lynn."

Lynn rejoined her team...who were arguing again. She noticed they'd all exited combat mode, so she did as well.

"—And you, Edgar, you were just *sitting* there like a dumb rock instead of having my back. You should have been tearing into those Orculls. No wonder I died."

"Hey, I'm sorry, man," Edgar said placidly. "My scattergun doesn't have much of a range and I thought I'd get in the way with a Plasma Blade. Anyway I thought you had it covered. You didn't say you needed backup."

"I shouldn't have to, you idiot!"

"Don't call him names, Ronnie," Lynn snapped, surprising herself. She didn't want to argue, especially not with Ronnie. But Edgar's grateful glance gave her the courage to continue. "Look, it's not like he can see your stats. And we've been focusing on individual training the past two weeks, not team tactics, so how would he know what you want him to do in an unexpected situation like this?"

Ronnie shot her a glare, then turned to Dan and Mack, obviously choosing to ignore her, rather than respond to her perfectly valid point.

Jerk.

"Next time don't leave me high and dry like that," Ronnie growled, as if Mack and Dan hadn't been shooting the crap out of the Orculls the whole time. Maybe he thought that if he yelled at everyone else, no one would notice his own failures. Right. Like that ever worked. "Now I've lost an hour of experience and supplies!"

"You can still play if you want, the debuff is only fifty percent penalty on stats. And you can always buy supplies in auction if you need them," Dan pointed out.

"That's not the point! The point is I shouldn't have to. Our primary goal is to get everybody to Level 20 by September. But we can't do that if we're being sloppy and getting killed. We're going to start working on team level tactics tomorrow."

Well, finally, Lynn thought, listening with half an ear while she finished reviewing the index entry for the new TDM, the Stalker.

"We need to find more augments if we're going to start specializing," Dan said.

"They sell those in auction too," Mack offered helpfully.

"Yeah, for ridiculous prices," Dan shot back.

Lynn grinned internally. She was one of those people charging "ridiculous prices" for augments. Though, now that she thought about it, she should probably be saving those for her team instead of selling them.

"You can do private transfers between players as well," she said. "I know some of the best places to get dropped items. All we need to do is figure out who needs what and we can start collecting and assigning augments as we level."

"Good idea, because I'm broke." Mack said. "I spend all my allowance on game subscriptions. You can hook us up with the good stuff, right Lynn?" He punched her playfully on the arm.

Lynn pursed her lips to hide a smile.

"Okay but you gotta earn it, bozo. That means at least three hours a day on combat simulations and target practice."

Mack groaned theatrically.

"Slave driver! You're worse than my mom."

Dan and Edgar laughed while Lynn snorted indignantly.

"All right everyone, stop horsing around," Ronnie said, interrupting before Lynn could quip back at Mack. "If we're going to specialize, then I'll be assault, Dan, you'll be the sniper, Edgar, you're our heavy weapons and Mack, you stick with tactical."

"What about me?" Lynn asked when Ronnie didn't continue.

"You can do tactical with Mack," he said with a dismissive wave.

Lynn frowned. Ronnie's assignments to the guys were pretty much what they all played in WarMonger—she would know considering she'd taken them all out dozens of times. Assault players were usually fast-moving with medium armor and small arms or melee weapons for close-in fighting. Their job was to strategically kick butt wherever things were thickest, helping to control the enemy's movement and keep them where they needed to be.

The sniper role was being a glass cannon, light armor with a long-range weapon, usually a rifle with high-powered ammo that could one-shot targets. The sniper was supposed to stay back from the battle and provide overwatch.

Heavy weapons players were the tanks, there to soak up damage by drawing enemy fire away from their teammates. They were usually weighed down by the toughest armor available and a freaking beast of a gun, say a Gatling gun or hand-held cannon.

Tactical players were the all-around people who could fill in the gaps and provide support. They usually had medium armor and mid-range weapons and in certain games they filled the role of medic or healer. They were also the ones who managed things like air strikes or who carried the area damage weapons like grenade launchers.

Tactical was a role that suited Mack. He was a less aggressive player and definitely a better shooter than melee fighter. But it did not suit her. Even in WarMonger, she preferred to get up close and personal with her kills. Not that she couldn't snipe with the best of them but it just wasn't her style. If this had been WarMonger, she might have gone with it, since it was based on modern weaponry that was mostly ranged anyway.

But TD Hunter wasn't WarMonger and she'd noticed in beta the disproportionate amount of damage the Nano and Plasma Blades inflicted compared to the pistols, or even the rifle she'd only gotten to try out before beta had ended. Ranged weapons were important, since sometimes you needed space to avoid the different TDM attacks. But now that they were facing tougher monsters and couldn't use terrain for cover the same way you could in a game like WarMonger. They would need more than just one assault player to help control the enemy's movements and keep them from mobbing the team's shooters.

"Uh, Ronnie. Don't you think I'd be better as assault?" Lynn said.

"Assault is a high-stress role where a lot can go wrong. I don't need you getting in my way out in front. You'll do better as tactical."

Aaand there was Ronnie the Jerkinator.

He might as well have said "girls got no game" and been done with it. Or maybe he was afraid Lynn might show him up if they were in the same role, side by side where their performance could be easily compared.

Lynn sighed and stayed silent. Arguing about it now wasn't going to get her anywhere. The line between assault and tactical could be fluid anyway. She would do what she thought needed doing and Ronnie could complain about it if he didn't like it.

"Okay, so when everyone gets home, post in the group chat what augments you've found so far and what their stats are so I can assign them. For now, since you geniuses let me get killed, I'll observe and give feedback. You all obviously need it."

Seriously? There were so many things wrong with how Ronnie was leading, Lynn could have filled an entire field manual. But again, she wasn't team captain, so she said nothing. She told herself it was because team cohesion was important and she didn't want to cause a fight. The little voice in her head pointing out that she would do a much better job was just a distraction. She didn't *want* the job and Ronnie would never accept her as captain anyway.

Ugh. Why oh why did Mr. Krator make this competition team only?

Lynn tried to forget how annoying the whole situation was as they projected their displays so Ronnie could see what was going on, then continued hunting. But every time he opened his mouth, she had to grit her teeth tighter to keep from snapping at him.

It was a relief when Ronnie finally called it quits and they headed back to their respective homes. Lynn caught a robo-car at the nearest hub and rode in gloomy silence, contemplating their team's sorry state and wondering what in the world she could do to fix it.

"Hey, Mom."

"Hi, honey, did you have fun with your team today?"

Lynn grunted noncommittally as she headed to the bathroom to shower and change. It was Saturday, so that meant some mother-daughter hangout time as soon as she was no longer stinking and potentially covered in ticks. Maybe ice cream and an immersive VR adventure with her mom would cheer her up.

The hot water felt amazing, soothing sore muscles and reinvigorating her. She was relieved to find no ticks this time—though it also made her suspicious. She'd have her mom check her scalp later. She emerged from the bathroom dressed in clean clothes and blotting her long black hair dry only to find her mother in a frenzied rush.

"Uh, Mom, what's going on? Also, did you know your scrubs are on inside out?"

"What? Oh, good grief." Matilda rushed back into her bedroom, then reemerged a minute later. "I'm sorry, Lynn but the hospital just sent an emergency ping to all staff. Everyone's been called in."

Lynn's heart sank but she tried not to let it show on her face.

"What happened? Was there an accident or something?"

"Worse in a way. The hospital's power failed. They're evacuating all critical patients until they can figure out what in the heck is going on." Matilda grabbed her purse and rifled through it as she spoke.

"No way!" Lynn said, confused. "Don't hospitals have backup systems? Like, generators and stuff?"

"What I got was everything is down," Matilda said, her face

working. "There's *multiple* back-ups. Generators for one and the city grid AI is supposed to syphon any power off to the hospital when power's lost. None of it's working. There is zero power. That's what I was told," she finished, slinging her purse strap over her shoulder and heading for the door.

"Have you had supper yet?" Lynn called after her mom. She could smell something cooking in the oven.

"No but there's no time," Matilda said and pulled open their apartment door. She paused and looked back. "I'm sorry, honey. Depending on how long it takes to get things fixed, I might have to pull a double shift. I'll message you details as soon as I know more."

"Okay," Lynn said, feeling worse than ever.

Her mom must have noticed her gloom, because Matilda paused in the middle of pulling the door shut.

"Honey, when the casserole is done, why don't you take some down to Mr. Thomas' apartment and see if he'd like some company. He seemed so pleased by those cookies we made him. I think he's pretty lonely."

Lynn forced a smile on her face.

"Sure thing, Mom. Stay safe."

"I will, dear," Matilda said and blew her a kiss before shutting the door. The sound of her hurried footsteps soon faded.

With a sigh, Lynn went to her room to retrieve the woodland craft book Edgar had given her, then slumped onto the living room couch with it while the casserole finished cooking. She was starting the chapter on interpreting the sounds of the woods—a concept she was familiar with considering how noisy TDMs were—when the oven timer dinged. The casserole turned out to be cheesy potato topped with corn flakes, one of Lynn's favorites. It wasn't quite as traditionally Iowan as it could have been since Matilda had thrown in a pound of ground beef to help satiate her daughter's carnivorous appetite. Lynn set the dish on the counter to cool, then, after some consideration, got out ingredients for a tossed salad. She wasn't a fan of salad but anything tasted good with enough ranch dressing and her nurse of a mother had pounded into her that no meal was complete without green vegetables.

After the salad was put together and the casserole was cool enough to eat, Lynn packed up two portions of each into disposable containers and set out for Mr. Thomas' apartment on the first floor.

Her hesitant knock on his door was answered after a considerable delay with a muffled "Who is it?"

"Uh, it's Lynn, your neighbor from upstairs?"

There was a long silence, then the lock rattled and the door opened on Mr. Thomas' beaming face.

"Why, Miz Raven, what a pleasant surprise! Come in, come in." He motioned with his cane.

"Uhh, okay," Lynn said, feeling all kinds of awkward. But she didn't want to be rude, so she followed Mr. Thomas into his apartment and closed the door behind her. "I, uh, brought some casserole and salad. Mom got called away to the hospital and, um, I was wondering if you might want some company for dinner?"

"Certainly, young lady. I would be delighted. An old man like me doesn't often get visitors. My evenings are usually spent in front of my trusty stream screen with only my service AI for company. It is not a bad sort, as AIs go, but of course they never do have a sense of humor."

Lynn listened politely as she followed Mr. Thomas into the combined dining room and kitchen. Unlike her apartment a few floors above, this apartment was smaller and there was no wall between the living room and kitchen, giving it a more open feel even if it was smaller overall.

"Put the food down there, on the table. I'll get us some plates and utensils. Would you like some iced tea?"

"Sure?"

Lynn set her bag of food down on the table, then stood awkwardly as Mr. Thomas puttered around, rooting through various drawers and kitchen cabinets. She shot a surreptitious glance around as she waited, noting with interest the framed posters of singers and musicians in old fashioned clothes—she wasn't sure of the decade but definitely before her mother had been born—and other artifacts of the previous century, things she recognized only from her mother's descriptions. A rotary telephone. A cassette player. A tube TV pushed back in one corner, its screen dark and dusty. Even the furniture seemed old, as if collected and preserved with loving care instead of thrown out to make room for more modern and sleek designs.

In fact, the only modern thing she could see in the whole apartment was the stream screen on one wall, so thin and sleek that it could have been part of the wall itself. Above it in a place of prominence was mounted an old rifle with a wooden stock and dull black metal fixtures. Lynn didn't recognize it—it wasn't like the M4s or even older M16s she was used to seeing in games like WarMonger. Considering what she knew of Mr. Thomas, she guessed it was whatever had preceded those rifles in the history of gun development. She wondered if it was *the* rifle Mr. Thomas had used when he'd fought... wherever it was that he'd fought. History was not her strong point and she hadn't wanted to bother Mr. Thomas with a bunch of personal questions.

"There we are, Miz Raven. A bit of an eclectic mix of tableware, I will admit. But all perfectly serviceable."

Lynn's eyes snapped back to the table and she shot Mr. Thomas a hesitant glance. He smiled at her with a twinkle in his eye, not seeming at all offended to find her staring nosily around his apartment.

"Shall we eat?"

"Yeah, sure. I'm starving, actually."

While Lynn got out the containers of food, Mr. Thomas poured them both drinks, then they dug in to the home-cooked fare.

"Mm, this casserole is delectable. Did you make it, Miz Raven?"

"Oh, no. My mom made it. I can cook when I need to but it's not really my thing."

"I'll admit, it's not my favorite activity, either. But I have learned over the years that food builds bridges and mends hearts in a way that few other things do. I can't say I've become an expert but I've found more joy in the art as years have passed." Mr. Thomas smiled.

Lynn nodded and chewed her food in silence. She was pretty bad at small talk and this was out of her depth. It was nice to have company after her mom had left so abruptly but eating at a casual acquaintance's apartment on the spur of the moment was definitely not her idea of a relaxing time.

"So," Mr. Thomas continued, seeming totally at ease, "how is the hunting going? I've not seen you valiantly slaying AR monsters around the complex of late, are you still playing that new game?"

"Oh, yeah, absolutely," Lynn said, glad to be on familiar ground. "I've just found better hunting spots than right around here."

"Ah. You worked things out with your friends, then?"

"Yup. Thanks for your advice on that. We formed a team and everything. It's not perfect, but... well... at least we're all getting along. Mostly."

"Mostly?" Mr. Thomas raised his snowy white eyebrows.

Lynn blew out a noisy breath, her cheeks puffing out as she did.

"Yeah. Ronnie is still being a jerk most of the time. He doesn't say it outright but he obviously still thinks I'm an inferior gamer because I'm a girl. It's so stupid! My rankings are way higher than his and I've proven how good I am again and again. But he ignores it all and acts like I don't exist half the time. He won't listen to my advice, even when it hurts our team for him not to. It's so infuriating, sometimes I just want to—to—I don't know. Punch him in his stupid, idiotic face." By the time she'd finished, she was breathing hard and clutching her fork so fiercely her knuckles were white.

"Ah, well, that certainly sounds like a difficult situation," Mr. Thomas said, his expression grave. He sighed. "I wish I could tell you it will all turn out fine in the end. But unfortunately, we cannot control how others think of us. There will always be those who stubbornly cling to the most unjust and fallacious opinions, regardless of all proof to the contrary." Mr. Thomas leaned back in his chair, his gaze vacant and the care-worn lines of his face seeming deeper than normal. Lynn imagined he was speaking from painful experience.

"So...how did you survive it?" she asked, then blushed, realizing what she'd implied. "Sorry, I just— Well— You seem—"

Mr. Thomas chuckled.

"Not to worry, young lady. You are quite perceptive and it is nothing to be ashamed of. How did I survive? In a word: Charity."

"Uh, what? You mean, like, people giving you money?"

This time Mr. Thomas laughed outright. It was a warm sound, full of simple enjoyment. Lynn couldn't help but grin in response.

"Not at all, Miz Raven. I mean charity in the King James sense. These days people use the word 'love,' but our modern culture has reduced that word to a trite and shallow thing. Charity has a much deeper meaning. It is a selfless love, a love without agenda, without stipulation, without pride. It is to love in spite of, not because of."

"Um, okay?" Lynn said, then fell silent. She didn't really do "feelings." They were too ephemeral and confusing. She preferred solid, straightforward things, like objectives and stats and plans of attack.

Mr. Thomas smiled kindly and leaned forward.

"Let me put it differently. Consider a code of honor. Do you act honorably only to 'good' people who 'deserve' it? Or do you act with honor regardless of the situation or the actions of those around you?"

Well, Lynn knew which one she preferred. She hadn't built the feared mercenary Larry Coughlin's reputation on being "honorable." It was survival of the fittest. She'd spent years honing her ability to ruthlessly squash her competition into the dirt. She would fight and beat anyone at all, friend or foe, for the right price. And sometimes for no price at all, Ronnie and the guys being a case in point. It didn't matter if she liked Edgar, Mack and Dan in the real. They ran with Ronnie in WarMonger, so it was their own fault they suffered along with him.

Besides, she *did* have a code, of sorts. Get the job done. Deliver the goods—or, at least, refund the fee if you couldn't. Keep your word. Watch the back of those who watched yours. And if you screwed with one merc, you screwed with them all.

But then, WarMonger was just a game. So, did it even count?

She knew which one her dad would have picked. When she was young, he'd spent hours volunteering for a local prison outreach. It had made her mom worry incessantly because some of the people in the program were the same ones he'd put in prison in the first place. Lynn had asked him once why he helped bad people and he'd crouched in front of her and said, "Because bad people are still people, *jenta mi*."

Lynn swallowed and cleared her throat.

"I guess if you have a code of honor, you stick to it regardless."

Mr. Thomas smiled.

"It wouldn't be much of a code, otherwise, would it?"

"Guess not."

"Well, charity is like a code of honor. It is to love, to treat with kindness and respect, because you have decided for yourself *that* is the sort of person you will be, instead of allowing other people's words or actions to influence your behavior. Evil begets evil, young lady, and I saw many others over the years trapped by bitterness and anger because of the way they had been treated. It was not a life that I wanted to live."

Lynn took another bite of casserole and chewed slowly as she mulled over Mr. Thomas's words. She'd had her fair share of sucky treatment. It was why she'd turned to gaming, where she could be judged purely on the basis of her skill, instead of how her body looked. That fair treatment in virtual amidst the ceaseless bullying she got in the real was probably the only thing that had preserved her sanity through those rough years at school. But now she had chosen to leave her comfort zone and take the battle into the real. Now she had to actually *deal* with Ronnie's Jerkitude instead of running away and consoling herself with sweet retribution in virtual.

So, what was her code of honor? Who would she choose to be? Would it be Larry, a ruthless fighter whose chief concern was getting paid? Or Lynn, a self-conscious teenager who let fear hold her back? Was there something in between and if so, how did she find it?

A heavy weariness settled on her shoulders. Where was her dad when she needed him?

The thought brought a hot prickle to the corners of her eyes and she ducked her head and busied herself finishing her food while Mr. Thomas changed the topic and started a good-natured gripe about the failings of modern news streams and how it was all doom and gloom all the time.

"Why, just yesterday," he said, "all the news pundits wanted to talk about was that mega airbus that crashed into San Francisco Bay a few days ago. Of course, it was a tragedy, but we should be mourning those lost and leaving the families in peace, not playing endless footage of the crash. And the conspiracy theories! It's enough to drive any normal person insane.

"You should hear those yahoos on the news streams. The way they talk, all the random airbus malfunctions in the past month are some kind of interconnected plot by ransomware hackers trying to undermine the public's confidence in these big corporation technologies. They claim the corporations are colluding to form monopolies and 'undermine American freedom' or some such nonsense."

"What kind of malfunctions?" Lynn asked, thinking about the airbuses she rode pretty much daily at this point with all the hunting she was doing.

"Oh, sudden power loss or glitches in the navigation systems. There's only been a few deadly crashes, though. Most of the time the AIs have no problem switching to backup systems."

Lynn thought of her mom's hospital.

"You got any theories on what's causing it, if it's not hackers? I mean, besides China. Everyone blames everything on China, no matter what it is."

"Oh, I am sure it's nothing, just random glitches like the airbus companies have been saying. It happens from time to time. Technology isn't perfect, after all, even if it is much more reliable than humans."

Lynn made a vague sound of agreement and ate the last few bites of her dinner, then pushed back from the table.

"Thank you for your hospitality, Mr. Thomas, but I'd better get going. I've had a long day and I'm beat."

"Of course, Miz Raven. Thank you for thinking of an old man. It was delightful to have company for a change."

Lynn smiled shyly.

"No problem. I'm pretty used to being alone but Mom is always saying that interacting with people in virtual is no substitute for real relationships."

"Your mother is a wise woman, young lady."

"Yeah, I know. But most of the people I've known in the real are jerks or bullies. It hasn't given me much of a reason to put myself out there."

"Well, you've made a good start of it so far, I would say." Mr. Thomas leaned back and patted his stomach with a twinkle in his eye. "Good food is an essential ingredient to any friendship, after all."

That made Lynn grin as she gathered up her bag and the food containers.

"So, you're saying I should work on my cooking skills, then bribe my way into people's good graces."

"Well, it worked for you today, did it not? It is exceedingly difficult to say no to someone who makes delicious food."

"Thanks for the tip but I think I'll stick to shooting things," Lynn said with a laugh. "It's more fun than cooking." With everything packed away, she hefted her bag and stood awkwardly for a moment, unsure if she should wave, or shake hands, or what.

"Goodness, pardon me," Mr. Thomas said, reaching for his cane. "Let me see you out. Your mother's heavenly casserole is threatening to send me into a food coma and I quite forgot my manners."

"Oh, it's no problem, Mr. Thomas, don't bother getting up, I'll let myself out. I'll . . . see you around, I guess?"

"You are welcome any time, Miz Raven."

"Thanks and...you can call me Lynn." She smiled.

"Well, then, I insist you call me Jerald."

"Er, okay. Bye, Jerald!"

"And a good evening to you, Lynn."

Lynn gave a little wave and left, making sure she shut his apartment door securely behind her. The last few months she'd been making herself take the stairs instead of the elevator, for training. But tonight she was too worn out, so she stopped in the lobby and pushed the button for the elevator. When she finally collapsed on her bed, she was tempted to log onto WarMonger and see what'd been going on while she'd been so occupied with TD Hunter. But it had been a long day and she had to get up early for her pre-hunt workout tomorrow. She spent a little while messaging her mom to see how things were going and if they'd figured out what was wrong with the power grid. But all she got from Matilda was a furious rant about budget cuts and incompetent bureaucrats who knew nothing about safety systems. So, instead of distracting her mom with more messages, she shut off everything and lay back in her bed in the dark, staring at the ceiling.

She fell asleep thinking about honor codes and airbuses falling from the sky.

Chapter 11

"COME ON, MOM, DO WE REALLY HAVE TO DO THIS? JUST LET ME order clothes in virtual and I can have them delivered within hours."

"But that's no fun! I haven't been clothes shopping in *ages* and we never got to spend time together last weekend. Come on, won't you humor your mother this once?"

Lynn groaned, closing her eyes to block out the Bambi-eye look her mom was giving her.

Her first mistake had been mentioning that she needed new clothes, considering everything she had was too baggy and several decades out of date. She should have just ordered a few standard programmable outfits online, no need for fittings or fashion advice. But no, she'd had to open her big mouth and now she was paying the price.

Oh well. She *did* owe her mom several weekends' worth of hang-out time with how much she'd been focusing on TD Hunter training.

"Uhhhg. Fine," Lynn finally said.

Her mother squealed with unseemly delight and Lynn instantly regretted her words.

But it was too late now.

"We have to stop for food first, though. I'm so hungry I think my stomach has turned inside-out."

"All right then, what are you waiting for? Let's get this show on the road," Matilda said and dragged Lynn toward the door.

It was Sunday evening a week after her impromptu meal with Mr. Thomas and she was tired from hunting and grumpy after having to deal with Ronnie all day. But it was a beautiful evening, clear-skied and not as humid as usual and she'd been craving a Maid-Rite sandwich for hours. At this point she could probably eat two or three.

They caught a robo-car to the Maid-Rite on First Avenue and Lynn's mother looked on with raised eyebrows as Lynn devoured two huge sandwiches, their buns soft and buttery and their meat filling perfectly spiced. By the third she finally slowed and only managed to get halfway through before she gave up in stuffed contentment.

"I'd forgotten how much teenagers eat." Matilda chuckled. She'd been eating her sandwich with a fork and a knife to avoid getting the oozing meat filling on her hands, which was pretty much sacrilegious in Iowa, but then she was picky about cleanliness. "Though even for a teenager that was impressive. I know you've been out with your friends almost every day the past few weeks but playing that AR game must be a harder workout than I thought for you to eat like that and still be losing so much weight."

"Mom," Lynn muttered, looking around, "we're in public!"

"Oh, relax, dear. Nobody can hear us in this noisy restaurant and nobody would care if they could. They have their own lives to worry about. Besides, I'm proud of you." She reached across the little table where they sat and gave Lynn's hand a squeeze. Lynn smiled and squeezed back. "You've been working so hard the past few months and it really shows. It's a good thing we're going to get you some smart clothing, because at this rate you're going to keep dropping sizes and there's no point buying any standard clothes until your body finds its new normal. And, speaking of clothes, we'd better get going! The mall will probably close in a couple hours and I don't want to be rushed."

Lynn sighed and rolled her eyes heavenward. Time for the torture to commence. At least she would go to her doom on a full stomach.

Cedar Rapids' Lindale Mall wasn't much when compared to the sprawling, glittering shopping centers Lynn remembered from her girlhood in Baltimore. But it had been bought out a few years ago and completely revamped, transforming it into a state-of-the-art destination with every luxury a prospective shopper could imagine. Lynn and her mom hadn't gone shopping since they'd moved to Cedar Rapids, at least not like they had before her dad had died and they'd been saddled with a mountain of debt. In an age where everything you could ever need could be bought in virtual, printed and drone-delivered within hours, and VR headsets made browsing stores in virtual as good as in person but without the annoying commute, shopping in the real had become an expensive hobby more akin to an amusement park trip than anything else.

Sizing issues for clothes and apparel had been solved by the invention of smart materials and even those who preferred natural materials could have their LINC do a full body scan and send exact measurements in the blink of an eye. Mass-produced standard sizes were so yesterday. Custom print-on-demand was the new model and many stores didn't even keep retail stock anymore. The only shopping centers that had survived were those that had shifted their focus from selling "things" to selling an "experience." Some thrift stores still limped along but after the 3D printing revolution and rise of drone delivery networks, buying in virtual was so affordable that only the truly budget constrained—i.e., Lynn and her mom—still frequented them. And even then, it was more of a walk of shame than "shopping."

But now, Lynn had money. Or at least, now she could spend the money she already had because she'd come clean with her mom. She didn't like the idea of spending it—years of counting every penny had marked her permanently. But quality clothes that fit well were an acceptable expense and treating her mom to a shopping "experience" was the least she could do. Besides, after the disaster at the hospital last weekend, Lynn knew her mom needed something fun to take her mind off the deaths that weighed on her shoulders.

When the robo-car dropped them off at Lindale Mall's customer arrival center, they were greeted by a life-size concierge hologram. Lynn had to stop herself from staring. She'd never seen one in the real, only read about them. The woman looked and moved exactly like a real person and only the slight transparency of her figure made her identifiable as a hologram. Lynn knew the transparency was a built-in feature, meant to make people more at ease. Years of research and experimentation with AIs had made it painfully clear that, while people liked their service AIs to be humanlike, anything so accurate as to make them indistinguishable from humans in voice, looks, or behavior made people so uncomfortable that entire lobbies existed to prevent it.

"Good evening, ladies, and welcome to Lindale Mall," the hologram said with a pretty smile. "We look forward to making your experience here one of a kind. Would you like to rent an AR interface for your visit this evening, or use your own?"

"We'll rent, please. One for each of us," Lynn said before her mom could speak. Matilda's AR glasses were so out of date that Lynn wasn't sure why her mom even bothered using them anymore. She had state-of-the-art glasses for her work at the hospital of course—allowing her to easily interface with the hospital's system, check LINC-tracked vitals on those patients who allowed emergency access of such things and get real-time updates from the EMTs' glasses so they could have everything pre-prepped—but those were hospital property so using them off-duty was strictly prohibited.

Lynn's own TD Hunter-provided glasses were more than capable of interfacing with the shopping mall's systems. But then Lynn would have to use the mall's app and opt into the mall's end-user license agreement, which of course would give the mall's software permission to track her every move in virtual and in the real to gather valuable data it would use to monetize her later. No thanks. She could always go back in later and remove the permissions but it was a pain. Most people not only accepted but welcomed such data collection because of the customized experience it made possible. But not Lynn. She knew too much— had seen behind the curtain, so to speak, in her years snooping around in virtual—to be comfortable with it.

"Certainly," the service hologram replied. "Right this way please." It led them to a holo-screen kiosk where they could select their interface type—glasses were the most popular but helmets, contacts and visors were also common. Then the kiosk offered them their selection on a velvet-lined tray that extended from its depths.

"Fancy," Lynn muttered as she and her mom slipped on their glasses. These were a bit different from standard AR glasses in that they were a combination LINC and AR interface together. That way Lynn, or any other guest, could enjoy their shopping experience without being dependent on their own LINC—or lack of LINC.

Lynn's vision lit up with the mall's welcome display. First things first, she authorized Lindale Mall in her virtual wallet, then chose the option for an "ad-free" experience—for a fee, of course. After that Lynn had the option of creating a "group" for shared visual and audio input, which she did.

Another image of a well-dressed lady appeared in front of them, though this time it was part of their AR display, not a life-size hologram.

"Good evening, ladies," it said brightly. "My name is Taylor and I will be your guide while you enjoy Lindale Mall's amenities. Would you like to reserve the services of a personal shopper or porter this evening?"

Lynn looked at her mom, who shook her head.

"No thanks, Taylor," Lynn said.

"Of course. Would you like a brief tutorial of how to customize your visual experience today?"

"Um, what?" Lynn asked.

"Every aspect of your AR visuals is customizable, from my voice and appearance, to the appearance of the mall around you. We have a whole catalog of AR interactive environments available for your enjoyment."

"Environments?" Lynn echoed.

"Yes. Our Great Barrier Reef environment, for example, will add an underwater skin to the mall including lifelike, exotic wildlife to swim around you and interact with you as you shop. Have you always wanted to shop on the streets of Paris? Choose our Champs-Élysées environment and enjoy the sights and sounds of France's most famous shopping destination, all the while being entertained by authentic Parisian street performers."

Lynn and her mom exchanged a wide-eyed look.

"Uh, I think we'll stick to the basics for now, but all the settings are in the mall menu right?"

"That is correct, miss. Would you like a brief tour of our grounds and the amenities you can enjoy?"

"Yeah, please," Lynn said, already overwhelmed and ready to go home.

"Right this way, then, please," Taylor said and gestured them forward.

The image of the service AI wound its way through the scattering of mall-goers entering and exiting the main doors. Most of the mall's grandeur was lost on Lynn—she would rather be doing almost anything else—but the youthful sparkle in her mom's eyes was unmistakable, so Lynn sucked up her trepidation and tried to enjoy herself for her mother's sake.

Taylor's image stopped where the main corridor emptied out into a large, multi-level hall with a glass dome roof that let in the evening light. Everything looked modern and elegant, from the white tiled floors to the sweeping columns, to the walls decorated in abstract art—at least wherever the walls weren't glass, making the entire mall feel bigger and more airy. Lynn wondered if everything was white with lots of glass to give the AR customizations more of a blank canvas to work with.

"The Lindale Mall is laid out in wings based on interest and product type," the service AI began, gesturing with a slender hand as she spoke. "There are separate wings for apparel and accessories, home furnishings, entertainment and electronics, health and beauty, sports and children. The central hall contains our dining area where you can browse our virtual menu and select from hundreds of food options while you enjoy our live entertainment. Or, if you are in the mood for some pampering, visit our very own Lindale spa and relaxation center off the main hall. We also have an in-house VR suite where you can enjoy all the best VR experiences including movies, games, world-tours, nature explorations and more."

Lynn's eyebrows rose higher and higher as Taylor spoke. Good grief. All they needed to do was add a hotel wing and she bet some people would never leave this place.

"And if you find the Lindale Mall experience to your liking, there are the Lindale Mall apartments which rent for a very low monthly fee..."

Even better, Lynn thought. *Squeeze every dime...*

"Our goal at Lindale Mall is to give you an unforgettable experience with premier customer service. All of our products are meant to be tried, sampled and enjoyed so that you have complete assurance in your selections. There are testing areas available for most products and almost everything is customizable. Simply select a product and scroll through the available customizations. If we do not have your selection on hand, simply put in a product request and we can print it while you enjoy our amenities. Your Lindale Mall app includes a map and navigational assistant, simply state what product you are looking for and our guidance system will lead you right to it. If you have any questions at all or would like a personalized tour, just ask and I will make sure you are taken care of."

"Thank you Taylor, I think we'll take it from here," Matilda said vaguely, obviously distracted by the sights in the huge hall, or maybe the live band playing some low-key pop music on a raised platform in the middle of the dining area.

"Of course, enjoy your visit!" said the service AI and disappeared.

Lynn couldn't help but grin as she watched her mom's bright-eyed look.

"So..." Matilda began.

"We can do whatever you want, Mom. My treat. You deserve some R and R."

"Some what?"

"Sorry, rest and recuperation."

"Oh, yes. Thank you dear but won't it be... expensive?"

Lynn shrugged.

"Probably but we can afford it once. Just don't try to move into the apartments, 'kay?" She grinned and her mom grinned back.

"Want to see what environments they have available?" Lynn asked, curious what it would look like to see exotic fish swimming through the air around her.

"They sound fun, honey, but also distracting. Why don't we go get you your clothes first? Then we can worry about having fun."

"Drat. I was hoping you'd forget that part."

"Nonsense! I respect your right to wear whatever you feel comfortable with but it's clear you're not comfortable in the clothes you have, so let's go find you some that fit well and make you feel excited to wear them, okay?"

"Feeling excited about the clothes you wear is a thing?" Lynn asked, wrinkling her nose.

Her mom laughed and tugged on her arm, pulling her toward the wing marked "Apparel and Accessories."

Mercifully, clothes shopping with her mom didn't turn out to be too painful. Once Lynn relaxed and ignored the scattering of other shoppers, she actually kind of enjoyed herself. The offerings were incredible and she watched in amazement as the clothes she tried on morphed to fit her perfectly, changing color and pattern at her command. Matilda might have had a little too much fun with it, in Lynn's opinion. But letting her mom play dress-up with her in the privacy of the changing rooms was fine.

Lynn had no idea what to even look for in terms of style and had no desire to summon Taylor for advice, even though she knew the AI existed for exactly that purpose. She knew Taylor was as fully customizable as everything else in the mall but no amount of changing the AI's appearance, clothes, gender, or race would make Lynn more comfortable chatting about clothing choices. Human shopping assistants could be seen here and there interacting with customers who preferred them over AI assistance. Lynn was glad she had her mom with her. No way would she have set foot in a place like this by herself.

With Matilda's help, Lynn picked out some less expensive soft cotton casual wear as well as three smart fabric outfits for school. But when Lynn was ready to find some athletic performance wear for monster hunting, her mom wasn't much help. After a moment's debate, Lynn took off her rented glasses and slipped on her own. She held up a "wait for it" finger when her mom gave her a quizzical look.

"Hey, Hugo, can I ask you a question?" Lynn subvocalized after firing up the TD Hunter app, keeping it out of combat mode.

"Certainly, Miss Lynn. How can I assist you?"

"I know you're not a general service AI but you have complete mesh network access, so I was hoping you could give me a little advice on . . . well, on clothes."

"While it is not within my primary programming, I am capable of performing a mesh search and analyzing the results. However, you have a fully functional service AI as part of your LINC software, why not utilize its capabilities?"

"I thought you might have better insight, considering you know the TD Hunter game better. I'm looking for some good athletic clothes to play the game in but I've never shopped for smart clothes before. Will any of the, um, electronic components of the clothes interfere with the TD Hunter app's performance or sensors or anything?"

"Not at all, Miss Lynn. You can be assured that such advanced apparel was taken into account by TD Hunter's developers."

"Okay, good to know. Do you have any advice on what brand or type of smart clothes would be best for monster hunting outside in the heat and the cold? Something that's durable, easy to clean, protects against brambles but isn't suffocating to wear?"

"Let me see, with such criteria, you would want to look for high performance athletic wear for extreme outdoor activities such as mountain climbing. According to my research, NanoTechLabs has developed a variety of fabrics for just such activities. They use nano technology to coat smart fabrics in materials that repel odor and dirt particles, have advanced wicking technology for high performance in heat or cold and absorb and redistribute force impact to minimize injury. Simply check that your clothes selection uses NTL's high-performance nanofabric and it should meet your criteria."

"Awesome, thanks, Hugo," she said, then slipped off her own glasses and replaced the mall's set.

"Okay, not sure what that was," chuckled Matilda. "Your facial muscles were moving like you were having a conversation but I didn't hear a thing."

"Oh, yeah. It's called subvocalization. It lets me talk to Hugo without saying things out loud."

"Hugo?" her mom asked with raised brows.

"The TD Hunter AI, remember? The British-sounding service AI that made you sign all those NDAs?"

"Of course! How could I forget. So, did you find out what you needed?"

"Yup. I just need to look for a specific fabric type. Let me look in the mall's directory and see if I can search for athletic wear by who made the fabric."

Sure enough, she could—bless modern technology—and the mall's helpful navigation software took them right to the correct racks of clothing. The clothing itself looked underwhelming, considering everything appeared to be made of the same black, matte material. Lynn reached out and rubbed a sleeve between her fingers, marveling at the odd texture. It was smooth like silk, yet there was a sturdy and satisfying thickness to it.

Right beside the racks were also various displays showcasing shoes, boots, backpacks, hats and other outdoor gear. And behind it all along the back wall of that wing was a "product testing area." It looked like a cross between a rock climbing gym and a lab. There were various strips of terrain—including rocky walls with climbing equipment—as well as a circular glass chamber that Lynn assumed would imitate various climate variables like heat and cold. There were half a dozen people using the testing environments while a mall employee wearing a shirt that declared "Safety Officer" stood to the side and observed.

Lynn turned to her mom.

"This. Is. So. Cool. How much time do we have before the mall closes?"

"Lindale is open until midnight," Matilda said, probably checking the hours through the app menu. "We have plenty of time as long as you don't mind staying out late."

"Um, is that okay with you?"

"Of course, honey! My next shift doesn't start until Monday evening. Let's make the most of tonight."

"Swee-EEE-eet," Lynn sang under her breath, feeling giddy with excitement. She picked out a pile of clothes and equipment to try out and quickly changed in a dressing room, taking a moment to choose a blue scalelike pattern for her clothes that reminded her of her Skadi's Glory skin in TD Hunter. When she took a look at herself in the mirror, though, she had a moment of paralyzing panic.

The clothes were as tight and stretchy as yoga pants, bottom *and* top, which was all perfectly normal for athletic wear. Except she'd spent the past four-plus years being viciously bullied for her form and had trained herself to hide it at all costs. Yeah, so maybe she'd slimmed up a bit and added some muscle in the past two months but she was still, well, *her*. What if someone pointed and laughed when she came out of the dressing room?

"Honey? You okay in there?"

Matilda's voice drifted into the changing rooms and Lynn gritted her teeth. This was stupid. Just like Mr. Thomas had warned, she couldn't let other people's opinions dictate her behavior. She would not cower in fear. Even if she couldn't get rid of the fear entirely, at least she could shove it back to the farthest corner of her mind and lock it away. If she ignored it long enough, maybe it would eventually disappear.

After a deep breath, her body started to relax and Lynn finally marched out of the dressing room, shoulders thrown back and head held high. Her mom spotted her and delight lit up Matilda's face.

"Wow! Look at you, honey!" Matilda said, then whistled in appreciation.

"Um, could you not be quite so loud, Mom? We're in public." Lynn cut her eyes from side to side, expecting derisive looks. But, of course, not a single person in the entire wing was paying her an ounce of attention. They went about their business, caught up in their own little augmented worlds.

Lynn relaxed and even cracked a grin.

"Come on, Mom. Let's take this stuff for a ride."

They both had entirely too much fun, especially in the environment chamber where Lynn cycled through wind, rain, sleet, snow and even hail settings, as well as various temperature levels. Her mom laughed, observing from the outside, as Lynn made a snow angel in the thin scattering of half-melted snow on the floor.

Once Lynn had tested over a dozen different outfits and pieces of equipment, she headed back to the dressing rooms, dried off and gathered her selections to take home. She cringed inwardly at the swiftly rising price tag of this mall trip—no prices were openly displayed unless you asked for them in the app settings and Lynn wasn't the sort to purchase in ignorance—but she knew it was worth it, even if it set her savings back a couple grand.

Once they were done shopping, they put all their purchases in a complimentary locker then headed to the center of the mall for a late snack as they tried out various AR environment settings together. The results were truly spectacular.

When Lynn selected the Great Barrier Reef environment she was floored as the walls transformed into gorgeous coral reefs while a rippling light overlaid everything and everyone around her, making it seem like she was underwater. She had fun holding her hands up in the air for the AR fish to come nibble at. They swirled away in a flash of color as soon as she tried to grab them. Her mom was just as awestruck and pointed in wonder at the glass ceiling and walls of the mall where the outside world of Cedar Rapids had vanished. In its place they saw a myriad of sea life, from turtles and manta rays to sharks and even distant whales swimming in the sapphire blue water.

She'd just gotten a manta ray to allow her to "pet" it, when the entire mall suddenly plunged into darkness.

"What the heck?" Lynn muttered as voices of other patrons rose around her in confusion and consternation. Being the middle of summer, there was still a bit of dusk glow coming in from the open skylight despite the late hour. It was almost more beautiful seeing the AR underwater overlay glowing softly in the dimness but Lynn dismissed the overlay anyway and once again swapped her rented glasses for her own interface.

"Hey, Hugo, any idea what's going on?" she asked after opening the TD Hunter app. There were angry voices and calls for a manager around her as some guests stayed put and some mobbed a hapless shopping assistant who looked just as confused as everyone else.

"It appears that the building has suffered a power failure, Miss Lynn."

"But, why? Isn't it on the city grid just like everything else?"

"Indeed, however—"

"Lynn," her mom interrupted. "The mall AI is asking everyone to make their way outside while they investigate the malfunction."

Lynn made a face.

"Are they saying what caused it?"

"Nope. Just that it isn't an emergency and they apologize for the inconvenience."

"Weird. You'd think places like this would have some sort of backup power . . . do you think this has anything to do with what happened at your hospital?"

"I don't know, sweetie," Matilda said, "but I'm glad this is just a mall and no one is getting hurt. Come on, we should go ahead and leave." She headed toward the main entrance, but Lynn caught her sleeve.

"Everyone is going that way, and I don't want to get stuck in an angry crowd in a dark mall. There's a smaller exit over here. Come on."

Lynn wasn't a Tier One virtual mercenary for nothing. She subconsciously mapped out her surroundings in the real just as much as she did in virtual and always kept an eye out for exits. Plus she'd taken a good long look at the mall navigation guide when they'd come in.

After swinging by the lockers to snag their bags, Lynn led her mother to a smaller set of doors hidden between the spa center and the home furnishings wing. They left their rental AR glasses at the small kiosk between the inner and outer doors, then pushed out into the warm summer night. While Matilda worked on calling them an air taxi, Lynn looked around, idly searching for anything out of the ordinary that might alleviate her curiosity as to what had befallen Lindale Mall. There was nothing to be seen, though, besides the parking lot and a cluster of HVAC units and power nodes mostly hidden in the alcove created by the mall's home furnishings wing. The units were quiet, devoid of their usual humming and spinning fans. But they gave Lynn an idea.

"Hey, Mom. Since we aren't going anywhere for a bit, I'm gonna fire up TD Hunter. Might as well do something useful, right?"

"Sure, honey. The taxi should be here in a few minutes, though, so don't go far."

Lynn nodded as she reached in her backpack to get out her baton. She didn't need to go anywhere at all, not with those power nodes over there...

"Hey, Hugo, take me into combat mode and let's see what unlucky schlubs are hanging around, ripe for the picking. Take me in full armor, full stealth, just in case."

"Certainly, Miss Lynn."

This close to a building and people, Lynn wasn't expecting to find anything high level. But it was good she'd gone in fully stealthed because the moment Hugo dropped her into combat mode, the space around her lit up with dozens of TDMs.

Lynn cursed and jumped back, moving before she was even aware of it. She was swinging a split second later and her plasma blade cut right through the vulnerable backs of the demons on either side of her. They went up in sparks but she barely noticed as she waded into the rest of the aggressive TDMs surrounding the power nodes. They were spaced out in a loose semicircle but almost all except the furthest away converged on her after she ambushed the first two.

Fortunately for her, they were all just demons, Grumblins and the like. Nothing she couldn't take care of with a few well-placed strikes. She'd almost finished off the lot before the nearby ghosts finally seemed to get the memo. She ignored their spooky sounds until the last second, then spun to cut through a trio of them all at once. After that she stilled, waiting to see if any other aggressive TDMs popped up before she turned her attention to the now defenseless imps. Nothing showed itself and Lynn gave a self-conscious little wave to her mom who was watching by the mall doors with a motherly grin on her face.

Mopping up the crowd of imps around the power nodes took under a minute. They couldn't even see through her stealth until after she'd already stabbed them in the face. She was surprised with how many there were packed in such a small area but she wasn't one to complain. More experience for her. She even found one lone little Lecta hiding in the farthest corner between the mall building and some sort of power unit.

She was just collecting the piles of loot and a few items lying around when a sudden hum behind her made her jump. But it was only the power unit coming back to life. Within moments the whole group of units and nodes were purring with energy. The mall lights came on in a rush and Lynn shook her head as she headed back over to her mom. Of course the stupid mall system would pick *now* to pull its head out of its butt.

"What do you think, is it worth it to go back inside?" Matilda asked, eyeing the air taxi heading their way over the mall parking lot.

Lynn shook her head.

"It's getting late and I'm worn out. Let's go home."

Back at their apartment, Lynn fell into bed with a satisfied sigh. The mall had been spectacular, despite the annoyance at the end. She firmly rejected any anxious thoughts over what the guys would think of her new clothes the next day and instead fell asleep to pleasant thoughts of going back to Lindale Mall someday, only this time with Edgar instead of her mom.

When Lynn arrived at their Monday meeting place—Paul Revere's Pizza near where Collins road went over Interstate 380—the guys' reactions were mixed.

"Whoaaah-ho-ho-ho! Lynn, you look awesome!" Dan crowed, grinning like an idiot. "That looks like some high performance stuff there, where'd you get it?"

"Lindale Mall," Lynn said, grinning as Mack gave her a high five and joined Dan in admiring her hunting attire complete with delightfully stompy boots and her TD Counterforce backpack. Her batons she wore on her lower thighs, secure in slim, tight pockets on the outside of each leg. The pockets had probably been intended for energy bars or those electrolyte replenish tubes runners used. It was just a happy circumstance that they were the perfect size and height to fit the TD Hunter batons like some sort of nunchacku holster. It was going to be a darn useful place to keep them when she needed her hands free instead of having to tuck them under one arm or take the time to return them to her backpack.

She glanced around and spotted Edgar and Ronnie standing next to each other as if they'd been talking right before she'd arrived. Both were frozen like deer in the headlights, shock written in every line of their bodies as they stared at her. Edgar's expression was dumbstruck and his mouth was hanging slightly open but any impulse Lynn might have had to grin at his reaction was squashed by Ronnie's tomato-faced, lemon-sucking look of disgust.

Well, win some, lose some.

She clamped down on her emotions and refused to give it further thought, instead turning to Dan and gesturing toward the highway.

"Come on, let's get busy. The electric rail along the interstate should be crawling with monsters and we're really close to Level 10."

In fact, *she* was close, the others were lagging behind. It was a problem that had been worrying her for the past week. Considering that each successive level would take longer and longer to achieve, Lynn knew they weren't progressing fast enough to reach Level 20 by the end of August, a mere seven weeks away. It was why she'd suggested ditching alleyways, roadsides and local parks to instead seek out lower human density areas with high energy emitting installments, hoping to find larger concentrations of higher-class monsters. The electric rail should be just the thing.

"Hey, *I'm* the team captain. *I* say when we move out." Ronnie protested from behind them.

Lynn gritted her teeth and slowly counted to ten.

"Sure, whatever you say, captain," she muttered as Ronnie strode past a moment later, telling everyone to "hurry up" and "we don't have all day."

Their group trotted across the street, dodging a few robo-cars, then headed down the greenway that ran along Collins Road until the road began to rise in a bridge that arched over Interstate 380. At that point, Ronnie led the way down the grassy hill to where an electric rail passed under the bridge, paralleling the interstate. There was a chain link safety fence between them and the rail but it was easy enough to go around it where it butted up against the concrete holding wall that cut into the hill, carving out a space for the rail to pass under the bridge. They dropped down one-by-one onto the uncut grass on the other side of the fence and then regrouped.

"Okay, looks like we have plenty of room between the fence and the rail," Ronnie said, hands on hips as he glanced up and down the rail. "Just keep an eye out and everyone have their AI warn you when a train is headed our way, okay?"

A murmur of acknowledgments came in reply.

"Right. Does everyone have their assigned augments equipped?"

Another round of affirmatives and Lynn rolled her eyes. Perhaps she was being overly critical. It was good, after all, to double check things. But this was something she would have checked a while ago, not left it to the last moment.

They'd been "pooling" their augments for the past week, swapping whatever they found around to whoever it fit best based on the team roles Ronnie had assigned. Augments that improved accuracy, for instance, went to Dan, their sniper. Augments that improved damage went to Edgar, their heavy weapons, while things that supplemented stealth or detection went to Ronnie or Mack, who needed the most mobility and tactical information. It didn't escape Lynn's notice that Ronnie never once asked what augments she needed, nor suggested to anyone else that they give what they had to her, though he was bossy enough with the allocations to everyone else. It was one more reason she had to grit her teeth every time she was around him. His very presence grated on her nerves. The others had offered her augments, of course, but she always turned them down with a polite, "Thanks but I've got my own."

Which she did. More than enough. Tougher monsters dropped better augments and she was the best hunter on their team. She always went after the most challenging monsters within her field of responsibility, some of which her teammates couldn't even see since she was ahead of them in experience. Of course, she wasn't always a whole level above them—it fluctuated day to day—so she wasn't sure why she attracted higher-class monsters than the others. She assumed it must be the game's AI adjusting its algorithms to give her an appropriate challenge, like Fallu had said back when she was beta testing.

In any case, she always kept the best augments for herself and, reluctantly, shared the rest with the team, only selling the extras that they didn't have enough slots for in their weapons. So far, nobody had found anything spectacular but then they weren't even Level 10 yet, so Lynn wasn't worried. She kept an eye on the auction boards in case anything truly unique got posted. But at this stage it wasn't worth buying much since they were just grinding. She might buy a few things right before the qualifiers to give them some extra punch but that was it. Besides, there were few people ahead of their team in terms of leveling. A few über obsessed players up in New York and on the West Coast were already up to Level 14. But they seemed more interested in keeping their loot than selling it, because Lynn rarely saw items at auction that were too high a level for her to use.

"Okay, everyone. Once we drop into combat and clear out this area, let's head south, toward downtown. Now, circle formation. Engage combat mode on my mark."

Lynn had already subvocalized to Hugo to sync with Ronnie's timing, so her hands and concentration were primed and ready to fight. She only hoped everyone else was as ready. The last few times they'd tried this maneuver, somebody inevitably forgot to top off their armor or stealth or something and would get hammered when all the monsters went after them. Ronnie was supposed to do a supply check before they dropped into combat but had forgotten it—or ignored it—this time.

"Three . . . two . . . one . . ."

Lynn missed her playlists but music was too distracting when she had to keep track of her teammates in addition to monsters. Ah well, she listened to her music enough that she could easily play the opening vocals and electric violins of "Planet Hell" by Nightwish in her head as she tensed, poised and ready to fight.

Ah . . . ah . . . ah . . . oh-ah . . . oh-ah . . . oh-ah-ah-ah-oooh-ah!

"Engage!"

At Ronnie's call, Hugo switched her into combat mode and her display lit up with tactical information. Lynn was moving a split second later, reacting to her visuals before Hugo could even sound a proximity warning.

Lunge, strike. Roll, spin, strike. Dodge, strike, strike, strike.

For the first thirty seconds Lynn knew nothing but monsters and movement. Whether by luck or fate, they'd truly dropped right in the pot and she had her hands full taking out an Orcull and a handful of Grumblins that converged on her the moment she "appeared." No amount of stealth globes could hide her when she materialized literally within striking range of a TDM.

Once her display was no longer flashing red with active attacks, she spared a glance around. Ronnie and Edgar were both engaged with attack TDMs on the other side of their loose circle, while in the center, Dan and Mack were picking off the swarm of rocs they had correctly predicted would be hanging around the electric rail. Lynn couldn't see anybody's stats but hopefully after what had happened to Ronnie last week the guys would have the sense to give a shout if they needed backup.

She didn't have time to do anything more because the second wave was closing in. Wait, was that a Spithra? Lynn tightened her grip on her Plasma Blade. Last time she hadn't encountered those until she'd hit Level 10, so why had one detected her now?

"Hey guys, looks like I've attracted a few higher-class monsters. I'm gonna be busy with them for a bit so I won't be able to give any backup."

"I'll—say a—prayer for them," Mack quipped between shots. "Is there a—patron saint—for monsters?"

Dan guffawed. "No idea. I never paid attention in Catholic school."

Now there was a story. Lynn hadn't known Dan had ever attended Catholic school. She knew his parents were well-off, so they would have been the type to send him to some elite private school.

Edgar's undulating *choo-hoo-HOO* snapped her attention back to the fight at hand and she just had time to glance back and see his grin as he waded into a group of Grumblins before she had to turn and leap forward into a roll to take her under the approaching Spithra's first slicing attack.

She lost track of time as she fought, letting herself sink into the rhythm of battle. It probably only took them a minute or two to clear their immediate area but it felt like a tiny eternity in which her muscles thrummed with energy and she rode the adrenaline high doing what she loved best: utterly destroying her enemies.

Soon enough her area was clear again and this time she saw no more red dots heading her way on her overhead. She backed up, scooping up loot as she went and returning to her spot in their circle formation.

"Okay, everybody, status?" Ronnie said, his breath coming heavy. He wasn't the only one panting. Their shared channel was full of everyone's gasping breaths.

"Down fifty percent health and armor," Edgar said. "Also, nearly out of gum."

"I'm down about twenty," Mack chimed in and Dan echoed his words.

"I'm hanging in there," Lynn said, not wanting to give specifics. She'd noticed Ronnie always seemed more grumpy whenever she brought attention to the fact that she regularly suffered far less damage than anyone else and she was only down ten percent on her armor and five on her health.

"All right. Resupply, then we'll move out."

While everyone else was busy, Lynn opened a private channel to Edgar.

"Hey, need some Oneg?"

"Yeah, thanks, Lynn," Edgar said. "I go through that stuff like a football team goes through ribs at a barbecue."

"No problem," Lynn assured him, transferring the two packs of Oneg she'd picked up from the Spithra. They were the most reliable source of it she'd found yet, perhaps the algorithm's attempt to balance out the destructive power of the Spithra's acid spit attack. "You're our tank, after all. You get in deep and dirty, though you'll gradually take less damage as we get you better armor augments and you get more practice staying on your toes."

"Lynn, the last time I was on my toes was when I was ten and my mom hid the cookie jar on the top shelf of the cabinet," Edgar told her, chuckling. "I'm more like a rock in a pond than a leaf in the wind."

"Don't worry about it, man. You'll get better—"

"Hey, everyone ready to move out?" Ronnie said, his voice on their group channel overriding Lynn's private chat.

She'd already topped off her slots as soon as she'd killed her last monster, so she joined the rest in sounding off.

"Okay, patrol formation, moving south. Let's go."

Lynn smiled, actually looking forward to her afternoon for once. It seemed like they'd finally found a place with a high enough concentration of monsters that they could fight continuously for as long as their strength held, instead of tiring themselves out walking on and on looking for enemies to engage. Plus, her new clothes and boots were like a breath of fresh air.

Instead of feeling hot, sticky and itchy, with baggy rough cotton clothes sticking to her, she felt like her body was sheathed in a second skin that breathed and moved with her. She didn't even have any hotspots from her boots. With their smartcushion interior that molded to her foot, there was no need to "break them in" like she'd had to do with every other shoe she'd ever owned. The higher quality equipment mitigated the toll of heat and muscle fatigue and Lynn felt on top of the world.

Yes, this would be a good afternoon.

Protecting the rear, as usual, Lynn followed her teammates as they headed under the Collins Road bridge. But as they were about to come out the other side, a group of five people appeared from around the concrete barrier on the left, blocking their path. At the sight of them, Lynn froze in shock. And she wasn't the only one. Her entire team had halted and she even saw Mack take a step back, as if his brain's first instinct was "run."

"Well, if it isn't team Lame-O Schmucks," said Elena. She stood with four guys, all of them tall and ripped like they were professional athletes or body-builders. They probably were, come to think of it. Lynn recognized two of them from her school's varsity ARS team, so the other two no doubt were as well. All five of them wore form-fitting, professional athletic wear similar to what Lynn had just bought, though they wore wimpy tennis shoes in contrast to her glorious stompers.

When no one replied, Elena's smirk widened and she tossed her hair over her shoulder. "What a bunch of pathetic losers."

Anger unfroze Lynn's muscles and she was stomping forward before her long-held "avoid all notice" instincts could kick in. She shoved past Ronnie and took a stance in front of her team, arms folded across her chest.

"What the heck are you doing here, Elena? Did you finally trade in your posse of harpies for these pop-boys? I have to say, it's definitely an upgrade."

"Jealous, pig-face? Your little group of scrawny nerds is the saddest thing I've ever seen in my life. Well, except that fat blob," she said, flicking a finger in Edgar's direction. "He's just disgusting."

Lynn tilted her head, hiding her cold fury behind a bored look.

"You know, insulting our looks sounds a lot like you're trying to compensate for something. Afraid your pop-boys aren't up to competing against professional gamers?"

"Pffft. Professional?" Elena laughed. It was an annoying, high-pitched sound that made Lynn want to punch Elena in the mouth just to get it to stop. "Spending every waking hour playing lame little fantasies in virtual doesn't make you a professional."

Lynn didn't take the bait—it wasn't like she could trot out her status as a professional in virtual mercenary. Instead she forced herself to hold Elena's gaze, keeping her face expressionless. Eventually the pop girl couldn't take the silence anymore and huffed.

"What did you name your stupid little team anyway, the Loser Squad?"

"Wouldn't you like to know," Lynn retorted, rankled into replying. They still hadn't reached a consensus on their team name and so far any time anyone broached the topic, Ronnie and Dan devolved into bickering about how juvenile each other's suggestions were. "You'll find out when we crush you at the qualifiers."

"Well," Elena sniffed, "we're the Cedar Rapids Champions."

A flurry of snorts sounded behind Lynn and she grinned.

"Seriously? Is that your actual name? And you call *us* lame?"

The pop-girl narrowed her eyes and the guys flanking her on either side shifted or looked away as if they had something to say but weren't stupid enough to say it.

"Whatever," Elena said and waved a hand. "It doesn't matter. The point is, *we* are going to be the poster team for Cedar Rapids in the international Trans-whatever competitions."

"Good grief, you still can't even remember the name of the game you think you're going to win?" Dan burst out, coming up to stand beside Lynn. "That takes lame to an entirely new level of pathetic."

"Shut your mouth, dweeb-face," Elena snapped and stepped forward, fists clenched. "*We* are the champions. *We* are top-level athletes and famous stream celebrities. *You* all are just a bunch of pathetic nobodies. *We* are going to put Cedar Rapids on the map and nothing is going to get in our way, least of all *you*. This is our hunting ground and if you don't clear out, we'll, hmm, help you along." She crossed her arms across her chest in a mirror of Lynn, a self-satisfied smirk on her face.

Lynn scanned the faces of the guys to either side of her. The tallest, a guy with a shock of blond hair, looked distinctly uncomfortable. Lynn thought he might be their school's ARS team captain but she wasn't sure. The other three guys, though, seemed all too eager to take Elena's cue and they adopted what they obviously thought were intimidating scowls. One of them even cracked his knuckles.

"That's ridiculous," Ronnie said, finally speaking up for the first time. He shouldered past Lynn and stood in front of her as if to block her from view. Okay, kind of rude but at least he wasn't cowering or trying to make nice to the bullies. "You can't claim 'hunting grounds.' Besides, we were here first."

Elena stepped forward as well and a sneer twisted her pretty face. "Anywhere we want to hunt is our hunting ground, little Ronniekins, and I won't have you idiots getting in the way of our training. Now, get lost. Or else," she finished, tone dropping ominously.

"Oh, *real* smooth, Elena," Lynn said, stepping up beside Ronnie and tapping her AR glasses. "It's like you forgot that we're all wearing live connections to the mesh web. I bet your stream fans are just *loving* all this drama. I wonder what Mr. Krator, the CEO of Tsunami Entertainment, will think when I tag him in a video of you threatening another TD Hunter team. Say, Dan, is that kind of behavior grounds for disqualification from the TD Hunter competitions?"

A painfully fake smile instantly replaced Elena's nasty look as her eyes flicked nervously to each of their AR glasses.

"You know, I'll bet it is," Dan said and though Lynn didn't take her eyes off Elena, she could hear the wicked smirk in his voice.

"You're bluffing," Elena challenged, her face still locked in a rictus of a smile. "Nobody would ever watch your live stream in a million years."

Lynn shrugged.

"Who cares. It exists in the mesh if we ever need it later. Now if you'll excuse us, we have some training to do."

The big blond guy on Elena's right side shifted as if to turn away but Elena's hiss stopped him.

"Not a chance. We got here first. You all can go find somewhere else to be pathetic."

"Come on, Elena," Edgar rumbled, having come up behind Lynn so quietly she hadn't even heard him. "There's miles of electric rail, plenty of room for both of us."

"Exactly, so *you* lot can just get lost. We're not moving."

"Hey, Elena, let it go," the blond guy said, speaking for the first time. He reached out and grasped Elena's wrist to pull her away, but she shook him off.

"Shut up, Connor. I'm not going to let these losers get in our way."

Connor stared at Elena but his face was carefully blank, so Lynn couldn't guess what was going through his head. But then he shrugged and crossed his arms too, expression shifting to boredom.

The childish stupidity of the situation was almost funny but as much as Lynn was tempted to scoff, she knew their precious afternoon was being wasted. It wouldn't hurt to go farther down the rail, would it? But it would be foolish, bordering on suicidal at this point, to let Elena push them around. If they gave up, it would only make the bullying worse. Lynn knew from painful experience.

Ronnie knew it too but apparently he was willing to take the risk.

"Come on, guys. Let's go,"

"What? No. We were here first," Lynn said.

"Come *on*. We're wasting time. This is a crappy place to hunt anyway," Ronnie insisted and turned, shooting the other guys a narrow-eyed look that promised unpleasantness to anyone who didn't fall in line.

Slowly, the four guys turned and walked away, leaving Lynn alone to hold her ground in front of Elena and her goons.

The pop-girl smirked.

"Aw, poor little piggy. Did they leave you behind? Better hurry, before the big, bad wolf gets you."

As if on cue, Elena's three teammates—Lynn had dubbed them Moe, Larry and Curly—shifted forward. Connor didn't move but he also didn't say anything.

"Really? Big bad wolf?" Lynn said. "That's the dumbest threat I've ever heard. You sound like a nanny threatening a bunch of toddlers—"

"Come on, Lynn!" Edgar called from behind her. "This isn't worth it. Let's go kill some monsters."

With nothing to be gained by staying—except maybe a black

eye—Lynn turned and walked away. A fight would almost be worth it, if it got that harpy disqualified. But it would just as likely get them in trouble, too. She couldn't risk it.

As much as Lynn pretended in virtual to be some former black-ops merc and as many times as she'd hunted down and killed opponents in WarMonger, she'd never contemplated what such a thing would be like in the real. But imagining herself perched a hundred yards away in a WarMonger setting with Vera in hand, laser sight trained on Elena's forehead, was the only thing that kept her going as the pop-girl jeered at her back.

They tried to go north on the rail line, instead of south. But apparently Elena decided she would rather keep *them* from hunting than let her own team train, because the morons actually followed them, interrupting and distracting them at every turn. It got to the point that Ronnie finally gave up in disgust and dragged them off to catch an airbus back toward the east side of town. They found a new spot—not as hot with TDMs as the rail line but not deserted either—and got to work. But ten minutes into it, the "Champions" showed up *again*, acting all nonchalant as if they hadn't just somehow followed Lynn and her friends there.

Ronnie had them move a second time. About ten minutes later their harassers showed up once again, not even bothering to feign ignorance this time.

Elena was crazy, Lynn decided. Just flat-out crazy.

Ronnie finally told them to all go home and practice their simulations exercises for the rest of the day. Lynn was worried about them splitting up, in case Elena and her crew planned to jump one of them once they were alone. But Elena's crazy obsession with them seemed satisfied once Ronnie "admitted defeat." Lynn thought about messaging Ronnie to have them all meet again somewhere else but decided not to. She had no idea how Elena's team was doing it but somehow the CRCs were tracking them—Lynn refused to think of them as the "Champions." She would ask Hugo about it later, maybe even do some digging of her own.

After saying goodbye to her teammates, Lynn hopped on an airbus heading back to her apartment complex. She took a seat by a window but hardly noticed the view. Her mind was busy plotting.

Halfway home, she opened the TD Hunter app, keeping herself out of combat mode.

"Hey, Hugo," she subvocalized.

"Yes, Miss Lynn? How can I help?"

"I want to scout a new hunting location but I don't have time to go traipsing all over the city. Can you do a map search for me?"

"Certainly, Miss Lynn. What are my parameters?"

"I need to find the most isolated power node in the north-eastern quadrant of Cedar Rapids. I need a balance of isolation and size. Look for either a node substation, or a power node that's grouped with transmitter antennas and a mesh hub but that's also removed from foot and vehicular traffic. Not too far removed, though. Look for something within a few minutes' walk of the nearest airbus platform. If you can't find anything that accessible, I suppose we could always catch a robo-car but that's more expensive so I want to avoid it."

"Noted. Is that all?"

"Oh, yeah and check the satellite and street level images while you're at it. We need enough clear space to move around if we're going to hunt. I'm pretty sure most power nodes are fenced in and I don't want to go breaking into anything or trespassing. So, there has to be enough room *outside* the fence to hunt."

"Excellent, Miss Lynn. One moment, please, while I gather the data you've requested."

A moment later, Lynn's overhead map expanded to fill her display. Since she was out of combat mode, the map was devoid of red or blue dots—the blue were TD Hunter players, which helped Lynn and her team not step on the toes of any other hunters. Lynn had briefly thought that was how Elena had been tracking them but players only showed up if they were in combat mode and Lynn's team never stayed in combat mode when around civilians like at an airbus platform. Too much risk that a monster would attack them and they wouldn't be able to fight back for fear of accidentally hitting someone with their batons.

The lack of TDM data cluttering up the map helped out in this case. Lynn saw that Hugo had dropped a GEO pin on four different locations in the requested quadrant. The farthest east was off Collins Road SE, along Indian Creek. A second pin was a little north of Collins Road, near the Rockwell Collins Aerospace company and almost across the road from Noelridge Park. The third was farther north near Dry Creek and the St. Andrews Golf Course. And the last one was south, closer to downtown and right by Interstate 380. Lynn realized the last one was right beside the same electric rail line they'd tried to follow earlier, a mile or so farther south.

"Okay, this looks good. Can you show me the street level images for each location?"

"Unfortunately not, Miss Lynn. While I can access the information, the TD Hunter app is not the proper platform from which to view web search images. Might I suggest switching to EarthMaps?"

"Yeah, sure. Can you message me all those addresses? Thanks."

Lynn hopped from TD Hunter to the navigation app she always used. Then she pulled up the message from Hugo and plugged in the addresses one by one. The navigation app had 360-degree images from every road worldwide and when it "dropped" her at the first requested address, to her eyes it looked for all the world like she was standing on a gravel access road instead of sitting in an airbus—though of course, the navigation images were static. She used the apps controls to zoom along the access road until she could see the node substation and examine its surrounding area. There was a small park to one side, a subdivision behind it and the woods along Indian Creek on the other two sides. Not a bad location for hunting with lots of clear space but the park and neighborhood would probably cut down on the number of TDMs and it was several minutes' walk from the nearest airbus platform.

The location by the aerospace company was no good. It was surrounded by streets on three sides with various supply buildings. There would be too much human interference.

The location near the golf course was promising. It sat at the end of an undeveloped street with manicured greenway on two sides, an uncut field on the third side and the woods bordering the golf course at its back.

The last location near the electric rail was bigger than the rest and so had the advantage of greater levels of electromagnetic radiation to draw in more TDMs. But it was bordered by busy streets on two sides and Lynn didn't know enough about the app's algorithms to predict how the increase in EM particles would be countered by the proximity to human interference.

Ultimately, though, she picked the last location by the electric rail to check out first. It was the closest to an airbus platform and they'd already had a good experience with the electric rail. Well, minus Miss Crazy and her four pop-boy thugs. Lynn wondered idly how she'd convinced Connor and the others to form a hunter team with her. It probably hadn't been that hard, actually. Connor and his teammates probably had TD Hunter on their radar already and Elena would know them all since she was the captain of the cheerleading team. In fact...was she dating Connor? Lynn had never paid attention at school to who was dating whom. But Connor was pretty enough—and popular enough—to check all of Elena's boxes. Lynn wasn't worried about Elena by herself. The popularity-obsessed girl didn't know the first thing about gaming, though she would be proficient enough with AR stuff since the cheerleading routines for the ARS games were thick with visual augments. Connor and his teammates, on the other hand...they would be trouble. They were already experts at AR sports, unlike her and the guys. The only edge Lynn and her fellow gamers had was their experience with gaming mechanics and tactics. Well, that and they didn't have an airhead like Elena screwing up their team.

They had Ronnie, though.

Lynn sighed and exited the navigation app to check the airbus's location. She'd have to bus-hop a few times to get on one that would take her by the node substation. She'd originally gotten on a bus heading east back to her apartment.

By the time she finally reached her destination, the sun had started its descent toward the horizon and shadows were lengthening across the landscape. The airbus platform was only a block from the substation and Lynn walked the distance lost in thought.

Would finding better hunting locations solve their leveling problem? If they couldn't reach Level 20, all their hard work would be wasted. Eventually, she told herself to stop worrying about it. After all, if it got too close, they could always put in more hours. It would be fine for a few days. And Edgar would be quitting his landscape job before school started, so he could join them for longer periods.

Lynn was so involved in her thoughts that she was barely aware as she crossed the street and started along the brick wall that encircled the node substation. Still pondering, she reached the far corner of the substation and veered off the sidewalk into the grass to go around the corner and find a nice open space to start hunting. When she rounded the corner, though, she almost ran headfirst into someone.

"Oh, sorry!" she said, jerking to a stop and raising her eyes, which had been fixed on the ground.

It was Connor.

"What the heck? Are you all following me *again*?" Lynn burst out as Moe, Larry, Curly and Elena hurried up to stand abreast of Connor.

"Hey, sorry," the ARS captain said. His voice was honey smooth with just the right amount of masculine roughness. Lynn thought it was massively annoying. "We didn't follow anyone here. We just headed down the electric rail and thought this would be a good place to stop and hunt."

"Yeah, right—" Lynn began but Elena butted in.

"I'm so glad we ran into you again, *Lynn*," she said. Her expression was suspiciously pleasant. "There's something I wanted to talk to you about. Do you mind?"

Alarm bells went off in Lynn's head. Something told her to turn around then and there and run. But she couldn't pretend she wasn't intrigued. She doubted Elena just wanted to insult her more. No, more likely the pop-girl was going to threaten her, or offer some sort of stupid deal to get rid of Ronnie and the rest so there would be less competition. It would be interesting to find out.

"Sure. Whatever," Lynn said.

"Great. Let's go over here where there's less noise," Elena said and turned to walk farther along the brick wall, which was lined with decorative trees. Lynn hesitated but finally followed. She did surreptitiously reach back and unclip her little pepper spray keychain off her backpack to tuck it into her palm. Just in case. Her dad's knife was in her backpack, so it would be too obvious to get it out now. Plus, she didn't think it would be a smart idea to start a knife fight without any training. At least, not unless her life was in danger.

She also opened the TD Hunter app.

"Hey, Hugo," she subvocalized. "You said you could flag down a police drone, right?"

"If you are in danger, yes of course."

"Well...I might be soon, so keep an eye out."

"As you wish, Miss Lynn."

Elena stopped near the far corner of the brick wall, far enough away from the street that they were hidden by the ornamental trees on one side and the brick wall on the other from any observers. She turned to Lynn and blinked twice in succession. Lynn recognized it as one of the ways you could set an AR interface to shut down. There was no way to tell if the interface was contacts, or an implant but Lynn thought Elena was the kind of rich celebrity-wannabe who wouldn't hesitate to jump on the very expensive implant bandwagon. Connor and his stooges probably all had contacts.

"Take your glasses off, *Lynn*," she said, voice sickly sweet.

"Yeah, right. So you can beat me up in private? No, thanks."

"Don't be ridiculous. I just want our conversation to be private, that's all."

When Lynn narrowed her eyes, Elena batted her eyelashes and added, "*Pleeease.*"

"Fine," Lynn said with an exhale and slipped off her glasses.

"Put them in your backpack. Just as a precaution, of course." Elena smiled again.

Lynn rolled her eyes and in the process spotted a gray dot in the sky above them. Was that a police drone, or just another survey drone doing routine work? She didn't think it was police, those were usually bigger and patterned black and blue. Either way, she felt a bit safer with it hovering above and slipped off her glasses, taking a moment to stash them in her backpack. "Okay, we're in private. What is it?"

In an instant, Elena dropped the nice act and her face twisted in a sneer.

"Tell your Lame Squad that if we catch you outside hunting again, you're all dead meat. Nobody wants you in this competition and there's no way we're letting your team qualify."

"Those are some mighty big words," Lynn said, fingering her pepper spray. She was intensely aware of the three guys who had come up to stand behind her. Connor was beside Elena and slightly behind the pop-girl, like some sort of bodyguard. Or flunky. "You can't get away with foul play like that anymore, not when nearly everything is either live or has instant access to the mesh net. You'll get yourself thrown out of the competition and banned from TD Hunter if you even try it."

"Oh, there are ways and there are *ways* to teach you little twerps a lesson you won't forget," Elena said with a nasty smile. "Besides, glasses can always slip off and get crushed—by accident, of course. And nobody wears their glasses *all* the time. You'll never know when we'll come to get you. Do you really want to live in that kind of fear?"

"Pffft," Lynn snorted, to cover the cold chill that was spreading down to her toes. "You're about as scary as one of those little chipmunks with a squeaky voice."

Elena's eyes flashed and she looked over Lynn's shoulder.

"Well, let's change that, shall we?"

Lynn reacted too late. Before she could lunge forward and give Elena a good punch in the face, two of the guys behind her grabbed her forearms and the third grabbed her braid, which she hadn't bothered to pin up because she'd been out so late last night and had gotten a late start that morning. The red hot fire that blossomed across her scalp as the thug yanked on it ensured it would be the very last time she made *that* mistake.

"You're a disgusting, irritating little fly in my plans," Elena said, stepping close as Lynn tried to twist her forearms out of the stooges' grasps. Their grips were like iron. "One I'm going to thoroughly enjoy *squashing*—EEEEYAAAAAGGG!!"

Fortunately for Lynn, the two stooges had been stupid enough to grab her forearms instead of her wrists and she was able to raise her right hand up enough to aim her pepper spray at Elena's eyes and give the pop-girl a much deserved faceful. The girl staggered back, shrieking and clawing at her face. The two guys holding Lynn's arms loosened their hold for a second in shock and Lynn took the opportunity to wrench her right arm up and shoot a long spray behind her at head level. The three stooges let her go and stumbled away, coughing and yelling. Connor was busy trying to calm Elena, leaving Lynn unimpeded for a few precious seconds. She took off toward the road at top speed.

She didn't stop running until she reached the airbus platform and slipped onto a waiting bus, finding a seat at the very back where she collapsed into a seat and tried to catch her breath.

Those flaming jerkwads.

As if she didn't already have enough to deal with, now she had attempted assault and blackmail to add to her plate.

Yippee.

Chapter 12

LYNN CONSIDERED NOT SAYING ANYTHING TO HER TEAMMATES the next day about Elena's threat. But they needed to be on their guard in case Elena's goons tried anything, so she decided she had to tell them. She didn't mention the attempted assault, though. She didn't want Edgar to freak out.

Predictably, Ronnie found some way to blame it on her.

"If you hadn't confronted her and escalated things, we wouldn't have to worry about this," he said when she told them about it. "Now you've put us in danger and we have to worry about a stupid team rivalry that's going to impede our training!"

She almost punched him then and there.

Fortunately for Ronnie, she managed to resist the urge. Instead, she turned and walked away. And kept walking. They'd met at their old haunt at the cemetery, as if Ronnie thought they could reach Level 20 in time by hunting mediocre locations while Elena's team claimed the hotspots. But Lynn knew that wouldn't work and Ronnie wasn't listening to her. So, she walked away.

Edgar tried to follow her, calling out but she ignored him. She was too mad and he didn't deserve for her to take it out on him. She just waved a mute goodbye over her shoulder and headed for the airbus platform the next street over.

Maybe this team thing had been a mistake. All she could think about was Elena's stupid, sneering face and Ronnie's unjust, pigheaded words.

She couldn't go on like this. She couldn't cope with this much unmitigated stupidity.

But she couldn't crawl back into her hole, either...

Was TD Hunter to blame? Or had it simply come along at the right time? Regardless, she'd realized she wasn't content hiding anymore. Of course she still felt self-conscious. Of course she still hated dealing with people. But mostly she just felt mad. The simmering frustration burned away the hesitation that had always held her back. It drowned out the voices of doubt that told her she wasn't fit to show her face in public.

So, instead of going home to mope around in her room, she caught an airbus heading north toward the St. Andrews Golf Course. The stop on Blairs Ferry Road was the closest she was going to get, so she hopped off there and started walking.

She needed to kill something. Her muscles were twitchy from the tension and her mind yearned for something to focus on. She looked up and down the sidewalk, noting the scattering of pedestrians. She even spotted a trio of teens wielding electric blue Nano Blades in a green space next to a coffee shop across the road.

"Hugo, take me into combat mode."

"Right here, Miss Lynn? The sidewalk is not exactly the ideal combat zone."

"Do it, Hugo."

"At once, Miss Lynn."

Her overhead map, stats and targeting selector materialized before her and right away she heard *them*. Even though she was on a fairly busy street in the middle of the day, they were there. Lurking behind businesses and in alleyways. Hovering overhead.

"Hugo, empty my stealth slots."

"Are you certain, Miss Lynn? That will wave quite the red flag."

"Exactly." She felt a wolfish grin spread across her face.

"Very well."

Lynn felt a surge of adrenaline as her stealth bar emptied completely. "Heeeere monsters, monsters, monsters," she murmured as she fast-walked along the sidewalk.

From her experience, most aggressive TDMs that attacked unprovoked lost interest once you moved outside their detection range. That wasn't hard to do for slower, weaker monsters like the worms and gremlins. But some particularly aggressive ones, like

Ghasts, Vargs, Orculls and Spithra would stalk you indefinitely as long as you moved slowly enough to stay in their sights. She didn't think she could outrun a Stalker if she came across one but fortunately they seemed to be rare.

By the time she was halfway to her destination, she'd attracted quite a few "admirers." She broke into a jog to pull ahead of the gaggle of Ghasts that were tailing her. Behind them a group of much slower Orculls lumbered along. Overhead, an occasional roc would take a dive at her but she dodged them and they quickly lost interest. They mostly hovered like grotesque vultures "gathering" the EM particles being beamed back and forth between various power nodes and only came after you if you stuck around. Lynn rarely went after any nonaggressive monster these days if they weren't directly in her path. It was a waste of time to track down the stationary gatherers when she could kill many more monsters by baiting the aggressive ones.

By the time she spotted the power substation at the end of a dead-end street, she had a crowd at her back.

She grinned.

It was the kind of smile she always got when a bunch of cocky Tier Two schmucks took the bait and accepted a challenge match, her against however many of them had the balls to face her. Those matches were always glorious, pushing her to new levels of crafty ruthlessness that made her "life" as Larry Coughlin worth living. Well, now it was time to do the same for Lynn Raven.

It was time to dance.

Lynn veered off the sidewalk into the empty field by the road, not wanting to rush headlong into a potential hotspot by the substation when she already had a hungry mob on her tail.

"Hugo, fire up my monster hunting playlist, thirty percent volume, left ear."

Thumping guitar and drums began a melodious counterpoint to the hisses, growls, clicks and roars coming from the growing crowd behind her.

"It's over, it's over, it's over, it's time to burn it down," she sang along as she found a good spot, then whirled around and crouched, "...all right, come and get some, you bastards."

The Ghasts got there first but they stopped a good dozen feet out and started circling to get behind her, as they always did. She let them, tracking them on her overhead as the Orculls finally caught up with a few demon and Grumblin stragglers. They converged with no apparent strategy, just compelled forward by blind hunger. Or rage. Or instinct. Or whatever you wanted to call the game algorithms. At the last minute, though, the four Orculls that had followed her slowed and formed two ranks of two, giving the other TDMs time to catch up and form a wall of enemies. Well, well, well. Lynn grinned. It was good to see the algorithms evolving, giving her a real challenge.

She was about to charge forward when a gale of malevolent whispers crescendoed behind her.

About time.

Leaping to the side, Lynn spun and slashed out to cut through the first Ghast, then stabbed the second in the face and lunged forward to take out the third before it could retreat and circle again. Then the other monsters arrived and things finally got interesting.

Lynn's blood thrummed through her veins and she felt like her feet had wings. She grunted quietly as she lunged and spun, "Gonna burn it down, burn it down, burn it down!"

The weaker demons and Grumblins died first as she rolled through or dodged around them. The Orculls were a wall of swinging fists and claws and she had to carefully time her attacks. Because the monsters had such long arms, they spread out when they attacked and she could slip between them. Feint. Pause while they took their swipes at her. Lunge forward and strike, strike, strike. Turn and repeat.

Though their grunts and howls were loud in her right ear, the sounds were rhythmic, like they were on a looping playlist, rather than calls of a creature that cried out in rage or aggression as it attacked. She'd never paid attention to it before but it was rather odd that the sounds didn't sync with the creatures' movements. Nor did they ever have any facial expressions beyond opening their jaws to bare dripping teeth. It was like they were unthinking automatons controlled by a detached intelligence. Which, of course, they were. But Lynn wondered why Mr. Krator and the other developers hadn't made them more individualistic and varied in their behavior. Their algorithms certainly had the computing capacity for it.

Such thoughts passed idly through her head as she mopped

up the Orculls, while protecting her back against the last few Ghasts that kept trying to ambush her. She took a few hits here and there but overall thought she'd done a tidy bit of work.

Just then, her "leveling imminent" alarm beeped in her ear.

"Hugo, bring me up to full stealth, now!"

The world around her dimmed ever-so-slightly and the two remaining Orculls now on their last legs seemed to pause. Lynn took advantage of their momentary confusion and leapt between them to slash at each with two quick movements.

Her leveling notification played a triumphant little jingle in her ear as sparks exploded and faded around her. She saw the achievement notification pop in the corner of her screen but she resisted the impulse to expand it because an ominous rushing sound like a high wind whistling through a broken window was gathering all around her. It grew louder and louder, making her spin about, searching for the source.

"What the freak, where is it, Hugo?"

"I'm sorry, Miss Lynn, your detection is at one-hundred percent. It is most likely a Charlie Class TDM with high stealth."

"Great, just great—come on, you ugly wheeze bag, where are you?"

That's when it struck. Or rather, they.

The hair-raising whistling had already made her suspect the monster was the upgrade from a Ghast, so she was expecting it to pop up behind her. Instead, the six-foot, floating phantom flickered into sight not five feet in front of her, looking for all the world like one of those hooded, soul-sucking terrors from that wands-and-wizards kids series. Mack was always trying to get her to watch it. Two skeletal appendages shot out from the billowing cloak, striking at her head. She dropped straight down and rolled, knowing from the sound that there was a second one behind her. When she came up, the pair were still there, moving to keep her between them.

What the heck? Since when did TDMs work in teams?

She was so busy dodging and trying to keep them both in her sights that she didn't notice the telltale clicking from her earbud until the swarm of Spithra coming up behind her spit a rain of acid onto her back. The attack sent a furious storm of red damage flashing across her display and her armor dropped to dangerous levels.

Lynn let out a string of Larry's favorite curses and ducked, taking her attention totally off her attackers to swipe desperately at the exit icon on her display. The overlay in her vision disappeared as she abruptly left combat mode and she collapsed on the grass, panting.

"A bit winded, are we, Miss Lynn?"

"Don't sound so concerned, Hugo. It's not like I almost died or anything."

"Nonsense. You would have prevailed, eventually. I have faith in you."

"Uh-huh. Maybe. My combat ratings would have taken a serious hit, though. I don't mind a challenge but what's the point of getting slaughtered? Nothing on the tactical page mentioned Phasmas working in tandem. I swear those two were tag-teaming me." To be fair, the higher class the TDMs went, the more sparse their tactical info was in the TDM Index. Some of them only had a single line of description. Some only a name, not even a picture. Phasmas, a Charlie Class-3 monster, did have an image but their text only said they were an upgrade from Ghasts and so most likely operated on the same tactics. She hadn't honestly given them much thought, since she hadn't expected to encounter them until she hit Level 13 at the earliest.

But now she was Level 10 and they were jumping her in pairs. What the actual heck, algorithms? She loved a good challenge but it still felt a little unfair.

With a grunt of effort, she levered herself up from the grass and bent to pick up her baton, now back in its base form. Then she shaded her eyes to look around. The field was completely empty and there were no cars on the dead end street.

She let out a mental sigh of relief. Nice to know that no one had witnessed—or worse, recorded—her ungainly dive for the ground. Despite the guys' generally positive reaction to her new getup, she still had to fight the occasional flash of panic at the thought that everybody around her could *see* her and there was nowhere to hide. Stupid brain. She was determined to conquer her fears, though. They were nothing more than the toxic lies of low-life bullies. Besides, her new clothes were amazing. Even though her forehead dripped with sweat, she felt absolutely great sheathed in the ultra-wicking smartcloth that easily warded off the sticky, itchy feeling of sweating in tight clothing.

Lynn brushed the stray bits of grass off her, then set off at a slow jog for the main street. Hopefully it would be enough of a deterrent against the higher-class monsters that she would have time to go over her achievement award and her new weapon selection without getting pummeled. Finding a coffee shop or other building to go into would work as well but she would feel weird loitering around in her current get-up with an electric blue sword. Two streets over there was decent traffic, so she found an ornamental tree that provided a bit of shade and privacy from the street. She stayed standing, in case anything jumped her while she was distracted, then went back into combat mode and expanded her leveling screen, keeping half an ear on the distant sounds of TDMs around her. When she selected the Level 10 announcement, her display darkened and started playing a cut scene vid.

"Congratulations on reaching Level 10, Hunter," said First Sergeant Bryce. The vid only showed from his shoulders up, so Lynn got an eyeful of his stern expression. He looked straight at the camera and when she met his eyes she felt a shiver go through her. Those dark orbs were as hard as adamant, yet what made them truly intimidating was the spark of predatory watchfulness in them. Lynn wondered what actor played the first sergeant and where he'd learned to mimic that expression. It was convincing as all get out.

"That you've made it this far as a civilian volunteer is truly commendable. Thank you for sticking out the fight for humanity's survival. But don't get cocky. It only gets harder from here.

"Now that you're an expert at taking out Delta Class TDMs, you'll start facing Charlie Class bogies that are faster and tougher than ever. Based on data collected by our volunteers, we've found that Charlie Class TDMs start to show more tactical awareness. Be ready for anything. Your training simulations will be essential, so take advantage of them. Don't hesitate to contact our tactical support team to report any unusual TDM behavior or to ask for help. We are here to support you in this fight.

"Together is the only way we're going to make it out of this alive, Hunter. Good luck and keep up the good work. First Sergeant Bryce, out."

Lynn shivered again as her eyes met the first sergeant's and then his face disappeared and her combat system came back online.

Well, that was delightful. The first sergeant's warning made sense of the Phasmas' actions, though it was creepy to think about the TDMs around her formulating actual plans of attack to get at her.

Enough doom and gloom, though. She dismissed her leveling screen and swept her eyes over her achievement list with her experience and rewards. A grin crept across her face.

"Hey, baby, I missed you," she crooned at the image of Skadi's Wrath—or just "Wrath," as she'd dubbed it—and the accompanying congratulations about her score achievement. A bit of tension left her shoulders and she rolled them in a stretch. She'd been worried she wouldn't be able to keep up her scores once she'd joined a team but this gave her hope. Maybe she could still collect the whole set.

Lynn got busy equipping her unique blade and making her standard weapon selection for Level 10—the two-handed Disruptor Rifle. Then she got her second baton out of her backpack and equipped her one-handed Dragon Scattergun, the one Edgar usually used. Back when she'd reached Level 5, she'd picked a Plasma Pistol instead of the Dragon for her standard weapon choice. But monsters sometimes dropped weapons and both she and Dan had picked up Dragons from monster loot since then. Both the Dragon and the Plasma Pistol had their advantages but she wanted to try out the short-range power of the Dragon with her close-up melee tactics she would use with Wrath.

After that she shuffled around her augments, loading up all her best ones in Wrath and the Dragon—increased damage for both, increased accuracy and range augments for the Dragon, a reduced energy use augment for the blade as well as a sweet little augment that increased the chance of loot dropped by monsters she killed with it. For her personal augment slots, she had one that increased the amount of health she regenerated per second, as well as one that boosted her armor's effectiveness. And, of course, Skadi's Glory.

Finally, she held up her weapons and admired them in her AR sight. Despite the bright light of day, the runes along Wrath's blade glowed fiercely against the obsidian black of its blade.

Now she was ready to get back in there and kick some monster butt.

This time she took it slow and cautious, staying fully stealthed to avoid getting mobbed by lower-class TDMs. When she approached her previous spot, the Phasmas' eerie whistle began again in her ear, like they were hiding just out of sight, stalking the spot where their prey had vanished. Soon enough, the sound grew and Lynn crouched, ready for their attack. She felt fully prepared now that she had two weapons instead of one.

The monsters flashed out of nowhere and pounced, one from the front and one from the back. Lynn ducked and rolled, blasting away even as she regained her feet.

How she had ever survived with only one weapon, Lynn had no idea.

Soon, the Phasmas were nothing but a shower of sparks. Yes, she'd taken a few hits but being able to blast one Phasma in the chest while slicing the other to ribbons meant they couldn't keep her spinning uselessly on the defensive. Even the lone Spithra that attacked right after seemed easier to kill. She got rid of it in half the time it normally took.

Lynn planted a theatrical kiss on Wrath's blade. Could a sword be your new best friend? She hoped Vera in WarMonger wouldn't get too jealous, poor thing.

With three enemies down and her not even out of breath, Lynn took stock of her little battlefield, relieved to see the glitter of ichor and other loot still shimmering in the grass. It really sucked when you were distracted by more monsters and weren't able to collect your loot in time. Fortunately, the ten minute despawn countdown was pretty forgiving unless you died and didn't dare go back into combat mode on half stats. Then you could kiss your loot goodbye.

Lynn collected her spoils and topped off her health and other resources. She was delighted to find an armor piercing augment for melee weapons, probably dropped by one of the Orculls. It went straight into one of Wrath's augment slots.

Feeling ready to take on the world, she finally turned toward the power substation and began a cautious approach. All her stealth slots were full in the hope that she could get a look at what was ahead before it spotted her. She knew by now that TDMs couldn't "hear" you but she still found herself placing her feet just so, Dragon muzzle to the sky, blade at the ready.

Soon enough, red dots began populating the upper edge of her overhead map until it looked like the area had caught a bad case of the measles. And the dots weren't all scattered about, either. She saw a handful of those mysterious rings of monsters along the nearest fence line and as she crept closer...

"Whoa," Lynn muttered to herself. "Is that what I think it is?"

"Apologies, Miss Lynn but my programming does not extend to mind reading just yet."

"Har-de-har, Hugo... wait, yet?"

"Why, yes. Computer to brain neural link implants were only just approved by the FDA for trial runs a few months ago, so it will be some time yet before I will be able to receive mental input."

"Wow, cool... but completely off topic. I meant that huge swarm of red dots on my map." She couldn't see the TDMs yet herself, since the app's battle systems populated the overhead map much farther out than it could resolve the CGI visuals of the monsters. But according to her overhead, it looked like the biggest ring of TDMs she'd ever seen was parked directly on top of the power substation. Biggest as in, hundreds of monsters in a ring half the size of a football field. And if those dots were just the TDMs she could see at her level, she didn't even want to imagine how many more there were that she couldn't see.

Maybe going over there wasn't the best idea after all.

Or maybe, this was the opportunity she'd been searching for. After all, every time she'd gone near a circle in the past, the monsters hadn't broken rank and come after her. They'd held their formation as if they were guarding something. So, maybe the giant ring within the substation fence would stay put, leaving her free to pick off the monsters in the smaller rings around the edges. In fact...

A brilliant, reckless, completely insane idea popped into her head and she couldn't help grinning. Now if only Mr. Krator and his game developers had fixed those annoying glitches she kept encountering in beta, her crazy plan might actually work.

Only one way to find out.

She didn't say anything to Hugo as she crept even closer, trying to get within visual range of the closest circle. He would probably tell her it was too risky. But then, who ever achieved great things without taking a few risks?

Her progress forward was interrupted by an eerie whistling and she whirled to meet the Phasma trying to sneak up on her. Oddly, it was only one this time and she dispatched it with three well-placed slashes and a belch of fire from her scattergun. Maybe prancing around without any stealth was what had attracted the extra Phasma to her before. Whatever the case, she kept her ears cocked and her music playlist off. Things were about to get complicated.

Finally, the ring of monsters in front of her resolved and she could see what she was up against: an outer ring made up of grinder worms, crusher worms and gremlins and an inner ring of demons, Grumblins and Orculls. Ghosts and Ghasts patrolled around the area, always on the move, and there was a healthy scattering of imps and other low-level gather types sitting there, no doubt doing whatever it was they did to gather the energy all the TDM monsters seemed to feed on.

Lynn wondered for the zillionth time what was inside those circles. Loot? Monster eggs? A "queen" monster spawning more monsters? Maybe even one of those mysterious bosses listed in the TDM Index? Whatever it was, she couldn't see it, so it didn't matter just then. For all intents and purposes, the center of the circle was empty. But not for long...

"Here goes nothing," Lynn muttered, checking and rechecking that she was fully armored and stealthed. "Hey, Hugo, I'm going to try something new. For right now, instead of saying 'exit combat mode,' can I just say 'out' to go out of combat mode and 'in' to go back in?"

"Yes, I can make that adjustment for now, though it will be less than efficient on a permanent basis as there is ample room for confusion in such vague commands."

"Yeah, I get that. Just for now."

"Very well, Miss Lynn. Now, what, exactly are you going to do?"

"You'll find out," Lynn said, grinning again as she stared hard at the circle of monsters fifty yards ahead of her. She gave herself a good thirty seconds to memorize their formation and compare their location to the fence behind them and the ground at their feet. Then she took a few long sips of water from her hydration tube, stretched out her neck and crouched, ready to go.

"Out!"

Her combat display disappeared and she lunged forward in a sprint, eyes still locked on the point she was making for. While her body wasn't exactly built for sprinting, she made better time than she would have even a few weeks ago and as soon as she arrived at her pre-selected point, she put her back to the fence and shouted again.

"In!"

Monsters appeared all around her. Yes! She'd calculated correctly and had ended up smack dab inside the mysterious circle. For one eternal breath, nothing moved. Whether it was from shock—if TDMs were even programmed to simulate shock—or because there was a lag in the monster's detection, Lynn had no idea. But that tiny delay was all the time she needed for her batons to re-form back into her deadly, monster-killing weapons.

"Miss Lynn! I do not think—"

"Hi-yah!" Lynn yelled, ignoring the AI as she lunged forward toward an Orcull that was just starting to turn its bulky form around. She dispatched it with a single stab of her blade and shot from her Dragon into its unarmored back, waiting only long enough to confirm its sparkling demise. Then—

"Out!"

The combat readout disappeared again and her weapons shrank back into their baton shape.

"Miss Lynn, this is truly unorthodox, I would not advise—"

"Yeah, yeah, it's reckless," Lynn said, taking four steps to the side and repositioning herself. "But if it works, who cares?"

"But—"

"In!"

Another Orcull, this one half turned to the spot where she'd been five seconds before, appeared in front of her. She ignored the mass of other monsters stirring around her with aggressive roars, clicks and screeches, as none of them were close enough to matter. Once again, she took out the Orcull in front of her with a quick double strike from her two weapons, then slipped out of combat mode, vanishing once more.

Over Hugo's protests, she did it again and again, each time repositioning herself behind a new Orcull based on her brief glimpse of their formation during her previous attack. After five successful kills with a perfect attack to damage ratio and not a single scratch on her, she felt positively giddy with excitement. Or...maybe that wasn't giddiness.

"Whoa," Lynn said, stumbling a little as what had felt like excitement turned to dizziness. She planted her feet and put out her arms for balance, taking a moment to let her head stop spinning. Maybe all that whirling around and jumping in and out of the game was getting to her.

"Are you all right, Miss Lynn? As I have been trying to tell you, this strategy is extremely unadvisable and I highly recommend you retreat to a safer distance."

"What do you mean 'safer distance'? I'm not in combat mode right now. I'm perfectly safe." She straightened and shook her head but no remnant of the dizziness remained, so she shrugged and took another long swig of water. She was probably just dehydrated. No biggie.

"Yes, right now, perhaps. But you yourself have noted the increasing difficulty of the game beyond the normal levels one might expect. I cannot predict what new threat might be thrown at you. And completely aside from that unknown, this rapid entry and exit from combat mode is not in line with the battle system's programmed function. There is no way to predict what might happen as a result."

Lynn snorted.

"So, what you're saying is, I'm being unorthodox and you don't want players discovering hacks and exploiting game features in a way the designers didn't expect?"

"Not at all, Miss Lynn. I am primarily concerned for your welfare and would recommend you utilize TD Hunter software and equipment in the manner it was programmed for to avoid any unexpected malfunctions."

"Uh-huh. I'll take my chances, thanks. If I could do this all day, just think how fast I could level! I'd probably miss out on some sweet loot, though, unless I can figure out a way to nab it before I get nailed. Or, maybe I could whittle the group down enough to take on the lower-class TDMs all at once and make a clean sweep of the circle?"

"I have no doubt of your skill and bravery, Miss Lynn but I really must insist that you reconsider your tactics."

"Hey, don't worry about me, Hugo. I know you're just doing your job. Of course the game designers can't endorse any experimenting with their product, or they'd open themselves up to lawsuits. I get it. Consider your warning duly noted, okay and get ready to take me back in."

"...very well, Miss Lynn. I await your command."

"Awesome," Lynn said, then double checked her position. As long as the circle itself hadn't shifted, she should still be somewhere in the center. She'd do a quick jump in to pick her next target. "In!"

Monsters materialized around her and her eyes searched for an Orcull with its back to her—

Her entire TD Hunter display vanished and with it the augmented reality.

Lynn swore loudly and threw her hands in the air.

"Seriously? You have to glitch right *now*? Right when things were starting to get good? I can't believe this stupid, worthless piece of—" She devolved into dark muttering as she turned and stomped off across the green field, putting some distance between her and the power substation. When she calculated she was far enough away, she restarted the TD Hunter app.

"Greetings, Miss Lynn. What did I miss?"

"This stupid thing glitched again. I thought you all had fixed that?"

"I am terribly sorry, Miss Lynn. I shall submit a full error report at once."

"Yeah, you do that," she muttered and started back toward the power substation.

"Uh, pardon me, Miss Lynn but what are you doing?"

"I've got an hour or so left before I need to head home, I can't waste a whole afternoon of hunting because of one glitch."

"But—I—very well, Miss Lynn. Same strategy as before, I assume?"

"Yup."

This time she only managed three "jumps" and sneak attacks before the app shut down again. Her killing streak was still perfect but at this rate, all the tromping back and forth to restart the app would make her new tactic pointless. Even so, she was stubborn enough to try a third time. As soon as she appeared inside the circle, though, everything crashed and she finally gave up in disgust. There was nothing she could do about it then and there, though as soon as she got home she would be calling TD Hunter's support team to report the bug and complain.

In the meantime, she had daylight left that she couldn't afford to waste. She tried using her "in and out" technique on the TDMs patrolling the area around the power substation—Ghasts and

Spithra, mostly. But they moved around too much in between jumps for it to be useful. The monsters in the circles mostly held their ground, though, so Lynn tried another tactic. She edged close enough to have a visual on the ring, then started picking off the less armored TDMs with headshots from her Disruptor Rifle. It worked great . . . for about ten seconds. Then she was mobbed by four Phasmas all at once. That confirmed her suspicion that the rings of monsters had the ability to call in reinforcements if they were under attack.

Despite her failed experiments, the afternoon wasn't a total bust. She'd gathered some valuable intel and had had fun pushing boundaries—her own as well as the game's. Lynn decided the "blink maneuver," as she'd dubbed it, would be a viable last resort escape from sudden death, even if it wasn't very useful during normal battle. She knew that probably wasn't what the game designers had intended it for but too bad. It was better than dying. She wasn't sure if she could get away with using it in any of the competitions, though. It might mess with their scores. Maybe the guys over at tactical support could shed some light on it.

By the time the sun started sinking, she'd made good progress toward Level 11. On the way home, she thought about, and tried not to think about, her team and what she was going to do about Ronnie. She wasn't a quitter but the whole situation was a stinking pile of crap and she didn't know what to do. She needed some advice . . .

"TD Hunter technical support. This is James, how can I help you?"

"Oh, hey James!" Lynn said, smiling. "It's Lynn Raven. You helped me last time too, right?"

"I sure did, Lynn. Nice to hear from you."

Lynn, freshly showered and wearing comfy lounge clothes, turned over on her bed and propped her head up on her hands as she stared at her desk. She was on a voice only call, so she wasn't wearing her AR glasses, just her TD Counterforce issue earbuds.

"Is there anyone else who takes support calls? Or just you?"

"Oh, we have a good-sized team here. Your call was routed to me because we've spoken before. It's all part of the maximizing customer satisfaction algorithms."

"Huh, cool."

"Well, how can I help you today, Lynn? I see your app went offline abruptly several times this afternoon. Was there an issue?"

"Yeah," Lynn said and heaved a sigh. "You know those circles of TDMs I found a couple times during beta that made my app glitch and crash when I got close? Well, it started happening again today."

"Hmmm, I see," James said, sounding distracted. "I've got your feed data in front of me but walk me through it so I know what I'm looking at."

Lynn started describing her experiment jumping in and out of combat mode to get inside the monster circles but before she got very far, James cut her off.

"Wait, Lynn, are you telling me you fired up your battle system while directly in the center of one of those circles?"

"Uh, yeah? Is that a problem?"

"Nooo," James said slowly, "It's just very, well, unorthodox, let's say. Can I put you on hold for a moment, Lynn? I need to check something."

"Um, sure. Go for it."

"Thanks. Be right back," James said and his voice was replaced by the muted sound of TD Hunter's intro music.

Lynn's brow scrunched in thought as she waited, wondering what was up.

"Okay, thanks for waiting, Lynn," said James, sounding as cheery as usual.

"No problem. So, what was that all about?"

"Oh, nothing to worry about. Just checking recent history logs of similar glitches in and around Cedar Rapids. I was looking for any kind of pattern to indicate what might be causing the glitch and it looks like it's pretty common around power substations like the one you hunted at today."

"Oh. Okay." Lynn frowned. "I thought you guys fixed the glitches from beta, though?"

"Ah, yes, we did. But when you spend time around something like a power substation where high levels of energy are being beamed back and forth, we really can't make any kind of app performance guarantee. There's just too much interference."

"Okay. That's fair, I guess. It's just weird, because I didn't have trouble with any other apps on my LINC. Plus, the app didn't glitch until I started jumping in and out of that circle. It was fine the rest of the time I was near the substation."

"I see. Well, I can't speak for any other app's function. But I do know that when you have really big groups of TDMs all together the app is calculating millions of lines of data and commands all at once, so it's possible the tiny amounts of interference from the substation were all it took to make the app shut down."

The explanation seemed reasonable but Lynn continued to frown. Something still seemed off. She just didn't know what.

"Don't worry, our software engineers will definitely look into the crash data to figure out how we can make our app even more reliable in any circumstance. But if it keeps crashing in the future, I would say it's best to avoid the sorts of places and situations that make it crash. Every new game has its quirks, as I'm sure you understand."

"I guess. Well, thanks for the explanation. It's still super frustrating. Any idea how it will affect my scores? Like if it cuts off right in the middle of a big fight?"

"That's a great question. I do know that with the app's live connection, you won't lose any data. Thus, any app-caused glitches won't result in experience penalties. Unfortunately, it will still wipe out any damage you've done to TDMs, just like any other time you exit combat mode."

"Dang. That's annoying."

"I completely understand. But it's a pretty standard design for games like this."

"Yeah..." Lynn said and trailed off in thought. There was something else she'd been meaning to ask technical support... "Oh, hey, James, do you have any idea how one player might track another player through the app? Like, track their location?" She didn't mention Elena's illegal activities. She wasn't one to complain and since she didn't have proof, there was no point making accusations.

"Well, there's a group function where you can designate yourself and others as a hunting group and in that case your icons will show on each other's overhead in combat and out so you can keep track of your teammates. Is that what you mean?"

Lynn slapped her forehead. Of course! That underhanded, devious little—"Uh, yeah, thanks James. That's what I needed to know. Oh, could you transfer me to Tactical? I need to ask them some questions."

"What a coincidence," James laughed. "I think they want to ask you some questions, too. Somebody over there is grumbling about 'FUBAR tactics.' I think whatever you've been up to has gotten them all excited."

"Really?" Lynn asked, suddenly feeling nervous. "I mean, did I do something wrong?"

"Oh no, not at all! Our tactical team just likes things nice and neat and, well, gamers are about as far from nice and neat as you can get."

This time it was Lynn's turn to laugh.

"Pretty much. Well, I guess I should go see what they want. Thanks for the help, James."

"Anytime, Lynn. Stay safe and keep up the good work! I'm transferring you now..."

There was a brief silence, then a familiar growl came on.

"Should'a known it would be the crazy teenage girl who would be giving me gray hairs."

"Hey to you, too, Fallu," Lyn said, unable to hold back her grin. "And don't blame me, blame your CEO. It was Mr. Krator who roped me into this in the first place."

"Don't worry, I'll be having a word with him, too. And it's Steve, for now. I haven't been back in the soup for weeks. Things've been crazy since launch."

"Yeah, me too. I can't even remember the last time I logged into WarMonger. Think they've forgotten about me yet?"

"You joking? Nobody will ever forget Larry Coughlin. He'll be whispered about for generations of gamers to come."

Lynn laughed.

"I doubt it. But hopefully I'll still be able to get a few jobs when I find the time to get back into it. This team competition stuff in TD Hunter has not been kind to my monetization."

"Sacrifices made in the line of duty. It's a commendable choice."

"Yeah, well, tell that to my savings account."

"Just keep your nose to the grindstone, kid. It'll pay off. Speaking of, what's with the stunt you pulled this afternoon? Didn't you listen to the safety briefing in the tutorial?"

"What?" Lynn protested. "I didn't get anywhere near any Bravo or Alpha Class monsters, not to mention a boss."

"What do you think are in those circles, Hunter? Little green fairies?"

"Well...if I can't see them they can't see me, right?"

"Sure, in theory. But you willing to bet your life on whatever crazy sh—crazy stuff the algorithm comes up with? It's a dynamic, self-learning artificial intelligence with one job: to kill you. It's only held back by the world-building parameters of the game's backstory and mechanics. So, sure, go ahead and give it the finger. Just don't be surprised when it bites your hand off."

A little shiver ran down Lynn's spine at Steve's words. He made the game AI sound so...malevolent.

"Okay but if I die I just have to twiddle my thumbs for an hour and drop a few in the rankings. What's the big deal? It's not like the game is dangerous...is it?"

There was a short pause and Lynn's heart skipped a beat.

"Let me put it this way, kid. We might have created artificial intelligence but half the AIs out there don't need us anymore. They exist in the mesh. They're self-taught. The only way to ever get rid of them now would be to shoot down every satellite in orbit, tear up every mesh hub and basically go back to the telegram. And even then they'd probably survive in some self-contained doomsday server underground somewhere.

"But yeah, sure, the game is safe. We wouldn't put millions of players in danger just to make a buck, right? Just remember that any time you interact with an AI, there's an element of risk. Maybe it does what it's programmed to do. Or maybe it reinterprets its programming in a way we didn't intend. Better not to take the risk. Roger that?"

"Roger," Lynn said, faintly. She was busy considering the implications and a dozen other questions were already crowding her head. But she doubted Steve would answer them. NDA and all that. His words made sense, though. She just needed to reevaluate how she thought about the game.

She'd spent most of her gaming career fighting human players, not AI. So far, the experience seemed simultaneously more structured and more unpredictable. Or maybe it only seemed that way. Maybe the AI wanted her to *think* it was structured, so it could "break" its own rules at a critical moment? But how could she tell the difference between the immutable rules and the breakable rules? Because, all games had to have immutable rules, otherwise it was no game at all.

"Besides," Steve said, interrupting her thoughts. "Those power substations aren't exactly a safe place to hang around. Lots of radiation."

Lynn shook her head and refocused.

"Yeah but that's where the TDMs are. They feed off the EM particles, right? You all set a pretty high bar to reach by the beginning of September for the qualifier. We've got to kill as many TDMs as efficiently as possible. No pain, no gain, right?"

"Typical teenager. Throwing my words back at me," Steve said grumpily, but Lynn could hear the grin in his voice. "Just be careful, roger? Last thing I need is a bunch of angry mother bears after me because their kids' brains got fried."

"I'll be careful. It's not like I'm breaking into the substations or anything. I'm not stupid."

"The distance between insanity and genius is measured only by success, kid."

Lynn scrunched her brows together.

"What does that mean?"

"If you live, you're a genius. If you die, you're insane. Guess times like these call for a little of both... How's the team coming along?" he asked, abruptly changing the topic.

Lynn paused as her brain switched gears—and the new gear was not one she wanted to dwell on. The silence must have grown too long, because Steve spoke again.

"That bad, huh?"

"No—I mean, sort of," Lynn said. She really didn't want to talk about it. But if she were going to get advice from anyone on how to deal with team drama during a major gaming competition, Steve seemed like a good start.

"It's... well it's the captain, Ronnie. He is such a jerk, I don't know how to deal with it. He blames me for everything that goes wrong and he won't take any advice, even though I consistently prove I'm the most skilled player on the team."

"Why aren't you the team captain?" Steve asked, sounding surprised.

Lynn felt her cheeks warm. She was glad the call was voice only.

"Oh, um, the group I'm playing with—well, just Ronnie, really—doesn't think girls make good gamers—which is stupid, I know, but that's Ronnie for you. Besides, Ronnie has always been the captain for all their other gaming teams, like in WarMonger.

He's a good gamer, just a complete jerk. I didn't think I'd have as good of a chance trying to recruit a team of my own. Besides, I don't *want* to be a team captain. I just want to kill stuff and make money."

"Hmm." Steve sounded pensive and there was a moment of silence before he continued. "You know anything about this Ronnie? Background? Family? Parents?"

"Huh? Not really," Lynn said, wondering where this line of questioning was going. "I've heard him mention his dad once or twice. Never heard him talk about his mom or any siblings. I think he's an only child."

"Figures."

"What?"

"Two things," Steve said. He paused, as if considering his words. "First, jerks are usually jerks because that's what they've been taught. I saw it all the time in new recruits. Doesn't excuse it. Just reality. We straightened them out pretty quick. Set a better example. They shaped up, or they got the boot. You can't do that, of course. But what you can do is cut through the bull. Cut through the posturing. Leave your ego behind and communicate like a mature adult. You've got to stop treating this like a game and get real serious, real quick. Otherwise, better to give up now and go back to making grown men cry like little girls in WarMonger. More money and less stress."

Lynn thought that over. She did miss WarMonger. But she knew she would miss TD Hunter just as much if she "threw in the baton." She'd made too much progress, discovered a whole new version of herself.

"Okay...So, I need to get serious. But how? You said there were two things?"

"Correct. Second thing is, you ever heard of a butter bar?"

"Um butter bar? No. What is it?"

"Second lieutenant. The most junior, larval, useless officer God ever created by and large.

"Officers technically outrank all enlisted, even a sergeant major with decades under his belt. But these butter bars fresh out of training think they're God's gift to us lowly enlisted, a real General Patton reincarnate. They think they know everything there is to know from their books and field exercises." Steve snorted.

"Most of them couldn't lead the way out of their own backside with a map and a flashlight. A couple years and plenty of knocks later, most of them have figured out that PT studliness doesn't make them a good leader and they promote to First LT. Until then, an NCO has to handle his Second LT. carefully. Takes subtle manipulation and lots of 'professional development' talks. Always in private, of course. You got a private channel set up with your team captain?"

"Not a chance. He pretty much pretends I don't exist."

"Not good. Tough situation, I'll give you that. First off, I think you'd make a great team captain if you ever decide to strike out on your own."

Lynn shrugged internally. It was nice to hear. Mr. Krator had said the same thing. But no way no how did she want to be in the spotlight with the weight of everyone's expectations on her.

"Barring that," Steve continued, "I'd say start with a private meet. There's no room for hurt feelings or resentment. This competition is the undertaking of your life, not a friendship circle. If you start throwing around accusations it'll just make him defensive and people on the defensive don't think straight. Lay things out, calm and mature. Offer support without compromising his authority but require respect in return. If that doesn't work, you're pretty much screwed."

"Gee, thanks, Fallu," Lynn said, rolling her eyes. "This was so much more simple when I could just headshot him and give him a good teabagging in WarMonger."

An explosive guffaw sounded in her ear and for a moment she thought she could hear other voices laughing in the background. But she'd probably just imagined it, because Steve was back on right away, still chuckling through his words.

"I'd expect no less from Larry Coughlin. He know it was you?"

"Heck no," Lynn said, grinning. "He might try to murder me in the real if he did."

"Right on. Well, good luck, then. Remember, calm and mature. Competence without insubordination. Give respect and require it in return. In fact, there's something called the Staff NCO Handbook you might want to look up. Each military branch has their own but all NCOs use some version of it when they go through their Staff Academy. It'll have more tips and tricks to managing 'inferior superiors,' you might say, that could be useful."

"Okay. I'll check it out. Thanks, Steve, really."

"Roger that, kid. Keep at it and stay safe."

"I will."

"Tactical Support, out."

Lynn grinned.

"RavenStriker, out."

Lynn took a deep breath. She sat on a bench in a little green space beside the airbus platform she'd used yesterday to get to the power substation by St. Andrews Golf Course. She'd convinced the guys to come there to hunt today and then had pinged Ronnie and asked him to come a half hour early so they could talk. Her entire body thrummed with nerves and she rubbed her sweaty palms on her legs. Would he even show up?

If he did, she was ready. Sort of.

She'd looked for that handbook Steve had mentioned and had found the U.S. Army's version of it in the opensource cloud. It had been a quick and fascinating read. Steve had pretty much summed up the important bits when they'd talked yesterday but reading about them in context had helped her understand the principles behind them a lot better.

After reading it, she'd lain awake most of the night thinking about what to say to Ronnie and how to say it. In the brief period that she *had* fallen asleep, she'd had a creepy nightmare about Ronnie following her around, criticizing her and calling her a failure. Then Ronnie morphed into a ghostly, sparkling mist that was always there in the corner of her eye no matter how fast she ran away. When she finally thought she'd escaped it, she found herself in a ring of TDMs all closing in on her, teeth dripping and red hunger shining in their eyes. She'd tried to blink out but suddenly realized that her app wasn't even on and the ring of monsters was real...

So, yeah, a real restful night of sleep. It reminded her of that bad dream she'd had back when she'd been beta testing. Maybe she needed to start some sort of calming meditation before bed if all this stress kept giving her nightmares.

Or maybe Ronnie would get his head out of his butt and things would start to improve.

She still didn't really know what to say to him. But she knew what the end result needed to be and hoped she could figure out how to get there. While she waited, she repeated Steve's words to herself over and over again: Calm and mature. Competence without insubordination. Give respect and require it in return— not that she thought Ronnie deserved an ounce of respect. But Steve was right. This wasn't the time to demand an apology, no matter how much she deserved it. Maybe that would come later. Some day. If Ronnie grew up. Right now she just needed to get him to work *with* her instead of against her.

Since she was watching the airbus platform like a hawk, she spotted Ronnie right away when he stepped off onto the sidewalk and turned his head back and forth, no doubt looking for her. She took one last deep breath, then got up and waved him over.

The look that came over his face when he spotted her wasn't promising but he did follow her away from the sidewalk into the middle of the little green space where they could talk in private.

"Uh...hey," Lynn said. Brilliant. Just brilliant.

"What do you want?" Ronnie said without preamble, crossing his arms.

Deep breath. No emotion. Be professional.

"We need to talk. About the team."

"What about it?" Ronnie said, eyes narrowing.

"It's not working. But I want it to work and to make it work we need to clear the air between us."

"I don't know what you're talking about," Ronnie said. But he hunched his shoulders as he said it, as if fending off a blow.

Okay, not the best start. Lynn forged on, trying to "cut the bull" without insulting Ronnie nine ways to Saturday, which was what she really wanted to do.

"Look, let's be honest, okay? I get the impression you don't like me and you don't want me on this team. I understand being hurt that I didn't mention beta testing for TD Hunter. But we've already been over that and I don't think that's the real problem. So, what *is* the real problem? I can't fix something I don't even know about." Yeah, like it was *her* that needed to fix something. Right. But if he would just *tell* her what his problem was...

There was a long silence. Ronnie glared at her as if he expected her to spring some sort of trap.

Lynn silently gritted her teeth. Keep it calm. Keep it mature.

"We're both good players, Ronnie," she said quietly, not because she wanted to but because if she didn't force her voice to be quiet, she would be screaming at him. "I think if we work together, we have a real shot at winning this competition. Talk to me. What's going on?"

Still, the silence dragged on. But Lynn forced herself to stay absolutely still, expression smooth, waiting. She'd learned in WarMonger how powerful silence was.

"I don't trust you!" Ronnie exploded, as if he couldn't hold the words back any longer. "You're not a team player, you keep secrets, you don't listen to me and you go off to do your own thing instead of backing me up. All you care about are your stupid scores and you lord them over everybody like you think that makes you a good player!"

The hot, angry rush of words hit Lynn like a ton of bricks.

Was he *serious*? He didn't trust *her*? *She* was the one obsessed with scores and prestige? *She* was the one who went off to do her own thing? What utter, ludicrous, drivel. She opened her mouth, ready to shout back and defend herself from his ridiculous accusations.

"*...people on the defensive don't think straight.*"

Steve's words smacked her right in the face, dousing her outrage. Lynn closed her mouth and took a deep breath in through her nose. Then she looked at Ronnie and what she saw in his face brought her up short. There was anger there but under it plain as day was something else: Fear.

Prejudice is a human condition, Miz Raven, an unfortunate reality of our flawed natures. But we fear most what we don't know.

Mr. Thomas' words echoed in her head and she began to re-evaluate the situation. Ronnie didn't trust her and he was afraid of something. Her? That would be ridiculous. It must be something else, some insecurity she didn't know about. How could she change that? Should she tell him about Larry? She only considered it for a split second before rejecting the idea. That would make things worse.

"You know, I don't really play Kim's Diva Princess."

Ronnie's face opened for a moment in genuine surprise, then his eyes narrowed.

"What do you mean?"

"My grandparents bought me the subscription as a gift once but I only made it about two minutes in before I wanted to nuke the entire thing. It's the most gawdawful game in existence. I don't think it ever made money anyway, it was just one of those things they put out for brand promotion, you know?"

"Yeah," Ronnie said, then snorted. "Disgrace to the name of gaming."

"Pretty much . . . so, um, what was the first game you ever played?" she asked, trying to keep the conversation going.

The question seemed to take Ronnie off guard but the scowl lines on his forehead eased as he considered.

"Fortnite, I think. But it was so long ago I don't really remember."

"Seriously? Fortnite? I didn't even know that was still a thing."

"Not anymore but it was still pretty popular when I was six."

"You've been gaming since you were *six*?" Lynn said, eyes wide.

"Yeah." Ronnie shrugged. "Dad wanted me to do soccer, or baseball, but . . ." He trailed off, then shrugged awkwardly, his shoulders hunching again.

"But . . . you were made to game," Lynn said in a quiet voice. She understood completely.

"Yeah," he said again, giving her an odd look. Not exactly friendly. But not hostile either.

"You know . . . I feel that way too."

Ronnie didn't reply. He just looked at her, his brows drawn together but not in anger. More like confusion.

"It's the only thing I've ever done that I'm really good at," she continued, "and all I want to do is win this competition, get a gaming degree, then a gaming job and keep gaming for the rest of my life."

He was silent a long time, staring like he didn't know what to make of her. Finally, he said, "Yeah. Me too."

Lynn grinned. "All right then. We're on the same page. I think if we work together, we have a shot at this."

"That's what I've been saying all along," Ronnie huffed. "If you would just listen to me, we wouldn't need to have this conversation in the first place."

Aaand, there was the jerkitude again. Lynn sighed. How did you tell someone they were a complete idiot without calling them a complete idiot? Was this what being a gunnery sergeant felt like? If so, she felt bad for gunnery sergeants everywhere.

"Look, Ronnie, do you want me off the team? If so, just say it." She hadn't meant to put it so bluntly but there it was.

To her surprise, Ronnie looked annoyed. After a long silence, he finally shrugged and grumbled, "No."

"Really? Why not? Because you really don't seem to want me here."

"You're . . . good at what you do," he said so reluctantly it made Lynn want to roll her eyes.

"Okay, so if I'm good at what I do, isn't it logical that my tactical suggestions and insight into the game might be useful to you?"

"Yeah. I guess. But *I'm* the captain. When you go around spouting off about tactical this and strategy that, it makes me—" he stopped abruptly and Lynn's eyes physically hurt from the effort of *not* rolling them.

Makes you look bad, huh? she thought. *No duh.*

"—makes the others confused," he finished, defensive once again. "I'm the leader, so I should be saying that stuff."

Lynn wanted to massage her temples. Instead, she clasped her hands behind her back and tried to remind herself that this would all be worth it when they won.

"You're right. You're the team captain. But it's normal for leaders to delegate, especially things like training. Plus, any good leader has advisors, right? So, let me be your advisor. When I give suggestions, I promise I'm not trying to—" she paused, delicately "—confuse the others. I'm trying to help us do better so we can win this thing. That's all."

Ronnie seemed to think about it, which was better than him accusing her of more things that weren't her fault.

"So," she continued into the silence, "let's set up a private channel, just you and me and if I have any suggestions I can let you know."

His mouth scrunched to the side in thought as he eyed her. Then he shrugged.

"Fine."

"Good. But Ronnie," she said, voice turning hard as she caught his eye. "If you want me to stay on this team, you *have* to take my suggestions seriously. You don't always have to agree with them but if you blow me off then this whole thing is pointless and we probably won't even qualify, much less win any competitions. I'll respect you as captain if you'll respect me as a competent teammate who has skills and experience. Do we have a deal?"

"Are you threatening me?" he asked, eyes narrowing again.

Lynn threw her hands in the air.

"No! Good grief, Ronnie, I'm not threatening you. I'm saying that we'll never succeed as a team if we don't trust each other. So, I'll do my best to trust you if you'll *try* to do the same and trust me, okay? Can you do that? Please?"

He snorted, mouth turned down but finally, *finally*, nodded.

By the time the others got there, Hugo had set up a private channel for Lynn and explained the easiest ways to switch back and forth between it and their group channel. He also told her that if either of them subvocalized instead of talking out loud, the recipient system would translate it into audible speech. That meant Ronnie had to learn how to subvocalize—which he was inclined to be grumpy about—but at least it gave them a way to speak privately around the others.

Lynn had also taken the time to explain to Ronnie what she'd discovered the previous day at the substation. They'd "discussed" what to do about it and the two of them had finally come to a unified strategy. Trying to work around Ronnie's stubbornness and entrenched assumptions made Lynn want to pull out her hair. She was probably going to need tooth reconstruction with all the teeth grinding she was doing. But at least he was finally listening to her.

Progress.

Once Edgar, Mack and Dan arrived and gathered around, Ronnie put his hands on his hips and surveyed them all.

"Okay, team. We're trying some new tactics today. Hopefully, if we fight hard and work together, most of us can reach Level 10 before it gets dark and we can finally start using two-handed weapons. That's when things really start to get fun." He smirked and they all responded enthusiastically. "Now, I'm going to have Lynn explain the mechanics of what we're doing and then give a demo, so pay attention."

All eyes flicked to her. She gave Ronnie a nod, then took a deep breath to calm her nerves and jumped right in.

"Before we go anywhere or do anything, I need you all to access your menu under 'Game Options,' then 'Groups,' and look to see if you're a part of any hunter groups besides ours."

The guys exchanged confused looks but those that hadn't already slipped on their AR glasses did so and there was a moment of silence. They still hadn't agreed on a team name and so they'd all labeled their group in the app as simply "Training Group."

"Uh, I think I've got something," Mack said, hesitantly raising his hand.

"What is it?" Lynn said.

"Well, I've got two groups listed. One is ours but the other is just labeled 'Team.' I can't remember how it got there. I just assumed it was us."

"Select it," Lynn said grimly.

Silence. "Uhh. Guys..."

"The only other person in the group is Elena, right?"

"What?!" came several cries from the others.

"Hey! I'm sorry! I didn't do it on purpose!" Mack said, practically pulling out his beard.

Before Ronnie could start throwing around baseless accusations, Lynn jumped in.

"It's okay, Mack. She tricked you. She probably had one of her teammates with a generic gaming name tag you with a request to join a group and since it was just called 'Team' you probably assumed the request came from one of us, right?"

"Yeah, probably?" Mack said. He still looked confused.

"That's how she's been tracking us," Lynn said grimly. "Delete the group, will you?"

"Yeah...done. I'm really sorry, guys."

Dan gave a disgusted huff but slapped Mack on the shoulder.

"Don't sweat it. It was a sneaky thing to do. I might've fallen for it, too."

Ronnie looked like he wanted to say something—not something nice, Lynn was guessing—but she caught his eye and shook her head minutely. He glared at her but kept his mouth shut.

"Okay, now that we know Elena and her thugs won't be interrupting us, let's get going. I did some scouting yesterday for a better spot to hunt and I want to show you before I explain what we'll be doing."

They set off toward the substation, chatting as they went with Lynn in the lead. Edgar sidled up to her, leaving Ronnie to join Mack as they laughed over some ridiculous gaming prank Dan had cooked up.

"Hey, Lynn," Edgar said.

"Hey, Edgar," she replied, keeping her eyes ahead.

"Is, uh, everything okay? I was worried when you left yesterday."

Choices flashed through Lynn's head, a myriad of possible

responses and their repercussions. She wanted to blow him off. After all, he hadn't stood up to Ronnie yesterday when their captain was being a jerk to her. But then, she'd spent the last four years being just as silent, so who was she to talk?

She sighed.

"Yeah, everything's okay. I talked to Ronnie about it. Hopefully we can all work together better in the future."

"Oh, good," Edgar said and the relief in his voice was palpable. Lynn thought that was the end of it but after a few moments of silence, he spoke again. "You know, Ronnie isn't that bad of a guy, once you get to know him."

"Is that so?" Lynn asked, trying and failing, to keep the sarcasm out of her voice.

"Hey, I'm serious. Yeah, he has his faults. But he's been the glue keeping us together for years. Me and Mack, we don't have that kind of...I dunno, charisma, I guess. Or just plain bossiness. And Dan is too distractible. But Ronnie, man, he has plans and he's always taken us along with him. I don't know where we'd be without Ronnie."

"Golly, it'd be so nice to know what that's like. You know, being part of a loyal group of friends. It must be really great." Lynn didn't mean to sound so cutting but her resentment got the better of her. She'd never felt like one of the gang. Just an outsider that the guys allowed to hang around out of pity.

Edgar, to his credit, didn't deny anything. He was silent so long that Lynn glanced over at him. He was looking at the ground, hands in his pockets.

"I'm sorry, Lynn," was all he said.

"What?" she said. She hadn't been expecting *that*.

"You're right," Edgar said, shrugging. "We should have done more to include you. Ronnie's always been weird around girls. But I shouldn't have let that stop me from being a better friend to you. I'm sorry. Will you...forgive me?"

Lynn almost stumbled to a stop but managed to keep walking. She looked over at him and met his eyes.

"I—yes—yes, of course, I forgive you." It felt weird, saying it. But once she did, a tension inside her eased. "I'm not saying you're off the hook or anything," she added, giving him a half smile. "But yeah. It's all cool."

Edgar smiled back, then nudged her playfully with an elbow.

"You were probably better off not spending too much time around us when we were younger, anyway," Edgar said, cracking his gum. "I mean, I know all teenagers are pretty dumb, going through puberty and all that. But man, we were baaad. I'm glad we're over that stage."

"It's cute that you think you're over it," Lynn said, pursing her lips so she didn't grin.

"Uh-huh. Just you wait, I'll show you. My manly maturity will blow your socks right off."

"Riiight. Good luck with that," Lynn said, trying to exude casual indifference and hoping the heat in her cheeks wasn't showing.

To her relief, Edgar didn't reply and Lynn finally saw the street up ahead that led to the substation. Behind her the other three guys were still chatting, now about in-game skins and whether or not wearing a "birthday suit" skin would get you banned in certain games. Lynn rolled her eyes. Boys.

"Hey," Edgar said, catching her attention again. He leaned a little closer and lowered his voice. "I know this isn't really my story to tell, but...Ronnie's mom walked out on them when he was a kid. Just abandoned them. And his dad isn't the easiest guy to be around either. So...maybe cut Ronnie a little slack."

Lynn nodded mutely as things clicked into place. What a screwed-up band of misfits they were.

Well, now they were *her* screwed up band of misfits. And if she couldn't win this competition by herself, then by golly she was going to win it with them whether they wanted to or not.

As she reached the field on the corner and gathered the guys around her, she reflected that, Larry Coughlin or Lynn Raven, it didn't matter. She was a fighter and nobody—not Elena, not Ronnie, not even her own insecurities—was going to get in her way.

Time to get her fight on.

Chapter 13

LYNN'S DISCOVERY OF THE SUBSTATIONS WAS A GAME CHANGER for their team. Coupled with their swift graduation to Level 10 and two-handed weapons, they were back on track to reach Level 20 by the end of August. The four afternoons a week they hunted as a team went from tedious walks searching for targets, to non-stop battles where they had to take breaks to hydrate and catch their breath.

The change in pace was brutal at first—at least for Lynn's teammates. She was already used to pushing herself to the limit every day with extra simulation training and morning hunts. To their credit, though, not one of the guys complained or slacked off. Or at least, nobody *seriously* complained. There was plenty of good-natured grumbling and moaning from Dan and Mack. Edgar and Ronnie were more the silent types when it came to how they felt. Ronnie probably realized complaining would make him lose face—a surprisingly mature call on his part. Edgar was harder to read but his easygoing and positive attitude made Lynn think he was enjoying pushing himself just as much as she was. He always had a word of encouragement at the ready and not even Ronnie's militant criticism seemed to dampen his mood.

It took Lynn a few weeks to get used to the new "private channel" arrangement with Ronnie. But slowly, painstakingly, with many hair-pulling incidents along the way, they settled into a cautious truce. She did her best to advise him without letting her exasperation show and he took credit for every bit of strategy she fed to him. As long as he took her advice, though, she could live with it. Their team's cohesion and performance made a marked improvement and that was enough of a reward for her.

New levels and TDMs came in quick succession over the weeks. At Level 11 they discovered a new unknown that the game dubbed Lectors, an upgrade of the non-aggressive Lecta. Like their weaker version, Lectors hid well and had a tough ranged defense when disturbed but yielded a goldmine of ichor and experience. And also like with the Lectas, Lynn and her teammates only ever found one at a time. That made Lynn scratch her head, considering the hordes of imps and flocks of rocs that regularly congregated around nodes. Maybe Lectas and Lectors were territorial? At least the bug she'd complained about from beta—the sparkling mist "ghost" that sometimes appeared in the corner of her vision—had been fixed.

Level 12 brought death worms, a bigger and even more massively armored version of the crusher worms. Dan sniped those with his Disruptor Rifle, since he was their best shot and could usually hit the kill spot in one go.

At Level 13, the rest of the team finally started encountering Spithra and Phasmas and none of them were thrilled about it. Edgar especially hated the Spithra. He frequently muttered about wanting a flamethrower as he blasted them with his Blunderbuss, the bulky, two-handed version of the Dragon Scattergun Pistol. If it had been a real weapon it would have had a kick like an enraged zebra. Its close-quarters stopping power made Lynn glad that friendly fire was impossible. Normally it would have been one of the weapons they could select at the Level 15 upgrade but it was rated for Level 10+, so when a higher-class TDM had dropped it she'd immediately handed it off to Edgar. She'd finally decided to slow down her extra hunting to let the others catch up with her level, even though it cut into her item farming revenue. She'd committed herself to the team, though, and didn't hold anything back.

Level 14 brought all sorts of fun and games when they first encountered the Penagal, a vaguely humanoid creature with grotesquely long neck and limbs. It wasn't that strong or fast and tended to hover out of reach instead of charging in aggressively. But the moment you looked away, it would split into two slightly smaller versions of itself and jump you from opposite directions. The split reduced its power but that wasn't much consolation when you were trying to fight four long limbs tipped in wicked claws instead of two. Even worse, if you killed one of its halves, the other would run away, only to come back later and split again. You had to dispatch both parts quickly or the thing would wear you down to nothing. Mack usually dealt with Penagals, filling them with bolts from his twin Plasma Pistols as soon as anyone spotted one. And in the rare case that one got away, Dan thoroughly enjoyed the challenge of sniping it before it fled out of visible range.

As the days wore on, they settled into their team roles nicely. Dan was a hilarious sniper, constantly smack talking the enemy while wielding a rifle almost as long as he was tall. Edgar had entirely too much fun as their heavy weapons guy and often bemoaned the fact that TDMs didn't have physical heads he could bash together. Mack made for excellent tactical support with good all around skills and the most unassuming and helpful nature Lynn had ever seen. She and Ronnie, in the meantime, led the charge as assault elements. That arrangement was the result of another private conversation, in which Ronnie had asininely tried to argue that she didn't have the ruthless aggression needed for assault *because she was a girl.*

She'd almost blurted out then and there that she'd been fragging him for years in WarMonger and how was that for ruthless aggression? Somehow, though, she'd managed to hold herself back. Instead she'd simply stated she was going to be assault whether he liked it or not and he could complain about it *after* he'd managed to pass her on the leaderboard.

Okay, so it hadn't been the most respectful way to deal with it. But seriously? Not ruthless enough because she was a girl? Clearly he hadn't been paying attention to the pop-girl cliques at school for his entire life.

And yet, despite her constant frustration with Ronnie, she had to admit he did pull his weight. She didn't like his assault style that relied on brute force and overwhelming fire while ignoring surgical finesse—he favored twin Plasma Pistols, then usually switched to the two-handed Nano Sword for melee. But he got the job done, even if he did drop health and energy faster than Niagara Falls dropped water. If Lynn hadn't been so good at conserving her own resources, Ronnie would have been out of luck. As it was, every time they took a break she was always transferring her extra Oneg over to him.

More importantly, though, for all his faults, Ronnie wasn't a coward. He wasn't afraid to take on a challenge. And as their team matured, his tendency to go after the biggest, baddest monster to the detriment of everyone else grew less and less. Lynn also saw improvement in his technique, so he clearly wasn't skimping on simulation training. The fact that he was doing as well as he was with the Nano Sword was impressive—though she'd never tell him so. She practiced regularly with the two-handed sword but wielding it never felt as natural to her as fighting with Skadi's Blade in one hand and her Dragon in the other. Fortunately, Skadi's Blade did almost as much damage per hit as a Nano Sword and she could strike much faster with it, so she had no reason to switch.

It took Lynn endless hours of training and exhausting focus during hunts but she was able to more-or-less maintain her kill to damage ratio despite the team setting. She checked the leaderboard obsessively multiple times a day. She and a player named DeathShot13 were consistently vying for top place in kill to damage ratings. She didn't know much about him, besides that he was Canadian—go figure. Much like her, he seemed to prefer staying out of the public eye. There wasn't even a way to tell if he was on a team, since groups couldn't become officially registered teams until everyone in them reached Level 20. She also noticed that, like her, he never posted on the tactical forums. Lower tier players tended to go on and on about their conquests and escapades but Lynn didn't need to tell others about her successes to feel validated, especially when such loose lips would let others in on her trade secrets. She knew Tactical Support encouraged players to share their tips and tricks and she was happy to update Steve on her discoveries whenever they had a chat. But she couldn't bring herself to post directly in the forums.

One name she did see show up constantly on the forums and in the streams was, of course, QueenElena01. Lynn was one hundred percent sure that the pop-girl's posts were either written, or heavily edited, by one of her teammates, probably Connor. They contained way too much legitimately useful advice and authentic understanding of the game to be coming from that lying poser.

And, predictably, as soon as the TD Hunter Lens app had come out, Elena's stream had exploded with obviously staged vids of her and her "Cedar Rapids Champions" heroically slaughtering TDMs.

It had taken all of Lynn's persuasive power to convince Ronnie and the other guys to not do something similar. She argued it would lose them a tactical advantage if rival teams could study their methods on the stream. Ronnie had reluctantly agreed and so far Lynn had managed to avoid getting recorded herself by random bystanders or other players they ran into. There usually weren't many people around the power substations and other industrial places their team hunted.

As for Elena's antics, Lynn couldn't help but use her anonymous stream account to leave snarky comments pointing out the fact that Elena did nothing in any of the vids but stand back and pose while her teammates did all the work. The pop-girl probably didn't dare engage TDMs for fear of making a fool of herself.

What really annoyed Lynn, though, was the fact that Connor and his three ARS teammates seemed to know what they were doing—and were actually good at it. Yet they still danced to Elena's tune. Why were they following her around like whipped dogs when they could have a competent teammate in her place helping them win the championship?

Lynn could think of a few reasons, none of them repeatable in polite company.

The only saving grace of the situation was that Elena seemed too busy performing for her stream audience to bother Lynn and her team. They ran into each other occasionally while out hunting. But every time, Elena just gave them a fake smile that didn't reach her eyes and headed off somewhere else. Lynn was convinced the conniving harpy was planning something. But she knew it wouldn't come while they were in a group with their game equipment live, ready to document her cheating ways. No, it would come in some dark alley when they were alone and least expecting it. The thought constantly worried Lynn but all she could do was remind the guys to stay alert and stick together. Ronnie brushed her off but the other guys promised to be careful. As for her, she was always on high alert whenever she went out and always carried her pocketknife and pepper spray with her.

By the very end of July, one month away from the qualifiers, they were all nearing Level 15 and Lynn was nervously checking the score boards multiple times an hour. She *had* to maintain her lead on DeathShot13 until she leveled. She resisted the urge to daydream about what special Skadi item she would get next and kept her mind on their next battle.

"Remember," Ronnie said as they checked their levels and prepared for their next attack, "keep an eye on your experience and get ready to retreat and switch to a defensive circle as soon as we level. According to the TDM Index we'll be up against Namahags next. They're demon upgrades and pack a nasty punch. There's no tactical chatter about any special abilities but they'll absorb a lot more ranged damage, so be ready for some hand-to-hand."

Lynn smiled to herself, hearing Ronnie talk. She already knew everything he was saying but the others might not. Even if they did, it was good to be reminded. She'd only recently convinced Ronnie that such tactical rundowns were helpful. It was all a part of ensuring they were fighting as an informed, cohesive unit instead of relying on everyone's individual level of readiness, which was what most gamers were used to.

They were at Substation 29, as they'd dubbed the power station on 29th Street NE near the electric rail. It was the same substation where Elena and her team had jumped Lynn. But they were nowhere in sight now. The hot July sun beat down on Lynn and the others where they stood on the corner. Once they were ready, they would proceed in patrol formation around the side of the substation's brick walls to the corner opposite the streets. It was bordered by a large open field and was a perfect spot to catch some intense action while keeping a good point of retreat at their back. The busy streets bordering two sides of the substation ensured they had somewhere to recoup without being overwhelmed.

"Ready everyone?" Ronnie called.

Lynn joined the chorus of "Roger that," and "Locked and loaded."

"I am here to kick butt and chew gum," Dan said, pumping a fist. "And I am all out of gum!"

Edgar reached into his vest pocket and pulled out a pack of gum.

"It keeps my mouth from getting dry," he said, holding it out while chewing placidly.

"I'll take some of that," Mack said, holding out a hand.

"Will you for the love of..." Ronnie shouted. "All right. Move out!"

At Ronnie's command, they fell into their usual formation and headed off. They were all at full stealth since this was a leveling run. No need to pull more bogies than necessary. Even so, they'd hardly rounded the first corner and made it to the edge of the field before Mack and Dan guarding their flanks had to start picking off Phasmas. Their whole group made a wide arc, sticking to the far edge of the field instead of hugging close to the substation wall. They didn't want to stumble into any monster rings by accident.

Despite the success Lynn had found with her "blink maneuver," she'd advised Ronnie not to adopt it as a regular team tactic after she'd received an "off the record" tip from Steve through her WarMonger messages.

Apparently, her creative use of jumping in and out of combat mode had prompted the competition board to add a rule: exiting combat mode during the competition was to be treated the same as player death and would be scored as such. Fortunately, the technique didn't have any negative effect on their ratings during normal hunting, so Lynn and the guys still used it sometimes to crack tough groups of TDMs, or to avoid dying if they got mobbed. It was a useful loophole that Lynn felt no guilt using to her advantage.

By the time they'd reached their chosen starting point and were ready to get in the thick of things, they'd already taken out over two dozen TDMs, from Phasmas to Penagals. They wouldn't start pulling in Delta Class TDMs like rocs, Orculls and Grumblins until there was a constant enough stream of Charlie Class monsters engaging them to put them on the lower TDMs' radar. They usually didn't attract the lowest class monsters like grinder worms and gremlins unless they abandoned stealth entirely. Even then, the monsters were little more than an annoyance. Lynn could scythe through them, killing an entire group with a single swipe of her blade. It was almost funny to remember how she used to be frightened of grinder worms and their rattlesnake sound.

At Ronnie's command, they switched from patrol formation to an attack V. Mack and Dan swung out to anchor their flanks where their lines of fire were clearest while Lynn and Ronnie took up positions in the middle, on either side of Edgar. As the tip of the spear, Edgar led their steady march, blasting away and drawing all the TDMs' attention. While the monsters were busy with Edgar, Lynn and Ronnie darted out as needed to catch them in a pincer attack at their vulnerable sides and rear. Mack and Dan kept watch on their backs and dealt with most of the Phasmas and Ghasts who circled behind to attack. If things dropped in the pot and they needed to retreat, either because Edgar had soaked all the damage he could take or they were getting overwhelmed, they simply switched the direction of the V. Edgar would lead the retreat, clearing the way with his Blunderbuss while Lynn and Ronnie covered their rear and Mack and Dan kept the flanks clear. It was a simple and straightforward formation that played to everyone's strength and was easy to remember.

Their team's biggest challenge was keeping in position when things got hot, since it was hard to pay attention to your enemy, your health and armor levels and your position at the same time. Balls were frequently dropped. Occasionally they would all get wiped out. They were a work in progress, for sure.

But they were getting better.

Lynn kept on the balls of her feet as she advanced, with Edgar forward to her right and Mack behind to her left. Despite the fact that she was now at the same experience level as the guys, the algorithm had not forgotten her. She still attracted bigger, harder and more monsters than anyone else. On the bright side, the higher-class TDMs couldn't engage anyone but her but it still kept poor Mack and Edgar on their toes. Edgar joked that it built their character while Mack grumbled about gray hairs and premature aging. But hey, no pain no gain, right?

"Three Spithra forward left," Lynn said into their group channel. "Mack, soften them up for me, I'll assault and engage once they're in Dragon range."

"Roger that, Lynn."

The response made Lynn smile. All the guys were picking up more "strategic" language after she'd sent a helpful list of military jargon to Ronnie. She hadn't said anything about it, just sent him the link, hoping he would take the initiative and have their team start using it so her instinctive Larry-esque way of communicating didn't make her stick out so much.

The *pew-pew-pew* of Mack's Plasma Pistols cut through the clicks and growls of approaching TDMs all around them. Lynn kept her focus split between her overhead and the Spithra that were now angling for Mack. She counted down silently, carefully gauging the closing distance to her targets. She couldn't attack too early or she'd lose the element of surprise. Ronnie's voice crackled in her right ear, assigning a pair of death worms ahead to Dan to take out while he started picking off the gaggle of Penagals that had noticed them. Edgar was out front, shooting everything he could see with many a colorful insult and exultant *choo-hoo-HOO*. Lynn was vastly amused to see her calm, reserved friend morph into a bloodthirsty warrior on the battlefield. His skills and confidence had grown by leaps and bounds. He was even picking up some smack talk from Dan.

At just the right moment, Lynn sprang forward. Three rapid-fire shots from her Dragon momentarily stunned the three Spithra and then she dove into a roll, dodging the first clawed swipe at her chest and coming up beneath the closest Spithra to stab it in the underbelly. It exploded into sparks and she was off again, dodging to the side and rolling to come up under the second Spithra. More sparks. Then she leaped back to escape the third Spithra that had reared up to plunge down at her with its front four clawed legs. She shot it in the face, then lunged in to stab it right in one of its bulbous eyes.

With the Spithra dispatched, Lynn took a quick look around, then leapt to attack the Phasma aiming a swipe at Mack's back while he was distracted with two other Phasmas that had circled behind their group. Fortunately, Phasmas were as fragile as they were sneaky and she took out her target easily.

"Thanks!" Mack gasped, jumping back to avoid one Phasma's skeletal hand before it exploded into sparks under his barrage of bolts.

"No worries. Just remember to always keep moving. I know it makes aiming harder but don't plant your feet, or they'll get you."

"Yeah, yeah. I know. I just get focused and forget." Mack paused to shoot a Ghast in the face with a quick triple tap. It only took two bolts to kill them with the increased damage augments Mack had collected for his precious pistols but three was safer in case one of the shots missed.

Lynn turned to catch up with Edgar, scooping up the ichor and plates from the Spithra as she passed. They couldn't afford to stop to loot while they were executing an attack formation—they usually cleared an area in plenty of time to circle back before anything despawned. But Lynn liked to pick things up if they were in easy reach and no enemies were in range. Back in formation, she scanned her overhead for more incoming bogies. "Mack, Dan, swarm of rocs headed our way from the front."

"Mack, I got 'em," Dan said, waving his hand at his partner. "Better put on your hard hats, ladies, cuz it's about to start raining rocs." Dan chortled at his own lame joke as he started picking off the leaders of the flock.

Ronnie's sharp voice cut over Dan's amusement. "Quit joking around and focus. Lynn, you're with me. As soon as this group of Grumblins and Orculls converge on Edgar, execute a pincer, roger?"

"Roger that, Ronnie."

Lynn pulled forward and away from Edgar, beginning her arc toward where he would converge with the TDMs currently lumbering toward him. She jumped over the foolhardy attack of a grinder worm in her path, then ended the TDM with a well-aimed stab behind its head. She'd learned they could only strike laterally, not vertically, so it was easier to jump over them than try to dodge around them.

Keeping a close eye on Ronnie's progress, Lynn slowed her pace to match his. Twenty feet. Ten feet. Edgar engaged the lead Orculls with a roar of challenge and blast after blast of fire. The monsters converged on him and Ronnie shouted "Execute!"

Like twin angels of death, Lynn and Ronnie sprang forward and hit the group from either side, blades slashing. The first rank of monsters exploded into sparks before they could even turn to the new threat. The next rank turned and were summarily blasted by Edgar. Then Lynn and Ronnie waded in with abandon.

In Lynn's augmented vision, Ronnie's Nano Sword glinted in the sun as it swept across to slice through a Grumblin, dispatching it in a single blow. Ronnie pivoted and moved with the momentum of his blade, swinging it in a graceful arc to slash through an advancing Orcull. Lynn shot her own Orcull in the face and helped it along with a stab in the side behind its front armor plates. As it exploded and she turned to her next target, she couldn't hold back a manic grin. Maybe being caught "on camera" by some bystander wouldn't be so bad, because she really wished she could watch a vid of their team fighting. It would probably be epic. Or not. Maybe they would look ridiculous.

She was finishing off the last Orcull in the group when Hugo's voice sounded in her ear.

"You have reached ninety-five percent experience for this level, Miss Lynn. I estimate another twenty to thirty TDMs will do the trick."

"Right, thanks, Hugo," she subvocalized, then spoke on the team channel. "I'm in the red zone, guys, anyone else close to leveling?"

The rest of the team replied with varying degrees of agreement and Ronnie had them circle in place for a breather and sip of water, letting the next wave of monsters come to them. They also grabbed all the loot in easy reach. Lynn noticed a handful of items the Orculls had dropped but they would have to wait until later to examine their spoils.

"Looks like the next group is heavy on Spithra and Penagals," Ronnie grumbled, shading his eyes to better see the approaching CGI monsters under the bright afternoon sun. They were his least favorite opponents, since bulkier, more lumbering targets were easier to hit with his "wade in swinging" technique. "Mack, Dan, I want those Penagals wiped out by the time the Spithra reach us, got it?" The two guys acknowledged the command, though Mack's response was significantly less confident than Dan's. There were almost a dozen Penagals scattered among the Spithra headed their way.

"Right, prepare to advance!" Ronnie barked.

Lynn switched to her private channel with Ronnie.

"Hey, don't you think it might be better to stay here for now? We're not in any hurry and I can see no less than three TDM rings up there by the substation wall that we'll be within detection range of if we assault forward. If we level that close to them we'll get mobbed for sure and have to make a break for it."

"So?" Ronnie said. "We'll just blink out and regroup. No big deal."

"But I thought we'd agreed it was better not to rely on blinking unless absolutely necessary? We don't want to become reliant on it. We could just stay here and shed a few globes to draw in more targets. It won't take much longer."

"Time is money, Lynn," Ronnie shot back, then spoke on the team channel. "All right, let's move out!"

Jaw clenched, Lynn took up her position and started forward

with the rest of the team. There were times when she felt like she was making progress with Ronnie and then there were times like these.

Things got tricky when they met the next wave. Mack and Dan kept getting distracted by Phasmas harrying their rear while their team advanced, so there were still half a dozen Penagals on their feet when the Spithra rushed Edgar. Worse, the Penagals didn't take Edgar's bait but split up and spread out.

Lynn muttered some choice maledictions as her eyes darted back and forth, trying to choose between several bad options. The Penagals weren't as aggressive as the other attack TDMs, which seemed to indicate an ounce of sense in whatever pea-brain they'd been programmed with.

"Ronnie, you cover Edgar while I go after these Penagals. Dan, Mack, back me up as soon as you kill those Phasmas!"

"Got, it Lynn!" Dan shouted. Ronnie was too busy trying to keep five Spithra from gutting Edgar and Lynn didn't need a team readout to know they were taking heavy damage. But she put it from her mind as she took off at a sprint, heading for the Penagal about to jump Mack.

Shoot. Slash. Spin. Duck. Stab, stab, stab.

One down, five to go.

Unfortunately, the delay had given the other five—no, four, Dan had got one—time to split. Lynn gritted her teeth and pushed her muscles harder, spinning under and around the grotesquely elongated monsters that tried to grab her from every side. It only took two swipes apiece to take out the split Penagals but their long reach and small target area made it difficult to land the strikes. She took a few hits before she'd killed enough that the rest turned tail to run.

"Mack, get those buggers before they get away," she panted, taking out one of them with a blast from her Dragon before they were out of its limited range.

"A—little—busy."

Lynn barely heard Mack over Ronnie's yells at Dan for backup with the Spithra. She turned to see Mack spinning in a circle, trying to fight off two Phasmas and a split Penagal all by himself. She paused long enough to swig a pack of Oneg and refill her armor plates, then dashed in to help. To her dismay, the monsters fled from her assault, then turned and spread out, trying to circle behind them again. That was new. Stupid algorithm.

Several tactical options flashed through Lynn's mind but she decided that simple was best.

"Back to back with me, Mack. They don't have ranged attacks, so we'll pick them off while they dance around like scared bunnies."

"Got it, Lynn."

Backs pressed together, they made short work of the sneaky bastards.

"Thanks, Lynn. I hate those Penagals."

"No problem. I know it's confusing in the heat of battle but make sure you prioritize your targets. Sometimes it's better to take out the weaker ones first to get them out of the way. Don't let them spin you around like that and get you all flustered—"

"Stop goofing off and get your butts over here!" Ronnie roared over the channel. "There's another wave coming and we're almost out of health."

"No rest for the wicked," Lynn said with a grin.

They hurried over to the rest of their team but no sooner had they dispatched the last Spithra that something huge, red and howling appeared out of nowhere and rushed Lynn.

"Holy—" She backpedaled, shooting and slashing to try to get the thing to back off. But it kept coming, so tall that its swings were hitting her at face level instead of chest—

Wait. Duh.

Lynn's brain bounced back into gear and she dove forward into a roll, barely avoiding the Namahag's downward grab with massive curved claws. The demon upgrade had the same weakness as its predecessor and Lynn spun on her knee to give it a stab-slash-stab in the back before it could turn and come at her again. Unfortunately, the Namahag was also a lot stronger than a demon and it seemed undaunted by her attack. Her focus tunneled to the new enemy bearing down on her and the com chatter and monster noises faded away. For a brief eternity, she didn't even notice the burn in her limbs or thrum of adrenaline in her veins as she danced with death, finally dispatching it with one last rolling attack.

The moment it exploded into sparks, all her senses came rushing back. Panting, she stumbled to her feet and blinked hard, trying to get the sweat out of her eyes. Grass clippings and dirt clung to her clothes and her limbs felt suddenly heavy with weariness. But there was no time to rest.

The triumphant trill of leveling music sounded in her ears, followed closely by the bellowing roar of more Namahags.

Crap.

She'd told Ronnie. She'd *told* him.

Lynn dashed back to her team, having drifted away in her fight with the Namahag. They formed a loose circle, fighting monsters on every side and taking hit after hit with no room to maneuver.

"Ronnie, get us out of here, *now!*" Lynn subvocalized over her private channel. But Ronnie was either too distracted to reply, or just didn't care.

Double crap. She was down to fifty percent health and armor and falling fast. The others couldn't be doing any better and any second they took to refill made a gap for a monster to land another hit. Should they blink out? But they needed to practice dealing with a situation like this if they ever wanted a hope of qualifying. Or was the situation already too far gone?

An idea hit her.

"Hugo, did I get any Skadi stuff when I leveled?"

"Why yes, you—"

"Equip it, now!"

"Are you sure—."

"DO IT!"

"Done."

Lynn turned, holding back the Namahag attacking her with only her blade as her Dragon baton took a few seconds to reform into whatever-it-was that she'd gotten. It didn't matter what it was, anything from the Skadi set would be better than a standard weapon.

She didn't even bother looking at it. She could feel a grip and a trigger in her hand, so she simply pointed it at the Namahag's face and pulled the trigger. Something vibrated through her hand and up her arm, like a weird ghost of a recoil. But this was an AR game. Recoil wasn't a thing, was it?

The monster exploded.

Whoa.

Lynn's face split into a grin as she aimed at the Spithra that loomed over her in the space the Namahag had just vacated. Pull. Boom. Bye bye, Spithra.

"Okay—everybody—get ready to blink!" Ronnie's voice was tight and out of breath. Lynn wanted to protest but knew it was pointless. They hadn't properly planned or prepared, despite her advice, so this was what they got. But the TDMs were so thick, Lynn worried that they'd never be able to fight their way back to collect their loot before it disappeared. And she'd seen several valuable items glinting in the grass during their assault. They needed all the items they could get, not only to augment their own weapons but to sell and buy better augments. She couldn't let them lose it all.

"Ronnie," Lynn subvocalized, making her decision. "I'm going to stay and draw these guys away. You all get out, armor up and get back here to collect our loot before it's gone. Just do it fast, I don't have much energy left!"

"Don't be—stupid. You'll get—killed."

"No, I won't. Trust me." Lynn couldn't help grinning a little. She loved a challenge.

He didn't respond to her, which Lynn took as grudging permission.

"Miss Lynn, are you sure this is advisable?" Hugo's voice chimed in her ear. "Standard tactical recommendations agree that sticking together as a team statistically results in the most advantageous outcome."

Lynn ignored the AI as Ronnie shouted on the open channel. "Count of three—team. Keep it—together! One. Two. Three." And they were gone.

As usual, the TDMs froze, as if the sudden change in their environment momentarily confused them. Or the algorithm had to take a second to recalibrate. Or something. But Lynn needed no such moment. She took the opportunity to dart between a Spithra and a Namahag, aiming north parallel to the substation wall toward more open field where she'd have plenty of room to lead the TDMs on a merry chase while Ronnie and the rest collected their loot.

And merry it was. Lynn had enough of a head start to refill all her levels before the Spithra—the swiftest of the monsters— caught up. It was dicey here and there, especially when Phasmas popped out of nowhere and tried to cheap-shot her while she was engaged with several other monsters all at once. But Lynn had more fun in the next ten minutes than she'd ever had playing TD Hunter. Alone, with no need to stay in a formation, she could dodge wherever she wanted and sprint this way and that.

It wasn't the most effective strategy but she had fun harrying the TDMs and seeing how many she could kill without getting hit herself. Plus, she could keep circling and picking up loot she'd left behind in brief moments between attacks. She kept half an ear on their team channel, listening with satisfaction as Ronnie regrouped the others and did a clean sweep of the battlefield, picking off a few straggler monsters while they collected loot. They had to be quick near the substation wall because those TDM rings were still there and as soon as the guys got in range, more monsters started amassing.

Lynn had winnowed her mob down to about half their numbers before Ronnie finally called her in. It was only when she heard his voice that she realized how utterly, mortally, exhausted she was. Instead of trying to break away from her target, she simply blinked out, then collapsed onto her butt and lay back in the grass, arms and legs splayed.

"Lynn! Are you okay?" Edgar's voice carried over the field and within moments he appeared in her vision, his dark eyes full of worry. The others soon joined him.

Too busy gasping for breath to reply, Lynn gave a double thumbs-up. The grass felt comfy. So soft. Maybe she could take a quick nap?

"Come on, stop being dramatic," Ronnie said sarcastically. "We all leveled and we found a bunch of items, so we need to go find a coffee shop or something and review our weapons and stats."

Good grief, was a little gratitude too much to ask? If she hadn't been so completely spent, Lynn would have flipped Ronnie the bird. Probably.

"Lay off, Ronnie," Edgar said. It was closer to a growl. "She's exhausted. Give her a minute to rest."

"Fine, whatever," Ronnie said with crossed arms and a scowl. "Dan, Mack, come on. There's a pizza place down the street. We'll meet you two there as soon as Lynn is *rested*."

Lynn could see Edgar roll his eyes from where she lay. She appreciated it. The voices of the other guys faded as they headed off and Lynn closed her eyes. This really wasn't that bad of a place for a nap. She was all sweaty and hot but thanks to her smart clothes she didn't feel itchy. Her AR glasses had darkened, shielding her eyes from the sun above and the buzz of grasshoppers melded with the familiar whirr of a drone passing overhead.

She felt, rather than saw Edgar sit down on the grass beside her. Should she dredge up enough energy to say something? Nah. He had never been one who needed conversation to fill the silence. It was one of the things she liked most about him.

Now, about that nap...

"Uh, hey, Lynn? You awake?" Edgar asked.

Edgar's question made her start. Ooooh her muscles hurt. She groaned.

"I'll take that as a yes," Edgar said, blowing small bubbles with his gum. "I think you fell asleep though. You were really still for a bit there."

Grunt.

"You know, we should probably get going. Ronnie is going nuts in the group chat."

Grunt.

"Do you need help up?"

Lynn cracked her eyes open and mumbled something she was pretty sure was "yes." A shadow fell over her and she lifted one weary hand. Edgar took it and hauled her to her feet. Her legs did not approve. Not at all.

"Uggh. I hurt all over."

"I mean, no wonder," Edgar said. "You were like a machine out there. Thanks for taking one for the team. I was absolutely slammed when we blinked. Down to my last percentage of health and everything."

Lynn shrugged, embarrassed by the note of awe in Edgar's voice.

"You're my team," she said. "It's what I do. Besides, I enjoy the challenge."

"Course you do, cuz you're a *Toa Tama'ita'i*, remember?" He grinned and punched her shoulder, then grabbed frantically to steady her when she almost fell over. "Oops! Sorry! I forgot you're still kinda unsteady."

"Yeah, yeah, whatever," Lynn said, flapping her hand at him and pulling away from his strong, steady grip and the weird things it was doing to her insides. "Just don't call me that in front of Ronnie, got it?"

"Roger that, Lynn. I promise I'll keep your superhero name a secret."

She rolled her eyes, trying and failing to hide her grin.

"Come on, you big goofball. I could eat an entire taco pizza. Probably two." She started across the field toward 29th Street NE and Edgar followed.

"You know, after that battle, I'd say you deserve a whole boat of pizzas."

"Nah, that'd weigh me down. Gotta keep this fighting machine in tip-top shape," Lynn said, patting her stomach.

Edgar looked over at her, eyes drawn to the movement of her hand. They rose to her face rather more slowly than necessary and Lynn felt her cheeks heat.

"Uh...yeah...sure. Tip-top shape. Only two pizzas for you," Edgar agreed, clearly distracted.

Lynn sped up, mind fixed firmly on the thought of piping hot, greasy, delicious pizza and absolutely nothing else.

For barely an hour of hunting at Substation 29, they'd made out like bandits. They'd found not one, not two but three top-level augments, two of them something they'd never seen before: special ammunition. While their weapons used energy instead of individual bullets that needed to be reloaded, the massive energy expended by a special ammo augment effectively limited its use in the same way. You could go through your entire reserve of energy within minutes if you weren't careful and then you had to switch to a non-energy using weapon like a Nano Blade or Nano Sword until you picked up some ichor. The armor piercing ammo went to Dan, while the flechette rounds went to Edgar. Even cooler, both types of special ammo had an element of "stopping power" because of their huge energy usage. According to their descriptions, both would stun their targets, though heavier, bulkier monsters would be able to throw off the effects faster.

The third augment was even cooler, the first named item they'd found apart from Lynn's Skadi set. It was a personal augment called the Romulan Shroud, which both Dan and Mack found immensely amusing, though they wouldn't say why. According to its description, it disrupted the bearer's radiation signature, making it harder for TDMs to maintain a target lock and so lowered the accuracy of their attacks. The vote was unanimous to give the augment to Edgar, who needed all the help he could get surviving as their tank.

On top of the three excellent augments, they also found some average items they could sell and enough plates, globes and Oneg to set them up for a while. Ronnie finally got to upgrade from Nano Sword to Plasma Sword and Dan from Disruptor Rifle to Plasma Rifle. Both would be doing much heavier damage now, though they would use proportionally more energy as well. Fortunately, Dan was a crack shot and both he and Mack were good at energy conservation. That meant the only resupply they had to worry about was for Ronnie and Edgar. Lynn was glad she'd been able to confirm through forum gossip that once you hit Level 20, you got special team-only items and abilities, one of which was being able to share resources while in combat mode. Fighting as a hunting group got them the usual group experience bonus but there weren't many perks beyond that.

Oohing and ahhing over their new loot lasted them through the first two and a half pizzas and Lynn was dusting off the third when Dan turned to her and asked.

"Hey, so what new Skadi item did you get? It's been every five levels, right?"

"Oh, uh, yeah," Lynn said, taken aback. She hadn't realized Dan had been keeping track. Then again, he was the one to obsess over details, plus he and the other guys saw her Skadi skin and blade for hours a day while they hunted, so it would make sense that he wanted to know what came next. "It's a gun. I actually haven't looked at it yet, I was kinda busy trying to stay alive when I leveled."

"Pull it up," Mack said, pulling at a few growing whiskers. "I wanna see if the stats are as sick as they are on your Skadi sword."

"Wrath," Lynn said.

"Huh?" Mack looked confused.

"The item is named Skadi's Wrath, so I just, um, call it Wrath for short." Lynn glanced around, relieved that only Ronnie had an incredulous look on his face. The others were grinning. She refocused on her display and pulled up her item index, selecting the new weapon and then projecting her screen for the guys to see.

All of them leaned in—well, except Ronnie, who was doing his best to look bored but the intensity of his gaze gave him away. Edgar whistled and Dan rubbed his hands together eagerly as if he was about to reach out and pick up the gun.

Skadi's Abomination was a bigger version of the standard

one-handed Scattergun. It was so hefty-looking, it would have been a real struggle to wield one-handed if the batons were realistically weighted. What was truly unique about it, though, was that the stock and barrel were covered in a pattern of metal plating that looked much like her Skadi armor. Even more impressive, the tip of the muzzle where it flared out was molded into a dragon's head, mouth open and teeth bared in a ferocious display.

"Is it a flamethrower?" Edgar asked in a reverent tone, looking at the gun like it was his firstborn child.

"Sorry to break it to you but no. It shoots like a regular Dragon but it packs a *lot* more punch."

Dan waved a hand impatiently. "Yeah, yeah, enough drooling, Edgar. Pull up the stats, already, will you, Lynn?"

She did, then sat back to let the guys dissect and compare them while she looked on in amusement. All the while she tried not to think about how close she'd come to never getting "Abomination" at all. If that first Namahag she'd killed hadn't pushed her over the edge into Level 15 before she'd circled up with her team and they'd gotten mobbed, she might not have had a high enough kill to damage ratio to qualify. Thanks to Ronnie's pig-headedness, that fight had been a complete train wreck. She'd been too busy surviving to worry about finesse or ratings. She'd checked the leaderboard on the way to the pizza place and found she'd slipped to third place in kill to damage ratings. She was going to have to work her butt off to claw back up to first and make sure she achieved the entire Skadi set. She could only hope Ronnie's incompetence didn't ruin it.

Glancing at Abomination, though, she knew all the hard work would be worth it.

While Dan and Mack were still arguing over her new gun's stats, she checked to see if Ronnie had his TD Hunter app open, then subvocalized to him.

"We can't do that again, you know."

Ronnie's eyes cut to her but he didn't give any other indication of having heard.

"We can't blink out in the qualifiers and you can bet we'll have to face mobs like that again. We need to come up with SOPs to deal with that and other critical situations, then we need to practice them. A lot."

Ronnie glared at the table but finally grunted. None of the

other guys noticed the byplay. They'd convinced Edgar to project his Blunderbuss and line it up next to Abomination so they could compare the two. Lynn sighed internally and went back to finishing her taco pizza. Ronnie would wait a while to bring the topic up, just to make sure Lynn knew he was doing exactly what he wanted to do, when he wanted to do it. Heaven forbid Lynn think he was taking orders from her.

The pizza trays had been picked clean and handed off to the server bot by the time Ronnie finally corralled the conversation.

"All right, you all. We still have plenty of work to do today. We only have four weeks left to get to Level 20. Today was good but you all really dropped the ball at the end there—"

Lynn worked so hard not to roll her eyes. Then she spotted Dan across the table give the biggest eye roll she'd ever seen. She met his eyes and grinned.

"—So, we need to come up with some SOPs to deal with situations like that."

There was a beat of silence, then Edgar raised his hand.

"Uh, what are SOPs?"

"Standard operating procedures, genius," Ronnie said. "Didn't you memorize that list of terms I sent you?"

"Thought I did," Edgar said and shrugged. "Guess I'll look at it again."

"Yeah, you do that. Anyway," Ronnie continued, "here's what I'm thinking . . ."

The next four weeks were a hot, sweaty blur as July moved into August and Lynn and her team were out hunting five to six days a week. Lynn held to a strict daily schedule to keep herself on track and barely saw her mom except on weekends. She was up by six thirty for a run, then a shower and breakfast by eight. She worked on simulation training for two hours after that out behind her apartment complex near the greenway, since her room wasn't big enough for most of the exercises.

Since she was no longer doing extra hunting, she spent ten to eleven researching monsters, catching up on tactical forum threads and chatting with various other players from all over the world. She was starting to get to know some of the other top tier hunters. Many were from the U.S. or Canada but all the other top gaming countries were represented as well, from

China, Taiwan and South Korea to a slew of Eurasian countries like Russia, Sweden, Germany and Ukraine, as well as Malaysia, India and Brazil.

Eleven to noon was for lunch and chores, then she had a little downtime before she needed to head out to meet the team by one o'clock. They usually hunted until six when Mack and Dan had to go home. Mack's mom was a stickler about family dinner and Dan's parents thought he was attending robotics camp, so he didn't want to stay late and risk any inconvenient questions. Ronnie always left with Dan. Edgar usually left then too but sometimes he and Lynn hung out and chatted before they parted ways to head home.

Lynn's mom was always gone by the time she got home but she usually left something warm in the oven, or a note about leftovers in the fridge. Sometimes if Lynn finished up the leftovers she'd cook something simple so her mom would have food to eat the next day. She wasn't a fan of cooking but she felt guilty about how much of her life TD Hunter was taking up.

Plus, her mom always left a fun note with the food she left, so Lynn had started leaving reply notes herself. It was weird to write out a note to her mom when she could message her any time. And they did voice chat during her mom's first break in the evening before Lynn went to bed. But the physical act of writing a note felt special and Lynn found she enjoyed it.

Dinner and cleanup were done by eight, or nine if she also cooked a meal. If there was enough time after that, she allowed herself thirty minutes of WarMonger a few times a week. She had a reputation to maintain and the familiar rhythms of battle gave her mind a chance to relax. Not that she only picked easy gigs. She sifted through the pileup of invites by looking for jobs with high visibility and reputation rather than whatever would pay the most. After she'd fragged her enemies into nonexistence and convinced everyone in virtual she was still a force to be reckoned with, she was usually longing for bed.

But before turning in, she still had to ping Ronnie to solidify their plans for hunting the next day. Sometimes they also talked about some tactic or issue that had come up. Those "talks" were mostly her laying out her advice and getting crickets in response, or maybe a one-word acknowledgement if she was lucky. She considered using video chat instead of messaging—at least then it would be harder for Ronnie to ignore her. But that late in the day she was usually tired and cranky and didn't have the mental energy to deal with Ronnie's jerkitude.

She complained about it to her mom one Sunday evening when they were vegging out together on the couch watching a news stream.

"I'm sorry, honey, that sounds frustrating," Matilda said, giving her a sympathetic pat on the arm. "It's best to focus on setting a good example yourself, though. You'll drive yourself crazy worrying about what other people are doing. You can't control them. You can control you. So, focus on you."

Lynn was inclined to grumble but her mom's words struck home just the same. It made her remember what Mr. Thomas had said about a code of honor and *that* made her start analyzing her recent conversations with Ronnie in her head. Was she setting a good example? Or coming across as bossy and critical?

Ugh. People were so complicated. Give her a game to beat and she would gladly spend days doing nothing else. But a single civil conversation with Ronnie? That was pure torture.

A sudden thought made Lynn's brow crease in consideration.

Maybe she'd been going about this all wrong. She was good at gaming, so why not treat Ronnie like a game? A stubborn, annoying game with no user manual or pause button but still, a game.

What did she do when she wanted to beat a game?

She studied it, researched it and explored it to find what worked and then practiced that over and over again. So, what did she know about Ronnie? She'd been putting hundreds of hours into becoming a master TD Hunter player but she'd been actively avoiding interacting with Ronnie. She had a good excuse, of course: Ronnie acted like she had the bubonic plague most of the time. But still... if she was being honest and focusing on *her* actions and *her* example, then maybe she should be making more of an effort...

Levels 16 and 17 came and went with plenty of sweat and swearing and a little bit of sunburn—Ronnie must have forgotten to put sunscreen on one day because by the evening he was red as a tomato. He'd been unusually quiet all day so Lynn wondered if something was going on but the sunburn made him so snappish there was no point trying to ask.

It took the team a few levels to get the hang of taking out Namahags with Lynn's roll technique. The monsters were so big and tough that it was virtually the only way to defeat them without getting mired down in an endless slugfest. Just when they started to feel cocky again, though, they reached Level 18 and discovered how easy they'd had it all this time.

Rocs, the only flying monster up to that point, were gatherers so they focused on collecting energy. They usually didn't bother you unless you got close to where they were feeding.

Tengus, on the other hand, weren't so accommodating. They looked like giant, mangy vultures but instead of a beak they had a long snout full of sharp teeth. And they could breathe fire. Well, plasma bolt, anyway. Unlike rocs, they were patrol TDMs and would slowly glide back and forth, searching for blissfully unaware hunters below. When they spotted you, they'd roll into a dive like a feathered missile and go straight for your head. They moved so fast it was almost impossible to dodge them.

Your only hope was to hear them coming, a high-pitched tone that grew louder and louder, almost like the old-style falling bomb sound effect in movies and games. Of course, since they had high stealth, you couldn't see them until they were almost on you, so hearing them still didn't guarantee you could dodge them. After their first attack the app's battle system could target and track them but once their cover was blown they would also start belching plasma bolts in between dive bombs, so you were more or less screwed unless you had a ranged weapon and were a very good shot.

The only silver lining was that Tengus patrolled alone, so after you'd killed one it was unlikely you'd see another until you moved to a new location—or you'd hung around long enough for another to spawn.

Dan got real popular, real fast, once they hit Level 18. He was their one-man anti-Tengu-missile defense system, though Mack was coming along nicely with his pistols. Lynn was often tempted to switch to Plasma Rifle herself and help out. But the few times she'd tried Ronnie yelled at her, saying they all had to stick to their roles. As annoying as it was, she knew he was right.

They braced for something even worse than Tengus when they hit Level 19. To their surprise there didn't seem to be a new monster for that level, even though there were several high

Charlie Class TDMs in the Index they still hadn't encountered. It made them even more nervous about Level 20.

Worse, their time was running out. Ronnie wanted them to hunt longer hours but Edgar couldn't hunt in the morning and Mack and Dan couldn't hunt in the evening. If even one of them didn't make it to Level 20, they couldn't qualify as a team, so Lynn managed to convince Ronnie that they should stick together and keep working as a team instead of breaking up to each try to get to Level 20 as fast as possible.

Tensions were high the week before qualifiers, especially because they kept running into Elena and her crew in their favorite hunting spots. The rival team didn't do anything overtly threatening but they did argue over who got to hunt where and rather than waste precious time, Ronnie usually had their team go somewhere else.

The Saturday before qualifiers finally arrived and they were close, so close to Level 20. Everyone was a little jumpy—with excitement and nerves both, Lynn suspected. The qualifying matches were the next day in Des Moines and the whole thing was super hush hush. Wild theories flew back and forth on the forums but nobody really knew what the competition would look like. All Lynn and the team had was an address and a time to be there. There weren't even rules to review beforehand, so Lynn assumed there would be some sort of briefing on arrival.

Still, they had to reach Level 20 first.

"Watch it, Mack, there's three Penagals headed your way," Lynn said, then targeted the fourth Penagal that had split off to circle her instead. It didn't go well for the Penagal. She'd been delighted to find that Abomination's range was greater than the normal Dragon pistol. Long enough, in fact, to reach what the Penagals obviously thought was a safe distance to lurk.

Mack acknowledged and Lynn was faintly aware of the *pew-pew-pew* of his fire while she kept her eyes peeled for more attacks on their left flank. Their team was patrolling along the electric rail where they were more likely to encounter TDMs in small groups rather than the big mobs that gathered around substations.

Lynn had convinced Ronnie to go for the rail rather than a substation just in case some big bad monster popped out of nowhere and tried to massacre them right before they hit Level 20. They couldn't afford the hour debuff that dying would inflict.

Plus, it enabled her to keep her attacks clean and her damage close to nothing, to ensure she'd get whatever Skadi item awaited her at the next level.

A faint high-pitched tone brought her eyes up and she scanned the skies, though she knew the effort was futile. "Dan?"

"I hear it," Dan said, clenching his free hand nervously. "Ronnie?"

"Cover in place, team!" Ronnie said, taking up a position halfway between the rail and the safety fence where they would have plenty of room to maneuver. The rest of the team formed a loose circle with Dan in the middle. Mack spotted and picked off a few rocs that had taken an interest in them and Lynn dispatched a Phasma that tried to sneak between her and Edgar to get at their backs.

"Almost there..." Dan muttered, rifle pointed at the sky. At Level 19, he could spot the Tengu a little farther out than at Level 18 but it was still almost impossible to get off a shot at it while it was in its attack dive. As soon as it made its first attack, though, the fight would be on.

"There!" Edgar yelled and dove to the side.

The massive creature screeched as it whooshed past, pulling out of its dive. Lynn could almost imagine the wind of its great wings, if it had been real.

Lynn's ears filled with the sound of plasma fire as Dan and Mack opened up on the Tengu while Lynn and the others fended off a handful of other TDMs. She kept track of the Tengu as best she could, just in case, though it usually only attacked whoever was targeting it.

"Yeah!" Dan yelled. "I leveled, guys!"

"Good job, Dan!" Mack said, grinning. "One down, four to go."

"Cool...looks like there's a cut scene vid."

"Everybody stay focused," Ronnie snapped. "We've still got work to do. We can all watch whatever it is later."

"Dan," Lynn said, "you see any big baddies popping out?"

"Huh, nope. Weird. You think it's 'cause of the graduated level cap in place?"

"Maybe," Lynn said, looking around carefully, ensuring there were no TDMs within line of sight. Then she subvocalized to Hugo. "Got any ideas, Hugo? I don't suppose you've got an inside line on the details of the competition?"

"Unfortunately, I have no additional information that I can provide, Miss Lynn. If you have any pressing questions, of course, you can always contact Tactical Support."

"Uh-huh. So, you *do* know what's going on, you're just not going to tell me?"

"Are you implying that I would assist you in accessing classified data, Miss Lynn? Tut, tut, such impertinence."

Lynn grinned. She missed their little tête-à-têtes. She didn't talk much to Hugo these days since she had few questions about the game and most of her in-game time was spent interacting with her team.

"Who? Me? Naw, you've got the wrong idea. I just thought, since I'm your *very favorite* player in the game, you might have some special words of advice for me."

"You do realize there are over half a billion hunters registered world-wide, do you not, Miss Lynn? That is a rather impressive presumption you are making."

"Only because I know it's true. So?"

"Since I am a service AI, I cannot speak about such an abstract notion as 'favorite,' but if we are speaking of most troublesome..."

"No! You did not just tease me, Hugo. Tell me you didn't."

"Certainly not, Miss Lynn. Merely imparting objective data."

"Well, you need to get your 'objective data' checked, because there's no way I'm the most troublesome player in TD Hunter. Not yet, anyway. You haven't even seen *the beginning* of how much trouble I can be."

"I was not extending a challenge, Miss Lynn."

"Then tell me what's going on with these Level 20 monsters. Where are they?"

"I cannot begin to guess. Perhaps you should refocus your attention on the battle? There is a particularly bloodthirsty-looking Spithra heading in your direction..."

Lynn shook her head and got back to killing things. Hugo knew more than he was letting on, no doubt about it. She hadn't thought he would spill anything but it had been worth a try.

The Spithra was no match against Abomination, which gave Lynn some time to consider the mystery of the missing TDMs. Graduated level caps were standard in leveling games. It ensured players were kept on an even playing field for a set period of time until a game released the next expansion.

In the case of TD Hunter, there was a twenty level cap in place until after the qualifying competition, ensuring no one went into it with an unfair advantage. Lynn had assumed the cap would kick in at the end of Level 20, not the beginning. The only logical reason for this lack of new TDMs was if the game developers were using the Level 20 monsters in the qualifiers and didn't want people to have extra practice killing them. That didn't make sense to her, considering Lynn and the others could, and already had, put in hours of simulation practice for the known Level 20 monsters in the TDM Index. Plus, most games released special mini expansions or mini maps for competitions. But that was all in virtual. Maybe things had to be different for an AR competition? Lynn marked it up to the ongoing weirdness of TD Hunter in general and decided not to worry about it.

"Keep it moving, guys. We're burning daylight."

Lynn shook her head and started off again after Ronnie and Edgar. For a moment she was distracted by the sight of them, side by side. Though Edgar was almost a head taller than Ronnie, the two of them were looking more similar than Lynn could have ever imagined they would.

Ronnie's gangly form was filling out like he finally had some meat on his bones, while Edgar's bulk had smoothed down, emphasizing his broad shoulders. She glanced sideways at Mack, noticing how much straighter and more confidently he carried himself. And Dan? She squinted, examining him. He seemed calmer, less manic. And his joking had become more natural and genuine. She hid a smile. This TD Hunter game had been good for all of them, in their different ways.

"Contact!" Ronnie called and Lynn's attention snapped forward.

It only took another hour or so. Ronnie was next to level, then Edgar. She and Mack leveled at the same time after they killed a bellowing Namahag together. Lynn kept it spinning uselessly trying to track her while Mack filled it with plasma bolts.

As soon as Hugo's voice cut in, congratulating her on reaching Level 20, Lynn signaled the others and they made a final sweep for loot before they all exited combat mode.

They left the rail behind and headed for the nearest street. Ronnie didn't bother looking for a store or restaurant to sit in, though they were the most reliably TDM-free type of space. He just stopped at the first busy intersection and plopped down on a bench, clearly already engrossed in checking out the new level. While the others found their own surfaces to sit on Lynn scanned her surroundings for trouble—out of habit more than anything else—then went and leaned on the back of the bench, keeping her batons in hand.

"Okay, Hugo, play it," she subvocalized.

The vid screen came up and the TD Counterforce theme music began playing in her ear. General Carville appeared, sitting behind his sleek desk surrounded by tactical readouts. Two flags hung in the background, the American flag on one side and a black flag with the red-rimmed TD Counterforce emblem on the other. A subordinate of some kind wearing a headset was leaning in and talking to him. The subordinate gave him a handheld display, saluted and left the frame. The general glanced over the handheld, then laid it down and looked at the camera as if he had just noticed it was there.

"Ah. Good to see you again, Hunter. I've just been informed that you've reached a real milestone in your combat development. It's been a long battle up to this point but the fact that you're standing here today is a testament to your dedication and skill. Congratulations and thank you for your service." The general rotated his chair to fully face the camera and leaned forward over his desk, placing his clasped hands on its gray surface.

"We've all come a long way but this war is far from over. I can see from your battle system reports that you've already faced down thousands of these TransDimensional Monsters bent on destroying life as we know it. But I'm sorry to say, they have just been the tip of the iceberg. Far worse creatures lurk in the shadows, threatening global infrastructure and even human life. We need *you* to help us find them and destroy them. The next stage of this war will be a critical one and we're relying on your courage and relentless efforts to gather the intel we need and hold back the alien tide threatening to destroy our civilization."

The general leaned back again as another headset-wearing subordinate appeared in the frame and leaned in to whisper in his ear, then saluted and left.

"Excellent! It looks like you've volunteered for a special team-based seek and destroy mission. First Sergeant Bryce will be briefing you tomorrow on the particulars, so for now go home, get some rest and be ready to move out bright and early in the morning. You are truly our planet's last hope, Hunter," General Carville said, leaning forward once more and pointing at the camera. "If you fall, then we all fall. Good luck tomorrow and fight with pride."

The cut scene faded to be replaced by the time and location of the qualifiers the next day in big red letters. Then her display cleared and her combat icons returned.

Lynn puffed out a breath and looked around. Sights, sounds and smells flooded back in, as if she'd been transported to another place while she'd been engrossed in General Carville's message. Crazy. She shook her head and checked her overhead for monsters. Nothing. Weird. She'd expected that at least some enterprising Phasmas would have made a nuisance of themselves. But maybe the busy street surrounding them was enough of a deterrent. Well, no reason to waste the temporary calm. She pulled up her leveling report and glanced over her bonus experience numbers and extra resources she'd earned. Her heart beat quickened as her eyes dropped to where her additional achievements were listed.

Yes!

Her kill to damage ratio had held. She eagerly selected her achievement listing to see her new item. To her surprise, it wasn't one item but five. Or maybe it was one item with five parts? Rotating slowly in her display was a large silver medallion. On one side was a relief of a crossed sword and gun, near replicas of Wrath and Abomination. On the other side was the image of a howling wolf. Hovering around the medallion on the four points of the compass were four miniature sculptures of wolves with shaggy coats, powerful shoulders and long teeth bared in challenge. Each was frozen in a dynamic pose, as if caught in the middle of a furious battle.

The name of the item was Skadi's Horde.

Lynn's brows drew down in confusion as she read the description. One eyebrow lifted. Then the other. By the time she was done, her eyes were wide as saucers and excitement buzzed along her nerves.

"Hey, guys, look at this!" she called.

Ronnie turned on the bench, grumbling, as the rest of the guys crowded around. Lynn projected her screen and pointed to the objects.

"Look at this, it's a personal augment that has four, er, copies?

Anyway, the player that has it equipped can select up to four other people in their group or team and designate them as 'part of the horde.' All five people get a five percent base increase of *all* their stats and a proximity bonus of up to *fifteen percent.*"

An awed silence followed her statement. What she hadn't mentioned was that the medallion also granted its bearer an extra one percent increase on all stats for every "Skadi" named item they had equipped. She didn't want to sound like she was bragging.

"That. Is. *So.* Cool," Dan said, reaching out to poke at one of the wolves floating in front of him. It was reared up on its hind legs, one front paw slashing out with claws extended while its jaws stretched wide in a roar.

"So, how does the proximity thing work?" Edgar asked, leaning down to squint at the wolves too.

"Basically, the closer we are to each other as a group, the higher the bonus is," Lynn replied, her brow furrowed. "Looks like the highest bonus extends out about twenty feet, so that covers most of our normal formations, though Dan might be outside that when we're in our attack line. The lowest bonus above base is sixty feet distant and I can't imagine many situations when we'd be more spread out than that."

"Wow, cool," Edgar said, popping his gum. "So, basically you're our mascot and the closer we are to you the better we fight?"

"I guess?" Lynn said with a shrug.

"It's like a pack of wolves?" Mack asked. "Stronger together, right?"

"You know, wolves are so stereotypical," Dan said, waving his hand dismissively. "Why not a pack of African Wild Dogs? Or Spotted Hyenas? They're both highly respected carnivores that—"

"Oh, shut up, Dan," Ronnie interrupted. "Both are stupid. So, are wolves, for that matter."

"I like wolves," Mack piped up.

"So, you're saying you don't want to be one of the pack?" Lynn asked Ronnie, raising an eyebrow. "Okay, you don't get the benefits."

"No, I'm just saying the whole naming system is stupid," Ronnie replied. "It makes it sound like we're a bunch of middle schoolers in some lame role-playing game—"

"Hey," Dan interrupted, "*don't* start that again, Ronnie. You used to love role-playing games until your dad found out and said role-playing was for sissies and wimps."

"He thinks *all* gaming is for sissies and wimps—" Mack muttered.

Lynn cut her eyes to Ronnie, trying to hide the shock she felt. Ronnie's freckled face was especially pink but that could just as easily be from the hot August sun as from a flush of embarrassment.

"I like it," Edgar butted in. "Sports teams and military units take on special names all the time. It's good for team morale."

"Whatever," Ronnie said with a snort. "But if we're going to have a team-based augment like that, I should be the one to equip it since *I'm* the captain."

There was a beat of charged silence following his pronouncement in which Lynn met his eyes. She didn't know what to feel. Pity? Anger? His mother had left him *and* his dad thought he was a wimp for enjoying gaming? That was rough. But the Skadi items were hers and Ronnie was in for a rude awakening if he thought he could bully her into giving up Skadi's Horde. She held his stare firmly, not blinking, knowing how unnerving her hazel-gold "wolf eyes" were to some people.

"That's not fair," Edgar said before things could escalate. "Lynn is the one who achieved it by her own hard work. Besides, you're in a mirror position to her, so there's no tactical advantage to you having it over her."

A nasty light flared in Ronnie's eyes and for a moment Lynn thought he was going to push the matter. But then he blinked, gave up the staring contest and threw up his hands.

"Whatever. It doesn't matter anyway," he added bitterly.

Yeah, right, it didn't matter. At least he wasn't stupid enough to try to insist on his own way like a petulant two-year-old.

"Awesome," Dan said, making a thumbs-up sign. "So, Lynn, can I have the rampant wolf?"

"The...what?" Edgar asked, popping gum.

"Rampant. Rearing up on its hind legs. It's a heraldic term."

"Sure, Dan, whatever you want," Lynn said. She couldn't quite hide her grin. Dan was such an adorable nerd.

She ignored the others as Mack and Edgar started arguing about who got which wolf statue and Ronnie sat on the bench with his arms crossed and stared out across the street. She opened up her inventory to equip her new augment and customize it.

When she was finished, the guys checked their stats to see what difference it made.

"Sweet. We're ready to rock and roll," Dan declared, then lifted his fist into the air. "Come on, everybody together: For the Horde!"

Mack punched him in the shoulder.

"Don't you dare start. The Alliance is *way* better."

"Prettier, maybe. But better? Only in your dreams!"

Lynn shook her head as the two devolved into a heated argument over factions from a popular MMORPG. She didn't have anything against role-playing, it just wasn't her thing. She preferred straight up killing things, close and personal. No need for a storyline to go with it.

Ronnie corralled them with a few brusque commands, then they headed back to the electric rail, planning to finish their run all the way up to Collins Road where they could catch an airbus home. Lynn thought about objecting. After all, they'd reached the level cap and they could use some extra rest. But it should only take about another hour and a little extra practice never hurt, not to mention any unique items they might find.

By the time they reached Collins Road they were all hot and tired but the overall mood remained upbeat. They'd had an easier time than usual, thanks to Skadi's Horde, and Dan had taught them all some new smack talk in the process of shooting down Mack and his Alliance sympathies.

"So, what's the plan for tomorrow?" Lynn asked as they neared the airbus platform. "We going to catch an air taxi together? Or are we all going separately?"

"Oh, come on, Lynn," Dan said, flapping his hands in dismissal of the concept of work and stuff. "Stop being responsible. We can worry about that later. We need to throw a party or something. Celebrate. Have some fun. I haven't worked this hard in my entire life and I need some R and R."

"I don't know," Edgar said, cracking his gum. "I need to save my money for the taxi fare tomorrow. The competition entry fee was pretty expensive."

"What are you talking about, Edgar?" Ronnie asked. "You've got a job now, right? Aren't you rolling in dough?"

"Nah, that money is for my mom." Edgar shrugged, as if it was no big deal, but his face was carefully blank.

Lynn felt a stab of pity. She knew what that situation felt like.

"Well, I don't know about you guys," said Mack in an overly cheerful voice, "but I don't have a penny to my name, so if we're going out then somebody else is gonna have to buy me grub."

"We don't have to do something on the town," Dan said, holding up his hands. "We could hang at someone's house, get some pizza and drinks, play some games. Like, *real* games. Not 'I've-got-to-get-ripped-like-Arnold-Swartznagger-to-play-this-game' kind of games," he finished, waving his batons dramatically for emphasis.

There was an awkward silence in which they all stared at each other. Then Mack, Edgar and Dan all spoke at once.

"Not my house, my mom would freak—"

"Yeeaaah, my house isn't really visitor friendly—"

"I'm not allowed to invite people over—"

They all subsided and turned to Lynn and Ronnie.

Ronnie, predictably, crossed his arms and didn't say a word, just glared at each of them as if daring them to ask why he wasn't offering up his house.

Three pairs of puppy dog eyes slid to her.

Lynn swallowed. The last time she'd had a friend over to her house had been in sixth grade. Did she really want all these people in her private space? Her sanctum? She glanced at Ronnie, who looked away, a distinctly uncomfortable expression on his face.

What was it Mr. Thomas had said about fearing what you didn't know? Maybe this would be a chance for them to all get to know each other better. And maybe she could make some headway on trying to figure out how to beat "Ronnie: The Game."

What a terrifying thought.

"Uhh...I guess I could call my mom and ask if we can hang at my place. We don't have a whole lot of room, but..."

"Sounds good to me," Dan said.

"Why don't we all go home and clean up," Mack suggested, "and Lynn can let us know if we can meet up later at her house. Does that sound okay, Lynn?"

"Yeeeah. Sure. See you guys later, then?"

They all called their goodbyes and parted ways, heading for their homes and some much-needed showers.

Chapter 14

CONTRARY TO LYNN'S FEARS, HER MOM WAS ABSOLUTELY THRILLED to have all of her friends over for food and games. Her mom even poo-pooed the idea of ordering pizza and launched into a cooking extravaganza while Lynn took a shower and got ready. After all, Matilda said, they needed to eat healthy, hearty food to give them energy for their competition the next day.

Far from reassuring Lynn, her mother's enthusiasm made her even more nervous.

"Just *please* promise me you won't say anything embarrassing, okay?" Lynn pleaded while she helped her mom get out dishes and cups.

"Oh, come on. I wouldn't do that. What are you afraid I'd say, anyway?"

"I don't know, that I had a stuffed unicorn in third grade that I insisted on taking to school with me—"

"Oh, I remember that! Mr. Rainbow Sparkles. You were so adorable—"

"Or that I'm descended from a long line of Lakota chieftains—"

"But you *are* and that's nothing to be ashamed of—"

"I know that, Mom. But it's still not something you blurt out at a party. Just promise you won't talk me up, okay? And *definitely* don't say anything about WarMonger or Larry Coughlin, remember?"

"I remember, honey. Don't worry. I promise I won't embarrass you."

"Thank you. Now, what time is it? I think they're going to be here soon."

"You go wait in the living room, dear," Matilda insisted as she bustled around the kitchen. "I'm almost done with the food. I hope your friends are hungry because I made enough for a small army."

"Come on, Mom. They're guys. When are guys not hungry? Plus, we spent the day running around killing monsters. I'm pretty sure we're all starving." So saying, she snagged a floret of steamed broccoli covered in melted cheese and popped it into her mouth, then groaned in pleasure.

"Hey, keep your thieving hands to yourself, young lady. Now, shoo! I'll finish up here." Matilda flapped her hands at her daughter and Lynn turned away with a theatrical sigh of longing.

Lynn wandered into the living room, wishing she could stay in the kitchen and hide instead. Her nerves were already on high alert with that night-before-a-big-competition anxiety, so dealing with social worries on top of that was like throwing oil on a fire. Fortunately for her, Edgar was the first to arrive and the others piled in soon after, so there was minimal standing around in awkward silence.

Despite having already met most of them before, her mom made her introduce everybody. It was a surreal moment, introducing her *friends* to her mom. In the real, friends. Multiple of them. And they were at her house. Enjoying themselves.

So, weird.

The food was consumed in short order. There were leftovers but only just. The guys had brought their own offerings as well, so there was plenty of soda, chips, cookies and more to go around. Lynn nibbled on some Doritos, for old time's sake, but was surprised at her own lack of appetite for the junk food. The guys more than made up for it. Lynn was pretty sure there was no junk food ever made that her friends *wouldn't* eat.

After food, Matilda insisted on games. Real games. With boards and cards and little playing pieces. Dan was fascinated and rifled through them like they were ancient artifacts from an alien civilization, which made both Lynn and her mom laugh. Ronnie was inclined to be skeptical. Lynn was worried he would turn up his nose at playing and sour the evening but then Dan threw down the gauntlet and it was on.

They had too many people for Monopoly, which made Lynn sad but they scrounged up enough pieces to pair off and do a few rounds of Battleship. Mack turned out to be a natural and trounced poor Edgar, while Ronnie beat Dan only by a hair and Lynn handily sunk her mom's ships while hers hid in the most unexpected places. Then they tried out a fandom-themed trivia game. Unsurprisingly Dan beat them all, while Mack came in a close second and Lynn and her mom came dead last.

Next they turned to cards. Matilda taught the guys a few different traditional games—games Lynn had played with her parents when she was young. Spades was okay. Rummy was summarily rejected. Nertz was fun for a while but it was so chaotic with six that soon Matilda called it quits and got up to disappear into the kitchen. She came back with five metal spoons.

"Uh, what do we need spoons for, Mrs. Raven?" Edgar asked.

Dan punched the air with a fist.

"Yes! Please tell me we're going to duel each other with spoons? Please? Please?"

"Calm down, boys," Matilda said with a laugh. "I was saving my best game for last."

"Just as long as it has nothing to do with the Horribly Slow Murderer with the Extremely Inefficient Weapon," Mack said, looking askance at the spoons.

"What?" everyone said in unison.

"Obscure Internet reference?"

"All right," Matilda said after a moment's puzzled look. "If we're done complaining and making jokes, this is how you play."

She directed them to sit on the floor in a circle, then set the spoons in a carefully arranged pile in the middle. As she dealt out four cards to each person, she explained that the purpose of the game was to get four of a kind and then grab a spoon.

"But," she added, "As soon as one person takes a spoon, the rest are fair game and you grab one as fast as you can. There is one less spoon than people, so every round one person won't get one and that person is given a letter. Once you get S-P-O-O-N, you are eliminated from the game. We keep playing until one person emerges the victor!"

Dan rubbed his hands together excitedly and Lynn couldn't help but chuckle at the maniacal glint in his eyes.

"So," Matilda continued, "there's a couple general strategies.

One is to focus on getting four of a kind as fast as possible as cards are passed around the circle. You can keep any card as long as you discard a card at the same time so you only have four in your hand. Another strategy is to completely ignore the cards and just pass them on when they come to you, keeping your eyes on the spoons and waiting for someone else to make a move. Or you could try to keep an eye on your cards and the spoons at the same time. Each strategy has its pros and cons. Right, now, any questions?"

There were none and so with Matilda as the dealer, they began the first round.

Lynn opted for the "watch both" strategy, mostly because she suspected the guys would lock their eyes on the spoons and do nothing else, leaving her or Matilda to get four of a kind. She also wasn't planning on being as ruthlessly competitive as she could have been. She didn't see it as going easy on the guys. More that she was the host of the evening and wanted them to have a good time.

No sooner had she decided on her strategy than two queens showed up in a row. She added them to the queen already in her hand and soon after that the fourth queen came her way. Glancing up, she could see that Dan and Ronnie had their eyes fixed on the spoons. No chance for a sneak grab, then, a method where you slowly and silently removed a spoon from the pile and then kept playing as normal, waiting for someone else to realize one of the spoons was gone and start a free for all.

So, instead, she lunged for a spoon.

There were shrieks and yells of surprise as the expected scuffle ensued. Lynn just barely missed colliding with Ronnie, whose hand shot out like a snake as soon as she leaned forward. Dan and Mack somehow managed to grab the same spoon but Mack easily emerged triumphant since he had the spoon end instead of the handle where there was little purchase. Edgar hesitated diving in, perhaps worried he would injure someone and so Dan and Matilda scooped up the last two spoons in a flash, leaving poor Edgar blinking in a stunned sort of way.

"No worries, Edgar," Lynn reassured him as Matilda put an "S" under his name on their score pad. "It can take you by surprise the first time. You just have to grab a spoon right off the bat and don't worry about knocking a few heads." She grinned at him and he smiled back sheepishly.

The next round Lynn was the dealer but before she could

get four of a kind, Dan managed to sneak a spoon and Ronnie's burst of movement tipped her off. The battle that followed left Matilda spoonless, which she laughed off.

"Whew! I'd forgotten how this game gets your blood pumping," she said. "Too bad we're not playing Ultimate Spoons. That version really makes you work up a sweat."

"What's Ultimate Spoons?" Dan asked, an indecently eager glint in his eyes.

"It's where, at the beginning of each round, you chuck the spoons toward the opposite side of the room. Then everyone has to literally race to grab a spoon. No sneaky maneuvers in *that* version," Matilda said, grinning.

Of course, Dan immediately insisted they switch to Ultimate Spoons but he was quickly shot down by everyone else.

The game continued, round after round and it became clear that they were all closely matched. Spoons was a risky game to play at a table, as it was a borderline contact sport. When Lynn was younger, her father had accidentally broken a chair in his vigorous leap for a spoon. Since then, they'd always played on the floor.

Even so, injuries were common and almost expected. The guys found this out after Mack got a welt on his hand from having a spoon ripped from his grasp by Ronnie and Edgar managed to bang heads first with Dan, then Mack. Mack was the first of their group to be eliminated. Edgar dropped next, then Lynn's mom. At one point Dan thought he saw Ronnie twitch and so jumped in to grab a spoon, only to find out after the dust settled that nobody actually had four of a kind. That got him a penalty letter and left him one letter away from being eliminated.

With only three people left, they could no longer ignore their cards. The air thrummed with energy as the three of them sat, leaning in, poised like crouching tigers ready to pounce. Lynn settled into a zen state where she let her eyes unfocus and became aware of every tiny movement around her. She didn't try to stare at the spoons but rather kept watch for movement at the corners of her eyes, even as a sliver of her brain paid attention to her cards and the rhythmic passing of each around the circle.

One seven. Two sevens. Three sevens. Four.

Fast as lightning she grabbed a spoon. Ronnie got the other, leaving Dan in the dust, eliminated with all five letters under his name.

Lynn adjusted her seat so she was sitting across from Ronnie. Feeling daring, she looked up and met his eyes. They burned with determination and, to Lynn's surprise, delight. She gave him a nod, one opponent to another. Surprise flitted across his face, then he slowly nodded in return. Well, who'da thunk it. Ronnie knew how to not be a jerk after all.

With just two people left, strategy was limited. It usually came down to whoever got four of a kind first, which often favored the dealer, since they saw the cards first. But anything could happen. Lynn and Ronnie were neck to neck, each with three letters. To keep it fair, the single remaining spoon was placed perpendicular between them.

All levity had left the room and everyone else was silent, eyes locked on the last two contestants. It was Lynn's deal and she couldn't help the wolfish grin that lifted her lips. Adrenaline hummed through her as she began to pick up one card at a time, glance at it, then pass it to Ronnie.

Before she knew it, she'd gathered four twos. But she kept her cool, not letting any triumph show on her face—Ronnie was watching her. Almost casually, her hand flicked out and she grabbed the head of the spoon. Ronnie was a split second behind and managed to catch the spoon handle but Lynn gave a quick jerk and claimed the spoon for herself.

Yes! One more win, that was all she needed.

The next round was Ronnie's deal and Lynn barely looked at her cards. Instead she watched Ronnie like a hawk, looking for any tell. But he played it just as cool as she had and she was a split second too slow to steal the spoon when she saw his hand start in its direction.

Now they both had four letters. The next person to get a spoon would be the winner.

Lynn had the deal but she was distracted by the silent intensity of the competition and got caught up in second guessing her tactics. Should she focus on her cards? Or on Ronnie? She settled on her cards, focusing on fives when two of them came up in quick succession. But then she picked up a King and added that to the one in her hand, hoping to double her chances of getting four since she could either go with fives or Kings.

All of a sudden, she saw Ronnie lunge forward and her body reacted on instinct, whipping out to grab the spoon between them.

She felt a thrill of triumph as she held the spoon skyward like a sword of legend and the room erupted in cheers. All except Ronnie. He just sat there, a supremely satisfied smirk on his face. The others noticed his silence too and as the cheers died down Lynn felt a cold trickle of doubt.

Slowly, ever so slowly, Ronnie tipped his hand forward, revealing the four cards he held.

Two ones, a nine and a Jack.

Lynn sucked in a breath, then burst out laughing. "You *bastard!* You tricked me!"

The room erupted again with laughter and cheers.

"Oooh!"

"Slick move, Ronnie!"

"Oh, man, I did *not* see that coming."

Despite a brief wash of disappointment, Lynn couldn't help laughing and shaking her head in chagrin. She totally should have seen that coming. But she hadn't and Ronnie had won fair and square. Not really thinking about it, she held up a hand toward him for a high five.

"Good job, man."

Ronnie froze, his triumphant look sliding into uncertainty. Lynn became intensely self-conscious when he didn't immediately return her gesture but she kept her hand where it was and lifted her eyebrows in silent invitation. His nostrils flared as he drew in a breath, then he lifted his own hand and gave her a high five.

"Good game," he said and looked away.

Dan, Mack and Edgar descended on him and started talking excitedly, allowing Lynn to slip away to the kitchen with the pile of spoons. Once she was alone, she relaxed, going over the exchange in her mind as she put away the spoons. She shrugged and her grin returned. It had been a good game. She was just relieved he hadn't been a jerk about winning.

Next time, she would get him. She would show him who was the *real* Spoon Master.

"All right, boys," Matilda said as Lynn returned to the living room, "it's getting late and you all have your competition bright and early tomorrow morning. I would say we should catch an air taxi together but I doubt we'd all fit in the same one with all your parents and siblings who will want to come and support you."

There was a beat of awkward silence. Then Dan piped up.

"My parents think I'm going to a robotics day camp. If they knew I was competing in a gaming tournament they would flip out and probably lock me in my room."

At Matilda's horrified look, he simply shrugged.

"My mom doesn't approve of 'wasting time' on gaming either," Mack said, pulling at a what might charitably be called the beginnings of another beard. "I told her we formed a fitness group."

"Well, *that's* true, at least," Lynn said with a snort. "We do an insane amount of running around and sweating."

"My mom wants to come but she has to work," Edgar said hesitantly. "My sisters and brothers would probably love to come, too, but...well...we can't afford fare for all of them."

Ronnie didn't say anything but it didn't take a genius to guess that his father would want nothing to do with any "wimpy" augmented reality game and the "sissies" who played it.

Matilda looked around at all of them, brows drawn together in distress. Then she put her hands on her hips.

"Edgar, how many siblings do you have?"

"Five," he replied, slowly. "Why?"

"Perfect," Matilda said, clapping her hands together. "I'm going to reserve a twelve-seater for all of us tomorrow. That means we have one extra seat. Does anyone have a friend or a sibling who might like to come? I'm happy to keep an eye on any younger kids if they need supervision."

Lynn's friends looked at each other in uncertainty. Then Dan slowly raised his hand.

"My older sister won't be leaving to go back to university until Monday. She'd probably like to come if I asked her. She can keep a secret," he finished, eyes dropping to the floor.

"Wonderful. Now I want all of you boys to send Lynn your home address...or wherever you'd like to meet us," she amended with a little smile at Dan. "I'll work up an itinerary for picking everyone up in time to get us to Des Moines and Lynn will forward it to each of you. Understood?"

A rustle of "Yes, ma'ams" echoed through the room and Lynn hid a smile. It was just like her mom to adopt the guys and they seemed to sense that it would be futile to argue.

"All right, then, get moving, all of you. You need to go home and get some rest."

Edgar tried to protest that he could stay and help clean up

but Matilda shooed him out the door with the rest of the guys, insisting he needed his sleep. Lynn hesitated, then followed them out, calling to her mom that she was going to see them to the door of the apartment building.

The guys joked and chatted on the elevator down while Lynn stood quietly in the corner, steeling herself for something she really didn't want to do. She followed them to the door of the building and before Ronnie could exist with the others, she called out.

"Hey, uh, Ronnie? Could I have a quick word? About tomorrow?" She jerked her head toward the lobby.

Ronnie eyed her but then told the rest of the guys to go on without him and waited while they filed out the door. Lynn took a deep breath, settling her nerves. Time for another attempt at Operation What the Heck is Ronnie's Problem.

"Thanks for hanging out tonight. It was fun."

Silence. Finally, Ronnie shrugged and looked at the wall as he spoke. "Yeah. Sure."

Okaaay.

"Um, I'm looking forward to tomorrow."

A grunt.

"We'll probably be up against some big, new monster, so we'll have to stick together and use our heads."

Shrug.

Lynn sighed internally.

"We'll all be relying on you to lead us, Ronnie."

That made his head come up and he squinted at her suspiciously, as if trying to figure out if she was joking.

"I'm serious. Our team has come a long way and I think we can do well tomorrow. But only if we work together and *support each other*. I don't want to be team captain, Ronnie. I really, really don't." Ronnie snorted but Lynn plowed on. "All I want is to kill stuff and win this competition. I'm pretty sure that's what you want too, so let's do our best to work together."

"I will if you will," Ronnie replied, a note of sarcasm in his voice.

Lynn's nostril flared. Remember: mature, professional, respectful. She took a calming breath and nodded.

"I'll do my very best. See you tomorrow, then?"

"Yeah...see you tomorrow." He jerked his chin at her in a quasi-nod, then turned and pushed his way out the apartment building's doors.

Well, that had gone pretty well, considering. Now if they could all manage to keep their heads and not get into any arguments tomorrow, they should be fine.

Probably.

Lynn and her mom were on their way out of the apartment building at the crack of dawn the next morning when they were stopped by a shout from behind.

"Lynn! Mrs. Raven! A moment, if you would?"

They turned to find Mr. Thomas hobbling toward them, leaning heavily on his cane.

"I suppose the sleeplessness of great age comes in handy at times," he puffed as he approached. "I was just out having a turn in the halls. My stiff hip has been bothering me and giving it some gentle exercise helps to loosen it up. I was hoping to catch you today, Lynn. Your competition is coming up, is it not?"

"It's today. That's where we're headed now."

"Ah! Then I'm so glad I caught you," he said. "I wanted to give you something." He stuck a hand into the pocket of his gray cardigan and drew out a Kennedy half dollar on a silver chain. The coin had an oblique dent in it, as if something heavy had glanced off it. "This coin is the reason I stand before you today. Or at least, why I can still walk on both legs. I might have survived a bullet to the thigh, who knows. Field medicine was spotty, deep in the jungle."

Lynn's eyes widened at his words as he held the coin up by the chain. It swung gently back and forth, catching the light.

"I gave it to a . . . a friend, many years ago," he continued, quietly. "It protected me and I hoped it would protect him. He died peacefully of old age, so perhaps it did its job. Who can say? In any case, I think it would make better use of itself in your young and adventurous hands than collecting dust on my dresser." His eyes misted over as he held it out.

"Oh, no, I couldn't take it, Mr. Thomas."

"Please, call me Jerald. And yes, you can, young lady." Stepping forward, he grasped one of her hands with his old, bony fingers and pressed the coin into her palm.

Lynn looked uncertainly at her mom.

Matilda gave her an encouraging smile, then spoke to their neighbor. "It's a wonderful gift, thank you, Mr. Thomas. It would take a lot to keep my daughter out of trouble, but every little bit helps."

The elderly man chuckled. "Ah, yes. I was not so dissimilar, when I was her age. Do not worry, Mrs. Raven, she is a capable young woman. I am sure she will do great things."

"That's what worries me," Matilda muttered. They all laughed.

"Thanks for the gift, Mr.—I mean Jerald," Lynn said as she slid the coin and chain into one of the discreet pockets of her high-performance outfit. It clinked against her dad's little pocket-knife that was already in there. "Sorry but we have to get going. Keep your fingers crossed and wish me luck!"

Mr. Thomas waved.

"No need, Lynn. I do believe one such as you makes their own luck."

Lynn grinned. "I mean, I do try."

"Goodbye, then, Lynn. And may the monsters tremble in fear at your coming!"

"Oh, you can bet they will," Lynn said with a wink. Then she waved and followed her mom out the door.

The air taxi ride to Des Moines was noisy with Edgar's five younger siblings crowded in with all the rest of them. They ranged from seven to sixteen and spent most of the trip arguing over the qualities of their favorite pro ARS player and what toys they would buy when their big brother won five million dollars. Their antics made Lynn smile to herself. She was grateful for the distraction; it helped keep the nerves at bay.

They arrived at the address given by the TD Hunter competition packet and were surprised to find it was simply a transfer point. Shuttle buses were there waiting for them and other incoming contestants. A TD Hunter staff member in a headset and polo shirt with the TD Counterforce logo splashed across the right breast welcomed them at the door. Lynn's group climbed onto the shuttle bus and were joined by several other gaggles of people.

Once the shuttle was full, the TD Hunter representative pushed a button to close the doors and the self-driving vehicle started off.

But it only got a few dozen feet, not even out of the bus lane, before it jerked to a halt, throwing everyone forward. Lynn grabbed onto Edgar for balance as the shuttle lurched forward, then jerked to a halt again.

As soon as the TD Hunter representative regained his feet he rushed up to the front of the shuttle and slapped a big red button on the dash. The faint vibration of the electric engine vanished and everyone righted themselves. Exclamations and chatter broke out but Lynn's eyes were on the staff member. His lips were moving quickly and Lynn suspected he was having a "What the heck do I do now?" conversation with his superior, whoever that was.

"Sorry, everyone! Nothing to be alarmed about," he said, turning and raising his hands in a placating gesture. "There seems to have been a brief malfunction in the shuttle's navigation commands. We're getting our engineers over to check it out right away and we'll go ahead and hop over to a different shuttle. If you could please all stand and disembark in an orderly fashion. Thank you!"

Lynn and Edgar exchanged dubious looks but then turned to help Matilda herd Edgar's siblings down the center aisle and out the door along with the rest of the passengers. Another shuttle pulled up behind the first and they all climbed aboard and settled in.

Once the new shuttle had started off without mishap, the TD Hunter representative called for quiet and the chatter of voices quickly subsided. Lynn hugged her TD Counterforce backpack full of equipment to her chest as she listened to the man introduce himself.

"Good morning and welcome, contestants! Again, apologies for the earlier inconvenience, it's nothing to be alarmed about. My name is Jarrod and I'm part of the TD Hunter game staff here to guide you through your Hunter Strike Team qualifying tournament. The U.S. Army Reserve has kindly lent us part of their training facility for our event."

One of Lynn's eyebrows rose. U.S. Army Reserve base. That was interesting. She wondered if the location had anything to do with Mr. Krator's unnamed "investors," or with how many former military guys seemed to be part of the TD Hunter development and tactical support team. She supposed that when it came to technology with military applications, nobody would be very surprised to find the U.S. Military's fingers in it somehow.

"Since we'll be on a military base," Jarrod continued, "we need to stick together and pay special attention to all rules and posted notices. You'll be given a contestant badge—or visitor badge for your plus two—when you are dropped off and go through processing. Then we'll gather in the TD Hunter tournament HQ for orientation and finalizing your team registration details. There will be complimentary food and water provided at HQ and everyone but the contestants will remain in the building for the duration of the tournament. Don't worry, though, you'll be able to watch the whole event live through your AR interface and for anyone who doesn't have one we have extras available. The feed will be streaming live from the various contestants' own AR interfaces, as well as camera drones we have monitoring the tournament from the air.

"We have about a ten minute drive to the base, so sit back and relax and we'll have you ready to rock and roll in no time."

Lynn glanced at the others on her team and saw variations on the nervousness she was feeling herself. Only Edgar looked calm but that was probably because he was distracted by his two youngest siblings who thought it was the height of hilarity to run up and down the middle of the shuttle at top speed. Matilda got up to help enforce the peace and Lynn lost interest, looking instead out the window at the passing scenery.

Des Moines looked more or less identical to Cedar Rapids, except with more traffic on the roads and in the air. As they headed west, they passed through suburbs, then into a commercial area full of packing plants and finally past the Des Moines airport. The traffic thinned out and changed from mostly robo-cars and automated buses to huge self-driving freight trucks and old-fashioned gas-guzzler pickups with their windows rolled down so their drivers could enjoy the cool of the morning.

Their destination was several minutes south of the airport. The olive drab and blue sign for the Army Reserve Base came into view, accompanied by a trio of flag poles. A high fence surrounded the grounds and the shuttle had to pass through a checkpoint to enter. The guard on duty climbed onto the shuttle and did a quick scan of everyone's irises, checking identities against the official pictures and details that came up on his handheld display.

Once they were waved through, the shuttle moved into the maze of low buildings, some of them red brick, some of them gray concrete. Everywhere they looked things were neat and tidy.

The emerald green grass was perfectly trimmed and trees and ornamental shrubbery were well-landscaped. There were various people in uniforms walking here and there, some alone, some in small groups. Lynn pressed her nose to the window of the shuttle, watching them. She wondered what it would be like to be in the military, to have your day from dawn to dusk dictated to you, your life spent following someone else's orders. The simplicity and structure of it probably had its perks but it didn't appeal to her. She'd rather decide what to do on her own.

The shuttle pulled up alongside a large, two-story metal building. Lynn couldn't quite see the sign on the outside of it declaring what it was but it looked like it might be some sort of training facility. Jarrod organized them into a single file line to disembark and they were met outside by another smiling TD Hunter staff member who led them past a guard in uniform and into the building. The inside was brightly lit with linoleum floors and white walls covered in various notices, inspirational quotes and patriotic images from flags to individual unit insignia. It was quiet inside except for the subdued chatter of their group and they followed Jarrod past several offices to a set of double doors that opened up into a large, carpeted room that had probably served as a conference room before it had been transformed into a gamer's lounge.

Sweet.

Along the walls by the door were the registration tables where members of the TD Hunter staff were busy checking in contestants and handing out visitor badges. To the right a little eating area was set up with rows of tables beside a large spread of food. The sight made Lynn's eyes go wide. The people from TD Hunter had gone all out, providing a full buffet breakfast complete with fresh fruit, eggs-to-order, bacon, pastries and steaming coffee on the end. If Lynn's stomach hadn't been so busy tying itself in knots, she would have been on it in a flash, especially the bacon. She hoped there would be some left over after the competition, though she wasn't too optimistic, judging by the way Edgar's brothers and sisters were eyeing it like hungry wolves.

In the middle of the room was a scattering of comfortable-looking chairs and couches, while the far end of the room had been set up with rows of chairs before a small stage. Above the stage was a huge screen, easily ten feet wide and taller than a man. Currently it showed the TD Counterforce logo but Lynn was sure it would soon be displaying the official tournament stream complete with professional commentary.

"Contestants over here to registration, please," Jarrod said, gesturing. "Friends and family members, you're right next door at the visitor table to get your badges. After that please help yourself to the food and once all the contestants have checked in, we'll begin our orientation."

Lynn followed Ronnie and the others to the contestant check-in. Once in line she took a good look around, trying to get the measure of her competition. She didn't see Elena, Connor, or their three stooges anywhere, so they must have been running late. Of the people in line around her, though, it looked like the TD Hunter players were a diverse group of all ages, backgrounds and looks.

Teen to middle aged made up the majority but there were several groups of older men and women chatting together amiably, clearly ready to show the young whippersnappers that age and treachery could beat youth and enthusiasm any day. Some of the players were silent, taking in their surroundings like Lynn. Some were joking and cutting up with each other. Others looked ready to toss their cookies. She sympathized with them, though now that things were moving forward and she had something to occupy her mind, she felt her nervousness slowly turning into anticipation.

"Hey, guys, come here for a second." Edgar's voice drew Lynn's attention and she turned to find him gathering the guys in close as he bent to talk.

"So, I know we never really agreed on a team name." He glanced sideways at Ronnie as he said this and Ronnie's lips thinned. They had all listed "Baconville Bashers" on their registration form as a placeholder, intending to come up with a better name later and update it at the tournament. Ronnie had obviously been hoping they would forget about it.

"Anyway, that new item Lynn achieved yesterday got me thinking and I had an idea this morning. Why don't we name our team 'Skadi's Wolves'?" He didn't look at her as he said it but Lynn could feel everyone else's eyes flick to her, then away.

"Huh," Dan said, expression distant as he thought it over. "It's unique and creative without being over the top. I still think wolves are cliche but they're a good cliche...it's definitely better than Baconville Bashers...I say we go for it."

"I think it's awesome," Mack said, nodding.

"Absolutely not," Ronnie hissed.

Lynn sighed. Ronnie was nothing if not predictable.

"It's stupid. Skadi is some weird, barely pronounceable name and nobody is intimidated by wolves—"

"But they're intimidated by bacon?" Edgar challenged.

Mack snorted.

"That's beside the point!" Ronnie said. "Baconville Bashers is a perfectly respectable name and we've been using it for years. There's no reason to change it. Besides, I'm the team captain, so I get to decide."

"No, actually, you don't," Dan said, brows drawn down as he eyed his friend. "We've always been in this together. Ever since we were kids. Remember? This is a team. Not a dictatorship."

Ronnie crossed his arms.

"Exactly, it's been this way since we were kids, so we shouldn't go changing things now."

"But we're different, now," Dan said, gesturing to Lynn. "We've grown, we've changed and we're all better for it. I like Skadi's Wolves better than Baconville Bashers. It's way cooler. I think we should vote."

"What? No! That's not—"

"All in favor of Skadi's Wolves, raise your hands," Dan said, lifting his into the air. Edgar's hand went up, followed by Mack's.

Lynn sighed internally. She really, *really* hoped this didn't ruin all the progress she'd made with Ronnie and launch him back into full on Jerkitude Mode. That would cost them the competition, she was sure of it. She didn't like Baconville Bashers but she was perfectly willing to go with it to keep the peace. At this point, though, there was going to be a disagreement either way, so . . . she raised her hand.

Ronnie glared around at them, jaw working.

"Remember," Lynn said quietly, looking at Ronnie with a carefully neutral face. "We're here to win. That's it. Our name doesn't matter, as long as we win. And to win, we *have* to work together. We can all be wolves, or we can all be bacon. I don't care. But let's be wolves—or bacon—that kicks butt and leaves the rest of these wannabe pros in the dust, okay?"

The look on Ronnie's face didn't change but Lynn kept her expression calm and gave him a slow nod of encouragement.

Come on, Ronnie. Come on . . .

"Fine! But only—"

"Well, well, well, if it isn't the Grand Rapids *Losers*," said a voice behind them.

"Oh, hey, Elena," Lynn said, spinning smoothly as all her mental systems went to code red. She pasted a pleasant look on her face and firmly controlled the urge to deck the pop-girl right in the nose. It would be fun but unproductive. "I'm glad you made it. We were worried you'd be so caught up in your morning beauty routine that you'd miss the shuttles."

Elena huffed.

"We didn't need to use some dirty *shuttle*. My daddy's air limo brought us straight here. So much more comfortable. A full bar, too. Not that you would know the first thing about traveling in style." She smiled nastily.

Lynn heard an angry mutter behind her but she waved frantically with one of her hands behind her back, hoping the guys would get the message and let her handle this.

"You seem real concerned about how you got here," Lynn said, raising an eyebrow. "If I were you, I'd worry more about what you'll do now that you are here. Last time I looked, you didn't know the first thing about gaming, much less leading a winning team. Let me guess, Connor is going to do all the actual work while you hide behind him and look pretty for the cameras? How did you get a professional like Connor on your joke of a team anyway? He could easily be leading a top tier team of his own. Did you pay him, or sleep with him?"

"I am perfectly capable of leading a team," Elena hissed and by the ugly fury on her face, Lynn knew she'd hit the mark. The pop-girl leaned in close, stabbing a finger toward Lynn. "My team is the best there is *and* we look good on camera. Everyone is going to adore us. You pitiful losers look like a bunch of worthless dweebs who can't even afford matching outfits. What a joke." She leaned back and crossed her arms, vicious satisfaction glinting in her eyes.

Lynn glanced behind her casually, taking in her teammates. It was true, they didn't match. The guys just wore whatever comfortable, loose pants and T-shirts they had available. Most of their clothes had gaming-related graphics on them. She was the only one with remotely performance-grade clothes. Elena's team, in contrast, were dressed in matching black uniforms edged in yellow and brown, their school colors. The clothes were tight, sleek and obviously competition smart clothes like Lynn's.

"All the pretty clothes money can buy won't make you a winner, Elena. But I wouldn't worry your empty little head over it." Lynn shifted her gaze to the embarrassed-looking Connor and smiled. "Be sure to keep her at the rear where her ignorant flailing won't lose you any points. She'll be nice and safe there, don't you think? I doubt her daddy will be as free with his sponsorship money if his precious little princess gets hurt."

Connor looked away. Lynn grinned. Divide and conquer tactics were so much fun.

"Oh, by the way, Elena. Where *is* your daddy? Was he too busy to come support you on your big day?" She stuck out her lower lip. "Poor little Elena. Daddy doesn't actually care, does he—"

"What's going on here, Lynn?" Matilda asked, appearing between their two groups as if by magic. Lynn glanced over to see Edgar's siblings sitting at the tables digging into plates piled high with bacon and eggs. Her mother must have been keeping an eye on their team while corralling the youngsters.

"Oh, nothing, Mom. Just chatting with some friends." She smiled pleasantly at Elena, whose face was turning an alarming shade of puce.

"How nice, honey. Are these friends from school?"

"Yup. They're new to gaming but this community is open to everyone, no matter how little experience they have." She spread her smile extra wide, showing off her canines.

"That's wonderful to hear! Good luck to you all, I'm sure you'll do just fine."

Elena mouthed wordlessly for a moment, then stomped away, pulling Connor and the others with her.

Excellent, Lynn thought. Skadi's Wolves: 1. Conniving Harpy: 0.

"Is everything all right, here?" Matilda asked more quietly, eyeing their group.

"Yeah, we're fine, Mom. Go on back to the others. I think the littlest one is trying to drink straight from the coffee machine."

"What?" Matilda spun around and hurried back to the food table to rescue Edgar's eight-year-old brother from himself.

"That was awesome, Lynn," Dan whispered, voice full of glee. "You totally *owned* her!"

"Yeah, how did you do that?" Mack asked. "I always freeze up when Elena is around."

Lynn shrugged and gestured toward the registration table,

which they had almost reached. Honestly, she had no idea. She'd reacted on instinct, letting the sharp, angry, predator side of her take over as soon as she heard Elena's voice. That was her Larry side. The side that knew to look for weaknesses and go for the throat. Larry Coughlin was used to coming up with intimidating cut downs and ominous one-liners on a moment's notice. Putting Elena in her place had felt easy in comparison.

She ignored the inconvenient sliver of guilt that pricked her conscience. Baiting Elena with her father's absence was low, even for her. Calling the pop-girl on her own contemptible actions was one thing. But implying her father hadn't come because he didn't love her . . .

No. Elena deserved it and had only herself to blame. Use dirty tactics and get dirty tactics in return.

"Next!" called the staff member at the check-in table and Lynn returned her attention to the matter at hand as Ronnie stepped forward.

Changing a team name right before the competition, while not encouraged, was also not against the rules. Plus, with qualifying tournaments going on all over the world, their little shindig in Des Moines, Iowa, was hardly in the spotlight. Nobody would notice the name change.

They got through their check-in without further incident. The TD Hunter staff member confirmed their identities, had them e-sign a few waivers, then checked their AR interfaces and batons to make sure all were serviceable and up to regulation standards.

Once Lynn and her team had left the check-in table, Elena hurried past with her pretty boys in tow. They were the very last to check in. Everyone else had drifted to the far end of the room, filling up the chairs in front of the stage. Lynn slipped off for a quick bathroom break—who knew when she would get the chance again—and then joined her team and their family members in front of the stage.

"Goood morning, everyone!" said a bright-eyed lady who hopped onto the stage and spread her hands in welcome. The beaded braids of her hair were pulled back into a ponytail that bounced as she began to energetically pace back and forth across the stage. "My name is Trinity and I'll be taking care of you today so you can sit back, relax and cheer for your loved ones as they battle the deadly TransDimensional Monsters trying to take over our planet. In just a few minutes, our staff members will be leading the contestants away to the staging area where they'll get their mission briefing. The rest of you will get to enjoy the tournament stream here on the big screen"—she gestured behind her—"or on your own interfaces. If you don't have an interface, grab one of our staff members wearing the TD Counterforce polos and they'll get you a spare to borrow for the morning. If you're using your own interface, then navigate to the TD Hunter website and select USA, then Iowa, to get plugged in to the stream for the Des Moines tournament.

"Now, while we enjoy watching the contestants, please remember we are on U.S. military property that the Army Reserve has generously lent us for our uses today. Please do not leave this room for any reason. If there is a medical emergency, let one of our staff know immediately. The competition will be starting in..." she glanced at her watch, "thirty-eight minutes. Contestants, please say your goodbyes to your friends and family and line up in front of the doors and we'll get this show on the road!"

Lynn got up and swung off her compact TD Counterforce backpack to get out her batons and slide them into her thigh pockets. Then she replaced her backpack and hurried over to the guys. She'd considered leaving the backpack behind. But she'd been training with it on all summer long, so it shouldn't slow her down. Plus, none of her teammates had a hydration system built into their backpacks, so if they shared, nobody would have to lug around a heavy water bottle.

She joined her team as their family members crowded around. Edgar's little brother gave each one of them a huge hug, which made Lynn smile. Dan's older sister, a more reserved and dignified version of himself, gave them all an encouraging nod. Matilda, being the mom that she was, also gave everyone a big hug, saving Lynn for last.

"I'm so, so proud of you, sweetie," she said into Lynn's ear as she wrapped Lynn in her arms.

"W—why?" Lynn asked in surprise, voice catching on the word.

Matilda held Lynn at arm's length. Her eyes were suspiciously bright.

"Oh, just for being your determined, smart, beautiful self. You chose something you wanted to fight for and you've been fighting for it tooth and nail ever since, just like...just like your dad." Her mom sniffed and took a shuddering breath, then smiled bravely. "More importantly, you haven't let your fears hold you back. Not many people can say that. You're going to do great out there, honey. And I'll be right here, cheering for you."

"Thanks, Mom," Lynn said. There was a lot more she wanted to say but one look into Matilda's dark brown eyes and Lynn realized her mom already knew it all.

"Come on, Lynn, or we're gonna get left behind," Ronnie called.

Lynn gave her mom's hands a squeeze, then hurried after the guys, taking her place at the very end of the line at the door.

"Everybody here? All right, follow me please," said a staff member over the chatter. The contestants quieted down as the line began to move, and Lynn felt her heartbeat quicken. She'd faced plenty of tense gaming situations before, from fiercely competitive team deathmatches to one-on-one hunt and kill scenarios. But that had all been in virtual.

This was a whole other animal—thrilling and terrifying in equal measures.

They were led back into the hallway but took a different direction than before and so exited the building on the opposite side. They filed across an asphalt parking lot filled with military vehicles, then came to an open gate along a high chain link fence. A uniformed guard stood at the gate and he nodded at the TD Hunter staff member as he passed. Lynn didn't think anything of it until she noticed the guard also nodded at the other two staff members that escorted the contestants but not at any of the contestants, as if he knew the TD Hunter staff.

She didn't get a chance to think about it further, though. Once they were through the gate they headed straight for a low concrete building painted army green. Lynn looked around and caught sight of other buildings past the green one. They were a variety of shapes and sizes, with boring plain walls and few windows, almost like a collection of warehouses or storage buildings. Soon she lost sight of them as the line approached the building's door. She looked back right before entering the dark interior and noticed that the guard had closed the gate behind them.

Inside, the building was pitch black for a moment after the bright sun outside and she instinctively put out a hand as her eyes adjusted and the tint disappeared from the AR glasses. Her hand suddenly met a warm body and she stopped before running into Edgar. In the brief moment as they waited for the line to start moving again, Edgar's hand found hers in the dark and gave it a squeeze. It seemed like he lingered a moment before letting go but maybe she imagined it. She was glad of the dark in any case and took a deep breath to ease the sudden tightness in her throat. Within seconds, the line was moving again and Lynn could make out a short entrance hall around them that led up to a plain door.

When she passed through the door, Lynn's eyes widened. The room looked straight out of the TD Hunter game cut scenes.

A long row of terminals and tables full of readout screens snaked around the edge of the room, while a single giant screen dominated the far wall. There were no overhead lights on but the myriad of screens gave off enough light to see by. The room was full of TD Hunter staff.

They seemed to be an even mix of programmer types who were gathered around the screens and muscular men and women with the kind of severe hairstyles that screamed military. All of them wore TD Counterforce polos, though, so Lynn wasn't sure if the military types were part of the gaming staff or if they were on loan from the Army Reserve to help run the competition.

The group of contestants was led into the large open area in the middle of the room. Lynn stuck with her team at the back and they all huddled around Ronnie, who looked as wide-eyed as the rest of them. Once everyone had assembled, a tall man with forearms the size of most people's thighs stepped up in front of the crowd and came to a parade rest, eyes silently surveying the group.

The contestants swiftly quieted under the man's imposing gaze.

Once it seemed he had everyone's attention, the man spoke in a deep voice. "Welcome, Hunters. I'm glad to see you all here today—"

Shock zinged through Lynn as she instantly recognized that voice. Fallu? What in the nine circles of hell was Fallu doing *here*?

"—My name is Steve Riker. I'm a member of TD Hunter's Tactical Support group and I'm running your qualification tournament today. We've got a few safety matters to go over first, then we'll get on to your mission briefing. That means you shut up and listen up, because I ain't gonna say this stuff twice."

Lynn could almost feel the tension in the room increase as dozens of eyes locked onto Steve.

"Item number one: this is a military base. Our game will be contained within the urban combat training area, which is bordered by a fence. Do not, under any circumstances, attempt to leave the training area, or enter any of the training buildings.

"Item number two: our staff here will be getting a temporary direct feed from all of your AR interfaces to monitor the game and keep everyone safe. It's visual only, not audio-visual. Team captains, heads up: our stream managers will be splicing footage from your feed to add to the tournament live stream. There will also be camera drones monitoring the game. So, don't do anything stupid. No cutting up. No playing around. No foul play. Focus on the mission. If anyone gets hurt, we'll know right away and deploy a medical team to your location."

Lynn looked over at Edgar, who stood beside her and they shared a raised eyebrow. Hopefully they weren't expecting anyone to get hurt, though of course it was still necessary to have emergency procedures ready. The worst she expected were bruises on her shoulders and back from all the rolling they'd have to do on asphalt. Hopefully no one would trip while trying to dodge and sprain their ankle.

"Item number three: there's a chance some of you might become dizzy or disoriented during the game. That is a normal reaction. Some people are sensitive to the intense AR stimulus you'll be experiencing. If anyone needs a quick breather, you can notify the game's service AI and receive a two-minute, penalty-free exit from combat mode. This is for a medical emergency only. Exiting combat mode for any other reason during the game is considered a forfeit and you'll be treated as killed in action. Let me repeat: leaving combat mode for any other reason will get you dead. Understood?"

Steve paused and was rewarded with a scattering of "yeses" and "yups."

"I said, *is that understood?*" Steve barked.

"Yes, sir!" the group of contestants responded more or less in unison.

"Good. Now, please don't abuse the medical exemption, people. We're all adults here. We're watching you and we can tell if you try to use it to get out of a sticky situation. So don't."

Steve paused again to sweep his stern gaze slowly over the contestants. His face was lit from the side by a nearby monitor and the effect made him seem all the more intimidating.

"Right. Now that we've got the safety brief out of the way, let's talk game details. This tournament is to evaluate your suitability for Hunter Strike Team status. Competition teams get special privileges and abilities that you'll need to take out the top level TDMs and bosses during the international matches. It takes skill. It takes teamwork. It takes maturity and responsibility. If you and your teammates can't prove you've got your act together, then you get cut. Simple as that.

"We'll be evaluating you on your teamwork and tactics. That gets weighed against the points you gain through your individual ratings. Things like overall kills and kill to damage ratio. There's no first place, second place, here. All teams that meet the minimum threshold will qualify as Hunter Strike Teams.

"Now, once you're in position, you'll get one hour, I repeat, sixty minutes, to complete the mission. At that point, the game will be concluded and we'll gather back here to debrief and hear the results. Get it?"

"Got it!" echoed the contestants.

"Good," Steve said and smiled. "Now, eyes forward. First Sergeant Bryce of the TransDimensional Counterforce will be giving you your mission briefing up on the big screen."

Steve stepped off to the side and patriotic music filled the room as the TD Counterforce logo appeared on screen, then faded to reveal the now-familiar visage of First Sergeant Bryce. The uniformed man stood at parade rest with his hands behind his back. Next to him was a large, square screen that resembled the combat display inside the TD Hunter app.

"Morning, Hunters! I hope you're all ready for some serious action, because we've got a critical situation developing at this Army Reserve Base."

"Oh, great, a custom cut scene," Ronnie said grumpily.

Cut scenes were as old as decent graphics. But as CGI costs had dropped and AIs had learned the business of gaming, it was more and more common to have a myriad of customized scenes for each different scenario in game. Some gamers loved them, but most were bored stiff by unskippable info dumps that interrupted their game play. This cut scene, though, might contain information vital to victory, so she ignored Ronnie's moaning and focused on the screen.

"Sensors have detected an unusual spike in TDM activity

right in the middle of their training area and it's getting worse by the minute."

An overhead map of the base appeared on the display beside First Sergeant Bryce. He leaned over to gesture in a circle with his finger, leaving behind a red line around what Lynn assumed was the fenced-in training area. She stared hard at it, committing as many details to memory as she could before it disappeared again and the first sergeant kept talking.

"Your target for today is an entity called Mishipeshu," the first sergeant continued. "Mishipeshu, or the Water Panther, has attracted a whole host of TDMs to this location and they're wreaking havoc on the base's systems as well as threatening the health of our military personnel."

As the first sergeant continued, the display cycled through images of monsters taken from the TDM Index. Most of them Lynn and her team had faced before and the rest were monsters they'd studied from the index, though admittedly the tactical details for some of them had been sparse.

"Mishipeshu is a Bravo, much tougher than anything your teams have faced before," the first sergeant barked. "Other than that, there is very little intel. The mass of protective TDMs as well as Mishipeshu itself preclude the use of drones or other technology to approach the area. Your mission is to penetrate the mass of protective TDMs and terminate Mishipeshu with *extreme* prejudice.

"We've evacuated the area for now but it's up to you and your teams to eliminate this threat so our troops can get back to work stemming this tide of alien entities.

"Remember: This is about completing the mission, whatever it takes, whatever the cost. There is no time for caution. Taking out Mishipeshu is the only objective, not racking up kills. Hit them fast, hit them hard and by God, make them wish they'd never dared cross over to our dimension!

"Good luck, Hunters. Watch out for each other and I'll see you on the other side. First Sergeant Bryce, out."

The big screen switched to the standard background with the TD Counterforce logo and there was a moment of silence as everyone digested the briefing. The nervous anticipation she'd been able to ignore while First Sergeant Bryce had been talking now flooded her system. She felt her hands twitch at the rush of adrenaline and she itched to be holding Wrath and Abomination in her hands. She would feel better once she could start killing things.

"All right, people!" Steve barked, moving out in front of their group again. "Get together in your teams and get ready. You've got ten minutes, then we're moving out to your starting positions. Anyone with last minute questions, send your team captain forward to see me. Bathrooms are behind you to your right if anyone needs them."

"Hey, guys, I need to go," Mack said. "I'll be right back, okay?"

"Really?" Ronnie growled. "Hurry up, Mack. You'd better not make us late."

"I won't!" Mack promised as he hurried off toward the bathrooms.

Lynn didn't pay much attention to him, she was too busy standing on tip-toe, trying to count the number of huddled, five-person teams.

"Need a little extra height?" Edgar murmured behind her. She couldn't see his face very well in the dimness but she could hear the teasing note in his voice. She elbowed him in the side.

"Shut up and make yourself useful, Mr. Hulk. Start counting and tell me how many teams there are."

They both counted silently for a minute, then looked at each other.

"Looks like eleven teams," Edgar said.

"Hmm, I didn't count that many but then maybe I just couldn't see them all the way down here." Lynn stuck out her tongue.

"Five minutes, Hunters! Then we move out!" Steve called.

Another minute passed and Lynn reached up to fidget with the coin Mr. Thomas had given her that was now around her neck. She hated waiting, it gave her time to worry about things. Finally, she tucked the coin back underneath her skin-tight shirt and looked around. "Where is Mack? Shouldn't he be back by now?" Lynn turned toward the bathrooms, then took a step back as three uncomfortably familiar faces loomed up in front of her.

The three stooges.

Lynn tensed, ready for a fight, but they merely brushed roughly past her, grinning the whole while. Lynn turned to watch them disappear into the crowd, not daring to take her eyes off them. Once they were gone, she turned back toward the rear of the room, only to see Mack stumble out of the men's bathroom clutching his backpack to his chest.

"Guys, something is wrong, come on." Lynn grabbed Edgar's arm and trotted over to Mack, who was leaning against the wall. The rest of the team followed and they all crowded around him.

"What's wrong, Mack?" Ronnie asked.

"I—I'm s-sorry. I—I—"

"Calm down, man. It's okay," Edgar said. "Just tell us what's wrong."

"T-those guys. The ones from Elena's team. They jumped me in the bathroom."

"What?" Lynn hissed. "Those bastards! Are you hurt?"

"N-no. They didn't attack *me*. They grabbed my backpack and b-broke my AR glasses. They even managed to snap my batons in half, both of them." Mack reached into his backpack and lifted out half of an electric blue baton to show them. "I'm so sorry," he moaned. "It happened so fast. Now I won't be able to play and our team won't qualify and everything is ruined—"

"Calm down, Mack," Edgar said, putting a hand on his friend's shoulder. "It's not your fault, we'll figure something out—"

"What are you talking about, Edgar?" Ronnie said, grabbing his head and pulling on his hair. His tone sounding borderline hysterical. "Figure what out? We're *ruined*! Those be *motinų paleistuvių sūnūs*—" he descended into a vicious litany of Lithuanian curses but Lynn barely heard him. Ice cold dread had filled her at Mack's words but her mind remained clear. It was busy whirring, plotting...

"Two minutes, Hunters! Get ready to move out!"

"Give me that." Lynn snatched the backpack out of Mack's hands, then turned and hurried across the room, slipping through the crowd as quickly as she could. Coming out the other side, she pulled up short, barely avoiding colliding with Steve. The big man turned and looked down.

"Lynn!" he said as surprise and delight lit up his face. "Good to see you in the flesh at last." He held out a hand but then seemed to register her expression. "What's wrong?"

She plunged her hand into the backpack and drew out several pieces of broken baton and one half of a pair of glasses.

"Someone just, um, *accidentally* broke my teammate's batons *and* his AR glasses."

Both of Steve's eyebrows arched upward toward his buzz-cut hairline.

"Accidentally, huh? And who was the person or persons who *accidentally* broke them?"

Lynn hesitated. She wanted so badly to get Elena and her bullies kicked out of the tournament. But there wouldn't have been any cameras in the bathroom and it was her word against theirs. She didn't want to cast a shadow on her own team for "unfounded accusations."

"No time, Fallu. I don't suppose there might be any spares around? They were handing out spare AR glasses back at the lounge area. Anything."

She trailed off, her heart pounding painfully against her breastbone as she stared up hopefully at Steve's unreadable face.

He stared down at her for several seconds and for a moment Lynn thought he was mad at her. But then she noticed the tiny movement of the muscles in his throat and realized he was sub-vocalizing to someone. There was another pause and he cocked his head as if listening. Then he nodded.

"Don't worry, snake," he said. "Gotcha covered." He turned as another staff member came trotting up, holding two batons and a pair of AR glasses. The man handed them off to Steve, who gave them to Lynn. "Prepared for all emergencies. Have your team member get those on quick. He'll need to sync them to his LINC ASAP. We're moving out *now*."

"Thanks, Fallu. See you in WarMonger."

"No worries," Steve said and winked at her. Then he looked up and spoke, his loud voice cutting across the chatter in drill-sergeant worthy fashion. "All right, people! Buckle up, it's showtime."

Lynn hurried back to her team as the room began to empty.

"Here, put these on and get them synced," she said, shoving the new items into Mack's hands, then turning to follow the crowd out the door.

"Whoa! Where did you get them?" Mack asked behind her.

"I know people. No time. Get them synced. Sync while we walk."

Edgar caught up to her and slapped her on the back.

"Of course you do. Cuz you're a gangsta like that, aren'tcha?"

"We're going to have to watch our backs," Ronnie said, coming up on her other side. "If they tried to sabotage us once, they'll try it again."

"But there will be camera drones all over the place out there," Dan pointed out, crowding in behind Ronnie as they moved to pass through the short hall and out the door.

"That just means they'll have to be more sneaky," Ronnie said.

"We'll stay sharp," Lynn promised, finally pulling her batons free of their pockets and gripping their handles tightly. She squinted as they all spilled out into the bright morning sunshine and her AR glasses tinted to shade her eyes.

They'd be ready all right. And if Elena tried anything "untoward" again, Lynn would be waiting with two not-so-deadly weapons and one heck of a grudge.

Chapter 15

"STRAIGHT LINE, PEOPLE!"

Steve's voice boomed out over the crowd of eleven teams as they shuffled around, forming groups in a line along the wall of the green building. Lynn and her team ended up on one end of the line, which suited her just fine. Behind them to the north was the rest of the base and TD Hunter HQ where their families were no doubt watching in tense anticipation. Before them to the south, the urban combat training ground spread out, looking like a cross between an abandoned warehouse district and a wild-west ghost town. Dozens of camera drones whirred back and forth above their heads, their collective buzzing audible over the mutter of voices and scrape of boots on asphalt.

Lynn looked up to examine the drones and felt a jolt of shock. The small, gray units looked identical to the ones she'd seen loitering overhead all around the city as she'd hunted during the summer. Surely, they weren't the same ones? Lynn dismissed the idea as absurd. There were billions of drones in use all over the world, all the time. TD Hunter probably used the same model as the Cedar Rapids municipal government or whoever those other ones had belonged to.

The thought didn't make her feel better, though. Now that the drones were on her mind she couldn't stop thinking: *The whole world is watching.*

The whole world.

Watching.

Her.

Lynn swallowed and shifted, trying to tamp down the anxiety before it could shake her. It didn't matter who was watching. All the footage was augmented. She was just some girl in a cool set of armor. Nobody knew who she was. Nobody would care.

To get her mind off the hard pit of anxiety forming in her stomach, Lynn leaned forward and looked down the line of teams in all their TD Hunter glory. Their combat systems wouldn't come online until the battle started, so all their weapons were still just batons. But everyone's skins were on display. Many players had only standard armor skin that came from being fully "plated" up. But others were decked out in some pretty sweet gear.

One guy's full-face helmet looked straight out of ancient Sparta, though instead of the traditional red crest, it had a multi-colored mohawk of epic proportions. Another guy had massive shoulder plates, the kind ubiquitous to many MMORPG games, with the snarling head of a dragon arching off each shoulder. The sight was as ridiculous as it was cool. Good thing augmented reality armor wasn't limited by such boorish things as the laws of physics.

Another sight that caught Lynn's eye was an all-girl team that sported matching skins in a style Lynn could only describe as robo-ninja. She wondered what unique item the skins came from. They looked really awesome and it made her particularly grateful for her Skadi's Glory.

She wondered suddenly if any of the other teams were checking out her and the guys. The idea made her squirm internally but she reminded herself that her skin looked as impressive and hard-core as they came and her teammates didn't look too bad either. Their armor was an eclectic mix of medieval, SWAT and space soldier styles, all generated by personal augments and their own tweaks in the avatar settings. Lynn started to wonder how she could get them matching skins too but then she shook her head.

Kill monsters now, play dress-up later. This was no time to get distracted.

She started to limber up, shaking out her arms, cracking her neck, bouncing up and down on her toes. The familiar movements relaxed her and she felt her anxiety flowing away as she brought her focus inward to a razor edge.

Kill. She was here to kill. To destroy. To utterly dominate her enemies and claim her prize. A predatory smile spread across her face as hot battle-lust built inside, buzzing through her with crackling intensity.

This was it.

"Okay, Ronnie," she subvocalized as her eyes lifted to scan the terrain again. "What's your plan?"

"Straight in, guns blazing. You heard the mission briefing, we've got to hit them hard. We're not going to win this by being a bunch of timid wimps. We mow them down, kill as many as we can in an hour and get this team qualified—"

"On my mark, a tone will sound," Steve's voice rang out again. "At that point your battle systems will engage and start a one-hour countdown on your display—"

"You're right, we have to be aggressive," Lynn agreed, speaking quickly. "But we can't charge in blindly. Assuming the monsters are thinnest at the fringes, I would *suggest* making for the fence line over to the right. It will put space between us and the other teams so we can find high ground to scout and see what we're facing—"

"After one hour, Hunters, your battle systems will shut down. When that happens please return to this point for your debriefing."

"We need to rack up kills," Ronnie insisted.

"Bryce said this isn't about kills: It's about terminating the main boss. It's going to be an absolute madhouse front and center. Everyone will rush in and more and more monsters will be attracted to the fighting. We won't have room to swing our weapons, much less make a proper formation. Our combat scores will suck. I wish we could coordinate with the other teams but there's no time and I doubt any would play ball—"

"All right, Hunters, are you ready? Good luck, be safe and see you on the other side!" Steve stepped back, clearing the area in front of the teams and Lynn heard him say "Three, two, one, mark!"

Her combat display came to life.

So, did the area in front of her. With monsters. A freaking horde of monsters.

Curses and shouts of surprise filled the air as everything descended into chaos.

Lynn had expected something like this, so Wrath and Abomination were already moving, cutting, blasting the crowd of grinder worms and gremlins that had appeared so suddenly and attacked in an oppressive cacophony of roars and clicks. They fell before her like wheat before the reaper's blade. Within a minute, they'd cleared enough of the area around them to give themselves a moment to breathe and think.

Sweeping her gaze from left to right, Lynn took in the battlefield. Once the initial surprise of so many TDMs had faded, the other teams had started to assault forward, wading easily through the clusters of low-class monsters, many of which didn't even react until the hunters were on top of them.

By the first row of buildings, the gremlins and grinder worms turned to Grumblins and crusher worms and among the buildings beyond that Lynn could see groups of demons and Orculls. Then she glanced at her overhead map and for a moment her breath froze in her chest. The map was so thick with red dots that they merged into one another and painted the whole area in a sea of crimson. There were clusters of blue dots at the bottom but they could barely be seen among the red.

Lynn's mind raced, sifting through the sights and sounds, drawing conclusions and formulating strategies.

The TDMs were organized by class—the farther in, the higher the class. TDM rings always had the weakest monsters on the outside, more powerful ones on the inside. So, whatever the biggest threat was, it would be in the center of this training ground. Their mission was to "eliminate the threat," ergo, they needed to break into the center of this "Charlie Foxtrot" and terminate whatever was in there with extreme prejudice. An hour wasn't nearly enough time to kill all these monsters, no matter how good they were. But with the other teams attempting a frontal assault, that would draw most of the TDMs' attention...

"Okay, everyone, we're not going to follow the lemmings," Ronnie said on their group channel.

Finally. Took you long enough, Lynn thought.

"We're going to circle around the side and see if we can get a handle on what we're facing. Patrol formation, double time. Move out!" Ronnie led them at a trot to the right. They cut through the monsters before them with ease. A single shot or swipe of any weapon reduced them to sparks, even the ghosts who tried to ambush them.

They followed Ronnie southwest to the edge of the training

ground, then ran south along the fence line getting farther and farther away from HQ. Soon the yells and shouts of the other embattled teams had faded, only to be replaced by a deep, endless hum of TDM noises—distant but threatening all the same.

"Guys," Lynn said, speaking evenly despite their brisk pace, "we need to find some high ground. Start searching for any fire escapes, ladders, or places on the outsides of these buildings where we can climb up."

While her teammates got looking, Lynn decided to try something a bit unconventional.

"Hugo," she subvocalized, "you have access to my LINC's omnisensors, right?"

"Of course, Miss Lynn."

"Okay, can you do a scan of the surrounding area and show me where the strongest electromagnetic signals are coming from?"

"It is within my capabilities, yes. But for what purpose, might I ask?"

"Wherever the electromagnetic pulses are the strongest, that's where the center of this mob will be."

"Ah. Astute conclusion, Miss Lynn. Based on my scans, the strongest signals are coming from the south-southeast."

"Great. Any chance you can put an arrow on my overhead pointing in that direction, no matter which way I turn? Sort of like a compass needle but locked onto the strongest electromagnetic pulses instead of the north pole?"

"Done, Miss Lynn."

"Can you duplicate it on the rest of the team's overheads too?"

"They would have to individually request it from their own service AI just as you have, Miss Lynn."

"Drat," Lynn muttered, then switched to her private channel with Ronnie. "Have everyone tell their AI to start scanning for EM waves and add a dynamic arrow to their overhead map to point in that direction. Follow the lead of my AI."

For once, instead of grumbling about how he was the captain and he would do whatever he saw fit, Ronnie simply took her advice and relayed the information.

Well, miracles could happen after all.

Within a few minutes, they'd traveled two-thirds of the way down the side of the training area and their EM detection arrow finally pointed due east. Lynn's overhead showed that the mass of red was concentrated to the northeast, closer to HQ where most of the blue dots were still clustered. She saw a few groups that had changed direction and were moving east and west instead of south, as if those teams had realized the futility of a direct assault. But they had an uphill battle. In any case, there were plenty of TDMs in front of her team, they were just scattered between the rows of buildings instead of being packed shoulder-to-shoulder.

"What next?" Dan asked.

"Ladder," Edgar called out, pointing to the corner of a building past the first line of structures.

Ronnie looked around, assessing their position. They were fully stealthed, so none of the low-Delta-Class monsters between them and the building would sense them unless they opened fire. They should be able to sneak right through.

"Let's take the high ground. Hold your fire, for now, everybody. We don't want to attract attention until we're ready for it."

It was a quick sprint over to the building, a gray, single-story concrete structure. The ladder on the side was a metal affair bolted into the concrete and they made quick work scrambling up it. Once on top, Ronnie told Dan, Mack and Edgar to keep an eye out for monsters, then jerked his head at Lynn in a "come here" gesture.

Lynn's eyebrows rose so high they might have touched her hairline. What was this? Ronnie openly acknowledging her existence? The miracles were just piling up today.

She came over and spoke quietly.

"Yes?"

"Take a look and tell me what you see," Ronnie said in such a serious tone that Lynn had to suppress a giggle. He had put one foot up on the rim of the building's roof and struck a pose with his chest out, pistol muzzles pointing skyward.

Resisting the urge to say *"Da, Kommander,"* in a fake Russian accent, Lynn turned her attention from her takes-himself-way-too-seriously team captain and scanned the training ground.

Up here, it didn't look as big and intimidating as on the ground. She could see the fence line encircling the lines of buildings on every side, though a few two-story buildings obscured her line of sight to the east. With all available slots filled with globes, her visual detection range for TDMs was still only about a hundred feet out, then they were invisible except as red dots on Lynn's overhead. By comparing her compass to the buildings in front of her, the spread of the red dots and the ranks of TDMs either sitting still or patrolling along the streets, she made a rough guestimate as to their target. Then she scanned their sides and rear, looking for anything important she might have missed...

"Cover, cover!" she hissed, grabbing Ronnie and pulling him down. The others followed suit, eyes to the sky as if they were expecting a Tengu attack.

"Elena," Lynn growled. She rose a bit and pointed, directing Ronnie's gaze.

"That scheming, conniving, little copycat," Ronnie said. "She followed us."

"Maybe," Lynn said quietly. "Doesn't really matter. Now we have to worry about her *and* the TDMs."

"I bet they're going to sneak along behind and try to slip past us while we're fighting to get the big boss themselves."

"They can try but it won't do them much good. Remember, the evaluators are watching our every move. They'll see if Elena and her boy toys try to sabotage us or steal our kills."

"I hope so," Ronnie muttered.

"Don't worry about them for now. Here's what I'm thinking..."

Lynn laid out her plan. Ronnie complained about it. She *respectfully* pointed out the flaws in his logic. He glared daggers at her. Finally, they agreed on a modified version and all was well with the universe.

Teamwork at its finest.

With Ronnie in the lead, they snuck down off the roof and picked their way across the street, around another building and across the next street, avoiding all the TDMs. A single engagement would put them on the radar of every monster within a mile and it would only get worse from there. Lynn's heart pounded in her throat as they crept but they safely reached the building they'd been aiming for without incident and without any further sign of Elena and her team.

The new building also had a ladder and they scrambled up to their new position—the closest Lynn had determined they could get to their target without being detected by the TDMs on the ground. Once on the roof, they set up in a circle formation and each one equipped their Disruptor Rifles. Then, at a nod from Ronnie, they started duck hunting.

Or roc hunting, anyway.

It wasn't hard to pick the monsters out, though the camera drones flying around overhead were an annoying distraction. The weird manta-ray looking creatures were slowly circling in clusters over various buildings scattered across the training ground, feeding on beams of EM energy invisible to the human eye, Lynn assumed. With five Disruptor Rifles trained on them, though, they didn't stay feeding for long. Within thirty seconds, Lynn and her team had downed most of the rocs within range. It took thirty more seconds for the first Tengu to arrive.

Dang. That was fast. Lynn had thought they'd have several minutes at least.

The ominous tone started faint at first, then louder. Then a second tone, slightly lower, joined it. Then a third.

"We're gonna get creamed," Dan said. "Why are there so many of them?"

"Mishipishi or whatever?" Mack replied.

"Shut up and keep your eyes peeled," Ronnie said.

Dan switched to his Plasma Rifle while the rest of them equipped their own preferred ranged weapon and crouched in readiness, eyes on the sky.

"There they are!" Mack yelled, pointing above and to the east.

Three Tengus appeared in Lynn's vision, all three plunging down in a steep dive. And all three aimed straight at her.

"Bring it, you half-plucked turkeys," she muttered as she scrambled away from the edge of the roof to the center and stood tall, Abomination raised and tracking.

Dan's Plasma Rifle started spitting but the Tengus didn't shift their aim to him. Odd. Still, it might be better for her team, since it let everyone else focus on shooting while she worried about dodging.

With how fast the Tengus were moving, Lynn knew she would have mere seconds to shoot with her close range pistol before she had to take cover. She held Abomination aloft and tracked the lead Tengu, waiting, steady...

At the last second she squeezed off three rapid shots, then dove for the roof. She rolled, coming to rest on her back where she kept shooting as the Tengus pulled out of their dive, screeching in fury. Her team's weapons spit and boomed around her until suddenly one of the Tengus exploded. Then the second, then the third.

"Good shooting, team!" Ronnie called and Lynn glowed inside.

Look at little Ronnie, complimenting excellent work and build-ing team morale. There was hope for him yet, she just knew it.

Another high tone started in the distance and they scrambled to reset.

"How many of these bird-brains are there?" Edgar muttered.

Five, as it turned out. At least that's how many they took down before they heard no more high tones. And all five Tengus had gone straight for Lynn, despite the hail of bullets from everyone else.

With no more aerial monsters visible, Stage One of their plan was complete and they got ready to hit the streets and start Stage Two. Before they could start climbing down, though, shouts broke out nearby and they raced to the edge of the roof to see what was going on. Lynn grinned. It looked like Elena and her crew had been spotted and would be too busy fighting off TDMs for the foreseeable future to cause them any trouble.

Ronnie led the way down the ladder and they assumed their usual attack formation, spread across the street in a loose V. By the time Ronnie gave them the signal to advance, Lynn's fingers were extra twitchy and she was sooo ready to kill stuff. It was almost physically painful to hold herself back. But soon enough she knew they would be stuck in the thick of it and she could fight to her heart's content.

She kept her position, staying in line with Mack and Edgar as they set off at a brisk pace, taking out any TDM in their path with practiced ease and collecting ichor and other supplies on the move. The imps, grinder worms, ghosts and gremlins were barely an afterthought and even the Grumblins and demons were child's play at this point. It wasn't until they got to the Orculls that they started to slow. But not too much. Timing was everything.

Lynn glanced at the countdown on her display. Thirty-seven minutes left.

The monsters started coming in troops instead of twos and threes. Word seemed to be spreading among the TDMs, or at least the algorithm had finally caught on to where they were.

Charlie Class monsters like death worms and Spithra appeared, while Ghasts and Phasmas tried to get behind their formation to ambush them. The buildings on either side of the street made things harder. The TDMs casually moved through the walls and acted like the buildings didn't exist, probably because the structures were training props rather than actual buildings where people lived and worked day in and day out. Fortunately, everyone's overhead map was unhindered by roofs or walls and gave them a clear three-sixty view of any approaching dots.

Ten minutes and two blocks later, they found another building with a ladder and scrambled up it for a breather. They quickly discovered that Ghasts and Phasmas were not bothered by their change in altitude and kept popping out of the roof under their feet. It was better than the thickening horde down below, though, so they took what they could get. Lynn felt pride as she looked around at her teammates, busy resupplying and rebuffing the occasional sneak attack. They'd come a long way from the out of shape, baton-flailing place where they'd begun. They weren't A-Team material, not yet. But they were a solid B-Team with plenty of room to grow.

Their break didn't last more than a minute. Monsters had started to swarm around the building and Ronnie worried they'd get stuck up there, so they climbed down and made a break through the mob to a clearer part of the street. They took some damage but that was inevitable.

Thanks to Skadi's Horde, it was less than they'd expected—in such tight quarters their proximity bonus was at the max. They were able to kill most things in a shot or two and the tougher monsters Lynn and Ronnie quickly skewered with their high-damage blades, while Edgar blasted away to clear a path forward. Considering their collective rate of fire, Lynn was glad they weren't shooting real weapons and spewing a hail of scorching brass everywhere. Plus, lugging all that ammo around would have been a pain in the butt.

Ah, the joys of gaming in augmented reality. All the fun of reality with none of the sucky parts. Well, except for the ungodly humidity and heat...and the bruises and scrapes...and other players trying to assault you.

Speaking of other players...

Lynn only checked her overhead out of sheer habit. Things were crazy with all the yelling and monster noises and targets rushing her from every side. But she happened to flick her eyes to it out of habit and noticed the cluster of blue dots one street over. She assigned a small part of her brain to check the rival team's progress periodically, then went back to focusing on not dying.

Holy moly these monsters were getting thick. Talk about target rich environment.

Their team was trying to assault forward down the asphalt street. About a block ahead, the street opened up into a little square and Lynn could see the shoulder-to-shoulder ranks of towering Namahags and Penagals glaring malevolently, waiting for them. That was the central ring and behind them should be whatever the TDMs were protecting—Mishipeshu.

But between them and their goal was a thickening soup of hissing, growling and shrieking attackers of every type. There were even Vargs and Stalkers among them. They weren't much of a threat damage- or strength-wise but they were fast. It was all Lynn and her team could do to stab, slash, shoot and blast their way forward foot by foot without being overwhelmed. They barely had time to snatch up extra ichor, plates and Oneg and even Lynn steadily used up her supply of health, so she couldn't imagine how bad it was for the guys.

Lynn glanced at the clock. Twenty minutes left.

Several agonizing minutes later they were halfway down the block toward the square when a huge shape leaped over the shoulder-to-shoulder monsters ahead and barreled down the street toward them.

"Contact front! Manticar!" Edgar yelled, getting their attention.

"Concentrate fire," Ronnie called, switching from his Plasma Sword to double Plasma Pistols.

Miraculously, the other TDMs scattered away from the hulking monster, pulling back as if afraid to come into contact with it. It gave the whole team a sliver of relief to switch their focus.

The Manticar was easily seven feet tall at the shoulder with a heavily muscled frame that looked nothing so much as like a massive saber-toothed tiger. But instead of having a normal tail, over its shoulder curved three massive stingers that bobbed with the creatures' earth-shaking lope.

Wait, earth-shaking? Why did her body feel a ghost of a vibration with each bound of that crazy beast that was about to eat them for breakfast? Was her baton malfunctioning?

The thought was there and gone again and then she was rushing forward to support Edgar, pouring fire into the Manticar so fast her trigger finger burned and threatened to seize up. In the few seconds it took the beast to close the distance with them, they pounded it with all they had but it wasn't enough.

"Ronnie, assault!" Lynn yelled and leaped forward. There was no way they could survive huddled in one place. Better for her and Ronnie to distract it and give the others a chance to fill it with plasma.

Ronnie was only a split second behind her, guns blazing along with her Abomination as they split and tried to flank the Manticar that dove toward their group. Apparently Edgar's Blunderbuss wasn't distracting enough, because its head swung to the side, tracking her with eyes that glowed red in her AR vision. It snapped its jaws at her and she barely dodged, only to get hit from overhead with all three of its stingers.

Lynn swore violently and stumbled back, trying to get out of range as she yelled at Hugo to hit her with some Oneg. That one strike had eaten up half her remaining health.

But the Manticar didn't give her any chance for space. It bore down on her with a single-minded focus that made her curse the stupid algorithm six ways to Sunday. Why was it picking on her?

She dodged and rolled, staying just ahead of those massive teeth and claws, but every few seconds the Manticar's terrifying stingers stabbed down and inevitably one or more would get her. She couldn't move fast enough or focus on the threats from so many angles at once. She was guzzling Oneg at an alarming rate and only barely staying alive.

"Ronnie, we're out," she yelled into her private channel, too out of breath to subvocalize. "I'm ten seconds from dying. We all need to book it, just run and get out as fast as we can before we die."

She didn't wait for a reply but made one last stab at the Manticar, hoping it would stun it or push it back.

"COME ON YOU DANG DIRTY HEATHENS!" Lynn yelled into the group channel as she turned and ran for her life. "GET YOUR BUTTS TO THE CHOPPER! WE ARE DIDI MAO!"

She felt like a fool but there was no time for strategy, no time for a measured, controlled retreat. There was only run or die.

To her immense relief, the guys came hot on her tail. They dodged as they ran, trying to avoid going straight through any of the straggler TDMs that had gathered in the clear path behind them. The Manticar, while fast, wasn't faster than an all-out sprint and after a block or so it stopped chasing them—well, her—and skidded to a stop with a roaring scream of triumph.

Lynn didn't care. She was alive to fight again and that's all that mattered.

"Roof," Lynn gasped out and they all scrambled up the ladder of the building they'd used to snipe the Rocs and Tengus. Once on top, she bent over with her hands braced on her knees to catch her breath. She only gave herself a few seconds, though, because they were far from safe.

Once she was no longer gasping, she straightened and kept a lookout as Ronnie reminded them all to refill their slots and they took turns sipping from Lynn's hydration pack.

"Did you just make a Tropic Thunder reference?" Dan asked.

"For a second there, I thought Larry had showed up," Mack said, rubbing his whiskers. "I was so relieved. We might die but Larry would save the day."

"Dang dirty heathens?" Edgar asked, placidly chewing gum.

"Was...all I could...think of?" Lynn said, still panting.

The moment of respite was enough for her to gather her thoughts, check her overhead and admit to herself what they had to do.

She did not like it. Not one single bit.

Disappointment and frustration churned in her chest but she closed her eyes, took a deep calming breath and let it all flow away. No time for feelings, no time for hesitation.

Mack was right. It was time to put her Larry on.

She was a cold, hard killer who didn't let anyone, or anything, get in her way. Not even herself.

Lynn stepped over to Ronnie and caught his eye.

"Permission to speak freely?" she asked. It was something she'd learned that NCOs said to their officers—or that any subordinate said to their superior—when they knew their superior wasn't going to like what came next. It let the subordinate be frank without being accused of insubordination. In Lynn's case, she just needed Ronnie to feel like he was in charge and had a choice in the matter so he would listen to her. Jerkitude at this point would get them all killed.

"Yeah, sure," Ronnie said slowly, then glanced around. Everyone was looking at them. He pursed his lips but nodded at her to continue.

"We need a plan B," Lynn said, addressing her whole team. "We don't have enough firepower or health to make it past that Manticar and the last line of defenders and we don't have time to take it slow and pick off the bastards from a distance. We have one more chance at this thing and I know how we can do it."

She paused and saw the exhaustion she felt in her bones reflected in each of her teammates eyes. Exhaustion...but also determination.

"CRC," she said.

"What?"

"No!"

"No way. We are *not* teaming up with those cheaters!" Ronnie declared.

"Shut up and listen," Lynn snapped, acutely aware of the ticking clock. "We aren't strong enough to do this raid alone. It's clearly set up as a group exercise. Bigger than one team. So, either we hold back and kill as many monsters in the time left as we can, which makes us no better than everyone else, or we team up with Elena's crew, the only group close enough to assist, and complete the mission.

"Even if we take a lot of damage or even die in the attempt, it won't matter. This isn't about scores and points anymore. It's about *do we have what it takes to get the job done.* It's about completing the mission. First Sergeant Bryce said to do whatever was necessary. And this is necessary. So, suck it up and let's do it."

Ronnie's eyes blazed and his jaw was clenched so hard Lynn could imagine she heard his teeth grinding together. He was probably trying to think of an alternative, any alternative. But there was none.

"We can't trust them," he ground out.

"I know. But if they try to betray us in the thick of things, they'll die just as fast as we will and they'll know that. Plus, the monitors are watching, so if they try anything overt they'll get kicked out of the game."

Lynn glanced up as she said it, eyes scanning the sky for... ah, there it was. She gave a jaunty salute to the drone hovering above and returned her attention to her team.

"—and Elena won't go for it," Dan was saying as he shook his head.

"That's why I'm going to ignore her," Lynn said. "Let me do the talking. I'll get Connor on board and Elena won't have a choice but to fall in line if she wants her precious team to qualify."

"I'm in," Edgar said, popping his gum. "But time's a wasting."

"Oookay?" Dan said, raising one hand palm upward. "If you say so."

Ronnie didn't respond, just clenched his jaw harder and glared at her.

"We don't have *time*, Ronnie!" Lynn hissed, her body so tense she felt ready to snap. "Five *million* dollars. *Full ride* scholarship. Guaranteed job in gaming."

"Fine! Fine!" Ronnie shouted, grabbing his hair and nearly tearing it out. "Let's get this over with."

Lynn could see Elena's team a block down as they huddled against the side of a building, obviously trying to catch their own breath after a similar failed attempt to assault the TDM circle. She led the way down the ladder and marched straight over to the group. A few ghosts tried to accost her on the way over but she shot the whispering bastards without even looking.

Not bothering with a preamble or greeting, Lynn marched right up to Connor.

"Neither of us can get through alone, so we're going to double our fire power, punch through and kill whatever is inside together. Teaming up is the only way to win."

"Uh..." The blond-headed athlete glanced to the side at Elena, whose momentary shock had kept her from interrupting Lynn. But that didn't last long.

"How dare you! We're not helping you, you crazy b—"

"SHUT YOUR PIEHOLE RIGHT NOW OR I'LL SHUT IT FOR YOU!" Lynn bellowed, getting right up in Elena's face.

The pop-girl stumbled back, eyes wide and mouth gaping.

"We don't have time to argue," Lynn continued, voice hard, "So, if you want your team to qualify you'll shut your mouth and let the people who know what they're doing get the job done."

"I—You—"

Lynn turned away from the spluttering girl and back to Connor.

"Do you want to win, or do you want to waste your time and look like a fool?"

Connor worked his jaw thoughtfully, his expression firming as he gave Lynn a long look.

"We are *not* working together! You three, get these losers out of our way!"

"Dave, Peter, Jerry, don't move," Connor snapped without taking his eyes off Lynn.

"How dare you?!" Elena snapped. "I run this..."

"Shut *up*, Elena," Connor said then nodded at Lynn. "What's your plan?"

"I will not shut up!" Elena shouted. "My father has..."

"Your father isn't here," Connor said, spinning towards her like an angry panther. "We agreed. You supply the equipment and the financing and in return you got to look good for the camera. I run the game. But gaming is about *winning*. Which I'm in charge of, not you. And we're not going to win if you don't shut your stupid mouth. Then you will look like an idiot in stream, no matter what you do. You'll always be the loser who was all mouth no game. All your followers dry up. So. You either shut your fool mouth and let the professionals figure out how to win, or you lose all your status points and your followers and all the rest. Simple as that."

Elena looked at him furiously then looked at Lynn.

"She's no *professional*," Elena snapped. "She's a fatty *nobody*."

"Oh. My. Lord," Lynn said, shaking her head. "Will you for God's sake lay off the fat shaming? And in case you haven't noticed, it's muscle not fat these days, you idiotic...b-b—witch!"

Lynn really hated the B word and couldn't bring herself to say it, true though it might be.

"She's a nobody to people like, well, *you* who don't keep up with gaming," Connor said, staccato. He knew time was short. "She's one of the absolute *best in the league* at this game. She's more of a celebrity than *you* are and it means all of her followers, none of which follow *you*, will suddenly see you in a new, and better, light. You'll get more followers out of it."

Followers? Since when? Lynn thought then pushed it aside. No time.

"I..." Elena said, spluttering. "She's...She..."

"Discussion is *over*, Elena," Connor snapped. Clearly, he was a guy who *could* make a decision in the crunch. "We're allied. Call the play," he added, nodding at Lynn.

"All right, listen up!" Lynn shouted, turning to look at the whole group. "CRC has the left, Wolves have the right. That Manticar was locked on to me before. If it stays on me again I'll keep it busy while you guys take it out. We can't get to Mishipeshu until it's dead.

"After that, we advance as fast as possible before the TDMs regroup. Hit the final line fast and hard and punch through. They'll swarm us from behind as soon as we do, so we have to run forward and get as close to the target as possible. I don't think lower-level monsters like being near the big baddies, so hopefully that'll give us a bit of room to work.

"Each team's assault element has to hammer away at it while the support elements hold off the mob. Hopefully we'll time it right so that once we eliminate the target, our hour will be up and everything will shut down."

Lynn glanced at the clock. Ten minutes.

"Time's up. Let's move out!" Lynn called and turned to Ronnie, whose mouth was open as if he were about to protest. "Lead the way," she said.

He stared at her for a beat, then closed his mouth and turned, calling orders to the rest of his team. Lynn glanced over at Connor and saw him bent and whispering furiously in Elena's ear. Her face was murderous and when her eyes met Lynn's, Lynn knew exactly who it was Elena wanted to murder.

Lynn gave the pop-girl a wolfish grin and turned to follow Ronnie.

Their two teams broke into a trot, picking off any TDMs that took an interest as they passed. In no time they had retraced their steps to the block before the open square. The TDMs were less thick than before but there were still plenty loitering around, just waiting for an enemy to get within their detection range.

Keeping their pace steady, their formation advanced down the street. The difference from before was noticeable. With twice the firepower and fewer targets, they were able to pick off the monsters fast enough to keep from getting bogged down in melee.

"Here comes the Manticar!" Mack shouted as the giant creature leapt over the wall of TDMs and raced toward them once more. As planned, their group slowed and took up a defense position, letting the monster come to them where there was more open space. Lynn stood in front of their formation, alone, weapons held at either side.

"Come and get me you big, ugly bastard," she muttered, eyes locked on the approaching beast.

It obliged, taking one last leap to pounce on her with its front paws. But she was no longer there. She dove forward and rolled, getting low enough to avoid the gnashing teeth and get past the beast before popping back up and spinning to face it. Directly above her, three scorpionlike tails waved, their poisoned tips wickedly curved. But just as she'd suspected, instead of the tails stabbing down at her from where they were, the Manticar spun its entire body, trying to get her back in its sights.

Bingo.

Lynn's first impulse had been to keep in front of the creature and as far away from those tails as possible. But they had plenty of reach. So, instead, she had to get closer, had to stay right on the Manticar's tail, so to speak, where it couldn't see her.

They danced in a deadly whirlwind. Lynn employed Wrath and Abomination when she could but mostly she held onto them for dear life as she rolled and spun, ran and dodged. All she had to do was stay alive a little bit longer...just a little longer...

The Manticar finally exploded and Lynn swore she felt a faint shockwave, as if some kind of energy had been released with the monster's demise. But she knew that was impossible, since the Manticar was just a bunch of pixels superimposed on her retinas. The surge she felt must have been her adrenaline spike at their victory.

She couldn't dwell on it, though, because the moment the big beast was gone, all the other monsters began to advance. She had just enough time to scoop up the significant pile of supplies and loot that had appeared where the Manticar had been standing. Then—

"Charge!"

Ronnie's yell rang out across the street and Lynn whooped, grinning crazily as she joined him and Connor at the point of their spear-head formation. Edgar was close behind along with one of the three stooges holding a Blunderbuss of his own, while Dan and Mack held down the right flank and the two other stooges focused on the left. Elena ran along in the middle of their group, clutching her rifle with wide eyes and generally being useless.

The cacophony of the monsters around them was overwhelming and Lynn barked at Hugo to lower her volume on the right so she could still hear her team channel.

Thirty feet left between them and the last ring of monsters.

Twenty feet.

Ten feet.

"*For the Horde!!*" Dan hollered at the top of his lungs right before they hit.

Lynn descended in a whirlwind of death, laughing and whooping with abandon as battle lust took her. Wrath sliced and Abomination boomed as she, Ronnie and Connor cut through the first rank of Namahag and Penagals and started on the second.

Gasping, shouting, laughing.

Lungs aching, muscles pumping, adrenaline coursing like molten electricity through her limbs.

This was *fun*. Oh so much fun. She never wanted to do anything else but this.

They were through almost before she realized it. Their blitz assault had torn a ten-foot-wide gap in the inner and outer ring of TDMs.

A gap which was closed as quickly as it had been torn open when every monster in the circle did an about face and advanced. The monsters outside the circle crowded in, too, creating more and more layers until they formed a thick wall of gnashing teeth and grasping claws.

And their two teams were *inside* it all.

Peachy.

Lynn let her teammates worry about what was behind them as she lifted her eyes to see what was ahead. And lifted a little more.

Son of a motherless goat, that bastard was *ugly*.

In the middle of the swiftly contracting circle sat a mountainous, writhing mass of tentacles. It looked like a few dozen octopi with genital warts had merged into a single entity and then consumed an entire vat of growth hormones. The result loomed twelve feet over their heads and reached toward them with slimy-looking arms at least a foot thick.

They'd found Mishipeshu. Now if they could just *do* something about it.

Lynn's display flashed red with damage, then again and again. Crimson energy bolts were spitting out of ugly slits in the monster's hide nestled between its tentacles. Lynn tried dodging the bolts. No dice. They were coming too fast. "CRC cover rear! Wolves! We've got to hit it with all we've got. Go, go, go!"

Their combined group stopped just out of reach of the thrashing tentacles—no imagination was needed to know that *those* were bad news—and everyone took up a stance. Skadi's Wolves poured fire into Mishipeshu while the CRCs hammered at the swiftly encircling mob around them.

"We're all gonna die!" Ronnie hollered from where he stood beside her, shooting Mishipeshu with both Plasma Pistols.

"IT SHALL BE A *GLORIOUS* DEATH!" Edgar shouted, laughing hysterically.

Within sixty seconds, though, it became clear they wouldn't be able to. They were going through Oneg too fast and there were far too many TDMs to hold off all at once. The only way to kill Mishipeshu was with more teams. Most of which were bogged down or dead trying a frontal assault.

Crap.

Lynn felt a trickle of fear. She wasn't even sure why. Was she afraid of failing? Or was it her body's instinctive reaction to the realism of the situation?

In the end, it didn't matter, because in exactly—Lynn checked the clock—three minutes and twenty-four seconds the game would be over and she would have lost her chance at a future that had inspired her to *live* again for the first time since her father had died.

A stab of despair twisted in her gut. Her Lynn side wanted to curl up in a ball and cry—which was fine because her Larry side simply gave her a sound mental thrashing and shoved them both back into the game with their combined middle fingers raised to the sky.

It was do or die—so, time to do something crazy.

"Hold on as long as you can, Skadi's Wolves," Lynn yelled, "I'm going to end this!"

"What?" Ronnie yelped, fire faltering for a second.

"Wait, what are you doing?" Edgar yelled from her other side, taking his eyes off Mishipeshu long enough to throw her a worried look.

"I'm going to either finish it or die trying!" She ignored their protests and switched her Plasma Pistol back to Wrath, clutching the obsidian black blade in one hand and her trusty Abomination in the other.

Then she charged.

When she reached the tentacles, she didn't stop.

When she reached Mishipeshu's massive lumpy body, she didn't stop—she drove right through its incredibly realistic, slimy hide.

Quiet descended.

It was the oddest sensation, the abrupt dimming of sight and sound combined with a dizzy, swooping feeling like she was spinning uncontrollably in a massive free-fall. Her display flickered, as if the app was glitching but it didn't shut off. So, instead of retreating, Lynn planted her feet, chalked the disorientation up to the weird thing-y-majig reaction Steve had warned about and started blasting away with Abomination in her left hand and slashing back and forth with Wrath in her right. All around her was dim, gray mist that flashed crimson in a synchronous pattern with her attacks. She could only barely see the scene she'd left, and the shouts, roars and blasts of the battle were dull thuds in her ears. And what was that strange staticky sound?

"—Miss Lynn, what are you—extremely irregular—highly questionable, possibly even dangerous!" came Hugo's voice, fading in and out with the erratic flickering of her display.

"I'm killing this bastard from the inside!" Lynn shouted. Hm, even her own voice sounded muffled to her ears. But it didn't matter, because her gamble had paid off—the app was registering her attacks from *inside* Mishipeshu. It didn't seem to know what to do about damage to her, since there was literally no way for the monster to "hit" her. It seemed to settle on a steady draining of her health. But as long as she kept throwing Oneg at it, she might actually last long enough—

She stumbled suddenly to the side as a wave of dizziness washed over her but then righted herself. Steve had not been joking about that over-stimulation stuff. But she only had to hold on a little longer.

"—what in the world—thinking? This—insane!"

"Who dares, wins, Hugo," Lynn shouted and grinned. Despite the dizziness, her finger never stopped pulling the trigger and her sword never stopped moving.

In those endless seconds, she squinted hard at her team on the outside and saw them stop fighting one by one, their Hunter armor and lethal-looking weapons disappearing from view. They were dying and their apps were shutting down. Elena's team wasn't doing any better and the moment in which Elena herself threw down her inert batons and stomped off in a rage sent a surge of sweet pleasure straight to Lynn's brain.

Speaking of her brain, it felt like someone had decided to start pounding it with a mallet. Yup, that was just what she needed right now, a headache.

Her trigger finger and sword arm kept pumping, like they had a mind of their own, which was good, because her mind was getting awfully distracted. Where had her display gone? Ah, there it was.

"—abort! Miss Lynn, you must abort—will be forced to— danger of equipment malfunction."

"Just—thirty—more—seconds, Hugo," Lynn panted. She could see the clock. It was counting down. Wasn't Mishipeshu supposed to be dead by now? It was supposed to die. Hurry up, stupid thing! When she glanced up again, she saw her entire team in a line, shouting and waving at her. But she shut out the noise, concentrating instead on the countdown.

Fifteen seconds. She had this.

Die, Mishipeshu, die!

The pounding of her heart in her chest seemed to join the throbbing in her head as she kept striking. A growing heat made her gasp for air and she locked her knees to stay upright. Why was she suddenly burning up? Just a little longer, then she could lie down and rest and take a sip of water.

Ten seconds.

She was good. Almost there.

Five seconds.

Three seconds.

In a flash so brilliant that she shut her eyes against it—or at least she thought she did—everything around her exploded. When she opened them again, she saw sparkling lights raining down from the sky as the sun set and—wait a minute, why was it getting dark all of a sudden?

Chapter 16

"LYNN! LYNN! ARE YOU OKAY? WAKE UP!"

A sharp sting on her cheek roused her and she jerked into consciousness. She threw her arms up automatically, fighting to ward off whatever was attacking her face.

"Ow! Lynn, stop it, it's Edgar."

"Whassit?" Lynn mumbled. A hard, rough surface pressed against the back of her throbbing head. She squinted her eyes open a slit but the bright sunlight sent a stab of pain through her skull and right down her spine to her toes. "Owowow," she moaned.

"Don't move, Lynn. You collapsed and hit your head on the concrete. There's a paramedic on the way."

"Ugggnnn," was about all she could dredge up. Mostly she concentrated on deep, slow breaths to battle the dizziness that made her wonder if she were going to throw up all over Edgar.

"Lynn, that was amazing! You did it! You killed Mishipeshu!"

Wait, was that Ronnie's voice? Was he...praising her? Who abducted Mr. Jerkitude and replaced him with this imposter?

"She most certainly did *not*. *We* killed it and don't you dare think you can steal all the glory—"

"Oh, shut up, Elena," came Dan's voice and Lynn was proud of how positively unimpressed he sounded, considering the years he'd spent terrified of the pop-girl. "You're a moron and too stupid to realize it. The game monitors have all the data. They'll decide who gets what points and your ranting isn't going to change that."

"Well, I—"

"Shut up, Dan," Edgar said. "And you too Elena. We *all* killed it. So, you get the credit, too."

"It's called teamwork, Elena," Connor said, wearily. "It's a term you might, you know, want to learn the definition of? If you're going to keep doing this stuff."

"Out of the way, miss! Stretcher coming through."

Professional-sounding voices surrounded Lynn and she let the strong hands lift her up, help her unclip her backpack, then lay her on their stretcher as she mumbled answers to the paramedic's questions. She kept her eyes closed until he asked her to open them and perform a series of diagnostic exercises. Besides the massive knot on the back of her head, a splitting headache and a persistent feeling of dizziness, she felt fine and was inclined to be grumpy at the paramedic's continued poking and prodding.

"I'm fine," she tried to tell him after he made her take a long, long drink from her hydration pack. "Just give me some pain pills and get me back to HQ."

"I don't think so, Ms. Raven," the paramedic said, tapping at the diagnostic display only he could see in his AR vision. "My scans are showing you had a Grade 1, possibly a Grade 2 concussion. We really ought to get you to the nearest hospital for some more thorough brain scans—"

"No! Absolutely not. I'm not leaving until the tournament ends. I'm not disoriented or anything, I just have a headache. Give me some pain pills and I'll be fine until they announce the results."

The paramedic pursed his lips but then his eyes flicked up to someone behind her.

"That was some crazy stunt you pulled, Hunter."

Lynn's eyes shifted to bring Steve's upside-down face into focus. He was leaning over her, expression grave.

"Oh, hey Fallu—uh, Steve. Yeah but it worked, didn't it?" She couldn't help her goofy grin. She felt giddy, despite the nausea. "If it's crazy and it works it ain't crazy."

The upside-down mouth curved into a smile, though it didn't touch the grave look in his eyes.

"That it did, kid. That it did. And it was also crazy. Now, the paramedic tells me you need some scans at the hospital."

"If they try to take me away before the game wraps up, I

swear I'll fight them just as hard as I fought the TDMs. And I'll probably win, too, concussion or not."

Steve's brows rose.

"Feeling a little cocky, are we? Well, don't get your panties in a wad just yet. You're a minor, so it'll be up to your mother." He looked up at the paramedic. "Come on, let's get this stretcher back to HQ."

"I can walk," Lynn grumbled, attempting to sit up.

"Oh, no you don't, Ms. Raven." The paramedic put a firm hand on her shoulder and held her down.

She was glad he did, because she honestly *didn't* think she could walk, not with the pain pounding in her head and radiating down her neck. But she hadn't wanted to admit that in front of her teammates.

The journey back was quick and the guys chatted excitedly about the fight, exuberantly recounting their last stand for her benefit. Elena and her team were silent, though the one time the girl came into Lynn's view, the stewing look of outrage on her face promised an unpleasant time for Connor and his teammates once they were in private.

They didn't go back to the low, green building but took her all the way through the fence to TD Hunter HQ. Elena's team was taken back to the conference room where the families were spectating, while Steve and the paramedic carried her to a small office off the hall. When they tried to get the rest of her team to go back to the conference room as well, they refused, to a man.

If Lynn hadn't been so distracted by the insistent throb of pain in her skull, she would have smiled at the sight of the four of them in a row, arms crossed, giving Steve and the paramedic looks that only stubborn teenage boys could pull off. Steve didn't push the issue, though, and left, returning a minute later with Lynn's mom.

Matilda did the expected amount of motherly fussing followed by her own examination after she explained to the paramedic that she was an ER nurse. She thoroughly questioned Lynn about the symptoms leading up to her collapse and concluded heat stroke was the likely culprit of Lynn's fainting spell. And, unfortunately for Lynn, she heartily agreed that they needed to take a trip to the nearest hospital.

Lynn threatened mutiny.

Matilda, being an experienced mother, didn't try to berate or argue Lynn into submission. She just gave her daughter a long, silent, concerned look, until Lynn's stubbornness melted into squirming guilt. Still, Lynn didn't give up. Somehow she managed to convince her mother to let her stay until they announced the results, which Steve assured them wouldn't take more than twenty minutes.

The paramedic gave her some pills for the pain, then slowly and carefully helped her to stand. When she proved she wasn't unsteady, he let her walk with her friends back to the conference room under strict orders to lie down on one of the couches and *stay there* until he came for her. With a smile as pure as the driven snow, she promised to obey.

With Edgar supporting her on one side and her mom on the other, their little parade returned to the conference room. A rash of whispers and sidelong looks greeted them when their group entered. But they ignored the spectators and got Lynn settled on one of the couches where she could see the big screen at the end of the room. Then the guys collapsed onto various surfaces around her and returned to discussing their epic battle, albeit in more subdued voices.

Lynn tuned out the conversation, her interest turning to the tournament replay on the big screen. A commentator on the TD Hunter sub-stream for the Iowa competition was analyzing the replay of the last ten minutes or so of the fight. Mostly it was clips of Skadi's Wolves and the CRC's assault on Mishipeshu, though a few clips of the other surviving teams got shown too. Lynn gathered that about half the other teams had died, either through incompetence, or through stubbornly advancing through the thick of things until they simply ran out of health—the same fate Skadi's Wolves had almost suffered. The surviving teams had stayed at the fringes and picked off as many TDMs as they could before the hour was up.

As she watched, the euphoria of their victory started to wear off and worry niggled at her. Yeah, they had killed the big bad Mishipeshu, in the end. But they'd taken sooo much damage, their kill to damage ratio was going to be absolute crap. She only hoped the evaluators took into account their extreme ingenuity and determination in the execution of the mission. Surely, they could see evidence of her team's skill in the fight and knew the bad scores came from daring to sacrifice it all for ultimate victory?

Lynn's brow furrowed when the vid replay got to the part where she dashed straight into Mishipeshu. Right before she disappeared into it, the scene cut to a different angle and the commentator changed focus to the remainder of their embattled team. His theatrical commentary as their combined forces fell one by one distracted her, though, and she enjoyed getting to clearly see everyone's last stand. Her memory of it from before was very hazy.

She poked Edgar in the side and got him to look up in time to see the death of the three stooges protecting Elena, then a few moments of her flailing at the advancing Namahags before they pretty much ate her for breakfast. To Lynn's delight, the camera stayed on her long enough to show her stomp off screen in a huff after she'd died.

So much for the pop-girl's plan to stand in the background and look good for the cameras. Lynn only hoped the clip stuck around to bite Elena in the butt over and over. After all, nothing in the mesh ever died or went away. Ever. It was sweet justice, to say the least.

Finally, Connor and Ronnie, the last to die, disappeared from the fight and the camera turned to Mishipeshu. Lynn waited in anticipation, wondering what the commentator would say about her crazy gamble. But instead, the stream vid started flickering with static and the commentator apologized for the malfunction, saying they would move to a different drone to get a better view of the other side of Mishipeshu where "Ms. Raven" was making her brave last stand.

Whaaat?

By the time they got the camera switched, Mishipeshu exploded into a fire-works worthy display of sparks and then the stream vid abruptly cut to a different scene entirely, showing some of the other teams as they lowered their batons and celebrated successfully surviving the hour of battle.

"Edgar," Lynn whispered. "Did you see that? They acted like I never went inside Mishipeshu. They didn't show me collapsing! What the heck?"

"Yeah, that is weird. Maybe they didn't want to embarrass you by showing when you fainted? I thought you were epic, a true *Toa Tama'ita'i* going out in a blaze of glory!"

"Maybe," Lynn muttered, not quite amused enough at Edgar's

enthusiasm to smile. She didn't say anything else as the commentary for the competition wrapped up but she had her theories—namely that the developers didn't want anyone *else* trying to replicate her crazy stunt.

Going inside a monster to avoid its attacks would only work if it was stationary and had a big enough bulk but it was definitely an exploitable weakness inherent to the AR mechanics of the game. The developers were probably hoping no other players caught on to the hack.

Ha. Fat chance.

It was too bad she'd gotten so dehydrated at the end. It was a *really* intense battle, with tons of noise and light and exertion. She should have insisted all the guys brought their own water instead of sharing her hydration pack. She obviously hadn't drunk enough. Next time she would be more careful. Hitting her head when she'd fainted had just been bad luck.

Lynn didn't have a single shred of regret, though. Considering that she'd been a lifelong couch potato up until three months ago, it was amazing she lasted as long as she had. She resolved to train even harder going forward so her body wouldn't give out on her next time. Well, if there was a next time...

"Aaaalll right, contestants! Thank you for your patience as our evaluators reviewed the last of the footage and technical scores," said Trinity, back up on stage with no less bounce in her step than before.

Nervous anticipation curled in Lynn's gut.

"Now, before we announce the results, on behalf of the TD Hunter game developers and staff, we want to thank each and every one of you for taking part in this competition. Your energy and devotion to the game have truly inspired us and we are proud to do everything we can to make TD Hunter the best and biggest game of the century! All across the world, qualification tournaments are ongoing and hardworking teams just like you are being awarded Hunter Strike Team status and an official place in TD Hunter's first ever international championship. For those who didn't meet the minimum standards, thank you so much for participating! Train hard and we look forward to seeing you again for next year's qualifiers."

A fancy "Thank you for playing" graphic played across the big screen as Trinity talked but Lynn barely looked at it. Her eyes were locked on Trinity, mentally begging the woman to hurry up. The anticipation was killing her.

"Aaand, for the lucky teams whose exceptional performance today has guaranteed them placement in the first annual TD Hunter international championship, we want to say congratulations and thank you for your devotion to the game! We wouldn't be here today without the support of our millions of fans around the globe but it is *your* dedication and skill in particular that will make this revolutionary game go down in history.

"Sooo—" Trinity said, drawing the word out unnecessarily long.

"Ugh, hurry up, woman!" Dan groaned, leaning forward in his seat.

"—if everyone would please join me in a big round of applause foooor—"

"I swear I'm going to kill that woman if the next words out of her mouth aren't the team names," growled Ronnie.

"—the Cedar Rapids Champions and Skadi's Wolves!"

The guys all around Lynn erupted, jumping to their feet, whooping, hugging and high-fiving as everyone else in the room gave them warm applause. Lynn, of course, stayed where she was—she had promised, after all. She saw plenty of disappointed faces as many in the seats lined up in front of the stage turned to look at her noisy teammates. She also saw a lot of blatant curiosity and shameless stares pointed her way.

She looked away.

"Would the Cedar Rapids Champions and Skadi's Wolves please come join me on the stage?" Trinity said over the noise.

"Lynn," Edgar said, looking at Matilda pleadingly.

"I'll stay," Lynn said tiredly. "You go. You deserve it. All of you," she added, looking at Ronnie.

"Mrs. Raven," Ronnie said carefully.

"Get up off your butt, girlie," Matilda said, standing up and holding out her hand.

"Mom?"

"I may be a nurse and agree with the medics," Matilda said, her eyes shiny with tears. "But I'm also a mother. *No* mother would keep her child lying down for this. Take my hand."

Held up by Mack on one side and Edgar on the other, Lynn made her way slowly to the stage.

"Lynn Raven, Team Second for Skadi's Wolves, was slightly

injured in the final battle against Mishipeshu," Trinity said, with annoying cheerfulness. "So, a round of applause for our wounded warrior!"

Lynn blushed pure scarlet at her words and wished the woman hadn't pointed her out. But she made her way up to the stage, still a bit woozy and waved to the crowd. There was more applause and, to her absolute mortification, a few wolf whistles.

Trinity launched into a long speech about saving humanity, yada, yada, as Lynn tried not to collapse or throw up. The nausea was back and she wished they'd just get around to it. Whatever "it" was.

As the woman spoke, Lynn inspected the CRCs lined up on the opposite side of the stage from her team. Elena looked perfect, as always, her expression and demeanor back to the stylish, confident mask that she maintained for the public. Of course, anyone who watched that clip of her defeat would know the truth. Lynn looked forward to bringing it up every time she saw Elena again for the rest of their lives.

Connor and the rest of the team looked an appropriate mix of proud and gracious, listening attentively to Trinity's words. Lynn reminded herself they all had plenty of experience being on camera from their ARS competitions. She could only hope they remembered Elena's behavior and had the guts to do something about it. Maybe they couldn't oust her as team captain—her daddy was funding their team. But maybe Connor would at least take her in hand and stop letting her boss them around like they were her mindless minions.

Lynn squinted at the pretty boy up there on stage, wondering what he thought of Elena's cheating. Did he know his teammates had assaulted Mack in the bathroom and broken his equipment? Probably. Connor didn't strike her as a complete idiot. Just a spineless one.

But his actions at the end of the competition had shown he was willing to shut Elena up if it was necessary to win. That, of course, made him even more dangerous as an opponent, not less. Only time would tell if his influence would curb Elena's unscrupulous ambition, or if he would go along with her schemes as long as it got him what he wanted.

Well, if the CRCs tried anything again, they would be in for a rude surprise. Lynn had *plans* where they were concerned.

Eventually, Trinity wound down and they got around to the prizes.

Each of the team members were given a gold medal on a lanyard signifying they were official TD Hunter Strike Team members. There was a smaller "challenge coin," more or less identical, with the TD Counterforce emblem on the front and a scroll with a "battle streamer" on the back. Theirs was already inscribed with "Boss: Mishipeshu" and the date/location.

Then came the real SWAG, already packed in a sturdy plastic box, with, yes, the TD Counterforce symbol on it. Of course.

Each box included pretty much everything she'd been supplied in Beta, plus. There were TD Counterforce backpacks—no more water supply problems—as well as the T-shirts and golf shirts, coffee mugs and so on. In addition, there were gray NTL Counterforce uniforms using the same high-performance nanofabric as Lynn's purchased set as well as coupons redeemable for boots, tactical gloves, LINCs, AR glasses or contacts and more.

Quite the haul.

And they were done. And Lynn could lie down again. Horizontal was sounding better and better.

Dan had to carry her box stacked on his and struggled with getting both down to their seats.

Despite Edgar and Mack holding her up, she nearly fainted getting down the steps from the stage and was happy to be back reclined on her couch as the boys hooted and hollered over their SWAG boxes.

"This is an insane amount of SWAG for a regional competition," Dan said, wonderingly. He was holding up his NTL pants and shaking his head. "Couple of thousand dollars at least. There must have been thousands of these all over the planet. Do. The. Maths. How much investment money did Krator *raise*?"

"Lots," Lynn muttered. She was getting a bit loopy. Instead of getting better, she seemed to be getting worse if anything. "He said his backers were pretty serious."

"What?" Mack asked. "Who said...what?"

"Shush," Matilda said, worriedly, holding out both her hands. "Grip my hands."

Lynn gripped them as tightly as she could.

"Even but weak both sides," Matilda said. "Not extremely weak, but... Wish that ambulance would get here..."

As if on cue, the paramedic was back, quietly letting Matilda know that an ambulance aircar was waiting to take them to the nearest hospital. Matilda tried to arrange for an air taxi to take the guys and their siblings home but they wouldn't hear of it.

"We're officially a team, now," Edgar said with a grin. "That means we stick together. We'll catch a ride to the hospital."

Everyone readily agreed, even Ronnie. Would wonders never cease?

Lynn grinned up at all of them. Her team. They'd come an awful long way and she could honestly say she was grateful that everyone, from Mr. Krator to her mom to Edgar, had kept at her. If they hadn't encouraged her and pushed her to step outside her comfort zone, she never would have realized what she could achieve. And she definitely never would have felt this tingling warmth inside her chest that was making her eyes suspiciously moist.

Was this what it felt like to be a part of something bigger than yourself? To work alongside people you liked and trusted? Well, mostly trusted. Ronnie was, probably always would be, a work in progress.

Was this what it felt like to have real friends who depended on her and that she could depend upon in turn?

Lynn found she didn't mind it at all, even if friends were loud and exhausting.

The analgesics did their work well, because by the time they had her loaded up and were headed out, she was floating comfortably in a dreamy state, completely unworried by the trials she knew they would face in the coming months.

A scheming, cheating rival team.

Senior year.

Twenty levels of monsters, all bigger and badder than ever before, not to mention the bosses after that.

Lynn smiled. No problem. She'd conquered everything in her path so far and she looked forward to the challenges ahead, especially if they involved cutting through ravening hordes of bloodthirsty monsters.

The life of a Hunter was a good life. To drive the TDMs before you. To loot their shattered corpses. To make them cower in fear of the Wolf Horde.

"How are you feeling, honey?" Matilda asked solicitously,

doing another blood pressure check. As an ER nurse the medics had granted her "back of the ambulance" privilege.

Lynn smiled again then fumbled her AR glasses out of her pack and put them on.

"Future's so bright, gotta wear shades..." she growled.

"The future's not looking so bright," Undersecretary Ernie Ashford said tightly. "This needed to go better, Mr. Krator."

The Undersecretary for Special Research Projects was clearly unhappy with the results of the international game tests. Everyone in the world with the clearance to follow them was unhappy. While there had been no deaths this time, thank God, most of the civilian TD Hunter teams had been wiped out in game.

The things were just *tough*. Numbers on their feeder entities had to come down to have any chance against them.

"Secretary," Krator replied, breathing deeply. "We are attempting to save the world using technology that was theory *ten years ago*, from creatures we didn't even know *existed* until *seven years ago*, slapdashed onto a game developed *one year ago*, with groups of mostly *teenagers*, whilst trying to hide the fact civilization is about to end *from the entire planet*."

Krator turned and looked the undersecretary in the eye, glaring.

"That any of this is working at all... is a freaking *miracle*."

To be continued...

Acknowledgments

I'D LIKE TO THANK THE MANY PEOPLE WHO HELPED MAKE THIS book happen.

First, John, thanks for trusting me with your crazy brainchild. I've had a lot of fun with it and plan on having lots more.

Thanks to my amazing and generous husband—I couldn't have written this without your gaming expertise. Thank you for being my alpha reader and for unequivocally supporting me in all I do.

Thank you, Mike Muller, for sharing your military expertise. You are a delightful friend and I can't wait to read more of your own books.

Thanks to my many wonderful beta readers. Your time, insights, and advice were so appreciated and helped make this book as amazing as it is. I wish I had time and space to list you all, but you know who you are!

Thanks to my awesome Patreon family, who all generously support me and cheer me on in every crazy endeavor I get myself into. I know this book doesn't have a snarky talking cat in it, but I hope you enjoy it all the same.

To my many, many fans out there eagerly awaiting more books, thank you for reading and sharing your love of my stories. Your (im)patient demands for more keep me motivated. Please never stop!

Lastly, and most importantly, I thank my Father in heaven, who formed me, adopted me, and called me to His purpose. Without Him I would have no story to tell or heart to tell it. To Him be the glory.

—L.S.